TE 11/16
Teb 03/18

2013

ASHTON PARK

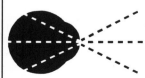

This Large Print Book carries the
Seal of Approval of N.A.V.H.

THE DANFORTHS OF LANCASHIRE, BOOK 1

ASHTON PARK

MURRAY PURA

THORNDIKE PRESS

A part of Gale, Cengage Learning

Detroit • New York • San Francisco • New Haven, Conn • Waterville, Maine • London

GALE
CENGAGE Learning®

LIBRARY OF CONGRESS CATALOGING-IN-PUBLICATION DATA

Pura, Murray, 1954–
    Ashton Park : the Danforths of Lancashire / by Murray Pura. — Large print edition.
        pages ; cm. — (Thorndike Press large print Christian historical fiction)
    ISBN-13: 978-1-4104-5916-9 (hardcover)
    ISBN-10: 1-4104-5916-0 (hardcover)
    1. Aristocracy (social class)—England—History—20th century—Fiction. 2. Social classes—England—History—20th century—Fiction. 3. World War, 1914-1918—England—Fiction. 4. Baptists—England—Fiction. 5. Lancashire (England)—Fiction 6. Domestic fiction. 7. Large type books. I. Title.
    PR9199.4.P87A88 2013b
    813'.6—dc23   2013010816

Published in 2013 by arrangement with Harvest House Publishers

Printed in Mexico
1 2 3 4 5 6 7 17 16 15 14 13

For my sister June, who taught me my letters, with all my love.

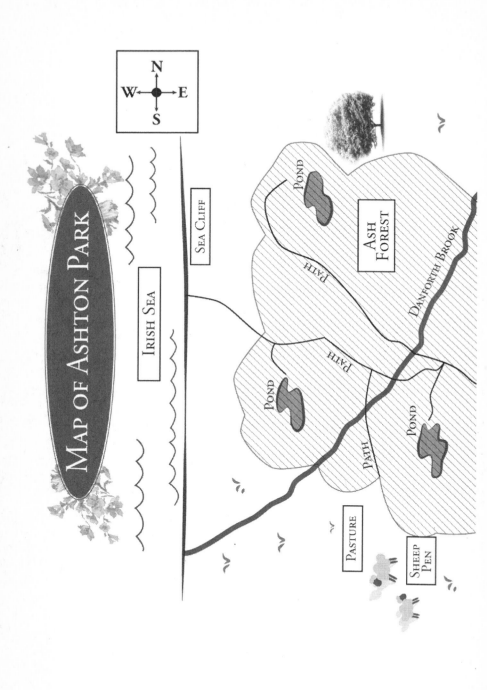

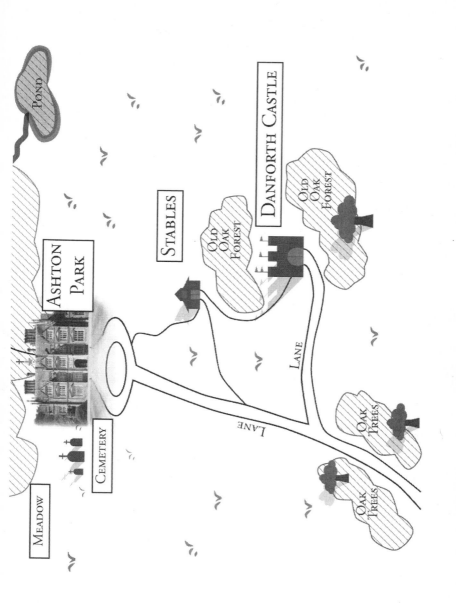

THE CHARACTERS

Sir William Danforth — husband to Lady Elizabeth, father, Member of Parliament (MP), and master of Ashton Park estate

Lady Elizabeth Danforth — wife to Sir William and mother to the seven Danforth children

Sir Arthur — Lady Elizabeth's father

Lady Grace — Sir William's mother

Aunt Holly — Sir William's younger sister

Edward Danforth — eldest son, Royal Navy

Kipp Danforth — son, Royal Air Force

Robbie Danforth — youngest son, British Army

Emma (Danforth) Sweet — eldest daughter and wife of Reverend Jeremiah Sweet

Catherine (Danforth) Moore — daughter and wife of Albert Moore

Elizabeth (Libby) Danforth — daughter

Victoria Danforth — youngest daughter

Mr. and Mrs. Seabrooke — managers of the household staff

Tavy — butler

Mrs. Longstaff — head cook

Norah Cole — maid

Harrison — groundskeeper

Todd Turpin — assistant groundskeeper

Skitt — assistant groundskeeper and Sheep-
herder

Ben Whitecross — groom and coach driver

Tanner Buchanan — groundskeeper at Danforth hunting lodge in Scotland

Lord Francis Scarborough — wealthy aris-
tocrat

Lady Madeleine Scarborough — his wife

Lady Caroline Scarborough — daughter of
Lord and Lady Scarborough

Reverend Jeremiah Sweet — Anglican
minister, husband to Emma

Albert Moore — husband of Catherine and
manager of Danforth shipyards in Belfast

Michael Woodhaven IV — American pilot
from wealthy family

Charlotte Squire — maid

Christelle Cevenne — waitress at café in
France

Shannon Dungarvan — young woman from
Dublin

**Pilots of Kipp Danforth's squadron in
France**
Bobby Scott
Kent Wales

Ian Hannam
Teddy Irving
Gladstone and Wellington — the Danforth
German Shepherds

1
1916

April 1916

"Go, girl, go!"

Victoria Danforth leaned into her horse's neck as it broke out of the forest and drove toward the sea cliff at full gallop.

"Come on, Robin! The man is gaining!"

A green ribbon flew from Victoria's head and her long auburn hair burst loose. She struck the sorrel's flanks with the heels of her black leather boots.

"Give me more, my girl, just a bit more!"

The shining sea drew closer and closer. A wind that carried the bite of salt water stung Victoria's nostrils. Face flushed by the wild ride, eyes glittering like a cat's, she cried out a final time.

"All you've got, my beauty!"

And then she hauled back on the reins, turned the mare's head to the left, sprang from the saddle, and hit the ground boots-first with a shout. The horse dug in all its hooves and tossed up mud and stone and grass. The cliff edge was only a few yards away when she stopped.

"Good, girl, that was lovely, that was grand!" Victoria stroked the animal's neck and mane. Both horse and rider were panting. "What a gorgeous view! I'll never tire of it."

The brisk ocean breeze pushed back the auburn hair from Victoria's face, bringing its deep red color out to the light, then turning it over and bringing back its rich browns. It plucked at her forest green riding coat, her white blouse, and the green silk scarf at her throat. The scarf brought out the emerald fire in her eyes.

"Miss Victoria," came a man's voice.

She had closed her eyes to better dream of sailing on a ship across the Atlantic to America or Canada. *There is land no white man has ever seen,* her brother Edward the naval officer had told her once. *Mountains where no man or woman has ever placed a foot. Animals that are the stuff of dreams.*

"Miss Victoria." The voice was more insistent.

"Mmm?"

"If ye want to be there to greet your father, we must head back. Even though he's using the coach he'll still be at the manor house inside a quarter hour. The train would have arrived at Lime Street Station in Liverpool well over an hour ago."

Victoria shook her head and laughed. "Old Todd Turpin, my highwayman, you are so particular about clocks and minutes. Is that because your great-great-grandfather's blood runs in your veins and you know where every coach is on any road at any given minute?"

Todd, a short and slender man of sixty with a flat tweed cap who sat astride a black gelding, flushed. "I'm not related to Dick Turpin. I told ye that before."

"Just as your mate Brendan Cook is not related to the famous sea captain who also met an untimely end. Though Captain Cook was eaten, while Dick Turpin was merely hanged."

"Sure, your mother Lady Elizabeth shouldn't like to hear ye talking like this."

"Well, she's not here, is she? Or are you her spy as well as my guardian?"

Todd's face flushed a deeper red. "I'm no spy neither."

Victoria gave him a sudden savage glare. "Let us hope not, Old Todd Turpin, or I should have to challenge you to a duel. And you know how quick I am with a blade." Seeing the startled look that sprang onto his face she laughed again, tossing her hair. "Oh, Todd, when will you ever get to know who I am? I wouldn't hurt a finger on your hand. You've served our family since I was eleven, after all."

"Well, but ye are not eleven anymore, are ye, Miss?"

Victoria swept up into her saddle, her long hair falling about her shoulders as she adjusted her black riding skirt and leather boots. "I may be eighteen but the eleven-year-old is still in there. Race you to Ashton Park."

She leaned forward and whistled softly in her mare's ear. The horse bolted forward, away from the sea cliff and down the path leading back into the forest of tall ash trees. Todd rolled his eyes and muttered, "Ah, dear Lord," and dug his heels into his gelding's sides, urging it after the mare. He knew he would never catch Victoria but at least he could keep her in sight.

The soaring ash trees, some two hundred feet high and hundreds of years old, flashed past on either side of Victoria as she and Robin hurtled along the track. She meant to get altogether out of sight of Todd Turpin, who, she was certain, reported to her mother all her goings-on, despite his protests to the contrary. Bending over the mare's neck, she took a different path and galloped full out over a trail she could have ridden with her eyes closed. It was a shortcut she was certain Todd had never used.

Sure enough, she erupted from the ash trees five minutes before a worried Todd emerged flustered from the main road through the grove. He saw her riding her mare slowly over the large green lawn that surrounded the manor house and called out to her.

"Ye little devil! Ye ought not to do that, Miss Victoria!"

Victoria smiled. "Do what, Old Todd Turpin? Outrace you?"

"Do some kind of witchcraft or spell or whatever it is ye did to vanish from the road and get here ahead of me!"

"Oh, I assure you I am still a good Christian girl, Todd, and all four of Robin's hooves were planted firmly on the ground. We may have taken flight but we were never in the clouds. You just don't know the ash grove like I do. Perhaps you don't have a highwayman's blood in your veins after all."

She rode Robin toward the great house with its stone walls and towering brick chimneys and hundreds of windows. Ivy grew green and lush over the entire back of the manor, the oldest part, completed in

17

1688. The newer wings, dating from the mid-1700s, were clear of growth and the stone shone, in some parts, a soft gray like pigeons, in other parts, a warm honey color, and in still other places, a ruby red that made her think of strawberries. She urged her mare onto the scores of flagstones that rimmed the house, and the horse's hooves clicked and clacked as Victoria guided her to the front of the ancient and sturdy manor. There were a hundred and sixteen rooms and Victoria had been into most of them at least twice, including the ones her mother had locked up tight.

A cluster of starlings burst from the trees and darted over her head, making the horse rear, nearly throwing her off. "Shhh, my lovely," she said, quieting the mare, tugging slightly on the reins. "It's all right." She stared after the birds as they raced for the far corner of the manor.

"Now what was that all about? Do you suppose they've seen hawks?" She glanced at the scores of windows. "Perhaps they saw a ghost. Old Todd Turpin always frightened me half to death with his stories of headless phantoms and Viking raiders swinging swords running with blood. The worst was the woman who burned to death when a candle set her gown on fire." The horse nickered and Victoria patted her neck. "That really happened. That's the trouble. A bride going up like a torch and no one could get her gown or corset off. The groom tried so hard and his hands were scarred forever from the flames. He never married again. She was a Danforth." Victoria shuddered. "Why did I have to start thinking about that gruesome event? Servants say they've seen her burning and screaming in the room where it happened. One butler quit over it." Robin nickered again.

"Miss Victoria!"

"What is it, Old Todd Turpin?" she asked in a tease. "Do you wish to have another race?"

"I'm looking at my watch. Your father will be along in another few minutes. I'm sure of it."

"Well, then, I bow to the wisdom of your hoary head, and Robin and I shall proceed to the drive. Thank you."

The sun had been in and out of the clouds all afternoon. Now a light shower fell softly on Ashton Park and its stone and ivy and grass. It glistened on Victoria's green sleeves and beaded on Robin's mane. The oak trees that grew around the old castle that was hundreds of yards away, its turrets just peeking above the treetops, glistened in the fall of the drops.

Victoria rode the mare over the front lawn to the drive and then toward the broad avenue through the gnarled and sweeping oaks, where she knew her father's coach would soon come. As Victoria watched, the sun slipped back out and the oak forest and castle and avenue caught fire. The beauty of the moment overwhelmed her. Then into the flame of leaves and bending tree trunks, like a moving photograph, a black coach suddenly appeared pulled by two nut-brown horses in harness. Robin threw up her head and gave a short whinny.

"Come on," she said. "Let's greet them."

She rode up to the coach as it slowed, its driver cloaked in black with a top hat and scarf. He lifted the hat to her.

"Miss Victoria."

"Mr. Whitecross. How was the traffic in Liverpool?"

"The usual dreadful mess of motorcars breaking down and wagons and carriages bottled up on narrow streets because of it."

"You look bundled up for February or March."

"The rains and winds of April, Miss Victoria. Are you out on your own?"

"Ah, no, I'm much too young for that, aren't I? Old Todd's with me."

"Where?"

"Oh, just back of the manor there." She bent down to the window of the coach. "Hello, Papa! It's so nice to have you home again! Happy Easter!"

A handsome head of brown hair with a dash of gray at the temples poked out, a smile opening up the man's face. "My dear Victoria! How good of you to ride out to meet me, my dear. Though I will reserve the Easter greeting for its proper moment on Sunday morning."

Victoria and her mare followed the coach around the circular drive until Ben Whitecross brought it to a halt in front of the large oak doors of the manor.

"Here you are, Sir William," Ben said. "Welcome home."

"Thank you, Ben. Thank you." Sir William climbed down from the coach and removed his top hat as his daughter swung down from the mare. He took her into his arms and held her tightly.

"Ah, it is always grand to come down that avenue through the oaks and see Ashton Park in all its glory in the sunlight." Sir William kissed Victoria on the top of her head. "How is my youngest? What trouble have you gotten into with the suffragettes this week, hmm?"

"I only marched three times while you were gone, Papa."

"Your mother wrote me. A number of your friends were arrested."

"Well, but not me."

"Not yet." Sir William stood at six-four and towered over his daughter in his long black coat, with his broad shoulders and two hundred and thirty pounds of weight. At fifty-two, his eyebrows were still as brown as his hair and eyes as they slanted downward. "You know what an arrest and jail time would do to your mother. Never mind yourself. Or the family name."

Victoria's own eyebrows came together sharply and her emerald eyes flickered. "You yourself made a speech in the House of Commons in support of votes for women. I read it in the newspaper."

"I do believe in it, yes. I've told you that before. But violence only makes the government resist your cause all the more."

"Yes, well, doing nothing ensures nothing happens, Papa."

He laid his two large hands on her shoulders. "I did not say to do nothing. But smashing windows and setting off bombs only hardens the public against you. And Parliament and the king become your enemies."

Victoria looked into her father's eyes. "Setting off bombs is something I will never do. Human life is precious to me, Father. That is why I protest the war."

"I thought the suffragette movement declared they were stopping the marches until the war was over. In fact, I read a number of the leaders support the war effort."

"That's the old group that's run by Mrs. Pankhurst and one of her daughters. The other daughter is completely against the war in France and started a new group. That's the one I belong to now, Father, the Workers' Suffrage Federation. We have proclaimed no amnesty on demonstrations for the duration of the war. Indeed, we feel we must hold rallies against the conflict in Europe every time we march for the right to vote."

He groaned. "Yes, there is that too, isn't there? Mass rallies against Britain's involvement in the war. Mother tells me the neighbors think you are unpatriotic."

"I am a true patriot. I want England to be known for preserving life, not taking it in the wanton slaughter of the trenches."

"For heaven's sakes, Victoria, you have three brothers in uniform —"

"I love them enough to want them out of

uniform and back safely at Ashton Park without a drop of blood on their hands and each of them with a clean conscience."

Victoria was aware of Ben Whitecross watching them uncomfortably as he stood by the team of horses, shifting his weight and averting his eyes, and of Old Todd Turpin approaching as slowly as he possibly could on foot, restraining two blond German shepherds on long leashes. Suddenly she smiled up at her father and put an arm through his. "I loved your speech about Home Rule for Ireland."

His lips curved up in a half smile. "But."

"No. I really did love it. I even cut it out for my diary."

"But."

She shrugged and began to lead him toward the house. "I think Ireland should have full independence. How would the English Parliament like to be ruled by a mob of politicians in Cardiff or Edinburgh?"

"One step at a time, my dear."

"You wouldn't say that if you wanted your freedom, Father. You always argue in the Commons that England is about liberty and English law is about justice for everyone."

He laughed. "I should end our subscription to all the newspapers that get delivered to this home."

The oak doors opened and a number of people rushed out toward the two of them. The first was a tall and slender lady, with hair the color of Victoria's piled pleasantly about her head and dark eyes smiling as warmly as her lips. She took Sir William in her arms and kissed him on the cheek. Lady Elizabeth was seven years younger and half a foot shorter than her husband and the differences in height and age were both noticeable.

"William, my dear, it has been too long. I'm so happy to see you. Have you lost weight again?"

He returned her kiss, smiling. "London food is difficult to digest. I'm sure our Mrs. Longstaff will soon fatten me up."

She pouted. "But you always want the meals to be so frugal and spare at this time of year."

"Oh, my goodness, Elizabeth, only for a few days as we remember our Lord's crucifixion and death." He hugged her. "On Sunday we celebrate His life and the new life He puts into all of us. There will be plenty of time for feasting then, eh?" He peered over her shoulder. "Who's this? Catherine and Albert? Are you here from Belfast? I didn't know. Emma's wedding isn't for another week."

"It is so rarely that we can surprise you," Lady Elizabeth spoke up. "It's nice for us to succeed at doing so now and then."

A tall woman with long black hair and a worried look behind her smiles came to Sir William and hugged him. "Hello, Father. We weren't sure Albert could get away this Easter but here we are just the same. I simply can't miss my sister's wedding."

"I'm overjoyed, Catherine. I haven't seen either of you in half a year."

Albert was short, with a broad brown mustache and a face given to red patches. Dressed in a three-piece gray tweed suit, he shook Sir William's hand. "Some matters came up, sir, that needed my particular attention. I have my concerns about —"

Sir William clapped him on the shoulder. "There will be time for that later, Albert. Much later. Baxter is coming down from Preston with the textile figures and Longbottom up from Liverpool with the ledgers on our shipping profits and losses. We'll wait until then. Let us relax, you and I, eh? You from running the shipyards and I from helping King George run the country. And who do we have here? Dear Emma, the blushing bride."

Another woman as tall as Catherine and

Lady Elizabeth, but with chestnut hair tied back, almost ran to her father, her plain face totally transformed by the strength of her smile. "Yes, Papa. I'm so glad you're here early. We will want your advice for so many things."

"Your mother is much better at advice than I am," said Sir William, holding her close with one long arm and Catherine close with the other.

Lady Elizabeth shook her head. "The manor chapel has always been your eighth child, William. No one knows how to dress it better than you."

"Is that what you think? Four daughters, three sons, and a chapel? Well, I hope my instructions for decorating it for Easter have been followed —"

Lady Elizabeth and Emma laughed.

"You see?" his wife teased. "Fussing over it already."

"I only wish —"

"Mr. and Mrs. Seabrooke have matters well in hand, my dear," his wife assured him. "You can have a look right after tea."

Mrs. Seabrooke peered out the window at the Danforth family gathered around Sir William. "I don't see Lady Grace."

Mr. Seabrooke looked over her shoulder.

"You know how it is. Sir William's mother never goes out of doors. Never takes tea either. She wanders about the rooms until dinner at eight."

"Sir Arthur and Aunt Holly said they would join us."

"They are in the library arguing, I believe, over some comment in a book. I have no idea what that is about. However, it is an amiable argument."

Mrs. Seabrooke continued to stare out the window. "Oh, now, Todd has let the dogs jump all over Sir William."

Mr. Seabrooke shook his head. "That's Sir William who has called them to his side. He dotes on that pair."

"A gift from an Austrian baron. He should have got rid of them once war was declared."

"Oh, we've been through that before, Mrs. Seabrooke. Remember what happened when Sir William got wind of that sort of talk from Clifford? Gone overnight. Sacked. *The dogs did not invade Belgium and France.* None of that from you, if you please, Missus."

"Ah, Mr. and Mrs. Seabrooke," came a voice behind them.

They both turned quickly from the window. It was Tavy the butler. He inclined his head at the husband and wife, both as tall and thin as reeds in a pond, while he stood round and sturdy as a boulder with his full stomach and firmly combed gray hair. Mrs. Seabrooke hesitated. When she realized he wasn't going to bring up her comments about the dogs, she smiled brightly.

"What is it, Tavy?"

"The household staff is assembled in the dining room as you requested, ma'arm. Did you wish to speak with them?"

"I did indeed. Thank you, Tavy. We'll be along directly."

"Do you think he heard?" she asked her husband when Tavy had left the room.

Mr. Seabrooke shrugged. "If he did, you'll find out about it when he wants a favor from you."

"Come, Tavy's not like that."

"You hardly know him. How long has Clifford been gone? Six months? And Tavy's only filled his shoes for three of them."

Mrs. Seabrooke pinched her lips together and rubbed the bridge of her nose with her thumb and index finger, closing her eyes. Suddenly she clapped her hands and headed for the hallway.

"They're waiting for us, Mr. Seabrooke."

The walnut table had been set for high tea with silver teapots and bone china. The maids and footmen and other staff were gathered in a half-circle at the far end of the long table from the Seabrookes and Tavy. Mrs. Seabrooke gave them a smile as bright as the one she'd given Tavy a few minutes before.

"The setting looks marvelous," she began. "We do not have tea while Sir William is away but when he is at the manor it will be served every day at four. Dinner, as usual, will be at eight. A few of you are new here and have never met Sir William. He is a good man. Fair. You know he is a great politician, our MP for this district, a key voice for the Conservative Party, His Majesty's Loyal Opposition. Very religious — there will be devotions at every breakfast and staff members are expected to attend if they are on duty. As with Lady Elizabeth, grace is said at every meal. What else? Ah, yes, do remember Sir William is left-handed when you set his place or serve him tea or coffee — Maggie, you will need to switch his fork and knife and spoon around — that's right — and his wine glass and water glass — excellent.

"Of course it is Easter week and tonight is Maundy Thursday. There will be a service in the manor chapel at ten. Completely voluntary in terms of attendance though both Sir William and Lady Elizabeth would be grateful to see you there. Bear in mind that Emma's fiancé, the Reverend Jeremiah Sweet, will be leading the service and giving the homily, so no doubt our dear Emma would be happy for your presence and show of support as well. The youngest, Victoria, will be singing 'O Sacred Head, Now Wounded.' I don't know what your religious beliefs are, but she has the voice of a lark — I would be hard put not to feel worshipful myself when that young lady lifts up her voice. Anything else, Mr. Seabrooke?"

His hands were folded behind his back and he nodded gravely. "Easter Sunday. The wedding."

"Of course. Sir William will want the black crepe taken down early Sunday morning from the chapel and replaced with fresh-cut flowers, as much color as we can find on the grounds and in the gardens. It's to celebrate our Lord's resurrection, you see. There will be a service here at eight Sunday, close to sunrise — well, not so close, but it is symbolical, you take my point. Then the family will attend Easter Sunday services at St. Mark's-among-the-Starlings. Our household staff is encouraged to attend if they do not have other pressing duties."

"Such as cooking the Sunday lunch?"

piped up Mrs. Longstaff, a small woman with curly, rust-colored hair and a voice and laugh that filled the room. The others laughed with her, easing some of the tension for those who were serving Sir William at his estate for the first time.

"Yes," replied Mrs. Seabrooke with a smile. "You and your assistants would indeed be hard-pressed to attend worship services and have the meal ready at one. Ben Whitecross and Todd Turpin will be busy driving the coaches back and forth from the church."

Loud voices could be heard from the front door, and footsteps began to echo down the long stone hallway. Mrs. Seabrooke clapped her hands together quickly. "Right. Here they come. No, just stay where you are for the present. Sir William will want to address you as a group. As for the wedding of Emma to Reverend Sweet, you already know it will take place next Friday in the chapel here. There'll be plenty of time to discuss arrangements after Easter Sunday is done."

Sir William and Lady Elizabeth entered the dining hall with its high ceiling and walls and rich oil paintings of ancestors who bore the Danforth name. Their family followed them. Sir William opened his arms to the staff.

"It is very good to see all of you. Sally, Norah, Mrs. Longstaff, Mr. and Mrs. Seabrooke, Tavy, Harrison — wonderful. And there are new faces too — welcome. I'll get to know you better this week, I'm sure, and Lady Elizabeth will help me put names to your faces as swiftly as possible. But for now, let us keep in mind that the days are upon us during which we remember our Savior's sacrifice for us. We will honor Him in quiet and with Mrs. Longstaff's good but simple meals for the first few days. But Sunday we will express our jubilation at His resurrection and His conquest of death. We'll enjoy a rather spare tea tonight — it is, after all, Maundy Thursday, when our Savior was betrayed and put in chains — and both tea and dinner will reflect that, as our meals on Good Friday and Holy Saturday shall reflect His death and burial and repose in the tomb. Very well. Shall we pray then?"

Heads bowed and Sir William spoke a few words of blessing, then the family sat while the staff moved about to serve them. Sir William asked after his daughter Libby, who was nursing in France, and then wondered if there was any news he had missed regarding his sons since he had been at Westminster. There was nothing to report, his wife told him — Edward, the eldest, remained with the Royal Navy and had seen no action at all, a great relief to her; Kipp, next in line, was flying with his squadron in France and had not been injured in the past fortnight, another relief; their youngest son, Robbie, was still with the army at Dublin, safely stationed with other officers in the Hotel Metropole, and chafing that he was not with the British army in France or Belgium — this also suited her admirably.

"I'm grateful everyone is where they are," she said, sipping at her water. "I hope the navy never has to fight and Robbie never has to leave Ireland. It's quite enough to worry about Kipp and Libby in France."

"Lib is far from the front lines, Mother," responded Emma. "I shouldn't worry too much about her."

Lady Elizabeth glanced across the table at Emma and Catherine and Victoria. "I have four daughters and I want to keep all of them. The front, as you call it, Emma, has a way of changing position altogether too frequently and putting persons where they have no business being — like nurses and doctors who are suddenly caught up in bombs and bullets and barbed wire. So I have committed my Easter prayers to Libby and Kipp. I will remember all of you, and all of my sons, but it is Kipp and Libby I shall be asking God to pay particular attention to this weekend."

Sir William nodded and rapped the table gently with his knuckles. "Hear, hear."

O sacred Head, now wounded, with grief
and shame weighed down,
Now scornfully surrounded with thorns,
Thine only crown.
How pale Thou art with anguish, with sore
abuse and scorn!
How doth that visage languish, which
once was bright as morn!

What Thou, my Lord, hast suffered, was
all for sinners' gain,
Mine, mine was the transgression, but
Thine the deadly pain.
Lo, here I fall, my Savior! 'Tis I deserve
Thy place,
Look on me with Thy favor, vouchsafe to
me Thy grace.

Victoria's pure, strong voice filled the chapel. The room was dark but for a dozen white candles placed at different stained glass windows. The chapel was connected to the manor and nestled in a rose garden.

Even at dusk light glowed in the windows. But now they were covered in black crepe so that moonlight could not penetrate. Victoria felt as if she were singing in a tomb.

The chapel could accommodate one hundred. Her family sat facing her in the flickering gloom as well as a dozen of the servants, including Tavy, Mr. and Mrs. Seabrooke, Harrison, Todd, and Norah, her own maid. As she sang she saw her father's eyes fill and he sank his head in his hands. It was never religion for religion's sake with him. He felt everything he believed deep in his heart and his blood. Her mother did as well, caring a great deal about the life and teachings of Christ, though she was never as emotional or as demonstrative as her husband.

The dimness of this space suits you, Catherine. Her sister's anxiety and weariness, cut in lines below her eyes and at the corners of her mouth, softened in the shadows and became the strokes of an artist working with sticks of charcoal. Her black hair, gathered at her neck, framed her face like a veil. *You feel the death and sufferings of Christ as deeply as father does.*

Emma smiled directly at her as Victoria began the fifth verse of the hymn. Dear Emma could never feel anguish like father or Catherine or even their mother. Of all of them, including Libby and her brothers, Emma was the most even-keeled, the one who never got into a flap, or laughed too loudly, or cried too long. She believed in the Christian faith, and was delighted to be marrying an Anglican minister — though Victoria was certain Emma would have married Jeremiah even if he were a brick-layer or fishmonger — but the flow of her faith through her heart was a gentle stream, never a torrent or a deep well.

Sir Arthur, with his large white curling mustache and shining bare head, her mother's father, sat with his cane across his knees and his eyes closed. Victoria knew he wasn't sleeping. It was his way of taking things in. He even did it in the middle of conversation at breakfast or dinner if he wanted to listen to what someone was saying as closely as possible.

On one side of him, Lady Grace, her father's mother, sat in a black dress trimmed in white lace, with a dark veil dropping over her face from a dark hat. Her eyes were wide and bewildered as they usually were. But it was a mistake, Victoria had long ago learned, to assume by her vacant gaze that she was not altogether there. Her mind was quite precise and she recalled details of incidents and dialogue that had taken place weeks before as if they were happening in front of her at the present moment. Yet she always seemed distracted, drifting about the rooms of the manor as if she were in another world, spending her hours among lords and ladies of Ashton Park who were long dead.

On the other side of Sir Arthur was Aunt Holly, her father's youngest sister. She was only in her thirties, and her teeth were white and straight, her figure slender and erect, her hair night-black and gleaming. The beauty of a young woman had never left her face or eyes or lips. One of her hands rested on Sir Arthur's arm. Always bickering but always together, as if they were husband and wife instead of quarrelsome friends. The skin of her face, thin over her cheekbones, seemed lit as if by a candle placed by her head, and her blue eyes glittered with an animation Victoria would have expected from Libby if she were present. Smiles were constant with Aunt Holly, but never fixed — every part of her was engaged when it was time to smile. She was a good aunt now and had been a good aunt when they were young, Victoria remembered — the one who had the best stories, the best sweets in her pocket, the best energy of any of the adults. She could always outrun and outclimb and outjump everyone. Why she had remained single was unknown to Victoria and her siblings, and their parents never talked of it, but Victoria and Catherine speculated that there had been a long-ago love gone bad. At any rate, she seemed content to live out her years here with her brother's family.

Victoria gathered her thoughts for the final verse of the hymn and left off thinking about her family to think about Christ instead. As she poured out her music from her throat, unaccompanied by any instrument, she knew Easter mattered to her as much as it did to anyone in the chapel, perhaps more, for she felt Christ cared about women, cared about the poor of Ireland, cared about the British and German and French soldiers dying in the mud of Flanders. That was why she worshipped Him. He was God with a human face.

My Savior, be Thou near me when death is at my door,
Then let Thy presence cheer me, forsake me nevermore!
When soul and body languish, oh, leave me not alone,
But, take away mine anguish by virtue of Thine own!

Be Thou my consolation, my shield when
    I must die,
Remind me of Thy passion when my last
    hour draws nigh.
Mine eyes shall then behold Thee, upon
    Thy cross shall dwell,
My heart by faith enfolds Thee. Who dieth
    thus dies well.

Jeremiah stood up in his clerical robes
once she had finished and clasped her hand
in both of his. The wooden limb and hand
that replaced the right arm blown off in
France eighteen months before pressed
firmly against her skin.

"God bless you, Sister," he said quietly,
almost whispering, candlelight moving
about on the lenses of his round glasses.

"It's an honor to sing on this night," she
responded.

Jeremiah took his place behind the small
hand-carved pulpit and delivered what
turned out to be a brief and to-the-point
homily — and yet, despite its brevity, here
and there in the room, there could be seen
the wiping away of a tear.

The service concluded with a benediction
and the family left first, followed by the
household staff, several of whom returned
to the various small duties that remained

before they could retire.

Long after the manor had gone to bed, her family and Jeremiah in upstairs rooms, the servants in the rooms below the main floor and just along the hallway from the kitchen, Victoria wrapped a deep green cloak about herself and went silently from the house to the stables, a night mist draping her shoulders and arms and head. A lantern was lit and hanging from a nail near a stall as she came inside. Several of the horses lifted their heads to stare, but picking up on her familiar scent, did nothing. Two arms suddenly enfolded her from behind.

"It's about time," said a man's voice.

He began to kiss the back of her neck. She closed her eyes a moment to take in the feeling before turning around and looking him in the face.

"You weren't at the chapel." She used an accusing tone but smiled as Ben Whitecross kissed her throat.

"Ah, you know me. I'm not one for the High-Church mumbo-jumbo."

"Jeremiah gave a nice message. Plain and simple."

"Plain and simple, was it?"

"And I sang."

"I know. That I would like to have heard.

41

But you can sing a hymn for me now."

"I will not."

Ben pulled her against him and pressed his lips to her damp hair. "You're perfect. Do you know that?"

"I certainly don't know it." She ran a hand through his dark curls. "I would like to have had you there."

"A good Methodist like me in a Church of England chapel?"

"I would have liked you there, Ben."

"Well. Maybe another time." He took her face in his hands and she saw him take pleasure in her green eyes. "How long do we have?"

"An hour. No more. Sometimes Harrison gets restless in those rooms of his in the Castle and walks about and checks on the barn and stables." Suddenly she laughed and stood on her toes in her boots and kissed him as hard as she could on the lips. "I think of you all the time, Ben Whitecross, with your black hair and blue eyes. You were so cute today bundled up in your coat and hat and scarf. I could be persuaded, oh, easily persuaded tonight, that I was falling in love with the curly-haired stable boy."

"Could you now? And what would your father say to that, my sweet?"

"I'd prefer not to think of that. Why bring

sadness to a night such as this?"

"Why indeed?"

2

The Easter weekend went by swiftly. Sir William spent a good deal of it walking with Harrison, the groundskeeper, who wore his perpetual adornment of tan corduroy jacket and brown fedora, wooden staff firmly in hand, while Sir William had on a tweed jacket and dark pants and flat cap. They wandered over the estate, examining the various stretches of forest and the half-dozen fish ponds where swan, geese, and ducks rested, Sir William wading in hip-high boots in Danforth Brook, which ran through the property into the sea, then taking a long look at the sheep and lambs Harrison and his assistant, Skitt, shepherded. The dogs, Gladstone and Wellington, were constantly at his heels but knew better than to chase the sheep.

Easter Sunday the sun came out of the clouds for a few hours. The windows in the chapel, although they faced southwest and did not catch the morning light, had their black crepe removed and glowed with blue sky that made the stained glass images bright and recognizable — Jesus feeding the four thousand, the healing of the lepers, the Sermon on the Mount. Bouquets of fresh flowers were laid on every sill.

Mrs. Longstaff prepared a pheasant for lunch and the spirit of mourning and somberness Sir William had insisted upon was banished as he called upon Ashton Park to honor Christ's resurrection.

"He is risen!" he called to the servants before his family sat down to lunch.

"He is risen indeed, sir," they responded as a body.

As Sir William tucked into the pheasant he glanced up at Tavy. "I trust Mrs. Longstaff followed my instructions."

Tavy poured water from a silver pitcher into Sir William's glass. "What instructions were those, sir?"

"A pheasant for the staff as well."

"She's cooked it to perfection."

"And you'll make sure everyone sits down to feast on it just as soon as we are done here?"

"We shall, sir."

"A Happy Easter to you, Tavy."

"And to you, Sir William."

The next day, Easter Monday, Sir William was up early to run his shepherds and meet Harrison at the Castle hidden among the oak trees. A tour was expected to arrive just after nine.

"Good morning, Harrison."

Harrison inclined his head. "Sir."

"Did that Sunday meal put some flesh on your bones?"

Harrison was a slender man with a quiet smile and eyes that always seemed to catch the light. "I look much the same as I did before the pheasant, sir."

"Do you?" Sir William snorted. "I shall have to ask Mrs. Longstaff to roast an ox for your birthday."

"Well, I love oxtail soup."

"Never mind the soup and the tail. I want you to eat the ox itself."

A horn sounded in the distance.

"There's an old custom," said Sir William, bringing his watch out of his coat pocket. "The coach driver announcing their arrival with a blast on the trumpet. Spot on nine. How many are we expecting?"

"Three coaches and two motorcars."

"So many? The note I received at my

rooms in London said only two coaches."

Harrison shrugged. "There's a lively interest in our English heritage these days. Perhaps it's the war brings people out."

"Hmm." Sir William clapped a hand on Harrison's shoulder. "Now you don't mind my leading the tour of the Castle? You do it so many times during the year when I'm down at Westminster. I'm sure you know the ins and outs of it far better than I do. You live in the Castle, not the manor, for heaven's sakes. But I take pleasure in doing it when I can."

Harrison shook his head as the first of the coaches rumbled along the avenue through the oak trees pulled by its four horse team. "It's your ancestors' home, sir. Please do us the honor."

The coaches pulled up followed by two shining black motorcars. Sir William greeted the people as they alighted while Harrison stood back. As Sir William spoke, introducing himself, the crowd gazed over his head at the Castle. To the left there were only walls, the roofs long gone and not yet restored, but to the right the keep soared three hundred feet, stone and mortar intact, no sinking into the mound of earth on which it was set, no leaning to the side, no crumbling at the turret. The buildings —

47

baileys — attached to it were also well preserved, the flat roofs of stone and timber having been repaired and fortified, the walls still sturdy and erect. A moat that had once been there had mostly been filled in with rock and dirt and grass over the centuries.

Sir William rubbed his hands together and smiled at a cluster of schoolboys standing in front. "Well, let me begin then. The date for the completion of the tower you see, the Castle Keep, is 1086, so far as we know. There are some descriptions in letters and journal entries of the time. The idea of building a keep came from Anjou and Normandy with the Norman Conquest of 1066. And it was as well the Danforths had it up — they called themselves the Danfordes then and came from the south of England. Yes, it was just as well, because there are county records that indicate a Viking raid took place in the summer of 1087, only a year later. Come closer."

The group walked up to the Castle behind him. He scooped up a fallen oak branch and tapped at streaks of black at the base of the Keep. "See that? The Norse raiders tried to bring the Keep down by building a fire to break up the mortar but it didn't work. The tower was too well constructed. They might have tried to keep the fire going for days but they didn't have the time. The oak forest here hid Lancashire men who began to pick off the invaders with their bows and arrows. So the Vikings beat a hasty retreat back through the oaks and ash trees to the sea cliff, where they climbed down a path to their ship."

Sir William straightened and pointed at the oak trees with his branch. "Now, most of this is new growth, of course; none of these trees saw the Norse raiders except — and it is a great exception — three we have here behind the Castle that experts have declared to be at least one thousand years old. Follow me." He began to stride around the left side of the castle and past the roofless buildings. "We've had to prop up the limbs of two of them to keep them from breaking off. But they certainly saw the Norse attack of 1087. And no doubt brave Lancashire men hid behind those ancient oaks and fired their arrows. Indeed, I will show you where a Norse spearhead is embedded in a trunk of one of the old girls — the Vikings sought to strike back at the bowmen. The tree has grown around the spearhead but you can still see it plainly. Rather large. We've never had it removed for fear of damaging the tree."

The crowd followed Sir William to the

back of the Castle, the schoolboys running up to get closer to him and closer to the Viking spearhead. Harrison smiled his smile and brought up the rear, while the coachmen and chauffeurs remained with the horses and the motorcars.

Victoria was about to slip out to the stables that evening, when a courier drove up by car from the nearby town with a cable from London. Instead of passing it on to Tavy to deliver, the courier's indication that the message was of some priority made Victoria decide to take it to her father herself. She found him sitting in his private study, a room full of books and chess pieces and telescopes and microscopes and globes, spectacles on his nose, reading documents and discussing shipyard matters with Albert, Catherine's husband.

"Ah, my girl." Her father smiled. "What is it?"

Albert gave her a smile but seemed perturbed at the interruption. "I was finally able to get your father to look into our business concerns in Belfast."

Sir William took off his glasses. "Plenty of time for that."

"A cable has come from London for you, Father," Victoria said. "The courier expressed concern that you receive it as soon as possible. I happened to be at the door so I decided to bring it to you myself rather than ring Tavy."

Her father's face dropped its smile. "He expressed concern, did he?" Taking the slip of paper from her hand he returned his glasses to his nose, opened the telegram, and read it. His face did not appear to change expression, but Victoria knew him well enough to understand the barely noticeable tightening of his lips.

"What is it, Father?" she asked him. "Something to do with Parliament?"

He put his glasses on the table strewn with sheets of paper and stood up. "I must speak with your mother first. Pray wait here."

He found Lady Elizabeth in her room. She was in her dressing gown and preparing for bed, brushing out her long auburn hair that, of all the children, only Victoria shared. She smiled as he knocked and entered.

"Hello, dear. Come to kiss me goodnight and tuck me in?"

But her husband did not smile back at her. "I've received a note from Westminster."

Lady Elizabeth put down her brush with a sharp look of annoyance. "Oh, no. They don't mean to bring you back early? They can't. Emma's wedding is Friday."

"There's some sort of trouble in Dublin. Irish revolutionaries have taken over key buildings in the city and mean to put up a fight. They've declared Ireland an independent nation. A republic."

Lady Elizabeth stood up. "What about Robbie? He's in Dublin."

"It just started yesterday. Easter Sunday. There haven't been any major engagements. I'm positive he's fine."

"William. I'm frightened."

"Come. Come here."

When she approached, he put his arms around her. "My dear, don't be anxious. This is what the Irish do. It shall be all over in another day or two. It's posturing on their part, nothing more. I can't imagine there will be any actual battle. They're simply trying to draw attention to their cause in the most dramatic of ways."

She closed her eyes. "I hope you're right. Not everyone thinks as rationally as you. It's bad enough having Kipp caught up in that awful air fighting but at least he can take care of himself, he always has. And Edward's at dock in Scotland and I can only pray the Grand Fleet remains at dock for the rest of the war. But Robbie — he's such an innocent . . . I thought Ireland would be so safe . . . and now this . . ."

Tears moved quickly down her cheeks.

Her husband patted her back. "Shh. Dublin is not the Western Front, why, it's part of Britain. There will be no war there. Those clashes are behind us and in the past."

"Must you return to Westminster?"

"No. The party hasn't asked me to do that. We're not in power, after all. Let us put this out of our thoughts and simply look forward to Emma's wedding. We won't breathe a word. There's no point in disturbing the household, when it will all blow over in a matter of days or hours. Though Victoria was present when I read the cable so she may pester me about its contents."

"The newspapers will write it up, William."

"When they do we shall discuss it with the family at that point. Until then, we put it aside and carry on with our plans as if nothing's happened."

Lady Elizabeth grasped the fabric of his coat tightly in her fingers. "How can a mother do that when her youngest son is in harm's way?"

"It's no easier for a father, but we must be brave when our children have taken on adult lives of their own. He shall be safe."

"Oh, surely not there, Elizabeth. Why, you'll smother the altar."

Lady Elizabeth blew an exasperated breath out of her nose and mouth. "Well, then, what do you suggest, Holly?"

"At its base. The very thing. It will look wonderful there."

Two footmen, Heatherington and Wallace, lifted a great heap of gold and green bunting down from the altar as Lady Elizabeth waved her hand. They placed it on the floor stones at the front of the altar. One of the maids, Lillian, knelt and began to fuss with it, molding it into a more pleasing shape. All around the chapel, people were putting up tall candles, or green and gold clusters of ribbons and sheets of fabric. Emma stood back with her sisters Catherine and Victoria, her fingers to her lips.

"I don't know if it's all coming together," she wondered out loud. "Mother is fretting so much."

Catherine shrugged. "Oh, it looks well enough. And it's only Tuesday. You have all week to fix it."

Victoria put an arm around Emma. "I absolutely love green and gold, Em. Like sunlight on the grass. It's perfect."

"Really?"

"Our gowns are going to be in green with gold sashes and scarves, aren't they?"

"Yes."

"It will have the most astonishing effect. All this riot of sun on green and you standing in the middle of it in pure white. Wonderful."

Catherine shrugged again. "Oh, well, any colors will do. I'm sure these are fine."

Victoria made a face. "Try to be a little more animated, Cath. Maundy Thursday is over and done with for this year. He's alive, remember? He's alive, we're alive, even you're alive."

"I'm tired from the weekend and all the back and forth to church and chapel."

Victoria hesitated. "Why, I always thought that was the very thing you liked. The worship. The kneeling. The prayers."

Catherine gazed ahead at Lillian, who was still working on the large heap of green and gold bunting, Aunt Holly at her side and offering her help. "I rather prefer staying in one place and in one room with one single candle burning."

Emma and Victoria stared at her.

"You sound like a nun," Emma said.

Catherine pondered this for a moment

and then said, "I don't think I'd much like being a nun."

"No, and I very much doubt the nuns would have you," Victoria said. "Now what's next to do? We want everything just so for your wedding, Em."

"It all looks lovely," Emma said. "Really. There's nothing amiss."

"And nothing shall go amiss," Lady Elizabeth said. "My daughters shall all have perfect weddings."

"And how about your daughters' marriages?" Catherine mused.

"That, my dears," Lady Elizabeth said, "shall be entirely up to you and your husbands. A mother can do only so much."

The British officer lifted the binoculars to his eyes again. The Irishmen were definitely armed and were all working feverishly to fortify Dublin's large post office. He caught glimpses of them in the windows. Then he raised the binoculars to the roof. Flags flew there. Not the Union Jack. Flags of the Irish Republic, which the rebels had put up on Easter Sunday.

"Now it's Tuesday," the officer said out loud.

"Sir?" A corporal behind him stepped forward.

"It will go hard on them, Collingwood. King George will not like the idea of a rebellion in Ireland when he's already fighting a war with Germany. There won't be any patience for this. The Crown will strike hard."

They were standing alone in an alleyway. On the street in front of them, rioters were running from shop to shop, breaking windows and smashing down doors, stealing hats and suits and shoes, carrying away chairs and sofas — whatever they could lay their hands on. Fires had been started and smoke drifted over the buildings near them.

"Anarchy." The officer made a note on a pad in his hand. "I count well over a hundred rebels in the post office so far. I'm making an estimate. I know I've likely counted some of them twice but —"

From behind him, came the Irish voice. "Put away the paper and pencil, limey. And don't move your hand to your sidearm."

The Irish voice was right in the officer's ear. A coldness went through his mind. He dropped the pad and pencil on the pavement. A gun barrel pushed into the back of his neck.

"Take his pistol, Seamus. You, limey, what's your name?"

"I am . . . Leftenant Robert Danforth."

"Well, Leftenant Robert Danforth, you and your corporal are prisoners of the army of the Irish Republic. Walk straight ahead, both of you. Get up with your hands. You're so interested in what we're doing at the post office, are you? So we'll take you along and give you a firsthand look. Don't try to run or you'll be shot."

Tall, like his father and mother, with the dark hair of Aunt Holly and his sister Catherine, Robbie moved out from the alleyway with his corporal beside him pale as sand, and the pair of them marched across the street, two gunmen at their backs, the one pointing his own pistol at him. The rioters paid the group of them no attention whatsoever, far more intent on looting and breaking open more shops. The four men continued past the dead horses of the Lancers that the Irish had shot and killed the day before.

Despite the roar of the mob, Robbie heard the sound of their boots on the street as if it were magnified. The same was true of the pumping of his blood and the noise of his breathing. His mother and father and Ashton Park passed through his thoughts, as well as images of the path on the sea cliff he had loved to slide down when he was a boy. His troops came to mind, stationed several streets back, and the cup of hot coffee and the hot cross bun he had been promised when he returned from his reconnaissance.

A door swung open when they reached the post office and he was prodded inside. Scores of men peered at him, all of them in rough clothing and gripping rifles in their hands. One jerked his chin at Robbie and the corporal.

"Hey. So you're standing on the soil o' the Free State o' Ireland. Take off your caps."

Robbie did so immediately.

"That's better." The man smiled. "Try not to look so tense, Leftenant. I may be wrong but I don't believe the Irish Republic shoots prisoners of war." Then he shrugged. "But maybe we do. I suppose it depends on how your king reacts to our declaration of independence."

Tavy smoothed his hands over his starched white shirt and his stomach and straightened his black suit jacket and tie. When he was ready he knocked on the door. After a moment, Mr. Seabrooke opened it a crack.

"Who is it?" came Mrs. Seabrooke's voice.

"Tavy, ma'arm."

"Oh, Mr. Seabrooke, open the door to him, for heaven's sakes."

Mr. Seabrooke swung the door as wide as he could and stood to one side as Tavy entered the room. Mrs. Seabrooke was bent over a ledger and jotting down numbers from slips of paper.

"A costly enterprise running this household," she muttered, her head still down.

"Indeed."

"Well. What is it?"

"There's an officer at the front door. A high-ranking army officer to see Sir William. I thought you should know."

Mrs. Seabrooke sat up and stared at him. "Is there? Why haven't you taken the officer to the man himself?"

"He's on the grounds somewhere with the dogs. I've sent two men to look for him."

"Will Lady Elizabeth do?"

"The officer did not wish to speak to Lady Elizabeth without Sir William present. I thought it best not to disturb her and her daughters while they decorate the chapel and work through the wedding details."

"What is the officer's rank?"

"He's a colonel, Mrs. Seabrooke."

"A colonel!"

"I believe this is a matter that has to do with Ireland."

She stood up, banging her knee against the desk. "It's about Robbie."

"I expect so."

"Oh, Lord, what has happened?"

Tavy cleared his throat quickly. "The colonel, of course, will not speak of it. I have him in the library with a tea. One of the staff — Wallace — was mentioning there was a bit of a to-do going on in Dublin. It hasn't received a great deal of reportage. Some Irishmen have taken over a post office, of all things. The article Wallace read did not offer a great deal of information."

"Surely Sir William has read the same article?"

"I think not. He would have said something. In fact, he has sworn off all newspapers during Parliament's Easter recess."

Mrs. Seabrooke blew out a lungful of air. "Who have you sent to find him?"

"Young Heatherington. And Todd Turpin. Todd is on horseback."

"Sir William!"

The blond shepherds ran barking up to the horse Todd Turpin was riding. Sir William waved a walking stick.

"Hullo, Todd. Felt I needed a breath of fresh air before tea. What are you up to then?"

Todd climbed down from the black gelding. "I've been sent to fetch ye, sir. There's an army officer up at the house who says he must speak with ye on a matter of some urgency."

Sir William frowned, reaching down to pet his dogs. "Army officer?"

"Aye, sir. Please take my horse. Ye know old Star. I'll bring the dogs along."

Sir William placed his walking stick in Todd's hands. "I am obliged to you."

He climbed into the saddle and turned the gelding's head with the reins. He urged Star into a gallop and moved rapidly across the field and onto a path through the ash trees.

Sir William, upon returning to the manor, gathered Lady Elizabeth and the two made their way to the library. A few moments later, Tavy opened the door and before he could usher the colonel in, Lady Elizabeth rushed up to the visitor and said, "Colonel, what is it? Is it my son? What's happened?"

The officer was a large man with square shoulders and jaw and a full mustache as dark as boot polish. He kept his arms at his side.

"Lady Elizabeth. Sir William. I am Colonel Harraway. I'm very sorry to tell you that your son, Leftenant Robert Danforth, has been captured by Irish rebels. As far as we know, he is perfectly fine."

"As far as you know?"

"Lady Elizabeth. Your son and a Corporal Collingwood were seen being marched into the Dublin post office at gunpoint. The post office is currently a rebel stronghold. Leftenant Danforth is a prisoner of war. That's the extent of our knowledge at this point."

Sir William put his hands behind his back. "I've received several notes from Westminster about the affair, Colonel. No doubt the papers will soon be full of whatever news they're allowed to print about the uprising. But I would like to hear your point of view as a military man."

"Very well. The rebels took over a number of buildings and intersections in Dublin on Easter Sunday. No one thought much of it. The next day they murdered a troop of British Lancers — shot them to death in the street. Tuesday the number of engagements between our forces and the rebels increased. Your son was on reconnaissance and attempting to assess the strength of the rebel position at the post office when he was captured. I can tell you the fighting has continued to intensify since then. We have already taken back some of the buildings the rebels have occupied. The fighting will continue until we have completely wrested Dublin out of their hands."

"And how long will that take?" demanded Sir William.

The colonel remained at attention. "Well, sir, the rebels do not enjoy popular support. Our troops are moving in on all fronts. It's Wednesday. We mean to have the city under the Union Jack by the weekend. If necessary we'll employ artillery."

"Artillery!"

"Yes, Sir William. We can't have this fire going on in our backyard when Europe is an inferno. It must be dealt with sharply. Artillery. Incendiaries. By whatever means necessary."

"Artillery can be — notoriously imprecise. You'll lay waste to whole streets."

The colonel nodded. "Can't be helped, sir. It's war."

Lady Elizabeth sat down and began to weep.

"Thank you for coming to tell us," Sir William said. "We do appreciate the effort.

With that, the colonel expressed his sympathies and turned to leave. Sir William sat beside his wife and took her hands in his.

"Bear up, my dear. Our Robbie will be safe. He must be safe."

3

Victoria lay beside Ben on a fresh bed of straw and ran her fingers through the dark curls on his head. A lantern hung from a beam one stall over.

"We don't have much more time," she said.

"Ah, love, just give me a minute."

"You know Em called off the wedding?" she asked.

"I did know that. Mrs. Seabrooke called the staff together this afternoon and explained the situation. I'm sorry for you and your family, Vic. Robbie was always decent to me, especially when we were boys and I had the job of mucking out the stables. He never put on airs. Not like your brother Edward."

"Oh, well, Edward. He's the firstborn son. That's the problem. Fancies himself lord of the manor already."

"How are your parents holding up?"

She leaned her head on one elbow so that she could look him in the face. "They take care of each other. He brings her to the chapel to pray. That helps."

"I'm praying."

"Are you?"

"I am. I believe in it. Though I can't say things always turn out the way I wish."

She ran her fingers over his lips. "Do you pray about us?"

"Always."

"What do you pray about then?"

"That you'll love me."

"I do love you."

He smiled and played with a strand of her hair. "I pray that you'll love me forever."

"Forever! That sounds serious."

He stopped smiling and sat up. He took her face in his hands. "So I am serious. I think about marrying you."

Her eyes widened in the lamplight. "Marriage."

"But it's mad. Your parents would never agree to it."

"We could persuade them if you really mean what you're saying."

He kissed her on the cheek. "How could we persuade them? I'm a poor stable groom who smells like horses. They'll want you wed to a duke."

"I don't fancy dukes. I fancy you."

"Sometimes I feel like going down to Liverpool and signing up. Ship over to France and do something brave and noble. Come back an officer. Decorated. A war hero. Then Sir William would sit up and take notice."

Victoria took her hand from his curls. "Don't talk that way, Ben. I don't want a dead man or an armless man. You don't need to kill yourself in that mess over there. They haven't come after you with an enlistment form, have they? So thank God and stay close to me and we'll work it out together. My father and mother aren't that set in their ways."

Ben groaned. "Of course they are. I'll have to do something, I tell you. They'll never consider a marriage otherwise."

She narrowed her eyes and brought one of her hands to his lips. "No more talk of your war ideas. Put them out of your head."

She drew him to herself and kissed him.

Sir William rubbed his forehead as he looked at the figures on the sheet of paper. "I'm sorry, Albert. What was that again? What am I looking for?"

Albert leaned back in his chair. "I think we should take a break, sir. You have a lot on your mind."

"No. It's best to do things. Not sit and fret. It's best to occupy the mind at such times."

Albert smoothed his mustache. Then he pointed to his left eye. "I wish I didn't have this bad eye, Sir William. I wish my vision was sharp as a hawk's. I'd have enlisted long ago. I'd have asked for Dublin too. I'd have taken proper care of those Republican sods by now. You and Lady Elizabeth wouldn't be grieving as you are."

"No one blames you for your eye, Albert. I'm glad I have you managing the family's affairs in Northern Ireland."

Albert made to say something, stopped, then leaned forward. "I know you think you're doing your best for them by trying to persuade them to adopt Home Rule. But it won't work. Remaining united to England is Ireland's future. It always has been. Do you think Ulster would ever vote for Home Rule? Or independence? We'd sooner die than be ruled by a Catholic majority."

Sir William removed his glasses and stared at him. "You have hard and fast opinions, Albert. It might be best if you did not voice them overmuch."

The splotches of red became more prominent on Albert's face. "You needn't fear I would speak in the wrong place at the wrong time and adversely affect the family business."

"I'm not afraid for the family business. I'm afraid for you. And for my daughter. I feel I misjudged not only the passion for independence a number of the Irish hold to — I misjudged their capacity to fight. I do not wish you to become a target as my son Robbie has become a target."

Albert shook his head. "No fear of that, Sir William. Belfast couldn't be a safer place for a fellow with my point of view. It's not Dublin, you know. It's a Protestant town. Loyal to the king."

Sir William returned his glasses to his face. "Nevertheless. I would prefer more prudence, Albert Moore. I think I make myself understood."

Albert stiffened in his chair and nodded. "Yes, sir. You do, sir."

Aunt Holly walked quietly down the hallway and peered in at the chapel. Afternoon light made the stained glass burn with colors. It also made it painfully obvious that the wedding decorations she had helped the maids lay out so carefully had all been removed. Not even a candle was left.

She stepped inside. Lady Elizabeth was

kneeling at the altar in a simple gray dress. Aunt Holly came up softly and knelt beside her. Lady Elizabeth lifted her head.

"Holly. I thought it was one of my daughters."

"No. It's just me. Sorry."

Lady Elizabeth did not want to smile but it formed on her lips anyway. "I'm not sorry. Just surprised. You never struck me as a praying person."

"I suppose I'm not."

"Then why join me here?"

"You never know. God might look down and take pity on you because you're saddled with me."

Lady Elizabeth was astonished to hear herself laugh. "Do you think that's the way it works?"

Aunt Holly put a hand on Lady Elizabeth's back. "I don't know how it works because prayer has never seemed to work for me. But who knows? Kneeling together might make a difference. The believer and the prodigal. God has a soft spot for prodigals, doesn't He?"

"What would you like to pray with me?"

"How about the Lord's Prayer? I still remember that. Or is it too common?"

"It's not too common at all. But you start, my dear."

Aunt Holly bowed her head, closed her eyes, and clasped her hands. "I feel like a fool. But I'll do it. God won't see me backing down. *Our Father, who art in heaven, hallowed be Thy name . . .*"

Ben Whitecross took off his cap and set it on a chair just outside the door. From the kitchen down the hall he heard Mrs. Longstaff giving instructions to her staff as they prepared dinner. He smoothed down his curls with both hands, shrugged his shoulders to loosen the tight fit of his best jacket, and knocked on the door. Mr. Seabrooke opened it a crack.

"Who is it?" came Mrs. Seabrooke's voice.

"Ben Whitecross, ma'am. You sent a message I should call on you today."

"I did. Come in. Please, Mr. Seabrooke, open the door."

Ben stepped into Mr. and Mrs. Seabrooke's office. The door was shut firmly behind him. Mrs. Seabrooke looked up from the ledger on her desk and turned in her chair to face him.

"Mr. Whitecross, have a seat."

Ben sat down. Immediately Mr. Seabrooke hovered over him.

"Well, that's it, lad," he growled. "You're done."

Ben glanced up at him, startled. "What's that?"

Mrs. Seabrooke tightened her lips. "There's no need for rudeness, Mr. Seabrooke. You are well aware that Mr. Whitecross has provided a fine service to the Danforth family up until now."

Ben stared at her. "What do you mean, Mrs. Seabrooke?"

She raised the thin eyebrows in her thin face. "Did you honestly think no one would notice your midnight . . . romance with the young Victoria? That no one else on this estate has nocturnal habits?"

Ben was surprised but his face darkened as quickly as the feeling of shock ran through him. "Who has been talking to you? Who has been spouting such nonsense?"

"Someone of impeccable reputation, I assure you. You needn't fear that this has spread over the entire estate or that Sir William or Lady Elizabeth knows of the matter. Mr. Seabrooke and I have kept it to ourselves. But there can be no more dallying with Miss Danforth on your part. You must leave the estate at once."

"I will not."

"You will, Ben Whitecross. I can assure you the repercussions of a refusal shall not be a pleasant experience."

Ben leaned forward in his chair. "I've done nothing wrong. I'm a decent Christian man, Mrs. Seabrooke."

"Oh, I'm sure you have not despoiled Miss Danforth in any way. But an embrace or two is enough. You are a groom, Mr. Whitecross, not a lord. Today you can leave with your reputation intact. We will provide you with excellent references to another noble family in Britain. Sir William and Lady Elizabeth continue to hold you in high regard for your loyalty and competence." She lowered her voice. "If you choose to fight me on this matter, I will destroy you."

Ben curled his hands into fists and said nothing. She waited. Finally he said, "I must have a few moments alone with Victoria."

Mrs. Seabrooke shook her head. "Out of the question."

"I must be allowed to say goodbye if I am to be forced out of Ashton Park today."

"Not just today. This minute. Victoria is off on a day excursion with her sisters." Mrs. Seabrooke picked up a pen and paper and extended them to Ben. "You may write a note. I will read it, so do not say anything foolish or she will never receive it."

"What am I supposed to say? That I am dismissed?"

"You are not dismissed. Unless you try to

make this a public scandal. You may tell her you have taken employment at an estate in Oxfordshire for the time being."

"She won't believe it. She knows I'd do anything to stay here beside her."

Mrs. Seabrooke tapped her fingers on her desktop. "You must vanish entirely, you understand. There can be no correspondence beyond this note. No address where she can find you." She stopped tapping. "Have you ever considered enlisting, Mr. Whitecross?"

Ben held the pen and paper loosely in his hands. "I have. Victoria is against it."

"But Sir William would be for it. He would hold you in high esteem. Perhaps he has wondered why you are here safe and sound while he has three sons in harm's way. His good opinion of you would secure your future." She leaned back in her chair, narrowed her eyes, and smiled. "Write the note. Bid her a noble and heroic farewell. Tell her you are bound by all that is holy to do your patriotic duty. Say you love her, if you must. Then go to the stables and gather your things and be off. Skitt will take you into Liverpool."

"Skitt!"

"Todd Turpin will be the new groom and Skitt will be his assistant."

Ben hesitated, reluctant to put pen to paper. She continued to smile and watched him, resuming the tapping of her fingers.

"It is the Germans or me, Mr. Whitecross," she said softly. "I believe you would be better off choosing the Germans."

Later that afternoon, Colonel Harraway came up from Liverpool. It was not a long drive in a motorcar. Leaving his driver with the vehicle, he knocked at the front door and was ushered by Tavy into the library once again, where Sir William and Lady Elizabeth quickly joined him. He refused tea or water.

"I wished you to hear from me directly," the colonel began as they sat together. "The game is pretty much up. The post office was the last position the rebels held and they are abandoning it. Scores have already surrendered. The fighting was brisk this week but it will all be over in matter of hours."

"What have you heard of our son?" asked Lady Elizabeth as soon as he paused. Her hands gripped her husband's.

"We have recovered some of the British soldiers the rebels held. Not all. They have been treated fairly, a factor that will tell in the rebels' favor when they are tried for treason. But there is no word yet of your

75

son. When there is, I promise you, I shall cable you or come in person."

Lady Elizabeth struggled with her words. "Have they . . . have the Irish . . . shot any of . . . their prisoners?"

"No, my lady, you may rest easy on that score at least. They know the world is watching. The Irish want their cause to appear noble and virtuous."

Sir William fixed the colonel with a sharp stare. "I take it the fighting was severe."

The colonel nodded. "Yes, Sir William. We used artillery and incendiary shells, as I expected. We did not have a month to play with the rebels, not with a war in France. Fires swept through city blocks — some, I grant you, were started by our shells, but others sprang up due to looters and vandals. Dozens of buildings were devastated — whole streets really. Better that shellfire level the rebel positions than our troops attack them head-on."

Sir William held the colonel's eye. "Quite."

The officer looked away and stood up. "I have every expectation your son will return to you unharmed."

Sir William also stood while Lady Elizabeth remained in her chair, a hand over her eyes. "Thank you, Colonel, for your personal concern. I too have every hope that my prayers will be answered." He shook the colonel's hand.

After the officer had left, escorted by Tavy, Sir William remained standing, hands in his pockets. "He knows about my speeches in favor of Home Rule. Likely doesn't approve. No more than I approve of His Majesty's forces shelling Dublin. Well, if we had treated Ireland fairly years ago none of this would be happening right now and Robbie wouldn't be in a fix. A lighter hand was what was needed. A lighter hand and a good dose of Christian charity."

He walked to the window and looked out over the lawn to the oak trees and the Castle they ringed with green. Lady Elizabeth glanced up and followed him with her eyes.

"Home Rule ought to have been in place for Ireland under Gladstone. Under Queen Victoria. Why, it ought to have been in place as far back as Pitt or Wellington. But none of them did it. So now this."

He turned to look at his wife, his face set in strong lines about his jaw and eyes. "We'll have him home again, mother. Through a maelstrom of botched politics and ill-tempered guns, by God's grace, we'll get him back."

That evening after dinner a cable was

brought to the house from a telegraph station in the nearby town. Sir William opened it at the door while Tavy looked on. Sir William clenched a fist and shouted.

I AM SAFE. AM RETURNED TO MY REGIMENT. NOT A SCRATCH. LETTER TO COME. LOVE. ROBBIE.

Candles and lamps were lit throughout the manor. Tavy scurried about gathering family and servants in the Great Hall with its massive stone fireplace that could manage eight-foot logs. Sir William waved the telegram in the air as people came together, Lady Elizabeth beaming beside him, and offered a prayer of thanks for Robbie's safe release. People began to clap. Sir William asked Mrs. Longstaff to bring up tubs of ice cream from the cellar and dish it all out in celebration.

Victoria noticed that Ben Whitecross was not present. While maids were handing out bowls and spoons she slipped out the door, cloak over her shoulders, and headed to the stables. They were dark and no lantern was lit, though she could see the horses that had been worked that day had been rubbed down and now stood quietly in their stalls. She lit a lantern she found dangling from a nail and went to Ben's room.

It was attached to the stables and contained a washstand, desk, wardrobe, a hearth for a turf fire, and a bed. All of his belongings were gone. The room was bare of pictures and clothing and boots. Mementoes she had given him were not on his desk.

"What is going on, Ben?" she whispered.

An envelope that bore her name lay on a chair at the foot of the bed. It was Ben's almost indecipherable handwriting. She opened it. A short note was inside. It did not take her long to read it. She sank down on the bed, lantern in one hand and the letter in the other.

"Enlisted!" she cried out. "France! It's hell, Ben! Hell on earth! Why? Why, Ben Whitecross?"

4

May and June 1916

"Thinking of home, sir? Or your girl?"

The tall officer with the dark red hair grunted. "None of your business, McGrail. But since the fleet's weighed anchor and we're bound to come to blows with the Germans, I'll tell you. I was thinking of my father's dogs. I miss them."

The two men were leaning against a guardrail as their battle cruiser sheared through water that looked like black glass. It was almost midnight and both had night watch. Over their heads, now and then, sharp, bright stars emerged from the cloud cover before disappearing a few minutes later. Neither of them noticed. Both had their eyes on the sea.

McGrail guffawed. "Dogs? You're joking, Commander Danforth."

"Never joke about an Englishman's dogs,

McGrail. What part of Ireland are you from?"

"Carlow, sir. The Garden of Ireland."

"Is it? What did you think about that little muck-up back in April?"

McGrail snorted. "Dublin? The rebellion? Rubbish." He dug into the pocket of his bridge coat, a pea coat that fell to his thighs. Danforth wore the same type of coat against rough weather. McGrail brought out a cigarette and lighter. "Would you care for a smoke, sir?"

"Not tonight."

"Do you mind if I — ?"

"Go ahead. Maybe it will warm us both up." Even though he wore gloves he rubbed his hands together. "It's almost June and the North Sea is still an icebox. *Join the army, Edward, and you can serve with your brother Robbie. Join the Royal Flying Corps and you can pilot a plane with your brother Kipp.* I should have listened to mother."

McGrail blew out a stream of white smoke. "I dunno. There's no way out of a burning plane. And no way out of a shell hole if the Hun have dropped one right on your head. We've got a better chance."

"If you can swim. If you get picked up before you freeze to death. If you're not below decks and go down with the ship."

81

McGrail smoked a moment. "Do you think the German's High Seas Fleet is out of port now too, Commander?"

"I should think so."

"You reckon they know about us being out of our Scottish dock?"

"We've been at sea, what now, an hour and a half? I'm sure their U-boats have reported in."

"I expect they can recognize us."

"Their crews have memorized our ships' silhouettes just like we have theirs. So many smokestacks. So many guns. Thus and thus high is the superstructure."

"Zere goes ze *Queen Mary,* Hans." McGrail imitated a German accent. "Yah, for sure zat's her, Fritzie. Quick, run und tell ze Kaiser." He flicked the butt of his cigarette into the sea. It glowed orange a moment and was gone. "Do you think the Kaiser has a battle cruiser named after *his* wife?"

Edward Danforth smiled in the cold dark. "I have no idea if any woman would have the Kaiser. Wife or otherwise."

"I heard he was Queen Victoria's grandson."

"True. But all resemblance to England ends there, McGrail. Those are his ships we're heading out to fight."

McGrail looked over his shoulder at the long barrels of one of the gun turrets looming in the blackness. "The thirteen-point-five inchers will take care of that business."

"I hope so, McGrail. I surely hope so."

"What on earth is she running around for?" grumbled Sir Arthur.

Aunt Holly glanced at him. "What on earth is *who* running around for?"

"My daughter."

"It's a wedding, Arthur. Her child's wedding. Your granddaughter. Heaven knows Elizabeth has had enough to fret about over the past few months. Let her enjoy herself."

"Enjoy herself?" Sir Arthur stamped the butt of his cane on the stone floor of the chapel where he was seated. "She has a thousand maids to do her running for her."

"Oh, don't be so medieval. The maids and footmen are doing their part. Elizabeth is simply bursting with good-natured energy. Don't you remember what that's like?"

"I have no idea why."

Aunt Holly slapped him on the leg. "I feel like pinching you. So you'll wake up. She has two of her sons home on leave for the wedding. The second attempt at the wedding, I might add. Sir William is due here from Lime Street Station in an hour. Do you understand now why she's bursting?"

"Which sons?"

"Well, if Edward is still at port in Scotland that only leaves two, doesn't it? Kipp and Robbie. You've dined with them the last three nights, for heaven's sakes."

Sir Arthur scowled as a footman dropped an armful of tall candles. "How is it that one of those boys has black hair and the other is blond?"

"The black hair comes from my side of the family. Any red or auburn from Elizabeth and your relatives. Any blond is from you yourself, you old fool. They say you had hair like sunlight when you were young."

"I did not."

"You did. There are photographs. Dozens of them. Shall I fetch them from the library?"

Sir Arthur frowned at a maid adjusting green and gold ribbons by a window. "I don't much care for photographs. Don't trust 'em. I think the Hottentots in Africa were right about that. Steal your soul."

"You mean the Khoikhoi."

Sir Arthur struck the floor with his cane again. "I mean the Hottentots."

The two younger Danforth sons had arrived home and Kipp was out on the lawns walking with Victoria. He took a white silk scarf out of the pocket of his heavy leather jacket and wrapped it around his sister's throat.

"There now," he said. "You're all ready."

Victoria laughed. "Ready to do what?"

"Ready to fly."

"Is that all it takes?"

One side of Kipp's mouth curled up in a half-smile. "Pretty much."

"Well, at the very least it will help keep me warm while we wait for Papa and his coach to come through the trees. He'll be so happy to see you and Robbie. He's missed you both very much. We all have."

Kipp grinned. "Papa and his coach. When will he break down and get a motorcar or two? And while he's at it, he could get the whole estate wired for electricity."

"Ah, you know our father. The incurable romantic. He says mother looks lovely in candlelight. And so she does."

"You can have electricity and still use candles and lamps when you want."

"How long are you with us?"

He shrugged. "I got here on Friday, right? Now it's, what, Tuesday afternoon? May thirty-first? So I told them the wedding would be on the first of June and they want me back three days after that."

"Oh, can't you stay longer?"

"Probably not."

Victoria pouted, squeezing his arm with her hands. "It isn't fair, is it? I've got my two favorite brothers at home with me and it's only for a few short days."

"Well, there's a war on, love."

Her emerald eyes flared in the sunlight. "How I wish there wasn't a war on. I wish the whole beastly thing would disappear into a great dark hole and leave all the men and women behind. Alive. Unwounded."

"Always dreaming, Vic."

She folded her arms over her chest and dark green cloak. Her eyes turned jade. "There is not much else to do stuck at Ashton Park."

"Stuck? Would you like to visit France?"

"And spend my days in a muddy trench wrapped up tight in barbed wire? No, thank you. Now if I could be up in the air with my golden-haired brother and flying through the fleecy clouds, that I might consider." She looked behind her. "And speaking of brothers, I thought Robbie was going to join us."

"I'm here!" A tall young man in army uniform called to them from the stables. "Be with you two in just a tick."

Victoria stared. "I thought you were in the

house with Mum. What are you doing down there?"

"Checking on my mare. Checking on Majestic."

"All's well?"

"Very well. Had her out yesterday. Either of you fancy a ride over the property this evening after Dad's arrived?"

"You're on!" called Kipp.

Victoria smiled at them. "I can't very well let you two go gallivanting off alone, can I? After tea then?"

Robbie walked across the lawn from the stables and joined them. "You don't suppose Cath or Em would have a go?"

"The night before her wedding?" Victoria lifted her eyebrows. "She might or might not. Cath won't."

"Are you sure?" asked Robbie.

"You see how glum she is. Worse than usual."

Kipp grunted. "Why is that?"

"Oh, who knows? She and Albert maybe?"

Robbie put his arm around his sister. "So maybe a ride is just the thing."

"Well, you can ask her at tea, if you'd like." Victoria looked her youngest brother up and down. "You're none the worse for wear after Dublin, are you?"

Robbie looked ahead at the avenue lined

with sweeping oaks. "They were gentlemen, Vic. Never had any intention of doing me harm. Did everything in their power to keep me safe from British machine guns and artillery. Then let me go when all was lost. Had no idea of using me as a hostage."

Victoria looked up at him. "You sound well-disposed toward the Irish. I expected it would be the other way round."

"I'm afraid we weren't so merciful to them, Vic. I dreaded getting the news about the executions."

"We had a couple of Irish in our squadron," Kipp spoke up. "Great chaps. Both brilliant fliers. I gather they didn't care much for the Easter uprising. Thought all the fuss it stirred up would quietly slip away like a tailwind. But they weren't happy about the secret trials and the executions by firing squad — what was it in the end, twelve or fifteen who were shot? That soured them. Last I saw they were talking independence like the most hotheaded Republicans."

"That's just it," replied Robbie. "The executions have made the whole Irish situation worse." He kicked at a loose stone. "And where are they, those two? Transferred?"

"Went down on the same afternoon a few

hours apart."

Victoria was grateful she could break up the conversation. "Here he comes."

Todd Turpin brought the coach smoothly around the drive to the door.

"Ah, there they are!" exclaimed Sir William, climbing out. "My two boys! Sound and healthy, I thank God!"

He took Robbie into his arms and kissed him on the cheek. "I'm so glad you're home and safe. So grateful. How we prayed."

Robbie returned the vigorous hug, closing his eyes. "Thank you, Father."

"How happy your mother must have been to see you." A glimmer of moisture came to Sir William's eyes as he stepped back to look at Robbie. "You seem well, Son."

"They didn't mistreat me. It's just as I wrote in my letter." He hesitated. "Father, thank you for your speech against the executions. I know you were jeered by the prime minister's people."

Sir William's face hardened for a few moments. "You'd think we were Kaiser Wilhelm's Germany the way we tried and shot those men. A disgrace. And a blow to all my good intentions for Ireland. There is another fight coming. The shootings opened the door wide to that." He smiled. "But you're alive and fit, so let's not despair." He gripped the shoulder of his other son. "And we have Kipp with us too. Welcome home, my boy."

They shook hands warmly and embraced.

Kipp grinned. "Hello, Father. You'd have reached Ashton Park faster in a car, you know."

His father laughed. "Or a plane. Well, we had a motor in 1914, you'll recall, before you joined up, and it wasn't much good, was it?"

"You can purchase far better ones now."

"Well, we'll see, we'll see. You look wonderful, Kipp. Still glad you're in the air and not on the ground?"

"Very much so. I love the flying."

"I can see that. They feed you pilots well?"

"Very well."

"The thing at hand now is the wedding. Victoria." He kissed his daughter. "How is Emma holding up?"

"She's very excited, Father. As you might expect."

"And why shouldn't she be? Perfect weather. The whole family here except for Libby and Edward. A second crack at getting married to Jeremiah. The poor girl has had to wait an entire month since the postponement at Easter." His voice dropped and his face took on its characteristic lines around the eyes and mouth. "I got word before I left London that the Grand Fleet, including Edward's ship, left Rosyth last night. They're expected to come to grips with the German High Seas Fleet, though where and when is anyone's guess. There was no action this morning. I'll tell your mother, of course, but I don't wish to postpone dear Emma's wedding a second time. We must get on with it. They'll courier cables up to the house here if anything happens."

He put his arms around his two sons and they walked toward the door. Victoria smiled at the sight: the older man walking with his very tall and very slender son, with the black hair of Aunt Holly and Catherine and the quiet smile of Libby, alongside another son with broad shoulders, hair like morning light, and eyes greener and more piercing than her own. She thought of Ben Whitecross's hair and eyes and her smile was gone instantly.

"Four o'clock!" her father called as they went in the door. "Time for tea, eh, Tavy?"

Tavy smiled and held the door. "It's all prepared. Welcome home, Sir William."

"The prime minister has two days respite from my strident voice, Tavy. No doubt he's as happy about the wedding as all the rest of us are."

Edward Danforth had snatched four hours sleep after his night watch and was back on deck at his battle station near one of the turrets. At 1520 hours the British light cruisers had signaled "enemy in sight" and opened fire. The Germans' big ships had begun to zero in on them less than ten minutes later and the British fleet had immediately started returning salvo for salvo. Edward had plugs in his ears to reduce the noise of the guns less than a hundred feet away, though the shock waves made his whole body shudder regardless. He lifted his binoculars and watched the high white geysers of the *Queen Mary*'s shellfire. They were still falling short. He turned to a sailor at his elbow after scribbling a note on a pad.

"They're not getting it. They need to increase the range."

"Yes, sir."

The sailor left with the slip of paper.

A whoosh cut the air over his head and a tower of water burst upward beside the ship, drenching his coat and officer's cap. Dark smoke to port indicated where the *Indefatigable* had exploded and sunk. To starboard there was another black plume from the wounded *Lion.* Edward checked his watch:

1620 hours, just twenty minutes after four in the afternoon, and already the fight seemed like a shambles, certainly no rout of the enemy like Lord Nelson's victory at Trafalgar in 1805.

More spray showered him. He had identified the *Seydlitz* as one of the German battle cruisers firing at them. Now he was sure they were being targeted by the *Derfflinger* as well. How long would it take before the combined fire of two ships finally scored a hit? Unless the *Queen Mary* sank them first. The turret nearby thundered again and the deck under his feet shook. He counted off the seconds, watching the guns of the German ships winking through his binoculars as more salvos came their way.

Suddenly the whole ship seemed to lift out of the water. Flames and smoke spewed into the air. Edward was hurled upward and then thrown to his hands and knees. He staggered to his feet, binoculars gone, cheek cut and bleeding, cold water on his face. Lurching up the deck alongside other sailors he tried to see where the ship had been damaged. One part of his mind was numb while the other part observed and made calculations. Twice they had been struck by German shells. Perhaps three times. All at once. If the German gunners adjusted nothing the next salvo would hit them too.

He spotted McGrail coming toward him. The chief petty officer was shouting. Edward struggled to move but the ship was listing and he stumbled. The air flashed red and black. He was picked up, twisted, and tossed into flames and oil and saltwater that bit his face and body with a fierce cold and a burning heat.

The five siblings had mounted their horses and were headed out toward the groves.

"I'm surprised you joined us, Cath," Victoria said.

"Sorry to disappoint you, Sis."

"Don't be silly." Victoria smiled at Catherine. "I love having all of us out here riding together."

"I had hoped it would lift my spirits to go through the green and gold of the ash grove. But I don't know that it will make a difference, Vic. I can't go back to my childhood. Sorry to be such a raincloud this visit."

Emma was riding on ahead through the trees with Robbie and Kipp. Victoria drew her mare, Robin, closer to Catherine's side and put a hand on her sister's arm briefly.

"What is it, Cath? Can I help?"

Catherine looked at her, glanced ahead at the others, then back at Victoria. She stopped, squared her shoulders, let them drop, and stared down at the horse's mane. "Albert would be furious. That I was talking about family matters. But here it is. It's this Irish thing, you see. It was bad enough before the rebellion. But now he's writing more and more letters to the editors of the Belfast and Dublin papers. No independence. No Home Rule. Union with Britain forever. He's gotten so many angry responses. Especially when he wrote that they didn't shoot enough of the rebels. Or that shooting was too good for them. One of the fellows who works at a local paper — well, we know him from church — he came by to see me when Albert was out and warned me — *warned* me Albert was being lumped in with the Protestant extremists — it would make him a target of the Irish Republican Brotherhood. If any kind of fighting broke out again . . . they would . . . assassinate him . . ."

Catherine drooped over her saddle. For a few minutes, she put her hand on Victoria's where it rested on her arm. Tears and a smile came at the same time. She slipped her eyes up to look at her younger sister.

"Remember when we both fought over Ben Whitecross two years ago?" Catherine asked.

The mention of Ben made Victoria cringe and conjured up swift images of severed heads in shell holes and dead bodies tangled in coils of barbed wire. But the other images of hair pulling with Catherine and kicking each other's shins by the sea cliff made her smile.

"Ben would have been quite the catch with his black hair and flashing blue eyes," said Catherine. "And, by rights, I should have had him, since I'm older than you. But ladies do not marry the grooms that work the estate's horses."

"So they say. Yes, quite the catch, I agree."

"Where is he now? Mum said he'd gone off to war with father's blessing."

Victoria's face tightened. "Oh, yes, bravely marching off to war, just because he felt guilty that Robbie was in danger. There's been not a word about his regiment or where he's been stationed. No letters to anyone in the household or to any of the servants."

"Maybe it's best that way, Victoria," Emma said. She had trotted back and pulled alongside her sisters as Robbie and Kipp raced each other through a sunny glade. Victoria glanced over at her in surprise.

"Why is it better to lose touch with a

trusted servant who has taken care of our horses and driven us safely everywhere we needed to go?"

Emma looked at Catherine and Victoria and shrugged. "Do we need secrets at our age? You were infatuated with him, Vic. You are a sensible girl but headstrong and passionate and you'd convinced yourself that you loved him."

"What?" Victoria reined in her horse.

"Were you going to have his child? Become his wife regardless of your social standing? Ruin our good name? Ruin yourself?"

"What are you talking about?"

"Midnight visit after midnight visit. We're not schoolgirls anymore, Victoria. We're women. We can't play those kinds of games. We can't indulge in those sorts of fantasies."

Victoria stared at her. "You told someone."

"I told Mrs. Seabrooke. No one else."

"And — she —"

"Dismissed him. Or rather, gave him a choice. Dismissal and a loss of references. Or enlisting and serving his country — and going far away from you and Ashton Park."

"You made him go to war. He could get killed, Em."

Emma's face colored. "Jeremiah went to war. No one forced him. He could have

97

been killed. Thank God he came back. Ben Whitecross can come back too, Victoria. But not to you."

Victoria hurled herself out of her saddle into Emma and they both slammed into the ground. Pinning her down, Victoria attacked her with her fists and nails. Emma warded off many of the blows, but not all — in moments her nose and lips were bleeding and there were scratches on her cheeks. Their horses snorted and shied and ran off. Catherine watched her sisters fighting in a kind of shock before finally jumping off her mount and hauling Victoria off Emma.

"How could you?" shrieked Victoria, her face dark with blood as Catherine held her back. "You spy! Ratting to Mrs. Seabrooke! You could get him killed! He made sure you never got killed all the years he drove you about in your coaches and carriages! Curse you, Emma Danforth! Murderer!"

She tried to struggle free and kick at Emma's head but Robbie and Kipp came galloping up, Kipp leaping down and seizing Victoria just as she broke free of Catherine's grip.

"Hullo, hullo, what's all this?" he demanded. "Fifteen minutes ago you two were best of friends. We leave you alone a few moments and you're scratching each other's eyes out?"

"She wants to kill Ben Whitecross!" spat Victoria, green eyes flaming.

Emma sat up, bleeding but not crying. Her face was defiant. "Vic was having a romantic relationship with Ben. I put a stop to it. It was my duty."

"Your *duty*?" Victoria almost broke free of Kipp. "You crucified him!"

"Don't talk nonsense!" snapped Emma, putting her hands to her cheeks. "He's not the Lord Jesus Christ, is he?" She looked at the blood on her palms. "I'm to be wed tomorrow afternoon."

"Soap and water. You'll be radiant, Em." Kipp shook Victoria. "Will you leave off?"

"I will not leave off. She doesn't deserve to be married. Not ever."

"Someone's coming," said Robbie. "One of the servants. He's approaching quite rapidly. It would be best if this incident did not become downstairs gossip."

Catherine helped Emma up as Todd Turpin galloped up to them.

"What happened here then?" he asked before saying anything else.

"I was thrown," replied Emma. "I'm a bit shook up. A few cuts and knocks."

"We must get ye back to the manor."

"Of course. We were just about to do that."

"I hope ye'll be all right, Miss Danforth."

"I'll be fine, Todd Turpin. Thank you." She forced a smile. "Why have you come looking for us in such a hurry? It's still an hour to dinner."

Todd quickly took the flat tweed cap off his head. "I'm sorry. A cable's just come to Sir William. He asked me to fetch you. There's been battle out at sea and it hasn't gone that well for us. Your brother's ship has been sunk. God help us, the *Queen Mary* has gone down and there are no survivors."

Mrs. Longstaff had cooked a special meal of roast pork and fresh apple-sauce but Lady Elizabeth wouldn't come down from her room for dinner. What was meant to be a family celebration on the eve of the wedding deteriorated into a listless and practically silent affair. Emma had argued the ceremony must be postponed again, struggling with her tears and disappointment, but her father would not hear of it.

"We must carry through with it this time," he insisted, grasping her hand. "Heaven knows we need it — your love for Jeremiah, the blessing of the bishop when he takes you through your vows, the holy moment when you two make your declarations. We cannot do without it."

Victoria sat in her room after dinner. Robbie visited with her for part of the evening, followed by Kipp, and then Catherine. If they were not with her they were with Emma. She felt no desire or compulsion to walk down the hall to Emma's room and certainly had no intention of offering an apology. Images of Ben's soft dark curls matted with blood haunted her. Anger toward her sister and Mrs. Seabrooke would not ebb. From time to time, as she sat on her bed, she wondered if her rage had abated, but every time stark impressions of Ben sprawled in the mud of Flanders resurfaced and whipped her indignation to a pitch of fury.

"I doubt I can forgive this, God!" she said out loud and alone. "It's murder, isn't it? How can I forgive such calculated, cold-blooded murder?" A few minutes later she added, "She does not even seek forgiveness. She is not sorry for what she has done."

Victoria was still up just before midnight when another cable arrived with the astonishing news that HMS *Tipperary* had picked up a handful of sailors from the *Queen Mary* and one of them was Commander Edward Danforth. The whole household — all those who were awake — seemed to relax and fall off to sleep in a kind of euphoria. But at four in the morning a courier brought unwelcome news of the sinking of the HMS *Tipperary* due to enemy action. Sir William did not inform his wife, he let her sleep on. Victoria, still up, sat with him in his private study as he talked and prayed and fretted.

"I do not see God's hand in this," he groaned. "I do not see it. That does not mean it isn't there but —"

"Are there survivors from the *Tipperary*, Father?" she asked, pouring him tea.

"I don't know. I expect that will be in the next cable. It's not unreasonable to suppose there were some."

At eight-thirty yet another cable relayed that twelve men had been plucked from the sea after the *Tipperary* had gone down. Most had been rescued by the Germans and were prisoners of war. Sir William shook his head as Victoria read the cable through twice. "I would not care. A son in a prison camp is better than one at the bottom of the sea."

Guests began arriving for the wedding after lunch. Despite the devastating news she awoke to, Lady Elizabeth greeted them with warmth and grace, clever work with cosmetics by her maid, Cynthia, disguising the redness and swollenness under her eyes. Tavy and his footmen ushered people to their seats in a chapel that gleamed with Emma's colors of green and gold and with the afternoon light. Lady Caroline Scarborough, tall and slender and fair as sunlight — the woman that everyone expected Kipp to marry — gave him a proper kiss on the cheek and sat with her family. The bishop was about to begin the ceremony when Tavy took Sir William aside and handed him a final telegram — Edward was one of the few seamen the Royal Navy had pulled from the water when the *Tipperary* went down. Sir William gripped Tavy's hand: "My boy is twice saved and we are twice blessed."

Ecstatic, he handed the cable to the bishop to read to begin the service. Many of the guests knew nothing about the sea battle or what had gone on at Ashton Park from one day to the next because of it. For Lady Elizabeth, the emotions that had ravaged her mind and body for the past day proved to be so exhausting she felt she was going to collapse in the tightly packed chapel. Aunt Holly bolstered her on one side and Sir William on the other. For Kipp and Robbie, who had both seen combat and knew the ending of the sea battle saga for their family was better than anything that could be expected, a marriage coming at the end of it all was something of a triumph, and they sat elated in their pew.

But for Victoria, happy as she was to hear Edward's life had been spared, the wedding was no more than a deeper cut in the wound of Emma's betrayal of Ben. Emma could marry the man she loved but Victoria could not. That possibility had been stolen from her by the sister she had grown up with under the ash trees and worshipped God with at St. Mark's. To her, the wedding was a scar on a perfect June day that had seen miracles. She sat rigidly next to Catherine without any expression on her face as Emma and Jeremiah exchanged vows. She knew something would have to be done about what her sister and Mrs. Seabrooke had set in motion against Ben Whitecross's life. She did not know what that something was, but when the opportunity presented itself she was certain she would recognize it for what it was. And she would act on it.

5
1917

February 1917

He had finally come home to Ashton Park. It seemed to Edward that nothing had changed since he had last been here. Indeed, he wondered if Ashton Park *could* ever change.

He hoped not, as he stood under the ash trees, hands in his pockets, staring up at the vast covering of green.

The rain was thin and light on his shoulders. Edward had experienced far worse standing on deck during the Battle of Jutland. He was sure the thousands of leaves kept the downpour from striking him with more force. Yet as the storm intensified, the branches flew back and forth, opening gaps that allowed the cloudburst to make its way through to the grass and to his head and body in fierce gusts. Drenched, he refused to move, testing himself against the elements.

It was much worse during the sinkings. And I could not get out of the cold sea, I could not. I can bear this.

"Mister Danforth, Mister Danforth, sir."

He glanced at a young maid in a long coat running toward him through the trees. She threw a heavy cape over his shoulders.

"You'll catch your death, sir. February rains are brutish."

"Why . . . thank you. Did Tavy send you out here?"

"I saw you myself from the window. Lord knows it should have been your valet Lewis, but he's off and tidying your room. I couldn't stand to see you get soaked through. And you having been through so much."

"I don't know you, do I?"

"No, sir. I was brought on after you left for your post on the *Queen Mary.* I'm Charlotte Squire, sir."

"Charlotte Squire. Do your friends call you Char very often?"

"Yes, sir." She smiled for the first time, raindrops sliding from her hood brim over her eyes so that she blinked.

Edward took her by the arm. "Not very gentlemanly to leave you out in the storm. Come with me."

"I should be getting back, sir."

But she let herself be led. He took her to one of the huts that dotted the estate, which were used for storing tools and other supplies. Inside there were three spades and a large saw. A scent of earth. Light came through a small window. She shook her cloak and pulled back her hood.

He looked at her in surprise. "Your hair —"

She reached up with her hands. "Oh. What's the matter then? Are the pins out — I can never keep them in once I've run a few steps —"

"I mean — it's so dark — and your eyes are as sharp blue as the sea —"

Charlotte laughed and didn't know what to do with her hands after bringing them down from her head. She looked away from him and at the floor. "From my father. He had the coal black hair and the eyes like a clear winter day."

Edward watched the silver light on her hair and face. She felt his gaze and kept her eyes on the puddles of water spreading out from their boots and clothing. He made to reach out and smooth back strands of wet hair from her cheek but she turned slightly.

"I'm sorry," he said.

Her eyes were still down. "You've not done anything to be sorry for, sir. But I should be getting back or Mrs. Seabrooke will have a fit. There's all the laundry, you see." But she did not move.

Edward stared out the window. "It's still blowing. Like a North Sea gale."

She lifted her face. The beauty was great, her skin shining with water and glowing with the sting of the wind she had run through to him. But he glanced away and back out the window again.

"At sea," he went on, "there are always the waves pitching into the ship and the deck moving under your feet. Sometimes hail that hits you like stones."

Charlotte folded her hands in front of her. "You have been through a great deal, Mister Danforth. I know that. I prayed for you. That long night. Went to the chapel, all decorated for your sister's wedding, and prayed for God to spare you even though so many others had died. Thousands of young lads."

Edward looked back at her. She did not drop her eyes.

"Do you believe in prayer?" he asked.

"I do, sir."

"Did you — tell me, did you stop praying for me after I was pronounced safe?"

Blood came to her lips and face. "Why, I —" She hesitated. "That's a strange thing to ask, sir."

"Forgive me then."

"No, I don't mind answering. But I shouldn't say, should I? And we shouldn't be in this hut alone either. But we're here. And you've asked. I'm ashamed to say I've never left off praying for you . . . there was the photograph every time I cleaned your mother's room. . .you looked . . . so fine in your officer's uniform on the deck of the ship and those great guns sitting just there over your shoulder . . . every time I saw your face I prayed for you . . ."

"That's nothing to be ashamed of."

"I shouldn't be thinking such thoughts. Fancying you like a schoolgirl."

"But you prayed."

"I did, sir."

"I find that odd."

"I suppose it is."

"Kipp was always the lady's man. Blond hair. Green eyes. I'd have thought you'd have daydreamed about him."

"I met your brother at Mistress Emma's wedding last June. He does look every inch the Royal Flying Corps type, if you know what I mean. But I much prefer your looks, sir. I apologize for being bold. You're darker, and warmer, and, somehow, deeper." More blood filled her face. "I'm sorry. I'm speaking rubbish."

Wind and rain cracked against the hut.

"Look at that," said Edward quietly. Water flooded the outside surface of the window-pane. "They said I'd soon be over it — the two sinkings. That war is war. I was unconscious the first time. After the *Queen Mary* blew up. The cold of the water and the heat of the burning oil gave me quite a jolt. I came to, and then swam for my life. The crew of the *Tipperary* hauled me on board. The second time I had both eyes open when I went into the sea. The *Tipperary* was breaking up behind me. I saw the German ship coming to pick up survivors and I swam away from them. Can you imagine? The water was like ice, it was night, I was five or ten minutes from drowning, but I swam away from the people who could save my life because I didn't want to be a prisoner of war. So the Royal Navy saved me instead. But what will my life accomplish in the end? There won't be another fleet action. All we'll do is hunt U-boats."

"Ah, don't say that, sir. Your mother and father thank God you're alive. Why, the whole household was rejoicing when they knew you'd been saved. It was not long after that I started looking at your picture. You're this young maid's daydream, if that pleases you, sir." She bit her lip and shook her head and yanked the hood back up. "I'm prattling. It means nothing." She put her hand on the door latch.

"Please — don't head back just yet, Charlotte."

"I must. I've been acting the fool. I must go."

"Please don't."

"Mrs. Seabrooke —"

"I'll handle Mrs. Seabrooke."

She stood at the door. "What do you want with me, sir?"

"It's . . . pleasant . . . and comforting to speak with you. You choose your words very well."

"Thank you, sir. We were poor but Da was always a great one for the newspapers and whatever books he could lay his hands on. We children were always reading something. Sometimes out loud to Da and Mum."

Edward rubbed his hands up and down over his damp face. "I'm . . . I'm not one for using words well . . . for talking."

"Many fine ladies come to Ashton Park. Once you spend time with them you'll not have any more trouble with your talk."

"I think you could outdo them all, don't you?"

"Oh, no, sir, I don't have the polish."

"You have a red rose North England beauty. It's rare."

"Sir. We shouldn't be talking like this. It will come to nothing. We don't know each other. You're of noble birth."

"Don't you believe attraction can sometimes . . . cross boundaries of class and race and religion?"

The hood brim shadowed her eyes. "I don't know, sir. You shouldn't be dallying with me. I'm dirt-poor. My family's dirt-poor. It's the ladies from the manor houses you'll want. The ones with the estates."

Edward stepped closer and slipped the hood back from her face and hair. The color and beauty of her eyes and lips and skin rushed over him again. Still he held back. Her mouth parted at his touch and she did not push his hands away.

"I was a dead man," he said. "I'm still a dead man. You know that."

"I've seen the pain in your face since you've come home. Yes."

"And you've prayed?"

"I have."

"And watched me from windows?"

There was a small smile. "Yes."

"Do you . . . feel something for me? A dead man the sea gave back twice?"

A strong white hand closed over one of his.

"I do feel something for you," she said. "But I have nothing to give. I'm no lady. Just a simple girl from the Pendle Hills."

"In ten minutes you've made me feel more of a sense of beauty and grace than I've felt in the nine months since the sea battle. It's as if I can breathe." He lifted her hand to his mouth and kissed it. "Do you believe me?"

"I . . . I don't . . . oh, nothing can come of it, sir. It's just a moment in a hut in a storm."

"Or something more."

"No, sir, it can't be more — please, you know that."

"I don't want to stop feeling alive." He began to draw the long pins from her hair and drop them at his feet. "It's been cold and black and wretched. Your eyes are a light."

Her hair was loose and dark and shining. He kissed it. He kissed her. Softly — then with strength. At first she only yielded to his kisses. But suddenly she responded with a burst of energy of her own, putting her arms around his neck and kissing him with a ferocity that stole his balance and his thoughts. Then she stopped and stepped back, dropping her arms.

"I'm sorry . . . that's too much . . . I don't . . ."

He twined several strands of her hair on his finger. "Don't stop. Don't imagine stopping."

"We ought to be done with this nonsense now, sir. I care for you, but . . ."

Edward kissed her white throat and she closed her eyes. She put her hands under his arms and over his back, gripping him tightly once again, as his lips moved over her cheeks and mouth.

"You are the most radiant soul in England," he murmured. "The most beautiful woman in Europe. You must be. Why else would I feel this way? A shooting star arcing over the sea in the dead of night."

She laughed and took a handful of her hair and brushed it over his face. "Now you're a poet. I suppose sailors can be poets. But you're teasing me. You can't feel that, sir."

"Edward."

"All right — just the times we're alone . . . if there will ever be another time . . ."

"Months and years, Charlotte."

"Char, then. But you can't mean that. Don't say those things. It only spoils it. Just tell me that you care for me right here in this wooden shack. That will be enough for the rest of my life."

Mr. Seabrooke scurried toward the front door of the manor. The March wind tugged at what was left of his hair and at the bundle of newspapers he carried in his arms.

He entered a side door and was immediately downstairs in the manor and a few feet from the office he shared with his wife.

"Ah, there you are, Mr. Seabrooke," his wife greeted him. "And you have the papers?"

"I do. I'll take them upstairs to the library directly after we've had a look."

She pulled a copy of the *Times* out from his bundle and began to read the casualty lists from the weekend. "Warton. Welke. White. Whitely. No, there's nothing. He's not there."

"Well. That's why we have the other papers, Mrs. Seabrooke. Sometimes even the *Times* misses a few."

"Let me see the Liverpool papers. You can glance over the other ones from London."

They sat in their chairs scanning the newspapers. Mrs. Seabrooke made a face as if she had eaten something bitter as she put a third one aside.

"Nothing. It's been almost a year." She

picked up a cold cup of tea that rested by her elbow and sipped at it as if it were hot. "I still maintain Ben Whitecross was killed on the first day of the Somme last July first. So many young men lost their lives that day. It only stands to reason he was among them."

"His name wasn't on those casualty lists either."

"The unknown dead. There are scads of the unknown dead. He could be one of them."

Mr. Seabrooke grinned, exposing black and crooked teeth. "If he never shows up at Ashton Park again then I expect you will be proven right."

Mrs. Seabrooke sniffed and sipped her tea. "If he never shows up at Ashton Park again it will be none too soon as far as I am concerned. I'll request a special service of thanksgiving at St. Mark's."

In the past, Ben Whitecross had always driven Victoria into Liverpool and been supportive of her suffragette marches. Now she had to rely on Old Todd Turpin, aged sixty-one, whose dark silences told her exactly what he thought of the protests and demonstrations. Her parents' disapproval had never amounted to them forbidding her to march so Old Todd waited glumly by Lime Street Station while she joined others in the streets, often taking horse-drawn cabs to different locations.

Several arrests had been made during the protest rally against the war that morning but, as usual, she had not been touched. She was in one of her black moods regarding Ben being coerced into the frontline trenches and would have welcomed being manhandled and hauled off. She could have kicked some policeman in the shins and felt better. Instead she began to look about for a cab to take her back to Todd. She had just begun to wave at one when a hand brought her arm down.

"Not yet, dear. There's someone wants a word with you."

Victoria recognized the woman, one of the protest leaders. "Oh, hullo, Mrs. Shakespeare. What's that?"

"Come with me. There's someone important wants to see you."

Victoria followed her across the street and down an alley to a door that looked half rotted through. It was locked. Mrs. Shakespeare opened it with a small key from her pocket and they stepped into a corridor that was black, Victoria thought, as two in the morning. But Mrs. Shakespeare seemed to know where she was going and did not hesitate, marching briskly ahead and turning left. There was another door that Victoria could just make out set into one side of the hall. At this door Mrs. Shakespeare did a strange kind of knock. A rough woman's voice asked who it was.

"Ella Shakespeare. I have the young Danforth woman with me."

"Send her in and be on your way."

The door opened from inside. Mrs. Shakespeare had already vanished back into the dark of the hallway. Slowly Victoria stepped into a room lit only by a small lamp with an even smaller flame. A tall woman in a black dress sat in a chair in the shadows, a veil covering her face so that none of her features could be distinguished.

"I'm sorry for the veil." It was the rough voice but not quite so harsh. "It's for your protection as well as mine. Miss Danforth, I've had my eye on you for some time. I have great admiration for your father."

"Thank you, ma'am."

"But he does not go far enough, does he? Ireland should have independence, not Home Rule. The war should be stopped, Britain should unilaterally withdraw her troops from the continent and bring them home — it is not a question of fighting the war to a successful conclusion, for there can be no successful conclusion when humans are slaughtered by the hundreds of thousands."

"I . . . I feel the same way."

"I was sure of it. I have heard you speak of these matters and others have reported back to me conversations with you as well. You take our cause seriously."

"I do, ma'am."

"That is why I have chosen you for a most important task. Others do not take us seriously, Miss Danforth, and we need to change that."

"I understand. What is it you want me to do?"

"Later this week a man will meet you at Lime Street Station and give you a suitcase. It will be large but not particularly heavy. You are a strapping young woman who will handle it without a problem. We need you to take it to a particular location and set it down."

"That sounds easy enough."

"The man will give you a key for the locks on the case. Once you have set it down at the correct place you will turn the key in each lock. This will engage the mechanism inside."

"Pardon me?"

119

"You will have primed the bomb, Miss Danforth. It will explode ten minutes after you have done this. Plenty of time for you to get safely away."

One part of Victoria's mind seemed to stop. "A bomb?"

"Every day hundreds of German, British, French, and Canadian boys are blown to pieces or lose arms and legs. But out of sight is out of mind for the British public. If we bring the war home to them they may change their thinking on keeping troops in France for another five or ten years. Let them see what the explosion of a shell is like firsthand. Let them see what a human body torn apart looks like. Let them see the color of blood. Then they will demand Britain make a speedy exit from the conflict." The woman paused. "But perhaps I was mistaken? Perhaps you are not the right person to perform this important task? It may be that you lack the moral fiber to do what is necessary. If so, please tell me, and you can be on your way. There are other promising candidates who will take your place."

Victoria was silent as she let everything the woman had said work its way through her. She saw Ben ripped up by a shell, possibly killed weeks or months ago, unidentifiable because he had no face. She thought of Emma at her cozy vicarage in Ribchester, where Jeremiah had just been assigned the church — safe and secure from all alarm, as the old hymn put it. And there was Mrs. Seabrooke, fussing with her ledgers, her husband fetching her cups of hot tea from the kitchen that she let sit and grow cold before she drank — Mrs. Seabrooke the witch. How quaint an existence Emma and Mrs. Seabrooke led. How far from the roaring guns and screaming shells they had forced Ben to endure.

"Well?" came the tall woman's voice. "Speak up, young lady. Arrangements must be made for this important mission. If not you, it will be someone else. On occasion, I am wrong about someone's character. You may be perfectly suited to the marching and shouting and not committed to —"

"Yes." Victoria heard her voice as if it were coming from another body on the other side of the room. Her heart beat faster as she spoke. "I will have no trouble doing what you need me to do with the suitcase."

The tall woman smiled. "I knew we could depend you. Your effort will save many lives. Yes, many lives."

Victoria envisioned only one life that she hoped to save — that of Ben Whitecross.

She would do this for all the others whose lives would be saved, but it was Ben whose life mattered most.

Emma put the letter down and rubbed her hand over her eyes. Her husband looked up from the bowl of oatmeal he was eating.

"What's wrong?" he asked.

"It's nothing." She stared at the oatmeal. "Why aren't you using brown sugar on that?"

"I said I'd give up sugar for Lent."

"Right. And I've given up tea with cream. I could use a cup."

"So what's in the letter from your sister?"

"Oh, Libby's going on about making amends with Victoria. As if it's so easy to do. She's across the Channel in France and we're up here at Ribchester."

"The train to Liverpool and Ashton Park is fast enough."

"Well, I don't have anything to say!" flared Emma. "Victoria attacked me. Almost broke my back in my fall off the horse. And those cuts and scratches took weeks to heal. And here is Libby —" she waved the letter in Jeremiah's face "preaching about forgiveness."

"It's Easter, isn't it?"

"Oh, don't you start. One sermon from

France is about all I can handle this morning. Victoria might try a measure of forgiveness too. But I'm the older sister so of course I'm expected to take the first step. I was only trying to spare her. Mother and Father would never have agreed to the marriage. Never in a million years. So my headstrong sister would have run off with him and ruined her life. No."

Emma got up from the table and went to the window that overlooked the river that ran nearby. Raindrops tap-tapped on the pane and she put her palm on the glass and spread her fingers.

"He's not been killed or wounded, you know."

Jeremiah bit into a piece of toast. "What's that?"

"I never look, but Harrison reads the casualty lists every day. Has done since the war started. Ben Whitecross has never shown up. At least not since the last time I spoke with Harrison. Thank God."

Jeremiah wiped his mouth with a napkin and leaned back in his seat. "What would you do if he returned to Ashton Park?"

"Let Mother and Father know about it. Let them deal with the problem. I tried to spare them, and look how that turned out. Vic and I were never the ones to quarrel with each other."

"I need to go down to Liverpool in a few days to see the bishop. I'll take the train. Would you like to join me? We could pop up to the manor after I've finished my business."

Emma turned away from the window. "An invitation from the Reverend Jeremiah Sweet. I can't let that one go by, can I?"

"Entirely up to you. I have no idea if you're ready to talk with your sister. You shouldn't do it if you're not ready."

"Oh, I suppose I'll be ready. Libby's right — as usual. It's past time. That doesn't mean she'll be open to patching things up, Jeremiah."

"I realize that."

"She can hold onto things for a long time. And she's done wild things when her temper's gotten the better of her. Set fire to one of the sheds in the forest once. She was twelve. Good thing the whole forest didn't go up. Another time she pitched a lot of Cath's clothes over the cliff into the sea. I can't remember what that was all about. She's mad, you know, when she wants to be. Completely mad." She tucked Libby's letter in a drawer in the kitchen. "So that's why I'll go down with you, whether I think I'm ready or not. I'd hate to have her set fire to the manor or throw Mrs. Seabrooke headfirst off the cliff."

Easter 1917

At first Victoria had slept well. Then at four in the morning she shot up in bed, gasping, her mind full of dead and dismembered bodies. At breakfast she had calmed down, though she could not smile. She barely noticed her brother Edward's new energy and enthusiasm, saying simply she was glad he was finally feeling better after what he'd been through on the *Queen Mary* and *Tipperary*. Her mother groaned when she said Todd was driving her into Liverpool.

"Not another march, Victoria. You just went on one. They'll certainly arrest you if you keep this up."

"I'm not marching, mother. Easter shopping. That's all."

Lady Elizabeth's face relaxed. "How delightful it is to hear a normal phrase come out of your mouth. *Easter shopping.* I do wish I was free to come with you. Or that you'd made plans to meet Emma there."

"I'll be fine. I hope to be home early."

"And Todd is accompanying you?"

"Just Old Todd. No one else."

But there was someone else. Harrison had things to pick up in the city and joined them for the trip, sitting next to Todd, who handled the horses from the driver's seat.

Harrison leaned down from his perch toward Victoria's open window. "I hope you don't mind."

Victoria sat back in her seat. "Why should I mind? Three's company."

"I expect there will be great crowds with Easter almost upon us."

Victoria looked out the window. She had no interest in chatting. The carriage moved onto the main road and the rush of air and rumble of wheels made conversation difficult. Harrison sat back up and spoke to Todd. Both of the men laughed.

She pushed everything from her mind. She only rehearsed taking the suitcase from the man and inserting the key in each lock and twisting it. Over and over again. When they reached the city, Harrison asked to be let off early and promised to meet them later. Todd and Victoria carried on to Lime Street Station, where Victoria alighted.

"I won't be more than an hour," she promised.

"That's short shopping for a lady."

"I don't need much. Make sure you're ready. I want to get home early."

He touched the brim of his tweed cap. "I'll be here."

Victoria walked into the station. She was dressed in a plain gray dress with an even plainer broad-brimmed black hat. Deciding it was best not to stand still or walk about in circles, she headed toward the first train platform. She had hardly gone a dozen steps before a voice behind her said, "Here's your case, Miss."

She turned. The man had a cheerful face with neatly trimmed mustache and beard. He tipped his bowler hat and put the case in her hand. As the tall woman in the room had promised, it was large but fairly light. He handed her a small brass key.

"There you are, my dear," the man said with a smile. "Set it by the cab stand in about fifteen minutes, please. Remain with it there for at least five. Then walk away. Make sure there a lot of people around you so that you are not noticed when you leave the case behind. I wish you a pleasant day."

He walked off into the interior of the station. After a moment, Victoria followed him, carrying the case in her right hand and the key in her left. She stopped at the large board that announced arrivals and departures and studied it along with other women and men. Then went to platform two and watched the hissing locomotive that squatted there, preparing to head to Birmingham. After a few minutes she wandered to platform one, set her case down, watched the train unload passengers for several minutes, then picked the case up and headed toward the arrival and departure board once again.

Her eyes saw nothing. She was in her head. She would set the case down where the horse-drawn cabs waited for fares. She would stand by the case a few minutes, looking about in her handbag. If a cabbie called to her she would say she had already made arrangements with another driver and was waiting on him. When it was busy she would insert the key in each lock and turn it. Hang about another five minutes and head to where Todd Turpin waited for her. If someone called and said she had forgotten her case she would thank them and tell them she would be back in a few minutes. If they persisted she would ask them to watch it for her until she returned.

She made her way to the cabstand but

stood back, not wanting to be hailed. She rooted around in her handbag, seeing none of the items inside. A train had arrived from up north and a crowd of passengers suddenly appeared, each of them calling out for a cab. She knelt by the case and put the key in one of the locks. She noticed that her hand was not shaking and that her palm was dry. She turned the key. Now her ears filled with the sound of her heart and the pumping of her blood. Now she hesitated as she prepared to insert the key in the second lock.

"How long will it take with the bishop?"

"An hour. We'll discuss the ministry at Ribchester and a few other matters. There is a beautiful garden you can sit in while you wait."

"It's a fine day. I like the sound of that."

"When I'm done we can shop a bit before we rent a coach and head up to Ashton Park."

"I like the sound of that too."

The blood seemed to run through Victoria's head and chest even more loudly. It was the voices of Emma and Jeremiah. She bent her head as low as she could and tugged on her wide hat brim. They hailed a cab, and she heard Emma laugh as Jeremiah helped her up. After counting to ten, she lifted her head and watched them pull away from the station, Emma still laughing, her ordinary face, as always, made radiant by her smile.

I could have killed her if I had primed the bomb sooner.

With this thought came a rush of fear. She could have blown her sister apart. Murdered her. She put a hand to her mouth and gagged. With all the anger and hatred she had nursed for a year she did not want her sister's death. Suddenly she saw the children and their mothers for the first time. The bomb would tear them to pieces. Little girls. Little boys. She put a hand to her head and drew in large breaths of air. People were all around her, shouting, whistling to cabbies, arguing.

As she stood up, the blood rushed to her feet and she almost fell. Regaining her balance, she threw the brass key as far as she could toward the street. Todd was only around the corner. She would get him to drive to the docks, where she could drop the case into the sea. He would ask her why they were throwing a perfectly good suitcase into the water to sink and disappear in the harbor muck. She would have an answer to that by the time she reached the coach. She began to walk rapidly away from the cabstand, holding the case tightly.

A hand gripped her arm and made her cry out. It was the man with the bowler hat who had given her the suitcase. His face was not cheerful now. It was scarlet with rage.

"Lost our nerve, did we? Did you think no one was watching? Give me the case!"

He grabbed at the handle but she pulled it away from him. "No!"

The man kept his voice down. "Surrender it, Miss Danforth. We should have known better than to trust a rich man's daughter. Surrender it or I'll cut your throat."

He hauled her into a corner of the station that was dark and stacked high with wooden pallets. They fought for the suitcase. Finally he got it from her.

"We're just a couple having a bit of a quarrel. No one is taking notice. If you scream, I'll tell the police I was stopping you from setting off a bomb. Where is the key?"

"I threw it away."

"You're lying."

"Why is it that killing people is always so important? Why is it that murdering children is always supposed to make the world a better place to live in?"

"Shut up. You don't have the brains to

argue philosophy or make policy. All you were was a foot soldier. And a not a very good one at that. Give me the key."

"I don't have it."

He grinned and put a hand into his pocket. "You're a fool. Don't you think we have a backup plan? Don't you think we have another key?" He brought out a small pocketknife. "I'm going to hug you. That's all anyone glancing our way is going to see. Hug and kiss and make up. But I'll put the blade into your heart and keep my mouth over yours until you're dead."

He flicked open the blade and pinned her to him, crushing his mouth down over hers. She struggled but could not break free. Where Ben had smelled of clean soap and fresh straw and smooth saddle leather, he reeked of tobacco and whiskey and dirt.

There's nothing I can do. God, don't let him set off the bomb. Never mind me. Don't let him hurt the others.

She could the feel the point of the blade pierce her dress and press into her skin. It would be fast. Perhaps she would faint. Or fall asleep after she had bled for a few minutes. She fought him and his arm only grew tighter. Then suddenly it was gone.

She staggered backward into the wall and collapsed, almost passing out. Dark shapes moved back and forth in front of her eyes. She pressed her hands against the wall and got up. The man was at her feet. Unconscious. The case sat on the concrete. She and the man were completely hidden behind the pallets. There was no one else near her.

The man began to groan and move his arms. Her mind whirling, Victoria picked up the case and ran from behind the pallets into the bright sunlight. Todd was where he was supposed to be and Harrison had rejoined him. They both doffed their caps.

"Miss Danforth," said Todd. "Are you all right?"

She sprang into the coach, her breath rushing in and out rapidly. "Get me home, please. And let's not take our time. I need to be back at Ashton Park."

"Miss Danforth —"

"Now, Mr. Turpin. Now, Mr. Harrison."

She clutched the case against her chest where her dress had a small tear and there was a pinprick of blood. She scarcely noticed the land they drove through. At the manor she thanked them and walked off into the ash trees carrying the suitcase. When she reached the cliff she glanced down at the sea boiling against its foot. It was high tide. She flung the case as far as she could out into the ocean. It bobbed on the surface a few moments, carried forward by the whitecaps. Then it sank.

"I thought you said they'd be gone until late," Charlotte said.

"It's only my sister," Edward replied.

"Where did she leave the suitcase she was carrying?"

"It doesn't matter, does it? It's her suitcase to do what she wants with."

The two were crouching behind a thick ash tree. Once Victoria was well out of sight on her way back to the manor, Charlotte put a hand to her mouth and began to giggle.

"What is it?" Edward asked.

"I'm with the lord's and lady's son and we're hiding behind a tree like children up to mischief, afraid of getting a spanking."

"Well, we are up to mischief of a sort."

She leaned back against the tree trunk, her hair black and gleaming about the shoulders of her maid's uniform, her lips a deep red from the warmth of the sun, her blue eyes caught up in all the light of the day.

"It's mischief, is it?" she teased. "Well, it must be. All we've done with our time together is lurk behind trees while your sister goes back and forth in front of us."

"She wasn't supposed to be here."

"And all because you were tired of meeting in the hut by night."

"Not tired of it. Just tired of not seeing you in the sunlight."

"Oh, sure you see me every day, Edward."

"But I can't touch you. I can't take the pins from your hair. I can't hold you in my arms and tell you what a beautiful woman you are. Absolutely stunning as the sea."

"You and your sailor words. That a girl should be so lucky. Come here." She stretched out her arms.

He came to her and she gathered him in, kissing his forehead and face. He did not respond, just closed his eyes and smiled, taking it all in — her arms tight around his back, her hair over his eyes, the heat of her kisses, her scent.

"What happens to us?" she murmured, kissing his ear. "What happens when you go back to Rosyth next week?"

"We write. You send me perfumed letters."

She drew her head back and her eyebrows arched. "Do I? And will your letters be scented with the North Sea? How do you expect me to get them without your mother noticing?"

"I have a plan."

"Yes? And what is it?"

"I will speak with Harrison. He can be trusted. I write to you and mail the letters to him. He will bring the letters to you. Discreetly."

"Every day?"

"Yes. Every day."

She laughed and laced her arms around his neck, the starched sleeves rubbing against his skin. "Not every day, love. It would be wonderful. But I am sure your mother would notice that too. Why on earth would you be writing Harrison every day? To ask after the ash trees and oak trees and sheep? Once a week will have to be enough."

"It won't be enough."

"Then write me every day and send them once a week." She ran her hand through his hair. "But I will write you every day. Every night. So you don't forget about me."

"No man forgets beauty like yours. No man breathing and likely few men dead."

She kissed him on the eyes. "Your silly words. I love them."

Victoria was not expecting the coach with her sister and Jeremiah. She was walking her mare Robin through the ash trees later in the day when she saw it drive up and Emma step down, followed by her husband. She had been brooding on the morning and all the things she had brewed in her heart for the past year. Seeing Emma was like a vision from God. She leaped from Robin's back and ran toward her sister.

Emma had been doing a lot of brooding of her own. In the bishops' garden, in the coach he had lent them along with his driver, in the miles leading up to Ashton Park. A dark feeling had settled over her. The last thing she expected to see was Victoria running across the lawn toward her, calling her name and crying. Before she knew it they were in each other's arms and Victoria was kissing her cheek again and again.

"Em, I'm sorry, so sorry, forgive me, I love you, I love you."

Her astonishment kept Emma from returning the embrace and affection for several seconds. But when she realized it really was happening, that Victoria really was weeping in her arms, something immediately broke inside her and the tears came and a rush of love for her younger sister. She hugged her fiercely.

"Never you mind then," Emma soothed. "We'll not let it happen again. Not ever again. And we'll get Ben back. I promise. We'll find his regiment and write him and we'll get him back."

"He . . . he might not be alive, Em . . ."

"No, Vic. He's alive. I swear to God. I have been praying every day now about that young man. It's in my bones. He has to be alive."

"There! There! It's done!"

Mrs. Seabrooke looked up from her newspaper. "What are you going on about?"

Mr. Seabrooke jumped to his feet and brought the *Times* to her, jabbing with his finger. "Look! Whitecross! It's him — he's dead! I knew he'd be with that great offensive at Arras!"

Mrs. Seabrooke bent over the paper. "Stop poking with your finger! I can't read a thing!"

Then she saw the name and she smiled. "Thank God then." For a moment her whole body relaxed — the Ben Whitecross problem was dealt with. But reading the full name across the line of type she came up with: *Whitecross. Peter. Major.*

She flung the paper at her husband. "You fool! It's the wrong Whitecross! Did you think to look at his Christian name then? Peter. Peter! And a major! Do you honestly think Ben Whitecross could have been promoted from private to major in one year?" She turned back to her ledgers in disgust, tossing her Liverpool paper to the floor. "The war will be over before he's killed and then what?"

Mr. Seabrooke picked up the *Times* and returned to his chair. "You said yourself he might be one of the unknown dead."

"So and what if he is then? We'd never be able to relax, would we, because we wouldn't know for certain. Five years after the war was over he could show up at the door with a wedding ring for Victoria Danforth. No, he has to be dead and dead. We must read about him in the papers. Nothing else will do."

Victoria saw Todd Turpin and Harrison standing by the stables in the lamplight a few evenings later and walked over to them.

"Gentlemen."

They both took off their caps. "Miss Danforth."

"I wanted to thank you for the other day. I was — a little worked up. The shopping hadn't gone well. Particularly the suitcase. I bought it and then I changed my mind but they wouldn't let me return it. It cost several pounds. I was upset about that."

"No harm, Miss Danforth," said Todd.

"Don't fret." Harrison smiled. "We all have our days, don't we?"

"I'd rather not have such days at all. But thank you both for your understanding. I wish you goodnight."

Todd put his cap back on his head. "Goodnight, Miss."

Before she turned away, Victoria hesitated, then smiled at Harrison. "I should convey Aunt Holly's best wishes. When she found out I was paying a visit to the two of you she requested that I ask after your health, Mr. Harrison. I take it she thinks highly of you and values your service to her and our family."

"Why, thank you, Miss Victoria. Please express my gratitude to Miss Holly, and you might mention I include her along with all the family in my daily prayers. I hope she is well."

"She is. Goodnight, Mr. Harrison."

Victoria had only gone a few steps before Harrison added, "One more thing, if I may, Miss Danforth."

She turned around. "Certainly. What is it?"

"Ben Whitecross had us promise to look after you, rain or shine."

"What? Has he written you?"

"I'm sorry. We've not heard a word from him. But before he went off to enlist last year he took me and Todd aside. *Keep an* eye on her, he said. *Don't let any harm come to her. Sometimes she gets wild notions in her head.* So we've done that. Kept an eye out."

"Why, thank you. I'm sure you have."

Harrison's face grew almost rigid as she watched. "Not only on the estate. But in the city. In the streets. At the train station. You understand."

Victoria felt everything inside her go completely still. "I believe I do."

"Todd was thinking you were acting off the last little while. That's why he asked me to ride along the other day. No harm done, I hope?"

"No. No harm done, Mr. Harrison."

"All's well that ends well, then." He put his brown fedora back on and winked. "G'night to you then, my lady."

"Thank you. But I need a lord. I'm no lady yet, Mr. Harrison."

He nodded. "Yes, you are."

7

May 1917

Smoke was blowing through the sky as Kipp put his Nieuport 17 into a quick dive. The German triplane corkscrewed past him to the left, still firing. Kipp quickly jumped on his tail, not thinking anything out, just acting and reacting. His guns erupted, hammering shells into the back of the red and white aircraft. A plume of smoke spurted from the plane's engine. A moment later it burst into a fireball of orange and black. Surprised, Kipp had no time to do anything but fly through the middle of the explosion. Burning debris showered his Nieuport and part of one wing narrowly missed slamming into the cockpit. Squinting through his goggles, he pushed through the thick smoke and flame until the sky was clear and blue and empty.

All the planes that had been snarling under and over one another five minutes before were gone. Kipp banked to the right and away from the parts of the German triplane that traced gray lines through the air as they fell. He lifted his goggles a moment and rubbed a gloved hand roughly over his face. He had never seen a plane blow up like that in combat. It had disintegrated in seconds. Along with the German pilot. He pulled the goggles back over his eyes. His fuel was low, his squadron gone. It was time to head back to the aerodrome near the town of Amiens.

Moments later a pair of Nieuports dropped into position on either side of him. He recognized Kent Wales and Bobby Scott, the squadron leader. They gave him the thumbs-up. Scott waved his hand forward for the airbase. Kipp gave the thumbs-up in return.

His mechanic was there when he landed. Kipp parked near the other aircraft of his squadron, including those of Wales and Scott, who had come in only minutes ahead of him and already were nowhere to be seen.

"Canadian troops confirmed the kill, sir," his mechanic said. "Not to mention Captain Scott and Leftenant Wales. That's five, Kipper. You're an ace!"

Kipp climbed down from his plane and shook his mechanic's hand. "Thank you,

144

Tommy. I'm surprised the Canucks spotted the German's crackup. The triplane flew apart with a bang. Right in my face. Just bits and pieces floating in the air."

"They said it was a bright flash in the sky, sir. No one could miss it."

"Well, I could use a hot bath and a hot meal, Tommy. That's how I intend to celebrate becoming an ace."

Tommy grinned. "None of that, Leftenant Danforth. At least not right away. The lads are in the mess hall and want to propose a toast in your honor. I'm to make sure you get there."

Kipp groaned and smiled at the same time. "Oh, the saints help us, is Bobby Scott doing the toast? Because if he is I'll never get a bath or bite to eat."

"You know he is, sir. He tells me it shouldn't go on for more than an hour or two. But he says he'll make it up."

Tommy and Kipp began to walk across the grass to the large French chateau that dominated the field, Kipp in his dark-brown leather jacket and holding his leather helmet and goggles in one hand.

Kipp snorted. "He'll make it up to me, will he? How will Bobby do that I wonder? A meal in Paris?"

Tommy winked. "How'd you know, sir? It

is a night out on the town. Not Paris, mind, but Amiens has some pretty neighborhoods, you've said so yourself. And you love the cathedral."

"I do indeed. Which restaurant, did he say?"

"Sans Souci. Right in the shadow of the cathedral but closer to the Somme River. Nice spot. He's in love with a woman there."

"Good! I'll be able to eat in peace as he whiles away his time romancing Claudette."

"I believe she's Christelle, sir."

"Christelle. Claudette. Josephine. It's much the same. I'll save my love affairs for England."

"Very good, sir. Perhaps your patriotism will rub off on some of the lads tonight."

Kipp did manage a hot bath and a tea after a ninety-minute toast. He had hardly set down his cup on its saucer in his room before the pounding on the door told him it was time for the drive into Amiens. It was a warm spring evening and the six men Kipp was with were in high spirits. They refused to let him spend a single *franc,* choosing his meal for him, trying to impress a waitress named Claire by ordering everything in rough and ready French, even deciding what he should drink.

Kipp leaned back in his seat and watched

his friends enjoy themselves. Why shouldn't they? A month before he'd been here with three other pilots and all of them had been shot down. The past few weeks had been a disaster, the Germans flying planes far better than their own. Who knew what daybreak would bring? If his squadron wanted to use his making ace as an excuse for a party, let them. The Lord knew they'd all been to enough military funerals to last a lifetime.

Kipp finished off the food on his plate, wiped his mouth with a red napkin, and looked about for Bobby Scott. Sans Souci was crammed with French, British, and Canadian airmen, so it was difficult to spot the short fireplug of a man. When he did, he noticed Scott was leaning on the bar and staring in his direction. Their eyes met and Scott raised the glass in his hand. Kipp prayed he wouldn't offer another toast to his making ace. But Scott simply drank and kept smiling at him. Kipp wondered where the love of Bobby Scott's life was if he was so head over heels for her.

"Excusez-moi, Monsieur Leftenant?"

Kipp turned around in his seat. A young French waitress with hair like fine silver and eyes as blue as the sky he'd flown through that afternoon was standing next to him, smiling shyly.

He did not know how to respond. "Uh . . . yes . . . *oui* . . . how may I help you?"

She spoke slowly in English, still smiling. Kipp noticed her small teeth were as white as cream. "I am told . . . you . . . today . . . have an ace become, yes? Putting down a German plane?"

"Yes. *Oui.* But how did you know?"

"Oh, *mon ami,* Bobby, he tells me."

Kipp glanced at the bar. Scott raised his glass again.

The young woman leaned over Kipp and took his face in her hands. Her perfume was sweet and spicy, the sensation of her fingers on his skin warm and overpowering. "Do you mind, Leftenant? *Je suis honorée de vous offrir un baiser.*"

She kissed him on the lips. It was not a long kiss, but to Kipp it seemed to go on for a blissful eternity. She started slowly and gently, gradually kissing with more strength, finally finishing with a flourish that seemed to pull his heart and breath out of him. As he sat back dazed in his seat, the other men at his table watching with their mouths open, she patted him on the cheek.

"Is that all right, Leftenant? I wished . . . to thank you . . . for fighting for my country. Yes? *Merci.*" She began to walk back through the crowded restaurant toward the bar, where Scott was grinning and clapping his hands together.

"So what do you think of Christelle?" asked Kent Wales.

"Is that her name? Bobby's girl?"

"Well. That's what he likes to think. But she's made it pretty clear she's no man's woman and won't be until France is free of the Germans."

Kipp was warm. He gulped a glass of water by his elbow and poured another from the pitcher.

"Does she kiss all the new aces like that?" he asked.

Kent shook his head, chewing on a toothpick. "I shouldn't think so. She never kissed me like that when I got my fifth. Nor Hannam when he got his tenth. Or just last week when Teddy Irving bagged his sixteenth."

"So Bobby put her up to it."

"No. Not her. He may have suggested it. But she's the one who decided to do it. And she wouldn't kiss you unless she really wanted to."

Kent followed Kipp's eyes over to the bar, where Christelle was laughing with Bobby Scott and two Canadian pilots from a squadron based near theirs. She glanced back at Kipp, held his eyes briefly, and smiled her shy smile again. After a moment, she went into the kitchen and emerged carrying three plates of *escargot* for a table on the other side of the room.

"What are you going to do now, Ace?" asked Kent.

"I honestly don't know. My head's a bit topsy-turvy at the moment."

Kent speared a black olive from Kipp's plate with his toothpick and popped it in his mouth. "Well, something's attracted her to you, mate. Once we find out what it is we'll bottle it."

Kipp sat back in his chair, arms folded across his chest, eyes closed, reliving the kiss. "Goodbye, Piccadilly."

Kent jabbed at another olive. "Farewell, Leicester Square."

Sir William tapped his soft-boiled egg with a butter knife before neatly slicing off its top.

"You see," he said, "things have been going along quite nicely for us since Easter. The Americans have come in, thanks to German U-boats sinking their ships. The Canadians took that dreadful Vimy Ridge, which has stymied us for years, and the Arras offensive has being going well. The air war has its ups and downs, but I must say we are giving as good as we get, though we need some changes in our aircraft. Did you receive my letter that Kipp is officially an ace?"

Lady Elizabeth buttered a piece of toast. "I'm simply grateful he's in one piece."

Sir William dug into his egg with a spoon. "Eh? They're all doing well, aren't they? Robbie back in Dublin. Edward back with the fleet in Rosyth, a new ship under his feet. Libby safe and sound at her hospital in France."

"I haven't seen Libby's face in two years. Why won't they give her leave?"

"We've been through that. Libby could have leave to visit us twice a year or more, but she refuses. She feels she's more needed there than here."

"But leave is only a week or two, what difference can that make?"

"It's the sort of girl she is, Mother. Pray for her. Keep her photograph by your bed. God will bring her home soon enough."

"Edward was positively bubbly when he left," Victoria spoke up. "Wasn't he, Mother?"

Lady Elizabeth found a small smile and nodded. "I thank the Lord for that. It seems he was out on the grounds all the time, William. Walking about with Harrison, of all people. The fresh air did him a world of good. Writes Harrison now quite regularly, did you know?"

"Does he?" Sir William replied.

"Heaven knows what they find to talk about. Harrison is not exactly a wizard with a pen. But they seem to get along."

"Grand. And Robbie chafing in Ireland?"

"Not chafing, William. I left his letter on the bedside table in your room. The executions that took place last year are still affecting the public mood. He and his fellow officers always go about in groups now. Things are tense."

"It is unfortunate. Leniency would have cooled matters down considerably. The firing squads have simply ensured there will be another uprising. I've said it before."

"I hope Robbie is well clear of Dublin before that happens. Charlotte dear, might I have another tea?"

"Of course, ma'am."

Charlotte Squire held the china pot firmly and poured a stream of hot tea into Lady Elizabeth's cup.

"Thank you, Charlotte. Catherine is well enough, William. Says Albert is very busy, works late most nights. I expect she finds the loneliness dreary."

"Can't be helped, Mother. There's a war on."

"Papa?" asked Victoria. "Did you manage to look into Ben Whitecross's whereabouts at all?"

"Hmm? I do have a person looking into it. It's a needle in a haystack, you understand. He hasn't written anyone, so we have no idea what area of the front his unit is stationed in. Why, we don't even know which regiment he's with."

"Aren't there any recruiting records?"

"Of course. But oddly nothing about a Benjamin Whitecross. Someone slipped up, I expect."

Victoria leaned toward him. "But you'll keep looking, won't you, Father? The servants ask about him. Harrison especially. And Old Todd."

"Of course I will. He's a brave lad. It meant a great deal to your mother and me to see him stand up and enlist when he saw what our sons were going through for country and king." He smiled at his daughter. "We'll find him. It's only a matter of time, my dear."

"Thank you, Papa."

Lady Elizabeth cleared her throat. "There's some news we haven't shared yet, William. Two pieces of news."

"Hmm?"

She looked across the table to her daughter. "Victoria, my dear, why don't you go ahead?"

"All right." Victoria set down her knife and fork. "I'm not marching anymore, Father."

Sir William looked up from his second egg. "What's that?"

"I still believe in the right of women to vote. Indeed, I am just as strongly committed to universal suffrage for all men and women over twenty-one. And I'm just as strongly opposed to the war in Europe. But I found the demonstrations were becoming too coarse. Too violent. That is not the manner in which I should like to voice my protest. I do not see the point in making war in order to end a war."

Her father sat back in his seat, wiping his mouth with a napkin. "I am astonished."

"So I prefer to avoid Liverpool for the time being. Letters to the editors of the various papers is my favorite mode of demonstration at the present."

Sir William laughed. "I am delighted. Your mother and I have fretted about your being arrested or hurt or worse. I'm very happy you've come in off the street, my darling."

"I'll still write the letters, Papa."

"Of course you will. What politician would mind that spirit in a daughter or son so long as the argument is elegant and sound and delivered with the proper amount of heat?" He attacked his third egg with knife and spoon. "My, my. This is most agreeable. What other news do you two have for me that can top that?"

Victoria sipped her tea. "Well, Em is with child."

Sir William put down his spoon. "What?"

Lady Elizabeth took his hand. "The baby is due in December, William. It's wonderful, isn't it?"

Sir William's face opened up in pleasure. "It is. Certainly it is." He looked from his wife to his daughter. "This is turning into one of the most splendid breakfasts I have ever eaten in this house. It's a pity Sir Arthur and Aunt Holly and Lady Grace ate early. I think I will spend the rest of the morning here and see what happens next."

Victoria stood up. "You may do that, Father, but I wish to go riding. I trust I may go about the estate without Old Todd Turpin as my shadow now that I'm nineteen?"

Sir William waved his free hand, the other still holding his wife's. "Of course."

Victoria looked at Charlotte as the maid set out a pot of cream and a plate of scones fresh from Mrs. Longstaff's oven. "Char, would you mind leaving the breakfast things for the other girls? I'd like you to help me with my riding outfit."

"Why —" Charlotte glanced at Victoria in surprise, stopping what she was doing with the sugar bowl. "I'll be right up, Miss Danforth."

Victoria stood in front of her freestanding oval mirror while Charlotte adjusted her jacket and scarf.

"That suits, Char, thank you."

"You're welcome, Miss Danforth."

"Tell me, Char. Do you miss my brother very much?"

"I . . . I don't quite know how to answer that, Miss Danforth." Charlotte straightened the shoulders of Victoria's green jacket several times. "I should find it wonderful if all your brothers were home from the war and safe."

Victoria looked at her in the mirror as Charlotte fussed over the trim of the jacket. "I saw you two that day. When I walked to the cliff and back. You were hiding behind a tree."

Charlotte's face filled with blood.

"So," continued Victoria, "are you good friends with my brother? Were you just out for a stroll together that day? Or are you in love?" Victoria turned around to face Charlotte. "I think it's love."

Charlotte smoothed her white apron and kept her eyes on the floor. "I'm sorry, Miss Danforth. I'm not sure what I can say to you."

"What are you sorry for? Do you care for Edward?"

Charlotte lifted her eyes. Victoria saw that they were clear and strong.

"I do, Miss Danforth. Very much. But I realize it's out of place."

"Why do you think that?"

"He's — Edward's of noble birth, Miss Danforth. Just as you are. We have no future together. I know that." Her eyes became a rich indigo color. "But he's so kind to me. His words are so wonderful. I have so little to offer him but he still treats me with such tenderness and respect."

"You have so little to offer? I've never seen my brother more cheerful and good-willed than he was his last few days with us. It wasn't the weather, Char. Or walks with Harrison in the woods. It was you."

Charlotte flushed a deeper scarlet. "You're kind to say so. But he's of noble birth and I am just a girl from a poor family. I know it can't last but I beg you not to tell your parents. I couldn't bear for them to punish

Edward in any way."

"Oh, Char." Victoria laughed and linked an arm through Charlotte's. "Do you think I or God in His heaven care how poor you are? If I can see the brilliance of your spirit, how much more clearly can He? No wonder Edward is dazzled. 'Poor Edward,' we should be saying. How can he ever escape your loveliness?"

"Are . . . are you not angry with me then?"

"For making a decent human being out of my brother? You are a complete delight. I'm glad Edward found you first because he needs you the most. Not Robbie or Kipp." She put a hand gently to Charlotte's face. "Is there not gossip about me among the servants?"

"Why, there's always gossip of some sort or the other about your family, Miss Danforth."

"About the man I love?"

"I've heard all sorts of things. I pay them no mind."

"It's Ben, you know. Ben Whitecross. A poor groom. Yet I love him, Char. I pray for him every minute I'm awake and I pray for him in my dreams, I'm sure. I want to marry him, Char. I beg God to bring him back alive from the war and I vow to marry him the day he sets foot at Ashton Park.

Now, do you see, both of us have the same sort of secret to share."

"Why — I'm happy for you, Miss Danforth. I never thought the rumors were true. I hope God returns Ben to you safely. And I pray your parents will accept the marriage. But they'll not accept you and Ben and me and Edward too. They'll feel the need to draw the line somewhere."

"Don't be so sure. They're set in their ways about some things but open-minded about others, especially if it involves the happiness of their children. The war is changing things. Not always in bad ways." She took Charlotte's hands in her own. "Do you think prayer accomplishes anything, Char?"

Charlotte met Victoria's gaze. "I do, I confess I do, Miss Danforth. I prayed over Edward's photograph in your mother's room every day for a year — and I had no idea that he would come to care for me in the way he has. It's a miracle."

"Then we shall pray together for our men, Char. Will you do that with me?"

Char smiled softly. "I will, Miss Danforth. It's very gracious of you."

"Let's begin now."

"It feels so strange, Miss Danforth. You being of the manor and I —"

"No more of that. God cares about the prayer prayed and not a family's name. Come here."

Victoria led Charlotte to a small couch with white and green fabric and intricately carved wooden legs. They sat down facing each other, Victoria's small hands closing around Charlotte's strong white fingers.

"I've never had anyone to pray about Ben with before," said Victoria. "This means a great deal to me. We should begin with the Lord's Prayer, Char. Is that all right? It seems to be a prayer we always pray in our family."

Charlotte closed her eyes. "Yes, Miss Danforth. There's no more perfect way to start."

Ian Hannam whistled as he walked past French civilians and British and Canadian pilots on a crooked street in the Saint-Leu district of Amiens. It was dark but the moon was almost full, the air was warm, and afternoon rain had opened blossoms and leaves, making the night's scent sweet and rich. He took in a lungful and almost laughed. He felt like a schoolboy again, helping his mates pass love notes back and forth to their girlfriends. He'd always been a good go-between back then. He never dreamed he'd pick it up again in the middle of a war.

Kipp was nursing a coffee at the Café Jules Verne. There were seven other airmen talking quietly in the candlelit room of rough wooden tables and checkered tablecloths that were worn and frayed. Ian came in the door, hands in his pockets, looking as if he'd just been shot down. Seeing his face, Kipp's stomach tightened.

Ian sat down at Kipp's table. "Sorry, old boy."

"What happened? What did she say?"

"Well, she asked why you hadn't approached her yourself. I was going to say you'd been wounded in the leg tangling with Richthofen but thought that might be stretching it considering you've never been wounded, not even a scratch on the —"

"For heaven's sake, Hannam!"

"Calmly, Danforth. Play the man. I said your French was *très miserable* and you required someone of my ability and charm to ask if you two could meet privately — *tête a tête.* She appreciated that and said she would be charmed, *enchantée,* but feared her English was no better than your French. I assured her that your French was much, much worse than her English and the two of you would get on splendidly.

161

Where there's a will there's a way."

"So what's wrong?"

"What's wrong, old chap, is that her boyfriend chose that moment to show up. Big as a gorilla. Mean as a Hun. Ferocious way about him. Eyes like machine guns. Well, perhaps I exaggerate."

"A boyfriend. I thought . . . Kent said she didn't —"

"Kent. Ah well, Kent, he went to Oxford you know, Christchurch, they made a frightful mess of his powers of reason. No, I'm afraid Teddy has won the day and taken home your Guinevere."

"Teddy!"

"Teddy Irving, ace of aces. I'm sorry. Did my best. Perhaps you'd like to head back to base rather than be here when the pair of them show up — oh, bad luck! Here they are. Steady, Danforth. Remember the king."

"The king? What does the king have to do with this disaster?" Kipp stared as Teddy held the door to the café open. He was in his uniform as were Ian and Kipp. In stepped Christelle, gleaming like the night stars, linking her arm with Teddy's. Smiling, the pair approached Kipp and Ian at their table. She was at least a head taller than him. Ian scrambled to his feet and did a quick bow.

"Mademoiselle."

She inclined her head. "Leftenant Ian."

Ian pumped Teddy's hand. "Congratulations, Teddy."

"Thank you, Hannam. I'm still a bit dizzy about it all, y'know."

"Don't blame you a bit." Ian turned to Kipp. "Faint heart never won fair lady. I'm sure you're up to offering the two of them your best wishes, Danforth."

Dazed, Kipp got to his feet. "Well done, Teddy."

Teddy ran his fingers over a thick brown mustache flecked with gray. "Thank you, Kipp. No hard feelings?"

"Best man wins."

Ian and Teddy looked at one another and seemed to be muffling a laugh. Then Ian counted out loud in French, *"Un, deux, trois, quatre, cinq . . ."* At five they both ran from the café and bolted down the street.

Rooted to the spot, Kipp watched them race out of sight. He glanced at Christelle, who had one hand over her mouth. The corners of her eyes crinkled and her shoulders shook.

"What's going on?" he demanded. "They made out you were Teddy's girl!"

Christelle finally laughed out loud, taking away her hand. *"J'en suis desolée.* I'm sorry

163

— they wanted to play a game. Your friend Ian asked if I would — go along. He said he would prove to me what a good sport you were."

"Is that what he said?" Kipp found his face growing warm with a mixture of anger and confusion. "What do you think?"

Christelle watched the battle in his face and stopped laughing. She took his hand. "I think . . . I am glad to be here with you, Leftenant. Sit with me."

Her touch sent a shock through his arm. She tugged him gently into a chair beside her. After a moment, he felt he ought to release her hand but when he tried she only tightened her fingers around his.

"May I . . . have a coffee also?" she asked. *"S'il vous plait?"*

Kipp was beginning to recover himself. "Why, yes, of course. Do you drink it very much?"

"I have not had it that often. With you, I would like to, *oui.*"

The sensation of her hand in his made it difficult for Kipp to remember what little French he knew, but he managed to ask the waiter for a second coffee properly.

She squeezed his hand. *"Chapeau!"* Kipp smiled. *"Merci."*

He sat looking at her, saying nothing

more, taking in her beauty, relief still running through him after the prank Ian and Teddy had pulled. He gazed on and on, enjoying her face, the way her hair fell about her shoulders, the changing color of her eyes. Christelle waited for him to speak, one eyebrow arching to emphasize the question in her features: *Eh bien? Well?* Finally she raised his hand to her mouth and kissed it.

"Don't you have anything to say to me?" she teased, her eyes catching the light of the candles in the café.

"Oui," Kipp said, taking her hand and bringing it to his lips.

Hours later, Ian and Teddy and Kent were jabbering away like madmen about their night on the town when they picked Kipp up. He had walked Christelle to her parents' home, where she lived, and returned to the café to wait for them. They peppered him with questions, none of which he answered, sitting in a dreamy silence in the back seat of the motorcar, until they looked at his eyes and gave up, preferring to talk about themselves again.

Once they made it to the aerodrome and chateau, Kipp stretched out on the bed in his room, arms under his head, and looked up at the dark ceiling, thinking over every moment of the evening, each facial expression Christelle had made, the different ways she laughed, how she mixed English with French when she spoke, the kiss at the door to her house that had lasted much longer than the one at Sans Souci the week before.

As he drifted off to sleep, recalling how the weight of her hair felt under his hand, his fingers touched an envelope that had been placed on his pillow. It had a whiff of perfume about it but not Christelle's. He groped for the wooden matches on his bedside table and lit a candle. The letter was from Lady Caroline Scarborough.

At first he was not going to read it. Then he was going to read it in the morning. Finally he opened it. The note was short, wishing him well, promising him her prayers, asking after his health. At the end, she wrote of their upcoming marriage.

Although there has not yet been a ring or a formal proposal, something we agreed to wait on until the end of the war, I think we are one regarding the matter and will wish to proceed with the wedding as soon as the politics of Europe allow. I would be grateful if we could discuss particulars as to when the ceremony ought to be held and where we ought to live once we are man and wife. I think the next time you are on furlough would be a perfect time to deal with such matters. I do love you so very much and look forward to your response to my letter and your return to England, my dear.

8

"The soup is quite good, Mrs. Longstaff."

"Thank you, ma'am. It was a new recipe."

Mrs. Seabrooke took another spoonful. "Did you receive it from someone who lives near us?"

"At a Baptist church in Liverpool. A lady there gave it to me."

The household servants were seated at their table just off the kitchen and eating supper. Some were listening to the two women discuss the soup recipe, a few were carrying on their own conversations, several had almost finished their meals and were ready to leave.

"Don't run off," said Mrs. Seabrooke, wiping her soup bowl with a thick slice of bread. "I wanted to announce that Sir William wishes for the servants to head down to the Danforth cottage in Dover and have it ready for Parliament's summer recess. Some, of course, must stay behind to maintain the house and property here. Harrison, you will remain. Skitt and Todd, you will take care of the horses and stables here. But Charlotte, you have been asked down to Dover to attend Victoria, and Norah, you will wait on Lady Elizabeth instead. Cynthia, you will be Aunt Holly's maid this summer. Tavy, you will naturally perform the same duties there as you do here. Wallace, you will be Sir William's valet, and Lewis, you will see to Sir Arthur and any of the sons who might pop up on furlough."

She paused to eat the bread. Then she tapped her spoon on the rim of the bowl. "Who else? There will be another maid or two and several footmen needed. For those of you who have never been there, the house at Dover is quite small compared to the manor here, only about forty rooms, but Sir William and Lady Elizabeth do like to entertain during July and August." She rapped the spoon sharply on the bowl. "Where is my head? Mrs. Longstaff, you will, of course, come with us to cook and you may ask two assistants to accompany you . . . Sally and Margaret, I should think. In any case, I shall pin the list of those going on the board here. If you haven't been selected to serve at Dover Sky this summer you may the next."

Tavy sipped his water. "What day will we be heading off?"

"The twenty-first or twenty-second of May. By coach to Lime Street Station and then by rail to London and Dover."

Charlotte gave a short laugh and twisted a fork about in her hand. "I've never been out of Lancashire, much less all the way down to the Channel."

"You'll adore it," said Norah, adjusting the pins in her brown hair with long white fingers.

"But won't the house be musty after a year all shut up?"

"No, dear girl," responded Tavy, wiping at a small stain on his sleeve with a damp napkin. "They have servants who live there all year round. Just to keep everything trim and proper. There are horses there too, y'see, as well as some lovely fields and orchards to maintain. About six or seven servants, I would say. They keep the place airy and bright."

"So they do." Mrs. Seabrooke clapped her hands together. "No more dilly-dallying. I'll post the list in a day or two after I've spoken with Lady Elizabeth again. Oh, and Harriet, we'll need you to tend to any lady guests' needs."

Harriet was small and white, with her hair

pulled back in a bun so tight it stretched the skin around her eyes. "What of Lady Grace?"

"Lady Grace does not travel to Dover for the summer. She prefers to remain at Ashton Park. The maids here will see to her."

Throughout April and May Sir William was busy at the House of Commons, and Lady Elizabeth took advantage of his absence to attend the Baptist church Mrs. Longstaff liked in Liverpool. A motorcar picked the two of them up at Ashton Park and brought them back after the service. The car belonged to a husband and wife who lived in a village nearby who were also members of the small church.

At her first visit, Lady Elizabeth found the singing noisy and the preaching loud and far too personal. She also felt the people took too many liberties and presumed too much when it came to striking up a friendship with her. And then there was the oddly musty smell of the building itself. She very nearly decided not to return and said as much to Mrs. Longstaff. But by the following Saturday night, she felt compelled to attend again. And by the third visit she found she preferred the enthusiastic style of the Baptist worshippers to what she considered the dull complacency of the congregation at St. Mark's. The preaching was easily understood and the friendship of the women and men, she had come to believe, was not affected or fawning as she had first supposed, but genuine and warm. She found herself praying in the pew and at home with an intensity that had not stirred her for years.

Lady Elizabeth's friendship with Mrs. Longstaff went back to the years when the children were growing up. The two had become close friends despite the social gap between lady and servant, Lady Elizabeth talking over difficulties with the children freely and frequently, growing to trust her. When Mrs. Longstaff had asked if she would come with her to her church, Lady Elizabeth had gone for the sake of their relationship, never expecting to go back again. By the time the household was to travel down to Dover Sky for the summer, Lady Elizabeth found she wished she could take the brick Baptist church — musty smell and all — and its congregation and minister with them.

"They'll still be here when we get back, ma'am," said Mrs. Longstaff. "You can count on that. I expect you'll still be wanting to worship with them come fall and winter."

"Of course," replied Lady Elizabeth as they privately shared a tea together in the front parlor. "So long as Sir William doesn't object."

"Why, he hasn't objected so far, has he?"

"He doesn't know. That's why we haven't heard a word from him."

"My heavens, ma'am, why would you keep it from him? Sir William is a good Christian man."

Lady Elizabeth stirred more sugar into her tea. "Sir William is a good Church of England Christian man, Mrs. Longstaff. That's the thing."

Catherine Moore hurried along the sidewalk toward the Belfast docks and her husband's office. Under one arm she had a roast-beef dinner she had placed in a box wrapped in brown paper and twine. The sooner she could reach Albert, the warmer his meal would be once he opened the box.

Thick fog the color of clay fastened itself to the larger buildings and shops as well as the high cranes that loomed over the harbor with their long necks. Catherine tightened a scarf around her neck as the cold damp tried to find its way past her coat to the thin blouse underneath. She did not want to miss him and quickened her pace.

There had been quarrels, usually over her father's Home Rule stance that granted Ireland a measure of independence, for Albert remained adamant that Northern Ireland in particular needed to stay firmly united to England. Over the past two months he had begun coming home later and later, skipping dinner with her altogether and snatching a plate of fish and chips at a local pub, showing up at the house smelling like beer and cigars. They had fought about that too. Several times he had slept on the leather couch in his den.

Catherine had decided that taking meals to him might be one way to heal the rift. Albert loved meat-and-potato dinners and was not likely to get those at a bar. She was certain it would bring a smile to his face and that they might be free to talk in a friendlier fashion to each other. It was worth a try.

Pigeons were clustered in front of her, jabbing their beaks at the cement. A man in a plum-colored vest was sweeping crumbs and cigarette butts out of a restaurant and onto the sidewalk and street. The pigeons hopped away from the broom but would not fly. They were too intent on getting the scraps he brushed out the door.

Catherine paused to let the man finish.

She glanced through the window of the restaurant. It was full of people eating and talking and smoking. There, at a far table, she saw Albert. He was laughing loudly, she could hear him through the open door, cigar in one hand, a plate of roast beef and potatoes and mushy peas on the table in front of him, a beautiful woman with raven hair, dark-red lips, dark eyes, and a sleeveless dress holding his other hand, constantly bringing it up to her mouth to kiss and then press against her cheek.

"Thank you, ma'am."

The man with the broom smiled and stepped back to let her pass.

"I've forgotten something!" blurted Catherine and began to walk quickly back the way she had come.

After a block, she went into an alley and put a hand to the brick wall of a law office to brace herself. She felt like she was going to collapse. A trashcan was lidless a few feet away and she pitched the box that held Albert's roast beef dinner into it. Her knees almost buckled. She took a dozen slow, deep breaths and finally straightened. Leaving the alley, she half-ran across the street in her long coat before another wave of traffic swept past. Gaining the other side, she turned up a boulevard with spreading green elms and walked as rapidly as she could up a slope and away from downtown. The house she lived in with Albert lay in the opposite direction and she had no intention of returning to it.

"I always love a train ride," Lady Elizabeth said as she stepped down from the rail car and looked around. "But I enjoy arriving even more. Ah, there's Fairburn!"

Fairburn, who managed what Sir William liked to call the Cottage at Dover Sky, stepped forward to greet Victoria and Lady Elizabeth, as well as Aunt Holly and Sir Arthur.

"The carriage is this way, milady," he said, directing them through the station and to the navy-blue and burgundy carriage waiting outside. A larger coach handled by his assistant Adkins was parked just behind, waiting for the servants to assemble on the platform. A third was picking up the steamer trunks and luggage. Motorcars and trucks mingled with coaches and wagons as Fairburn coaxed their carriage out of town and into the countryside. Every tree and bush and flowerbed was at least two to three weeks ahead of Lancashire. Victoria smiled as she gazed at long lilac hedges that were in full bloom and perfuming the air. The afternoon sun lay on the green fields like lace.

"I have enjoyed coming to Dover Sky since I was a child," Victoria said, holding her mother's hand.

"I love our visits too, dear. Late May is one of the loveliest times of the year in southern England."

Sir William's cottage of forty rooms was easy to spot from miles away because it stood alone on a small hilltop. Unlike Ashton Park it had no forest surrounding it, only neatly trimmed hedges and a small orchard of apples and plums, so its walls and chimneys of white stone shone unobstructed in the sunlight, while the sky over its roof seemed as limitless as the nearby sea.

"It looks like it's made of snow when it gleams like that," Victoria almost whispered. "Or ice."

"I think it looks like the cliffs themselves." Aunt Holly leaned out of the carriage window. "I look forward to my room here."

"What's special about it?" asked Victoria.

"I can catch a glimpse of the Channel from my window. Just a glint of light on water and a bit of the French coast. It's wonderful. The only thing missing is a few of the people I admire."

"What do you mean?"

"I wish some others could join us here from Ashton Park."

"Such as who?"

Aunt Holly kept her eyes on the green landscape they were moving through. "Harrison for one. I feel nothing bad can happen to us if he's nearby."

"Who else?"

Aunt Holly smiled. "He's the only one who comes to mind at the present."

One of the few trees near the house was an apple tree that grew near Victoria's window. As a girl, she had leaned out to pick the one or two apples that showed up in late August before they returned to Ashton Park. Now she opened the window to let the scent of the tree's white blossoms fill her room. She perched herself on the sill and closed her eyes.

"Heavenly," she murmured.

A thought of Ben sitting by the window with her brightened her face rather than darken it.

I will find you. I know you're alive.

The next day was Friday, May twenty-fifth. A group was leaving Dover Sky and going into Folkestone, a nearby town, to shop.

Mrs. Longstaff swore by a grocer in the main street. Fairburn took the family in the blue and burgundy carriage, and Adkins the Seabrookes, Mrs. Longstaff, and Tavy in a small black one.

"There's a barber in Folkestone I trust with my head," Tavy announced as their coach moved along the road, now and then passed by motorcars and trucks.

"Go on with you," teased Mrs. Longstaff. "You've scarce enough hair to nest a cricket."

"All the more reason to choose a good barber. I must take excellent care of what God's left me."

They arrived just after four. The day was still warm and brimming with spring light. Mr. Seabrooke wandered in and out of shops buying up various newspapers and took his time about it, chatting with the vendors, so that at six o'clock he still only had three or four in his hands. Mrs. Seabrooke had agreed to help Mrs. Longstaff select fresh vegetables from the green grocer, plums and pears from the fruiterer, as well as choice cuts from the butcher. Tavy spent the first two hours walking up and down the streets and looking out over the harbor where ships were anchored and troops milled about. No embarkations were

179

scheduled for France and the Western front. Eventually he found the barber and settled himself in his seat. Fairburn and Adkins had parked by a tobacco shop so they could sample the pipe weed available as well as keep an eye on the horses. Victoria drifted in and out of shops with her mother and Aunt Holly, looking over dresses and shoes and perfumes. Sir Arthur detached himself from the women and found himself a sturdy bench that enjoyed a good amount of sunlight and composed himself for a nap, cane across his knees.

At six o'clock, Victoria slipped out of a hat boutique where Lady Elizabeth and Aunt Holly were involved in the long process of purchasing eight new hats between them. She watched three girls skip rope in a side street, two of them turning the rope over and over and chanting a rhyme while the third jumped. A clattering noise began to grow louder and louder and she thought it was a train. As she continued to listen, she decided it did not sound anything like a train and must be a motorcar or one of the larger trucks she had seen driving about full of soldiers, and not just one of them, but four or five. She soon rejected this idea as well, for the growling of engines was coming out of the air and over her head.

She stepped away from the boutique so she could get a clearer view of the sky. Others were craning their necks upward and shielding their eyes from the sun with their hands. Planes sprang over the rooftops, flying in a ragged formation. Victoria had not seen many aircraft but she had observed enough to know these were enormous and had wings far longer than usual. Assuming they were British, she wondered what so many of them were doing on this side of the Channel instead of flying over the front.

"Germans!"

A man was pointing at one plane that had separated itself from the others. The black crosses on its tail and wings were unmistakable. Suddenly it dived and the rumble of its two engines became a screech. Dark objects hurtled from the plane. Fire broke the street open and a wall of hot air followed by a roar knocked Victoria to her knees. There was a second rush of air and noise and a third. She crawled against the wall of the hat shop as needles of glass and slivers of wood slashed through the streets and alleys. A chunk of brick, smoking with heat, smacked into her leg and she cried out. Black clouds and orange flame and shattering blasts forced her lower and lower.

A wounded horse screamed and lurched

past dragging its back legs. Victoria shielded her head with her hands as a large pane of glass above her head flew apart. Hats with feathers went spinning through the bomb blasts and rolling over the paving stones. Her mother's voice was shouting out her name. She tried to respond but her mouth filled with dust and ashes and she lost her breath, coughing violently into her hands while roaring in the sky and roaring in the streets blotted out any other sound.

We at the *Anglican Herald* wish to announce the birth of twins to Reverend Jeremiah Sweet, vicar of Ribchester in Lancashire, and his wife Emma, née Danforth, daughter of Sir William Danforth, MP, and Lady Elizabeth Danforth of Ashton Park. Peter and James were born at five in the morning on December third. Mother and sons are doing well. The christening will occur at eleven in the morning on Sunday, December ninth, after which the church will gather for a luncheon and a celebration of God's goodness to Reverend Sweet and his family. The Bishop of Liverpool is expected to be in attendance as well as Sir William and Lady Elizabeth. Sons are a gift from the Lord, the psalmist tells us. In such bleak times it is good to see His graciousness to the Sweets and the Danforths, and we thank God for new life where so much has been taken by war and pestilence.

9
1918

Spring 1918

"How is Mrs. Seabrooke?" asked Kipp.

Victoria shook her head. "It's been almost a year since the raid on Folkestone and she just gets worse and worse. At first we thought she would pull it together. During the summer she kept things running like a clock at Dover Sky. But once we returned to Ashton Park in the fall she simply unraveled. This winter has been horrid. You can see for yourself. She's much like Lady Grace now. Except she wanders through the ash trees in the forest and Lady Grace wanders through the rooms in the manor."

Kipp thrust his hands in his uniform pockets, a frown on his windburned face, as he watched Mrs. Seabrooke limp across the lawn with the help of a black cane, heading toward the woods. "Bad luck. How long did Mr. Seabrooke live then?"

Victoria had her arms folded over her

chest and wore a shawl against the March wind. "He was killed instantly. I'm sorry we didn't write you sooner about what happened. No one wanted to."

"I wish I had been there. My squadron would have made quick work of those Gothas. Bombing civilians like that is nothing short of murder."

"It wasn't the first time, was it? The Zeppelins did the same thing to Norfolk at the beginning of the war. The longer wars drag on, the nastier humans prove themselves to be. The Germans killed almost thirty children at Folkestone."

"No real aviator would do that. Richthofen and his Flying Circus wouldn't." He put his arm around his sister. "But mum wasn't hurt. You had a leg burn and a few others had cuts, but nothing bad, right? So I thank God for that. Is it true Sir Arthur hid under a bench?"

Despite watching Mrs. Seabrooke hobble along, Victoria could not suppress a quick smile. "The very bench he'd been napping on. Stuffed himself right underneath. When a bomb lifted it off him he just balled up and crouched lower."

"That's something." Kipp kept his eyes on Mrs. Seabrooke until he lost sight of her among the trees. "Did you say Tavy's been running the household now?"

"He is."

"Tavy's a good sort. He'll keep things going smoothly here. Who keeps an eye on her?"

"You see Skitt there at the edge of the trees? He's following her."

"I like Skitt. Grown up fast as a groom, hasn't he? Good for him. Speaking of the servants, just before I came out on furlough we got a batch of new lads for our squadron along with a brace of topnotch Sopwith Camels. Who do you suppose popped up with the pilots?"

Victoria shrugged one shoulder, still staring into the ash grove where Mrs. Seabrooke had vanished. "I haven't the foggiest."

"Do you remember a fellow by the name of Whitecross? Fancy seeing him there."

Victoria snapped her head around. "What?"

"He'd been with different infantry regiments for a year. Applied for the Royal Flying Corps. Took to planes like a hawk to air, I gather. I haven't been up with him yet. One of my mates, Ian Hannam, has young Whitecross under his wing —"

Victoria threw her arms around Kipp's neck. "Oh, thank you, thank you, that's the best news you could have brought me."

"What's all this?" Kipp kissed her on the forehead. "Do you care for this Whitecross fellow?"

"Yes — no . . . no, I'm just glad to get some good news from the war for once . . ."

Kipp looked at her eyes. She wiped at her face with the back of her hand.

"You don't need to keep secrets from me," he said. "I'm not Father. I don't expect you to marry the Duke of Marlborough. If you like Ben, that's perfectly fine as far as I'm concerned. He's an officer in the Royal Flying Corps now. Mum and Dad can hardly object to that."

She smiled up at him, still crying. "Do you think . . . do you think they might be favorably inclined towards him — one day?"

"As your suitor? If the war lasts a few more years he could be promoted to captain. So who knows? Look, I'll take a letter back to him if you like."

"I wouldn't want to be forward."

"Clearly you thought well of him before he enlisted. How could a letter be forward?"

"I'd prefer . . . that he dash a line off to me . . . if he wishes . . ."

"I'll tell him you'd like to hear from him. How's that?"

"Yes — all right."

Kipp hugged her. "I don't mind being a

go-between for you and Ben. Don't imagine me some sort of spectacular upper-class snob. I'm not Edward."

Victoria patted her eyes with a pale-green handkerchief that was the color of her dress. "As a matter of fact, Edward's not like that anymore."

"He's not? When did this startling change sweep over Lord High and Mighty, first son of Sir William and Lady Elizabeth Danforth and heir to the great manor of Ashton Park?"

She pinched his arm. "Don't be cheeky. I'm serious."

"Just tell me."

"I will later. It's quite a story."

"It would have to be. Fine then. We'll wait. When is Emma arriving with the boys?"

"This afternoon."

Kipp's green eyes lost their light quickly. "Caroline is due to show up after lunch as well."

"Why — what's wrong with that? She's practically your fiancée. You've always worshipped her."

"Worship is perhaps too strong a word, Vic. Let's go for a walk in the woods like Mrs. Seabrooke. If you have something to share about Ben Whitecross . . . well, I have some things to tell you myself."

"Here." A laughing Emma handed one baby off to Kipp and took the other from Jeremiah and offered it to Victoria. "Don't worry, Kipp, they've both been changed recently."

Kipp smiled into the baby's face. The child was calm and wide-eyed, not making any sounds or movements, gazing steadily at the person holding him.

"Which one do I have then?" he asked.

"Peter. They're not identical twins. Peter has green eyes like you. James has brown eyes. Like chocolate, mum says."

"I've seen plenty of babies and plenty of chocolate," said Lady Elizabeth, watching Kipp and Victoria holding Peter and James with clear delight.

"He'll fly," announced Kipp. "Look at how bright that face is. How sharp his eyes are. He'll fly, Jeremiah."

Jeremiah was wearing his collar. He laughed, happy with the welcome his sons were receiving at Ashton Park. "Not anytime soon, I hope, Kipp. You can do the honors until then."

"Yes. Me and Ben Whitecross. I didn't tell you I ran across him in France just before I came home on leave. He's a new recruit in my squadron."

Emma's face opened up in surprise. She looked at Victoria then back at her brother. "Are you quite sure?"

"Of course I'm sure. He was our groom and driver for years."

Emma seized Victoria's arm as she held James. "That's wonderful. Wonderful. Thank God, Vic!"

Victoria's face was as bright as Emma's. She kissed the baby's head. "I know. I couldn't believe it when Kipp told me."

Lady Elizabeth glanced from one daughter to the other. "Young Ben must have made quite an impression on our household. I'm glad to hear he is well. Your father had everyone but Winston Churchill and King George scouring Europe for him." She looked to Kipp, who was gently bouncing Peter in his hands. "I presume he's a flying officer then?"

"That's right, Mum. A leftenant just like me. Although I have seniority. He's quite handy with a kite, I hear. I'll get up with him when I return to Nancy next week."

Jeremiah had his hands behind his back, one of flesh, the other of wood. "That's exceptional news. Really splendid."

"It appears to be earth-shattering," responded Lady Elizabeth. She reached out for Peter. Kipp carefully placed the baby in her hands.

"There you are, my dear," she said. "Grandmother shall keep you firmly on the ground for the present. Even if others here have their heads in the clouds."

Tavy coughed as he approached the group by the fireplace with its logs burning yellow and orange. "Pardon me, ma'arm. But the Scarborough coach is just pulling up the drive."

Lady Elizabeth held Peter to her shoulder and patted his back. "Thank you, Tavy. Please show Lady Caroline in. We'll wait for her here."

"Very good."

"I expect you'll want to greet her at the door," Lady Elizabeth prompted Kipp.

Kipp inclined his head. "Yes. I was just thinking of doing that, Mother."

"What do you mean? Slow down? Darling, if we go much slower we'll both drop dead of old age before we're married."

Kipp had taken her to the library and its small turf fire, gently holding her hand. Lady Caroline was tall and blond like him, her hair swept up on her head and speckled with small jewels. A diamond necklace shone on the smooth white skin of her throat. Her blue eyes were large and seemed to take up her whole face. Matches seemed lit behind them. Kipp had often found himself gazing into their color and trying to think. Now he spoke quickly and quietly.

"Let the war end, Caroline. There will be plenty of time to discuss where you want the ceremony and where we ought to live once we have peace."

"Darling. It can't go on forever. I'd really like to work on something rather than stand around and wait. Or sit and roll bandages. I'm restless. So much time has gone by." She kissed him on the cheek and ran her hand through his short blond hair. "We're both changing. Look how bleached your hair has become."

"That comes from flying. Not from old age."

"But I'm so much older. Look at me."

Kipp laughed. "As if a chap could do anything else when you're in the room. Do you imagine you're falling apart?"

"Well, what do you think?"

"To borrow a phrase from the Yanks, you look *in the pink.*"

"Well, it sounds lovely. I hope it means good things." She placed her arms around his neck and her eyes smiled. Her perfume was sweet and made him think of lemons and sugar. "I've missed you. I know war can be a dreadful thing. No doubt you've experienced all sorts of things you'll never talk to me about. But leave that behind for now. It's just us here now. No bullets or bombs. Just us." She kissed him on the mouth. "Relax. I haven't learned to bite." She kissed him a second time. "What's wrong? Where are you, Kipp?"

"I'm right here with you, Caroline —"

"No, you're not." She examined his eyes, arms still around him. "I don't know if it's the war . . . or another woman. But you're not quite with me, are you? Perhaps it's that you're worried about the men in your squadron — did someone close to you get killed? No. I think it's another woman. Belgian? French? A British nurse? Well, you won't get shed of me that easily, Leftenant Danforth."

She moved her hands up to either side of his face and kissed him with as much strength as she had, locking his mouth onto hers. His reserve finally broke down under the onslaught of her fire and heat and he began to respond with more and more passion. Finally she pulled her head back and ran a finger slowly over his lips.

"At least you remembered how to kiss

with that one. So there's hope." She linked her arm through his. "Come, dear. I want to see the children. We'll have a marvelous afternoon despite your personal demons, won't we? If I can call her that. Where are the others?"

They began to walk down the hall. "In the great hall. They're looking forward to seeing you."

"Are they, darling? How pleasant that someone in the Danforth family still thinks well of me."

"Libby?"

A nurse was leaning in a doorway and letting the June sun play over skin she felt was far too white. The letter she had been reading hung loosely from her hand. Her eyes were closed.

They are six months now but mom says they look eight or nine. Both are growing so fast. Kipp says Peter is "made in his image" but the truth is his hair has the same ginger quality yours does — he's not a straight blond. He's lovely. They're both lovely. But James has more of Edward's and Robbie's dark looks. And Catherine's and Aunt Holly's, I suppose.

"Libby! Are you there, love?"

When she heard her name the second time, the young woman adjusted her uniform and cap and smoothed the sides of her blond hair — it was cut short just below the ears. She folded the letter away in a pocket in her apron. A tall lady, in the same type of uniform, approached her from inside the building. When she saw Libby, she smiled.

"There you are. I've been looking all over creation. Though heaven knows you deserve a rest. Did you read those letters that came for you?"

"Yes, Mrs. Turnbull. One from my sister who had the twin boys last December and another from my mum. Good letters. Better than coffee for perking me up."

Mrs. Turnbull had her hands on her hips. "Most of the girls have gone home on leave once a year if not twice. You've never gone."

"Neither have you, ma'am."

"Well. I don't have any family left alive. It's a different matter for you."

Libby shrugged with one shoulder. "I love them all well enough. But there are so many of them, I'm scarcely missed. Here I'm needed."

"I doubt your siblings and your mother would put it in those words. You're a rare

195

bird, Libby. I'm sure they notice that you're not there at the family gatherings. But suit yourself. I expect you'll find your way home whenever this horrid conflict is settled. Until then, I can't say as I'm displeased to have you all to myself. Follow me. We have a difficult patient."

They entered the hospital that had once been a convent and began to walk down a corridor. It smelled of soap and blood. Each room they passed was full of beds and the beds were full of the severely wounded.

"Do you mean difficult as in hard to manage or —"

"Difficult as in hard to keep him alive. That's why they sent him up to us here in Paris. They think we can work miracles."

"The doctors —"

"Have done all they can. He's a pilot. Made a crash landing. Broke both arms and both legs. His neck is not doing very well either but at least he's not been paralyzed. We're giving him plenty of morphine for the pain. What's needed not even the chaplain has been able to provide. A will to live."

Libby, though a foot shorter, matched Mrs. Turnbull's rapid pace. "Why shouldn't he want to live? Broken bones will heal in time."

"But not broken spirits." Mrs. Turnbull

stopped outside a closed door. She lowered her voice. "His brother was killed in the same air fight. Since they told him that last week he's scarcely eaten or had more than the briefest sips of water."

"And you want me to do exactly what?"

"Talk to him. Reason with him. Coax some food and drink into him. He's American. A captain. Squadron leader. I'm sure you'll get along famously."

"And why do you think that, Mrs. Turnbull?"

"You're both bluebloods. You'll understand one another. His family made their fortune in banking. His name is Michael. Michael Woodhaven. The Fourth. He's a millionaire, Libby. The Yanks want him to live. Our uppity-ups in the military want him to live. You've had success with other patients who thought just like him and wanted to cut their wrists."

"I don't think of myself as a blueblood. I don't like being called that."

"I know you don't, but it's what you are." Mrs. Turnbull opened the door. "He's got his own room. The American army insisted on that. And on his having a private nurse."

Libby felt her face grow warm. "All the other wounded deserve the same nursing care. Why should Captain Woodhaven be treated any differently?"

"Because he *is* different, my dear. His father owns half of New York."

"I'd rather not take on this assignment, Mrs. Turnbull. I'm sure you can get another nurse to fuss over him."

"He's your patient, Miss Danforth. That's orders. If you don't like them you might consider returning to England."

Libby narrowed her blue eyes. "If the Yanks are so worried, why don't they put him up at one of their own hospitals?"

"The American Red Cross told them this was the best one in Paris. I'll check in on you in an hour or two. Remember your vow to serve the sick and wounded, Libby."

"I don't need to be reminded of that, thank you very much."

Libby entered the room, shutting the door behind her. She saw the tall man in the bed, all four limbs in heavy white casts and up in traction. His neck had a cast as well. But he was able to turn his head when she crossed the floor toward him. His eyes were the deepest and darkest brown she had ever seen.

"Hullo," she greeted him, standing beside the bed. "I'm Libby Danforth. Your nurse. They tell me your name is Michael Woodhaven. The Fourth."

"Does that mean anything to you?"

"Not at all. Should it?" She knew her eyes had taken on their ice color. "It means something that you're a pilot, however. My brother's a pilot too. His aerodrome is near Amiens."

The man grunted. "What's his name?"

"Kipp. Kipp Danforth. He's just made captain."

"Probably because the other captain's dead. What's your brother fly?"

"Um." Libby thought a moment. "Sopwiths. Yes. Sopwith Camels."

"Yeah? We just got our SPADs. Good kites. Had mine a week before it got shot to pieces."

"Why don't you tell me about that?"

"Aw, you don't care. They just sent you in here to get me eating and drinking and making merry. Am I right?"

"They want you to get better."

"Sure they do. Can't have the heir to the crown jewels go bottoms up in France at twenty-four, can we?"

"I'm sorry about your brother."

"What? You didn't even know my brother. How can you be sorry?"

"Because I hate suffering and death, Captain. I hate war. And I'm sorry it took him."

"Yes. You're sorry it took the rich man's son."

"I'm sorry it took a mother's and a father's son." Libby put her hands on her hips. "Tell me, Captain Woodhaven. What do you see when you look at my eyes?"

"I see the pretty little Brit they stuck in my room to shake me up and make me feel like living and loving again."

"Then you're not looking hard enough, Yank. I don't care who you are. I don't care if you think I'm pretty or as ugly as a coal scuttle. I just care that you're wounded, you've lost family, and it's my job to help you get back on your feet again. I'd do it for anyone, rich or poor, tall or short, fat or skinny. Can you read my eyes now?"

"It's just your style, Pretty Patty. I've seen it all. Some come at me playing the shy barmaid. Others are down on their luck and need a shoulder to cry on. Then there are those who act like the Queen of England. Go practice your moves on some other poor sap."

"I beg your pardon?"

"I read about it. They get the prostitutes and jailbirds and the dirt poor from East London and ship them over here as nurses. The upper-class gals would never soil their precious little hands."

Libby's eyes widened and her mouth opened but she did not speak. Woodhaven lifted his head as far as he could off the pillow, glaring at her.

"What do you think, Patty? That I'm going to fall in love with you because you've got blue eyes? Because you're a strawberry blond with a flashy smile? An easy way to become an heiress overnight, huh? Go from the brothel to the rich man's mansion in the wink of one of your bright eyes. Well, not this flyboy. Go practice your charms on some simple-minded doughboy or Tommy. Or take a fast boat back to the alleys of London."

Lady Elizabeth had always warned Libby about her temper. Libby had fought to control it all her life and had reached a point where she felt she had it well in hand. But Woodhaven's stream of insults put a quick and sudden end to her self-control. While one part of her mind screamed it would be an end to her nursing in France and everywhere else, another part screamed equally as loudly that Michael Woodhaven was a scoundrel and a blackguard, and the death of his brother did not excuse his language or his behavior. Libby seized a glass on the table by his bed and dashed the water in Woodhaven's eyes. While he spluttered, she took his plate of beans and corned beef and mushy peas and smacked it into his face as if it were a pie. He stared at her in disbelief, his face a mess of brown beans and green peas and red beef dripping with water.

"You're finished!" he exploded.

Libby could feel the blood in her face that made her skin feel as if she were standing in a bonfire. "I'm not. You're a disgrace to your nation and your uniform. And your family name. If I ever set eyes on you again it will be the second-worst day in my life. This was the first. You're a cad. A brute. I have no doubt in my mind but that your brother was a far better man than you."

She stormed from the room, flinging open the door. To her surprise, Mrs. Turnbull and two doctors fell back from the doorway, where they had been crouched listening.

Libby's eyes were fierce blue flames. "I am done, Mrs. Turnbull. If you wish my resignation, you have it. I shall return to England at once."

Mrs. Turnbull was smiling. "Why, child, you're the only person who has ever stood up to him. It's precisely what was wanted. Doctors Bradshaw and Kincaid and I think you're off to a splendid start."

"That, Mrs. Turnbull, was a grand finale. He will never want me as his nurse again.

For which I thank God. All the oceans in the world could lie between us and it still wouldn't put enough distance between Captain Woodhaven and me. I utterly despise the man."

"Ma'am?"

"Yes, Norah. What is it?"

Norah Cole stepped into Lady Elizabeth's bedroom at Dover Sky. She held a dozen envelopes in her hand. "I don't wish to disturb you. But I found these letters addressed to Mister Harrison. As he's never at Dover Sky I'm at a loss as to how they came to be here or what I'm to do with them."

Lady Elizabeth had been sitting at her vanity. Placing down her hairbrush she extended her hand. "That is odd. Let me see them." She sorted through the envelopes. "Postmarked last year. And this year. How very strange that they are lying around in this house. Where did you say you found them?"

"On a chair in the servant's quarters, ma'am. By Miss Squire's room."

"I see. Well, thank you very much, I'm sure, Norah. I'll see you at breakfast."

"Do you need anything, ma'am?"

"Not at all. Goodnight."

"Goodnight, ma'am."

Norah left, shutting the door. At first, Lady Elizabeth put the stack of letters on the vanity, having no intention of opening them. But she realized they had been written by her son, so she couldn't resist picking up one of the envelopes for a peek. After all, he never wrote her as often as he wrote Harrison. What on earth was it the two men had to talk about? She drew Edward's letter out of the envelope in her hand. It was postmarked May thirty-first, 1918.

10

Summer 1918

Catherine tipped the man who had brought up her new furniture two shillings and closed the door firmly behind him. She looked around the flat. It was small and simply furnished and suited her perfectly. Perhaps there was a touch of the monastic in her — not a very desirable trait for a Protestant. But now that she was far away from Albert and her family perhaps she didn't have to be Church of England anymore.

She crossed to a window that looked out over a convent. She was in the Catholic section of Belfast by her own choice. Albert would be looking for her and he would not think — or dare — to come to this neighborhood. As she watched, several nuns stepped out of the large brick building and walked around a grass quadrangle enclosed by three high walls and the convent itself. One of them held a large umbrella over herself and the others to protect them from the summer rain. The four nuns were laughing as they walked.

Gray pigeons flew up from the convent roof and fluttered down to land at Catherine's windowsill. It happened so quickly it startled her. She peered at them through the glass. Whether they saw her or not, they weren't concerned, settling in, cooing and folding their wings. She had not smiled in many weeks but now she felt one cross her lips.

So have you come to invite me to Mass? Well, that's not a bad idea. That's another place Albert would never look for me. Though God might.

Victoria flung out her arms and danced about her room at Dover Sky. What a summer it had turned out to be — *Ben had written her!*

It had been five weeks since Kipp had promised to encourage him to drop her a note. Five long weeks. But now Victoria understood what the expression lighter than air meant.

I feel like I could fly as high as one of your aeroplanes, Ben Whitecross. I am most definitely up there among the starlings and the swallows.

Perhaps he had said too much too quickly. Perhaps he had promised more than he should have and made too many vows. But it made her feel like taking the path down the cliff to the shingle beach and flinging herself into the sea in her dress and shoes.

Today I feel like I could swim from here to America and back.

She desperately wanted to share the letter with someone. But who? Emma was with her boys and Jeremiah in Ribchester. Catherine was with Albert in Belfast. And Libby, well, who had seen her since 1915? There was no one in her family she could show the letter to.

Of course she would read it to Char. She would be ecstatic for Victoria. But somehow the news was bigger than the two of them and she needed to draw someone else into the secret. Who? She went through the list of maids at Dover Sky in her head and rejected all of them. Then Norah came to mind, her personal maid for years before Char. If anyone was trustworthy it was her. Tall, angular, plain, and trustworthy Norah. She could read the letter to her knowing it would never go any farther than that. Running down the stairs from her room she found Norah dusting shelves and straightening books in the library.

Her face was pink from her short run. "Norah. Could I see you a moment, please?"

Norah looked at her face. "Why, whatever is it, Miss Victoria? What has happened to agitate you so?"

"Nothing at all, my dear Norah. Everything is absolutely brilliant. Can you come with me?"

"Of course I can. But what's all this about?"

Victoria brought the letter out from behind her back. "I have something to share that makes me want to dance. Let's use Father's private study. He's out and about with Fairburn for the afternoon." She took Norah's hand. "Come. This will make your day just as it's made mine."

Libby placed her hand on the doorknob, closed her eyes, and cried out to God in her mind. Michael Woodhaven IV turned his head as she entered the room. Libby stopped as their eyes met.

"Please," said Woodhaven. "Come in, Miss Danforth."

Libby walked slowly to his side. "Captain Woodhaven."

He half-smiled. Her face was stone.

"I did not think you would return," he said quietly. "Even at my request. A request accompanied by an apology."

"I had no intention of returning, Captain. Mrs. Turnbull begged me. A Yank named Eddie Rickenbacker came all the way from his aerodrome near Nancy to plead your case. Then I made the mistake of praying about it. That's why I'm here."

"I thought it might have been my good looks and charm."

"I'm afraid not."

"No. I suppose I'm not much on looks with lunch covering my face."

"That was an improvement in my estimation."

Woodhaven lifted his head. "I know who you are. I'm dreadfully sorry for the way I treated you last week."

"Is that why you're apologizing? Because you found out I am a 'blueblood' like yourself?"

"I'm apologizing because of conduct unbecoming an officer and a gentleman. It would be easy to say it was my grief over Mark. But that's an insult to Mark. You were right when you said he was a better man than I am."

"All right then. How can I help you today? Is the traction for your arms and legs set

209

comfortably?"

"Oh, sure. I feel great. Like a turtle that's landed on its back and can't get up. Could I trouble you to light a cigarette for me?"

"No smoking in hospital rooms. You can slip out into the corridor if you wish."

"Or you could wheel me."

"The door's too narrow for the bed."

"If I can't smoke, perhaps we could chat."

"We have nothing to say to each other, Captain. I don't mind helping you with your breakfast."

"I'm not hungry."

Libby smoothed down the white apron of her uniform. "Then I'll be on my way. I'll pop back in an hour to check on things."

"You are a hard case, aren't you?"

"Nurses are not prostitutes, Captain Woodhaven. We are ladies. Whether we are of the manor born or not."

"I appreciate that. As I said, the other day was conduct unbecoming. Once again, I am sorry. I was a beast. I am trying to make it up to you."

"I doubt you can. I never met a man in my life I liked less. If you'll excuse me, I have to —"

"I do need something, Miss Danforth."

"What exactly is that?"

"A shave."

"A shave?"

"If I have one I guess I'll feel up to some scrambled eggs and toast."

Libby hesitated. "Very well. Let me step out and fetch a razor."

"A razor. Glad to hear it. I thought you'd be looking for a dull bayonet."

Libby's lips curved upward slightly. Then quickly returned to a thin line. "I'm grateful for the idea, Captain. I'll see what I can come up with."

She returned with a basin of hot water, soap, shaving brush, a towel, and a straight razor.

He grunted. "That looks almost as bad as a bayonet."

"Actually, it's much worse. A slip would be fatal. Do you still want me to go ahead, Captain?"

"My life's in your hands."

"Your life is in God's hands, Captain. I'm just a mortal, prone to mistakes."

Libby wet his beard and lathered it with the soap and the brush. Carefully, she began to apply the razor, frequently dipping it in the basin to free it of soap and whiskers. Woodhaven's eyes followed her hand. Neither of them spoke. Inch by inch beard and lather disappeared until his face was clean and pink. Surprising herself as well as him, she patted his face lightly with her hand.

"Smooth as a baby's bum, Captain. Is that East London enough for you? I expect you're ready to eat now."

"Considering I thought I'd be dead before you were done, yes."

"You never know, Captain. I could have put strychnine in the eggs."

"I'll take my chances."

She sat by his bed and fed him the scrambled eggs with a fork. Then she held the pieces of toast to his mouth, one after the other, so he could take bites until they were both gone. After the toast she offered him a slice of fried tomato.

"What's that?" he asked, suspiciously.

"It's what it looks like."

"Do you English fry everything?"

"Everything we can get our hands on. Including Yanks."

"I think I will forego the tomato, Miss Danforth. I eat them fresh with salt and pepper."

"An odd custom. Anything else then, Captain?"

"The bedpan. Please."

Libby brought a white ceramic bedpan out from under the bed and plopped it in his lap. "Help yourself."

"Yes. Well. I have no arms. And I can't move."

This time a full smile came to Libby's face and she let it stay there. "If I had a shilling for every time I've heard that line in East London I'd be a rich lady today."

"Mother, you called for me?"

"Ah. Victoria, dear. Please come in and shut the door."

Lady Elizabeth was seated in a white rattan chair at a small white table in a greenhouse that took in the sun from the south and west. Green plants and bright blossoms thrived all around her. Victoria sat in a chair next to her mother. A tea had been poured for her.

"I had Charlotte set that out for you only a minute ago," Lady Elizabeth said.

"Thank you." Victoria lifted the cup and took a sip. "It's lovely."

"A special blend from Ceylon. I forget its name. Look at your father."

Sir William was throwing sticks for his shepherds. Now and then he raced them and got hold of the sticks first. Mother and daughter laughed.

"He thinks he's twenty." Lady Elizabeth smiled. "Summer is so good for him. Away from Westminster and all that."

"I agree."

"He worked tirelessly on that voting legislation that received royal assent in February. Did it please you?"

"It pleased me to have all men over the age of twenty-one receive the vote, Mother. But there are still too many restrictions on the women. They have to be over thirty, they have —"

"Yes, my dear. But it is, as your father says, a step in the right direction."

"It is."

Lady Elizabeth patted her daughter's hand. "He'll be back at it in a week or two. We'll start packing up for our return to Ashton Park in a few days."

Victoria nodded. "I'll be ready."

Her mother poured herself fresh tea from a small white pot with a blue knitted cozy. "Charlotte Squire will not be making the trip, I'm afraid."

Victoria set down her cup. "What do you mean?"

"She has found a position at an estate on the Isle of Man. Wonderful family. We, of course, provided excellent references for her."

"I don't understand. She hasn't said a thing to me. I thought she was happy here. She is one of the best maids we have."

"Indeed she is. Graceful. Competent. Pleasant. Charming. Altogether too charming when it comes to my eldest son." Lady Elizabeth continued to look at Sir William playing with his dogs. "Honestly, my dear, did you have to encourage the affair? I appreciate she has lifted Edward's spirits but you must know nothing could ever have come of it. Out of the question. Why, her father is a grocer."

"Edward —"

"Edward thinks he's in love with her. Of course he does. I admit she is striking in appearance. But a few months at our hunting lodge in Scotland, where he can meet young women of his class, will soon put things right. Your father and I have agreed he is to go there once the war is over. Whenever that may be. Miss Squire, on the other hand, will be on her way the day we leave Dover Sky."

"But she has been so kind, Mother."

Lady Elizabeth nodded, sipping her tea. "She has. That is why arrangements were made to put her up with a fine family elsewhere. Tavy will inform her of all this tonight. That's why she's said nothing to you — she hasn't been made aware yet. It's for the best. Although we are not ungrateful for how she managed to lift Edward's spirits after the sinkings." She turned to face Victoria, cup still in her hand. "Then there is the matter of you and Ben Whitecross."

Victoria's cheeks lost what little color they still had after the news about Charlotte Squire. "What do you mean?"

Lady Elizabeth shook her head. "No more of that. You've played quite enough games with us this year, Victoria. I was informed of your correspondence with young Ben. Once again, a fine man for his class. Upright. Good with the horses. A superb driver. But he will not be returning to the Danforth estate after the war."

"Our correspondence. Who told you about that?"

"It doesn't matter."

"I only shared the letter with Char . . . and Norah —"

"As I said, it doesn't matter. Is it true?"

"Mother, I —"

"Shh. You love him. Or think you do. Once that nonsense in Europe is finished we will be having a good number of balls at Ashton Park and inviting a great many young men to come and call. Not a few of them will be officers and gentlemen as well the sons of noble families."

"Ben is an officer and a gentleman as well."

Lady Elizabeth saw her daughter's temper rising and held up one hand. "I do not wish to have a fight here. Your father and I are as fond of Ben as we are of Charlotte. Perhaps they would be suitable for each other? Nevertheless, if you wish to keep on writing him, you are welcome to do so. If he survives the war, he may come to call at Ashton Park. He will receive the warmest welcome. The Danforths know how to honor gallantry and courage, attributes young Ben seems to have in generous amounts."

Victoria's eyes were the darkest green. "But he cannot ask for my hand, can he?"

"I should think not."

"Even if he was a captain or a major or —"

"Which he is never likely to become."

"But if he were? If he came back a hero like my brothers are in your eyes? What then?"

Lady Elizabeth laughed at her daughter's persistence. "You are tenacious. It is true Ben has made his way up in the world. From a stable boy to a groom to our principal coach driver to an officer in the Royal Flying Corps. Your father and I recognize these are not small accomplishments for someone of his class. Who knows? He may become the great commoner who attains to loftier heights yet. So your father and I are prepared to strike a wager with you."

Victoria's hands were clenched together in her lap. "A wager? What do you mean?"

"We are not a gambling people. It is not the Christian thing to do. But this is not a wager quite like that. Though I should say the stakes would be considered quite high, especially from where you sit, my dear."

"You're speaking in riddles, Mum."

Lady Elizabeth nodded. "I am. Forgive me. This is going to sound frightfully medieval, but it was the only way your father and I thought we could appeal to your sense of fair play and keep you from running off the cliff."

"I am not going to run off the cliff!"

"Allow me to finish, my dear. Let Ben come back. Let him have a chestful of medals. Let him have the rank of captain or greater. Let him gain the eye of the king for some reason or other."

Color rushed back into Victoria's face and eyes. "The eye of the king! For heaven's sakes, Mother, there are millions of men fighting in this war, how can you expect Ben to be singled out no matter how brave he is?"

"I have no idea. You may pray about it. But now, listen, my dear, the Lord can do whatever needs to be done. We do not want the two of you coming up with outlandish schemes. Do not tell Ben of this wager. If something occurs, let it occur naturally. Or by divine appointment. But not by the two of you working out grand schemes in your letters to each other. He is not to know about any of this. Or you forfeit the wager."

"Forfeit the wager! You make it sound like a game!"

"On the contrary, Victoria, your father and I are deeply in earnest. Great things may come of Ben Whitecross. We are willing to give you the benefit of the doubt on that."

"I see. And suppose he meets or exceeds Danforth expectations? What if I take you up on this and I win the wager? Does he get to return to Ashton Park? Will you let him be employed here again? Would you dare to allow him to be close to me?"

Lady Elizabeth leaned over and kissed Victoria on the cheek. "Oh, you do not understand, do you? The stakes are infinitely higher than that, my sweet girl. Let Ben Whitecross show signs of becoming a great man and he shall win more than a position among the servants of Ashton Park. If you wish it, he shall have you as his bride."

Sir William knocked and came into his

wife's room in his robe, winding his pocket watch. "Came to say goodnight, my dear. So we're off to Ashton Park in the morning. The summer went by like a galloping horse."

Lady Elizabeth was in a red robe, sitting at her vanity and dabbing cream on her face. "It's always too brief a season."

"How is Charlotte Squire?"

Lady Elizabeth shrugged with one shoulder. "Reconciled."

"No more tears?"

"Not in front of me."

"Have you spoken to Victoria at all today?"

Lady Elizabeth wiped her hands with a white cloth. "No more than you. But she takes this wager about young Ben quite seriously, you know. It was quite the right thing to do. No hysterics. No shouting. None of her theatricals. I believe she is praying about the whole affair."

Sir William smiled, dropping his watch into a pocket of his robe. "Well, that's something, at any rate. And who knows? Who knows?"

"He is a fine young man. I just wish his last name was other than Whitecross."

"Hmm. The Duke of York perhaps? The Prince of Wales?"

Lady Elizabeth laughed. "I do not set my

sights so high. But if he were Sir Benjamin Whitecross that would be a start."

"Such things have happened."

She brushed her hair with long, firm strokes. "When the war finally ends, what a different world it shall be."

Sir William put his hands behind his back and stood as if he were in uniform. "So much has changed already. Mr. Seabrooke dead. Mrs. Seabrooke incapacitated. Charlotte Squire on her way to the Isle of Man. I must tell you — Mrs. Longstaff is on her way as well."

"On her way where? Is she leaving for Ashton Park before the rest of us?"

"She's already gone. But not to Ashton Park. I tried to set her up with another family but she would have none of that."

Lady Elizabeth set down her hairbrush and swung around in her chair. "What on earth are you going on about?"

Sir William moved his hands from behind his back and thrust them deep into the pockets of his robe. "You should have told me, Elizabeth. About the Baptist church. About attending worship services there with Mrs. Longstaff. Am I such an ogre you could not risk informing me about what you were up to?"

Lady Elizabeth sat up straighter in her

chair. "What did you do?"

"I released Mrs. Longstaff. I can't have her taking you to religious sects that meet in the back alleys of Liverpool behind my back."

"You released her without consulting me? You sent her on her way without even asking for my opinion?"

"I'm sorry, my dear. This was not a decision for you to make."

"She is my friend, not just my cook. How can you say that?"

Sir William cleared his throat. "I gave her money for her purse. She would not take it but I insisted. I am not unmindful of my duties as a Christian man. But I cannot have you or our estate or our family name associated with Methodists or Baptists or whatnot. I am a Member of Parliament, and Danforths have always been loyal to the Crown and to the Church of England. Even under persecution. Even under Bloody Mary."

"So where is she? How did all this happen without my knowledge?"

"It has only transpired over the past hour and a half."

"Where is she, William? Out in the dark at the side of the road?"

"Fairburn took her to the train. She's

quite safe in his hands. Apparently she has relatives in London. That's where she was planning to go. I had a position for her at the Roxboroughs' in Essex but she said she would only serve our family."

"What is she going to do then? How do you expect her to make a living?"

"I don't know." Sir William fished out the watch and glanced at it. "Almost eleven. I must turn in. I had no wish to upset you."

"Of course you've upset me. You speak about me going around behind your back. What have you just done? How have you treated our faithful servant, Mrs. Longstaff? She's not a young woman anymore, William. Do you really think she's in a position to fend for herself in London?"

"It was her choice. She has relations there."

"Relations! They are gin swillers! Pickpockets! Prostitutes! How on earth can she fit in among them?"

Sir William moved toward the door. "I must turn in. There was never any question of permitting you to continue attending the religious services of a sect. You knew that. But you thought I might not find out. A maid let it slip. Thank God. I've been able to nip this quickly before it became a matter of public knowledge and gossip."

The candles in the room began to waver. Light and dark ran back and forth over Sir William's and Lady Elizabeth's features. Her eyes were darker than the shadows.

"You should not have done it, William," she said in a low voice. "Turning her out will not bless or protect our family. It will bring a blight upon our name. Besides, she did not coerce me to go. I willingly accepted her invitation."

Sir William opened the door and stepped into the hall. He looked back at her, not happy, not sad, but resigned and determined. "Even under Bloody Mary, Elizabeth, when they burned a Danforth at the stake. Even then we remained loyal to our Church and our God. I will pray for Mrs. Longstaff. But I can do no more than that."

"Tell me about your brother," Libby asked.

"What for? You never met him."

"That's why I want you to tell me what he was like. Were the two of you very close? Did you do all those brotherly things together, go fishing and hunting? Fancy the same girl? Compete against one other at school?"

Libby was bathing Woodhaven's chest and neck with a cloth dipped in warm water and

224

soapsuds. He lay back, staring at the ceiling.

"Why would you ask me such things?"

"Because you never mention him. Yet I know you think about him all the time."

"You can't know what I think, Miss Danforth."

Libby squeezed out the cloth and wiped his brow. "I can. When your eyes wander and you cease to talk you are certainly not thinking of me. Perhaps you are conjuring up memories of home. Perhaps you have a sweetheart in America. But I don't think so. It's Mark who's on your mind."

She thought he was going to keep on arguing. But he said nothing more while she washed his face and dried it with a towel.

"He wanted me to be the leader," he said when Libby was preparing to leave. "Think of the games we'd play. Where we'd go on a Friday night. We never took out the same girl, but if I liked one he made every effort to like her sister." Woodhaven shook his head slowly and laughed. "Even if she was as plain as a brown paper bag or had no more personality than a wood tick. Crazy kid. But yeah, that was it. Mike decides which fishing hole. Mike decides where to buy a new suit. Mike says he's going to learn to fly, well, Mark has to fly too. Used to annoy me." Woodhaven grew quiet. "If I could have him back again I wouldn't give him grief about anything he did. Not a thing."

Libby had been standing when he started. Now she sat back down. She had missed a patch of soap under his ear and she flicked it away with her finger.

"So you flew before the war, Captain?"

"Long before. There was a flying club we joined when I was eighteen and he was seventeen. Pop paid for the lessons. A Jenny where you sit up front and the instructor sits behind you with the controls. Until it's time to sit in the backseat and handle everything yourself. It took Mark a while to catch on. I thought he was going to blow it for the first time in his life and get left behind. But he put his head down and dug in and pulled it off. I was sure he wouldn't make the cut for the United States Army Air Service last fall. We called it the Aviation Section of the US Signal Corps then. But he got in. Pop pulled some strings to make sure we wound up in the same squadron. I thought he'd dog my heels everywhere for the rest of my life. But he got to be his own man." He looked away from the ceiling at her. "He was starting to cut his own path. Know what I mean?"

"Of course."

"I was relieved and proud and worried about him messing up all at the same time." Woodhaven grinned. "What are you smiling at?"

"You, Captain. Your smile. You use it so little I thought the US Army hadn't assigned you one along with your wings and white flying scarf."

He glanced back at the ceiling. "You have any brothers and sisters?"

"There are four sisters altogether. And three brothers."

He looked back at her, smiling again. "No kidding. That's a full house. You all get along all the time?"

Libby smiled and shook her head. "I'm afraid not. More like a tale from Dickens actually."

"Which means what?"

"Always a lot going on. Some of it fun. Some of it wicked."

"Where did you fit in?"

"I didn't. Not much. Everyone was kind enough. I just liked to wander off and be by myself. It seemed more interesting."

"And no one tagged along like Mark did with me?"

"Oh. Vic did. Victoria. Funnily enough she was a loner herself. But if she wanted company or a partner in crime, she chose me." She patted his arm and got up. "I've got to run now and fetch your dinner. You will eat for me, won't you? You won't spoil our new record?"

"And what's that?"

"Seventeen meals in a row."

Woodhaven stared at her. "I haven't."

"You have."

"I'll get fat."

"You'll get healthy." She headed for the door. "Don't lose your smile, Captain. Hang on with both hands. I want to see it when I come back."

"Whatever you say."

Libby bit her lip as she walked quickly along the corridor to the kitchen. His eyes had been warm and deep and dark. His hair a rich, thick brown after she had washed and combed it. Woodhaven's rugged looks appealed to her. His rudeness had obscured them, but now that his rudeness was gone the brown of his eyes and hair and skin emerged along with the whiteness of his teeth and the smoothness of his voice. It made her feel strange. Part of her wished they hadn't talked so much. Part of her wanted to just do her job and never talk to him again, not because he was a monster anymore, but because he was too pleasant. She found it unnerving.

Picking up his warm plate she returned to his room. There was a part of her that wanted the talk and teasing to continue. Not to stop. Why was that? The loner in her wanted to drop the plate and run. But this other part of her she did not understand or recognize wanted to make him smile, wanted to feed him, wanted to think of an excuse to wash his hair again today and run her fingers through the warm water and soapsuds and the softness. It made no sense to her. But she carried on to his room just the same.

"Ah, the smile is still there," she greeted him as she opened the door.

He shrugged, the smile growing larger. "I couldn't disappoint you. Could I?"

11

September and October 1918

The stars became brighter and brighter as the sky fell into night. Norah Cole smiled and closed her eyes. Taking off her maid's cap she turned her face upward to the starlight as if it held the heat and light of the sun. She loved going to Dover Sky but she loved returning to Ashton Park even more. The crisp northern weather and brisk winds suited her more than the milder temperatures of the south.

"Casting a spell, are you, Miss Cole?"

Norah whipped her head around. It was Harrison in his fedora and corduroy jacket, holding his walking staff. She laughed a small laugh.

"You startled me, Mister Harrison. You shouldn't creep up on a person like that."

"Why, Miss Cole, isn't that what you do to the Danforth family?"

"What . . . what do you mean?"

"Nicking my letters and giving them to Lady Elizabeth so she could read all about Charlotte Squire and Edward. Telling Sir William about Mrs. Longstaff taking his missus to the Baptist church in Liverpool. Seeing to it Miss Victoria's letters to young Ben came to the awareness of her mother. Now Miss Squire's in exile on the Isle of Man. Sir William and Lady Elizabeth are scarcely on speaking terms since he let Mrs. Longstaff go. Miss Victoria's fretting that she'll not see Ben again or that he'll not make the grade with her parents — the Lord alone knows what reckless thing young Ben will do in France to try and win over Sir William and Lady Elizabeth. Miss Victoria knows it was you that told her mum about Ben. She'll never speak to you about it. But she told me she knew and that she could never trust you again. All this trouble in the family on account of your tongue, Miss Cole. Your tongue and your devilish ways."

She could see Harrison's face more clearly as her eyes adjusted to the dark. She tilted her chin. "I did what I believed was right before God. Everything I told Sir William and Lady Elizabeth was true."

"Before God, did you say? Do you mean yourself?"

"Don't talk rot."

Harrison pulled a pipe from his jacket pocket, placed it in his mouth, and lit it, puffing deeply and carefully to be sure the tobacco in the bowl caught. Then he waved the match several times to make sure it was out, tracing a pattern of light in the blackness. The flame in the bowl flared up. Norah took a step backward.

"You don't frighten me, Mister Harrison. I shall scream if you so much as touch me."

"Touch the likes of you? No, you go on to your bedchamber, Miss Cole, and see if your conscience will let you get any sleep. And while you're staring at the ceiling and wondering what scheme to hatch next, bear me in mind. I've served the Danforth family since I was nineteen — that's almost twenty-five years. Watched the little ones grow into handsome men and women. Watched them try to make their way. Then along you come. In the past, I've had to do many things to deliver this family from wickedness and harm. I'll do so again, Miss Cole."

Norah fought with streaks of fear and anger that shot through her body. "I've never been one to be afraid of the likes of you."

"Or I the likes of you. Keep that thought close to what heart you have left."

Michael Woodhaven IV's casts were off.

Libby couldn't resist clapping her hands. "Wonderful! You look splendid!"

"I do not," growled Woodhaven, sitting on the edge of the bed in his blue hospital pajamas. "My arms and legs are as thin as pipe cleaners. I'll never get my muscles back."

Libby put her hands on her hips. "Of course you will, my Lord Woodhaven. You just need to get up and move about."

"How do you presume I do that, my Lady Danforth, since I can barely stand on two legs?"

"You need four. Here. Up we go."

Before Woodhaven could protest further, Libby had looped one of his arms over her shoulders and helped him to his feet. She began to walk around the room, half-dragging him with her.

"This is ridiculous!" he snapped. "You don't have the strength!"

"Well, Yank, obviously I do have the strength or you wouldn't be prancing about like this, would you?"

"Prancing. You make it sound like I'm ten lords leaping."

"We'll get you there."

"It hurts."

"I don't care if it hurts. We'll do this seven times. Like Jericho in the Bible. Then you can rest for five minutes. After that, we're going outside."

Woodhaven snarled. "I can't go outside. I'll look like a fool. Being hauled about like some big overstuffed toy."

"Other men wouldn't mind. Or do you think I'm an ugly, ginger-haired Brit?"

"Even during our worst fights I never thought you were that."

"Well then, my Lord Woodhaven, the September air is lovely. Blue skies. Sunshine. A breeze. You're a horrid white color. Let's change that, shall we? Two more around the room and then you can sit on your bed and feel sorry for yourself a few minutes before we —"

"Outside."

"What?"

Woodhaven scowled. "Take me outside now. Lord knows I've had enough of your taunts. And these four walls with their depressing green plaster."

Libby steered him toward the door. "Right, my lord. So it's out and down the corridor to our right. There's a courtyard with a fountain and a rose garden where the nuns used to go to pray and meditate."

"No one told me this was a convent."

"It hasn't been since 1915."

They made their way down the hall to a door that opened on the grass and the fountain, Woodhaven leaning heavily on Libby. No one else was outside except two British soldiers who were sitting on a bench and smoking, their crutches resting beside them.

"Shall we sit then?" Libby asked.

"Why? You tired?"

"Not at all. You're light as a feather. Are all Yanks featherweights?"

Woodhaven snorted. "My legs are burning but I'm not going to tell you that." He glanced up at the sun, squinting. "The air does feel good. I haven't seen blue sky since —"

He stopped. He bent his head. Libby stopped walking and saw him wrestle with his emotions. A feeling went through her she had never expected to feel for Michael Woodhaven. One of the many feelings that had surged through her during July and August and that she had tried to fight off. She stared at three robins cocking their heads to listen for worms and pecking at the earth in the garden, yellow and white roses hanging above them. Finally she put a hand to his cheek.

"You can fly again," she said.

"With legs like strawberry jam?"

"You can fly again, Michael. And when you do your brother Mark will fly as well."

"That's crazy."

"He will. Now do you want to have a seat on that marble bench?"

Woodhaven's brown eyes glittered with light and he stared straight ahead. "I want to walk. If you're not tired."

"I'm fine."

He continued to look in front of him. "You've never used my Christian name before."

"I know." They began to walk again. "Pretty soon we'll have you in the pink."

He gave a sharp laugh. "I didn't know you knew American."

"I know lots of American now, Michael. It's been a good summer."

"Spent nursing the cantankerous war veteran from Manhattan Island?"

Libby kept helping him move around the yard as he pressed down weakly with his feet. The British soldiers watched and smoked. The robins took flight. Libby and Michael watched them spin into the sun.

"It's been one of the best summers of my life," she said.

"Make me proud of you. But I already am proud of you. So don't change a thing. Not the color of your eyes. Not the curl in your hair. Not one inch of your heart."

Victoria's sorrel mare twitched its left ear around to listen to her mistress' voice. Horse and rider continued to walk slowly through ash trees that were turning to gold from the change of seasons while light the same color streamed through the branches. Victoria reached forward and patted Robin's neck.

"I know. I am a bit mad, aren't I? But I find it best to compose a letter in my head before I commit it to paper. And I can't do that without speaking out loud. So riding through the woods with you is how I write my most important notes to people."

An October breeze whirled a dozen leaves in a tight circle of yellow. They passed through it and two leaves came to rest on the arm of Victoria's green riding jacket. She did not brush them off.

"Ben, autumn is lovely here as I expect it is in France. My father and mother have a row going on that is spoiling it for me. Not a screeching and throwing things row, which they have never done. Just long, cold, deadly silences. Of course, with Parliament sitting Father isn't here much anyways. But when he is around they speak to each other in the most formal manner as if they were strangers at some reception in a stuffy mansion. Well, it will sort itself out. It always has. Though every time the sorting out sorts out differently."

Victoria and Robin emerged from the gold of the ash forest into a field where Skitt was herding the sheep toward Danforth Brook. He did not notice her, too distracted by the antics of the flock — it tried to go in every direction possible at the same time. Victoria flicked the mare's reins and headed toward the sea cliff several hundred yards away. There she sat on her sorrel and thought and finally made up her mind while gulls swept overhead and whitecaps flashed in long ragged rows.

"I am not to tell you this. But I shall anyways because I think the news will bless you as it has blessed me. Mother and father are worried it might drive you to do something rash but I know you better, I think. So this is what has come up — my parents will consider you a fit man to marry their youngest daughter, Victoria Anne, if you continue your upward rise. Stable boy to groom,

groom to coach driver, coach driver to officer in the Royal Air Force, and so on up the ladder to heaven. They do not mean you should climb the ladder all at once. But suppose, my darling, you return a captain? Suppose you become squadron leader? What if King George comes by to inspect your aerodrome and your commanding officer points you out to him? Mum and Dad just want a strong indication that you are going to make something of your life. I think you only need to carry on just as you have been doing and it will all come out right as rain. You see, my dear? We really do have a chance to become man and wife with my family's blessing. Isn't that something to look forward to? So keep on going as you are going and we shall have a wedding at Ashton Park once the war is finished. Mum and Dad call it a friendly wager. I should like to win it."

She closed her eyes and waited a few moments. Then she opened them again so that the blue of the sky and the blue of the sea filled her with color and light.

"Please, God," she said.

Ben Whitecross looked gloomily at his Sopwith Camel, his face showing the cracks and fissures of hours of frustration. His eyes were as dark as the rainstorm that had just ended.

"What's the problem?" asked Kipp, walking up to him.

"We've been mucking about with this since four. The armorer says the guns aren't up to snuff. It could be another half hour yet. Maybe more."

"Are they jamming?"

"Jamming would be nice. They won't even fire long enough to jam in the first place. He's worried about them being out of synch with the propeller as well."

Three mechanics swarmed over the Sopwith's guns and cockpit and engine cowling. Kipp glanced to the east and Germany, where a bright autumn sun was clearing the cloudbank over brown and gold fields. He clapped a hand on Ben's shoulder.

"We can't wait. Look for us due west near Cambrai. The troops are pushing the Hun back farther and farther every day."

"The war will be over and I'll not have made ace at this rate."

"Why do you have to be made ace?"

"I . . ." Ben looked at the plane, not Kipp. "I should like Victoria to think well of me."

"She already does. Making ace won't get her to love you more than she already does."

"I should also like your father and mother

240

to think well of me."

Kipp smiled. "They're stuck in some of the old ways. Want you to be a duke or a knight. A lot of that rubbish will be cleared away by the war. So steady on, Ben. You've accomplished a great deal starting out as private in the infantry. But it's all for naught if you don't come home in one piece. My parents will give you the marriage once they see you at Ashton Park in your uniform and shiny leather boots."

"I'm not so sure."

"Well, we're both in the same boat. They expect me to marry Lady Caroline Scarborough and I want to marry a French girl whose father is a humble baker of bread and *croissants.* We both have to win my mum and dad over. Let's try and buck each other up." Kipp pulled on his leather flying helmet. "See you up there."

The squadron's planes roared over the grass airfield, taking off one after the other while Ben stood by his Sopwith Camel, watching them go. Kipp flashed a thumbs-up as he swept past and Ben returned the gesture without much enthusiasm.

"Any luck?" he asked his chief mechanic.

"We'll test fire the guns against the brick wall in twenty minutes. But we can't be sure they'll be spot on."

"All right. Keep at it."

The sun rose higher and blazed over the aerodrome. The blades of grass that were beaded with the morning rain sparked and burned.

Fifteen minutes out Kipp had not seen any enemy aircraft except a German observation plane a good distance to the north. Woodlands below the squadron that hadn't been blasted to stumps by artillery glowed orange and red as blue or green rivers and streams wound between them.

Stretching his neck, looking all around him, especially to his back, he had just begun to wonder about the thick white clouds high and to the north, when black shapes hurtled through them and dived on his men.

He recognized the yellow and black wasp camouflage of one of the newer German *Jagdstaffels* — *Jastas* for short — led by Wolfgang Zeltner. They flew Germany's most modern fighter, the Fokker D.VII. Except for Zeltner — he would not relinquish his Fokker triplane, and Kipp watched it swoop, guns flashing, three wings of yellow and black.

Bullets scorched the air around his cockpit. He frantically signaled his squadron to break, slashing with his arm, but the sleek black-crossed aircraft had already fastened onto the Sopwiths like claws, and one of his airmen went into a spin, gray smoke pouring from his plane's engine. As Kipp watched the aircraft wind itself into tighter and tighter circles, another of his men was struck out of the sky, his plane bursting into flames and streaking to earth like a shooting star.

Tracers cut through the fabric of his top wing and he shot a look over his left shoulder. One of the *Jasta* had locked onto his tail, guns crackling. More shells smacked into his seat and he thanked God the back had been reinforced with a plate of steel. But the German's bullets found his engine and blue flame spurted up and began to run along the cowling like water. Kipp threw his plane into a steep dive but the D.VII stayed with him. A corkscrew to the left did nothing to shake Kipp's pursuer. Hole after hole appeared in his wings. The dive put out the fire but oil still gushed into the air.

Banking sharply to the right, he looked at the black and yellow plane that was about to claim him as its victim. It banked with him, guns firing, tracers making their way toward his Sopwith Camel, floating and bobbing at first, then appearing to come faster and faster until they were howling past his head. Suddenly a plane with blue and white and red RAF roundels painted on its wings swooped down and raked the German with bullets, blowing off the D.VII's tailfin and riddling the fuselage so that fabric began to tear away in great pieces. Kipp could see that the German pilot was as surprised as he was, snapping his head around to look, swinging his plane from side to side to avoid the British plane's guns. But when he went to the right, fighting to control his damaged fighter, the shells that had been tearing into his tailfin and fuselage slammed into his engine and the front half of the Fokker broke away, flinging the pilot into the air while the torn halves of his plane tumbled in sparks and smoke to the ground.

The Sopwith Camel streaked through the debris and jumped on two D.VIIs that were flying side by side and pouring fire into three British planes just ahead and below them. It hammered both the D.VIIs at close range, setting one ablaze when several lucky shells broke open the engine so that oil and flame flew everywhere. The second German plane simply fell out of the fight and out of the sky, its pilot slumped in the cockpit, twisting down to the French farm fields without smoke or fire until it crashed into a small hill and exploded in red and black.

The Sopwith then went head to head with three D.VIIs, guns spurting yellow light. One of the German planes immediately streamed purple smoke and went into a dive from which it could not recover before plowing into a field of rocks and flying apart. Almost ramming the other two, the Sopwith scattered them to the left and right and carried on into the cluster of black and yellow aircraft behind them.

Now it seemed as if all the other German planes pulled away from their targets to concentrate their fire on this menace that had dropped out of the heavens like an avenging angel. Five D.VIIs converged on the Sopwith Camel's tail, guns chattering and flashing. The Sopwith pilot lowered his airspeed sharply, fighting a stall, and let the Germans sweep over him. Then he fired at their underbellies. One of them exploded twice and dropped like a stone. As the Sopwith turned away, Kipp could make out the letter B on the fuselage.

"Madness!" shouted Kipp. "Break clear, Ben! You've done enough!"

He knew he could not be heard. Nothing could be heard in a sky full of wheeling aircraft and pillars of dark smoke except the rush of wind over wings and the cracking of machine guns. Ben Whitecross would not disengage and the *Jasta* finally got him, two latching onto his tail and shattering his plane with gunfire until black smoke, shot through with waves of orange heat, wreathed the entire aircraft. Following him down, the Germans were quickly pounced upon by other Sopwith Camels in the squadron and a new air battle began to twist and turn through blue sky and gray clouds. It did not go on for long. Having lost seven planes in less than ten minutes, mostly due to one reckless British flier, the wasp-colored D.VIIs formed up and headed east behind German lines.

Kipp nursed his plane lower and lower. He watched as Ben's wounded Sopwith spiraled to earth boiling black smoke. It leveled out before it struck and mowed a path through a field of uncut hay before cracking open and belching fire. Kipp saw Ben stagger from the wreck and run through the hay. His plane exploded a second time, vanishing in flames.

Victoria set down her cup sharply.

She was having mid-morning tea with Aunt Holly and Lady Grace. Both of them looked up.

"What's the matter, child?" asked Aunt Holly, her cup to her lips.

Victoria put a hand over her eyes. "I don't know."

Reds and blacks stormed through her mind. She saw Ben standing in the middle of it all in a leather jacket and boots.

Lady Grace stared at her as if she were far away. Aunt Holly placed her cup in its saucer and moved to Victoria's side, taking her hand.

"What is it?" she asked again.

"I keep seeing Ben. I feel sharp and unpleasant things. When the *Titanic* went down there were stories of people far away sensing that something was wrong long before there was any news of the sinking. They had such an overpowering feeling that their loved ones were in danger."

Aunt Holly nodded, squeezing Victoria's hand. "I read several of those stories. Is that what you're feeling about Ben right now?"

"I think . . . I think it is. Many of the people prayed and their loved ones survived. I wish someone would pray for him . . ."

"I'm not the one to take the lead in such matters, dear, lapsed Anglican that I am. I wouldn't know what to pray for Ben."

"O God, our help in ages past, our hope for

247

years to come. Our shelter from the stormy past and our eternal home."

It was Lady Grace quoting the words from the hymn. Victoria hardly recognized her voice it was so calm and sure, as if from another person much younger. She was looking straight at Victoria and spoke a second time.

"Lord, we beseech thee, safeguard our family this day. Safeguard those we love. That death may not have dominion. That destruction may not wear us down with sorrow and loss. May your grace be triumphant. We beseech thee, have mercy, O Lord."

She still held her teacup in one hand but with the other she tapped upon the table. *"He that dwelleth in the secret place of the Most High shall abide under the shadow of the Almighty. I will say of the Lord, He is my refuge and my fortress: my God; in him will I trust."*

Kipp landed his plane in a field only fifty yards from where Ben's Sopwith lay burning. The hay had ignited and dark smoke laced with white fire towered over the wreckage. Vaulting from the cockpit, Kipp ran toward the hayfield, having no idea where Ben was. As he came closer he saw a body in the grass and dirt. The flames were only yards away. He lifted Ben's head off the ground. It was slippery with blood.

"Ben!"

The eyelids flickered. "Kipp — you all right?" The voice was a rough whisper.

"I'm all right," Kipp responded, wiping blood from Ben's face with his gloved hand. "You saved my neck. You saved the whole squadron's neck. It was madness. Absolute madness."

He picked Ben up in his arms and staggered from the hayfield, which was exploding with fire and heat.

"Your plane won't take . . . us both . . ." rasped Ben. "There's . . . no room —"

"There's room."

Kipp laid Ben in the cockpit and crammed himself in beside him. He gunned the engine and his Sopwith rolled across the field away from the inferno. It struggled and wobbled and finally lifted into the wind. The squadron dropped into formation to the front, back, and sides of Kipp and Ben. They maintained this box of protection all the way to Amiens and their airfield. Smoke curled from Kipp's plane and flames began to appear on the fuselage. He had scarcely landed and bounced to a stop before the engine blew apart in blue and red fire.

Mechanics ran across the field and hauled Kipp and Ben clear. An ambulance roared up and Kipp and the mechanics placed Ben in it.

Kipp slapped the roof of the truck. "Get him to the dressing station!"

"He'll need to go to the hospital in Amiens," the driver said.

"Then he'll go the hospital in Amiens! But get him patched up here first!"

The ambulance raced toward the chateau and hangars. The rest of the squadron were landing, their planes jolting across the grass. Kipp counted them. Two were missing. White, gray, and black smoke rolled over him as a tanker truck pumped water onto his burning plane. He looked down at his hands and saw they were red from fingertip to palm to wrist.

12

November 1918

Lady Elizabeth stood stiffly at the manor doors with Victoria as Todd Turpin drove the coach up. Sir William jumped down in the twilight, the lamps on the coach making the grimness of his features obvious. He came up the steps, pecked his wife on the cheek, and took Victoria into his arms.

"I'm sorry, my dear. I couldn't send the news by cable. I could not. Only that you should expect me. And that Ben was alive. Follow me into the library. Both of you."

Tavy opened the oak doors.

"Good to see you, Tavy," said Sir William quickly.

"Thank you, sir. May I say the servants' prayers are with young Ben."

"I'm grateful. Please tell them that."

A fire was burning in the library's small fireplace. Tavy lit three or four large candles and a lamp and withdrew. Sir William stood with his back to the fire.

"There was an air battle," he began. "A rather vicious one. Kipp's squadron was involved. Young Ben of course is a pilot in that squadron. He was shot down and remains in serious condition at the hospital in Amiens. I have requested that special prayers be said at St. Mark's tonight. We should leave for the church in the next quarter hour."

Lady Elizabeth took Victoria into her arms and kissed the top of her head. "The praying will help. The praying will give you strength."

Victoria's eyes were closed. "Could we . . . ask Lady Grace and Aunt Holly to join us?"

"Of course. Aunt Holly would be ready to come with us at the drop of a hat. But Lady Grace?"

"I am quite capable of getting in and out of a coach on short notice, thank you, Elizabeth." Lady Grace leaned on a cane in the library doorway. "It's Ben Whitecross, isn't it?"

"Yes, mother," replied Sir William. "He's been wounded in combat."

"We prayed for him just yesterday, Holly and Victoria and I. We must be off to St. Mark's at once. The prayer service will make a difference. Come along. Have Todd Turpin

252

bring the coach around."

Surprised by his mother's outburst, where for months and years she had spoken only in short sentences and monosyllables, Sir William nevertheless held his place at the fireplace and did not move. "You never leave the house, Mother."

"There has never been a good reason for leaving it up till now."

"I must fill in a few details first. Kipp sent me several cables. Ben was not with them when the Germans attacked. The Hun had Kipp's squadron by the throat. Ben arrived on the scene after repairs were made to his aircraft and immediately launched himself at the enemy. He shot down four or five of the Germans before they turned on him. He crashed in a field. Kipp landed and picked him up and flew him back to their aerodrome."

Lady Elizabeth stroked her daughter's hair as Victoria clung tightly to her mother. "That was a brave thing for our son to do."

Sir William remained by the fire, hands behind his back, and looked at his wife. "Ben shot down the plane that had our boy in his sights. He saved Kipp's life."

There was a soft knocking on her bedroom door but Victoria would not get up from her seat by the window. Tears moving across her face, she stared out at the trees and the moonlight. The knocking came again.

I told you about the wager. I shouldn't have but I couldn't resist. You put your life at risk to win my hand, didn't you? How could mother and father ever say no to the man who saved their son's life? But now you may lose yours, so in the end we have won nothing. I will never forgive myself for prompting you to do something heroic. I knew you would respond to what I wrote. I wanted you to respond. Now you're wounded . . . and perhaps, by now, dead.

The knocking stopped.

Why were they bothering her? She had gone to the prayer service with them. People had been lovely and gracious and kind. But what good were loveliness and graciousness and kindness when a person was in jagged pieces inside? The vicar had read from the Bible and then sunk to his knees to pray. All lovely. But she herself was dark.

There was a sliding sound. Paper on wood. A telegram was being slipped under the door, still in its envelope and unopened. Heavy footsteps walked away. Her father. She wiped at her eyes with her fingers to clear them. She gazed at the telegram a few moments and finally decided to walk over and pick it up. It was from Kipp.

BEN HAS THE STRENGTH TO
TALK FROM TIME TO TIME. HE
WANTS YOU TO KNOW HE IS GO-
ING TO FIGHT THROUGH AND
THAT HE'LL MAKE IT. HE SAYS
HE WOULD HAVE DONE WHAT HE
DID REGARDLESS OF WHAT YOU
WROTE. HE WOULD NOT HAVE
LET HIS SQUADRON DIE. HE
LOVES YOU.

Victoria sat down on the floor with the
telegram in her hand. She began to cry
again so that her body shuddered with huge
waves of emotion: pain, relief, hope. She
did not get up, finally stretching out on the
carpet and falling asleep, her face streaked,
the cable still in her grasp.

The sun seemed the reddest Libby had ever
seen. How much she had colored it with
her own feelings she did not know. The Sopwith Camels were lined up black against the
dawn light. An engine sputtered. Then
another. Soon the early morning shook with
thunder.

"I have to go," he said.

A hand rested lightly on her shoulder and

was gone.

"Please put it back," Libby asked him.

"I didn't want to presume too much."

"You didn't. Please put it back a moment."

Michael's large hand returned to her shoulder. She lifted her own hand to rest on his, glancing up. The sun was bright yellow now and had turned his brown eyes to gold. But it was about her eyes that he spoke.

"I've never seen such blue. Not in the sky. Not in the sea. Not in the rivers and streams of any mountain range I ever knew."

She smiled. "You promised not to do anything rash, Yank. These blue eyes want to see you again."

"And I want to see them. Believe me. But now that I've been restored to active duty I have to fly at least one more time. I have to."

"I know that. Go with God, Michael."

He kissed the top of her head, pressing his lips into her perfectly combed and gathered red and gold hair. He walked over to his plane, looked it over, shook the mechanic's hand, and climbed into the cockpit. Tightening his leather helmet, tugging his goggles over his eyes, adjusting the white silk scarf around his throat, he gave the thumbs-up. The engine roared and he turned his plane into the wind, following the others in his squadron as their Sopwiths rumbled over the grass and took off into the clear sky and clouds of early morning.

It was Sunday, November 10, 1918.

MY DEAR ELIZABETH
KAISER WILHELM HAS ABDI-
CATED. WE EXPECT AN ARMI-
STICE TO BE SIGNED ENDING
THE WAR. PERHAPS AS EARLY AS
TOMORROW THE 11TH. PRAY THE
BOYS STAY OUT OF HARM'S WAY.
PRAISE THE LORD. GOD SAVE THE
KING.

WILLIAM

Libby expected to see Michael and his squadron safely back by ten in the morning. It was two in the afternoon. She had requested a transfer from Paris to be closer to him at the hospital in Nancy. But she stayed on at the airfield's dressing station and waited, calming her nerves by feeding and cleaning the few patients they had, most of whom suffered from nothing more serious than mild forms of dysentery. An aide found her there.

"We just got word!" he told her. "Of

course we know they had to set down somewhere. They would have been out of fuel hours ago. They landed at an RAF aerodrome well north of here. They had a run-in with a *Jasta,* a German squadron, but don't worry, there weren't any casualties."

"Oh, thank goodness." Libby felt exhaustion and relief at the same time and wanted to sit down. "Are they coming back?"

She had scarcely asked when they both heard the drone at the same time. Running outside they saw aircraft approaching from the north and east. Libby began to count them as they came in to land.

"Missing three," said an officer on one side of her.

The aide frowned. "There weren't any missing when they left the RAF aerodrome, sir."

"No. Something happened between here and there."

Libby looked at him.

"Not necessarily a dogfight, Miss Danforth," he went on quickly. "Engine failure. Controls damaged by the action this morning. Could be any of a hundred things. They've probably put down somewhere else."

Libby fought a coldness that moved through her stomach and chest into her head. "Three of them?"

Not now, Lord. Not when I'm getting to know Michael. When we're becoming friends . . . and more. Not today.

But she knew before she was told that Michael was not with the squadron. She could sense that he had not landed.

"They didn't crash," the squadron leader told her. "We went through a lot of dirty, thick wet clouds and they disappeared. If they got disoriented they'll just put down somewhere else. Don't worry, Miss Danforth. Mike flew well this morning in the dogfight. And he was flying straight as an arrow the last I saw him. He'll be fine."

"Were there — any enemy aircraft nearby?"

The squadron leader looked at her for a moment. Then he made up his mind. "A ways off. But they were there."

"Who?"

"Do you know the German squadrons? Zeltner's *Jasta*? Black and yellow. But don't fret. Word is there will be peace in a few days. The Kaiser has abdicated. Germany's in an uproar. Zeltner's pilots want to get home in one piece too. I doubt they'll start a fight."

"You had a fight this morning."

He nodded. "Yeah. We did. This morning."

She stood watching the sky with him and the others in the squadron a few minutes more, but no other planes appeared. Eventually the pilots went to get something to eat and the squadron leader headed off to file his report. Libby walked back to the dressing station. She had promised several men she would clean their hair, cut their nails, and shave their beards.

As she began with a young American from Seattle, her mind argued it didn't matter whether Michael Woodhaven was alive or dead, they were just friends, and she was going back to England when the war was over no matter what happened to him. But her heart used different words and a different language — they had gone past friendship and were touching on something else, something greater, and it *did* matter to her whether he was alive or dead. But she'd no sooner feel this in her blood than her mind would speak up again and convince her that any romantic ideas she had were a flight of fancy — Ashton Park and Britain were her future, not Michael Woodhaven and America. Dead? She might shed a few tears. Alive? She'd give him a quick hug and a pat on the back and finish shaving her American fliers. Michael Woodhaven could never be a big part of her life.

"There! That's them! I swear it's Mike and Quincy and Wyatt!"

The shout made her drop her razor and spin around. She could see men running onto the field. At the same time she heard a growl of plane engines. She knocked over the basin of hot water she was using, fell over a chair, and bolted out of the hut, leaving the young pilot with one side of his face clean-shaven and the other sporting a five-day beard and white lather.

One. Two. Three. They dropped lower and lower until the first one touched down. Men were still running, heading toward the first Sopwith Camel as it rolled over the grass. She told herself to stay put and wait until all of them were down and they'd come to a stop. Spinning props were dangerous. What did it matter if she saw him on the landing strip or here at the dressing station or over in the mess hall? What difference did five or ten minutes make?

Then she saw his plane. She recognized the letters on its side. She saw its wheels throw up dust and stone as it touched. His goggles were up — and it was his face and eyes. She began to run as hard as she had run in her life.

261

Her nurse's cap spun from her head as she flew past pilots and ground crew toward his plane. The closer she got the more detail she saw — holes in his plane's fuselage, tears in the fabric of the wings, long streaks of black oil smearing the engine cowling.

"Michael! Michael!"

He had cut the engine but the Sopwith Camel had not rolled to a stop before he saw her and heard her as she raced toward him, her uniform white against the brown uniforms of the men that ran beside her, white against the green of the airfield, against the gray and blue of the November sky. He vaulted from the cockpit and she threw herself into him, her hands grabbing hold of his leather jacket, her lips covering his, tears making tracks through the grime and dust on both their faces.

Land of Hope and Glory, Mother of the
  Free,
How shall we extol thee, who are born of
  thee?
Wider still and wider shall thy bounds be
  set;
God, who made thee mighty, make thee
  mightier yet.

God, who made thee mighty, make thee mightier yet.

The choir finished singing and sat down in their loft behind Reverend Jeremiah Sweet. He stood in his collar and robes and faced the congregation, eyes soft and dark behind his round glasses.

"This is a service of thanksgiving," he began in his mild yet firm voice. "Thanksgiving that the war is over and that we remain a free people. I welcome you, in particular our many guests, including my wife's family who have traveled up to Ribchester by motorcar. I'm grateful you have joined us today."

Sir William acknowledged the welcome with a slight bow of his head. Lady Elizabeth, Sir William, and Victoria sat in a pew with Emma and the two boys. Aunt Holly, Lady Grace, and Sir Arthur were down the pew on the other side of Emma. Peter and James sat in small suits in their mother's lap, each just shy of turning a year old.

"I confess I have conflicting emotions this first Lord's Day after the Armistice. On the one hand, I am thankful to God that the fighting is over and that our armies have not been defeated. On the other hand, I know only too well from my service in the trenches what a price Britain and her allies have paid in securing our victory and our freedom. Indeed, all of Europe has paid a terrible price. There are many who will never sit in their church pew again in Oxford or York or Blackburn. Many more will never walk again. Or see with their eyes. Some will never speak. Some will never hear.

"Still others will not sleep again, not as they slept in 1913 before the artillery and machine guns and the bombs from the sky and the poison gas. Before they saw their friends dead beside them. Before they saw children lying motionless in their shattered homes. Before they themselves took another man's life. Now their pillow will seem thin to them and their bed hard. Now they will wake with a shout in the night thinking they have heard shellfire or the rush of approaching troops who come with rifles loaded and bayonets fixed. Now they will close their eyes and see the slain, and they will open them again and find no rest. The price war has exacted for our liberty and well-being in these islands has been dreadful beyond all that we feared when our sons and brothers and fathers and husbands marched along Piccadilly in 1914."

Jeremiah paused to turn the pages of the

large Bible in front of him with his good hand. "I am reading from the Gospel of St. Matthew, chapter 25, verses thirty-four to forty-six:

Then shall the King say unto them on his right hand, Come, ye blessed of my Father, inherit the kingdom prepared for you from the foundation of the world: For I was an hungred, and ye gave me meat: I was thirsty, and ye gave me drink: I was a stranger, and ye took me in: Naked, and ye clothed me: I was sick, and ye visited me: I was in prison, and ye came unto me.

Then shall the righteous answer him, saying, Lord, when saw we thee an hungred, and fed thee? Or thirsty, and gave thee drink? When saw we thee a stranger, and took thee in? or naked, and clothed thee? Or when saw we thee sick, or in prison, and came unto thee?

And the King shall answer and say unto them, Verily I say unto you, Inasmuch as ye have done it unto one of the least of these my brethren, ye have done it unto me.

Then shall he say also unto them on the

left hand, Depart from me, ye cursed, into everlasting fire, prepared for the devil and his angels: For I was an hungred, and ye gave me no meat: I was thirsty, and ye gave me no drink: I was a stranger, and ye took me not in: naked, and ye clothed me not: sick, and in prison, and ye visited me not.

Then shall they also answer him, saying, Lord, when saw we thee an hungred, or athirst, or a stranger, or naked, or sick, or in prison, and did not minister unto thee?

Then shall he answer them, saying, Verily I say unto you, Inasmuch as ye did it not to one of the least of these, ye did it not to me. And these shall go away into everlasting punishment: but the righteous into life eternal."

Jeremiah looked back up and his face was pale, almost deathly, so that his wife Emma shrank back into the pew, holding her sons more closely, startled at the change that had come over him. It looked as if he had been struck a blow by the words he had just read out loud to them all.

"Do you know what I fear? That the sacrifice will have all been in vain. That we shall go back to our daily lives and return to gossip, to slander and cheating and thievery. Even worse, that we shall once again hate and hurt and let our petty grievances and bigotries and prejudices rule the day. We told ourselves we were fighting for a better world, but if we make it the old world again, what have our fathers and sons died for? Why have we buried them in shallow graves from Flanders to Verdun? If it was just to make the world a crueler place, well, we didn't need to fight a war to do that. We had hoped the blood and the suffering and the bravery might lead to something more. Something extraordinary."

He ran his wooden hand over the pages of the Bible. "Care for the sick. Feed the hungry. Clothe the naked. Bring hope to those in prison. Can we do that? Are we able to extend that kind of mercy? Do we have that kind of heart? Can we treat the less fortunate as if they were Christ himself? That in their faces are set His eyes, that when we take their hands we touch the hands of God? I pray to the Lord we have that better world, and that we fight for it as valiantly now as we have just fought in the skies and in the fields and on the high seas. Let us come before our Savior."

Victoria was astonished to see her father

drop to his knees as Jeremiah prayed a final prayer. He knelt on the bare floor, hands clasped, head bowed. Even during the singing of the last hymn, as all rose, he remained where he was. Lady Elizabeth, who still only spoke to him when absolutely necessary and as briefly as possible, leaned down and placed a hand on his shoulder.

With the service over and people talking and moving and shaking hands, Sir William got to his feet. The first thing he did was take a startled Lady Elizabeth into his arms — they had scarcely touched in three months.

"I do not wish to embarrass you," he said in a voice rough with emotion, "but I see what a fool I have been. I have let the past determine my future instead of freeing myself from centuries of bitterness and forging a new destiny for the Danforth name. I pray to God it is not too late."

He hurried through the bodies around him and down the aisle to where Harrison and Todd Turpin sat.

"Have either of you heard from Mrs. Longstaff?" he asked abruptly.

"No, sir," responded Harrison.

"I have not, Sir William." Todd stood up. "None of the household has as far as I know."

268

"But if she were still in London, where is it she is likely to be?"

Harrison held his brown fedora in his hands. "She has kin down by the docks."

"Might she be there?"

"If she's still in London."

"Where else would she go?" Sir William tapped his top hat against the side of his leg. "I expect they have any number of eating establishments in that area for sailors and dockworkers?"

"So they do, Sir William, but no fit places for a lady."

Sir William set his hat down next to Harrison and pulled on his gloves, the lines around his mouth and under his eyes sharp. "I did not leave her much choice, did I, God forgive me. We must make haste. You will drive us to the nearest station and we will catch the first train south."

"What about the motorcar?" asked Harrison.

"We shall leave it parked at the station. Return for it once our task is completed."

"What of the rest of the family?"

"They can remain at the vicarage or join us as far as Liverpool. We three must carry on for London, where we shall stay until we have found dear Mrs. Longstaff and rescued her from my sin and my folly."

Harrison and Todd Turpin glanced at each other.

"If ye don't mind my saying so, sir," Todd spoke up, turning his flat tweed cap around in his hands, "London's waterfront is not a place for the likes of ye, a gentleman and a Member of Parliament and all. Let Harrison and me take care of matters."

Sir William shook his head. "I appreciate the gesture, Todd Turpin, but that's out of the question. I put Mrs. Longstaff there and I shall bring her out. Even if I must disguise myself as the scoundrel Bill Sykes in *Oliver Twist* or as a drunken sailor off a garbage scow." He glanced along the church's aisle and spotted his wife and Victoria approaching. "Gather them up, Harrison. Gather them up and let's be off."

Kipp sat with his arms folded and eyes closed outside Ben Whitecross's hospital room. Next to him Christelle was teaching Libby medical terms in French, smiling and speaking words and phrases that Libby repeated over and over again. Michael Woodhaven stepped quietly out of the room. Kipp opened his eyes.

"Still sleeping," said Michael softly.

"How's his breathing?" asked Libby.

"It's good. Better than yesterday when

they brought him down to Paris from Amiens."

Libby got up. "I should take a look. Thank you, Michael."

"My pleasure, Miss Danforth."

Libby laughed. "Stop that. I'm Libby to you. How long do I have to put up with this?"

"I have a two-week leave. The war's over. Uncle Sam doesn't need me anymore."

Kipp closed his eyes again. "They want my help in turning our aerodrome over to the French. But I've still got another week in Paris. Looks like you're stuck with me and the Yank."

Libby smiled. "I suppose I can bear up. But can you, Christelle?"

Christelle was smoothing back Kipp's hair as he tried to doze. She laughed. "I will do my best."

Two officers marched down the hallway toward them and stopped.

"You are Major Kipp Danforth?" asked the tallest one, who sported a trim black mustache. "Son of Sir William Danforth MP of Ashton Park in Lancashire?"

Kipp rose quickly to his feet and saluted. "I am, sir."

"Colonel Byrd, RAF, and this is my adjutant, Leftenant Arbuckle."

271

Arbuckle saluted. "Major."

Kipp returned the salute. "What's this about?"

"Stand easy, Major. It's about a chap in your squadron. I've spoken with every one of your men and not a few German pilots and now I'd like to hear from the squadron leader. Congratulations on your promotion, by the way. I understand it's only a day or two old."

"Thank you, sir. I'm not quite used to being addressed by that rank yet."

"It grows on you, Danforth. Now about this fellow —" He consulted a clipboard. "Leftenant Benjamin Whitecross. Though I suppose that's no longer technically correct. His promotion is approved even if nothing else is settled. Were you flying with Captain Whitecross on the morning of October twenty-fifth?"

"I was."

"How would you describe what occurred at that time? When you were jumped by Wolfgang Zeltner's *Jasta* near Cambrai?"

"We were in a bad way, Colonel. Their whole group came out of the clouds and were upon us in seconds. Our squadron lost two aircraft almost immediately."

"What of Whitecross's actions?"

"He was just catching up with us, sir. He'd

been delayed at the aerodrome due to problems with his plane's machine guns. When he reached us and saw what was going on he launched himself at the German aircraft."

"What sort of aircraft?"

"Fokker D.VIIs."

Colonel Byrd glanced at his clipboard. "The formidable D.VII. What was their paint scheme?"

"Black and yellow."

"Did you spot Zeltner?"

"Briefly, sir."

"Did he engage?"

"Yes, sir. In his Fokker triplane."

The colonel grunted. "Eccentric Prussian baron. Flying an outdated plane the Germans pulled off frontline duty last summer." He wrote with a pencil on a sheet of paper attached to the clipboard. "What happened exactly when Captain Whitecross intervened?"

"He shot down the plane that was in the process of shooting me down. Then he bagged another just ahead of me. After that he bounced a group of two or three that were firing on other planes in our squadron."

"You're quite sure about the sequence?"

"Yes, sir."

Byrd continued to scribble, not looking up. "It was definitely Whitecross?"

"It was his letter B on the fuselage. No one else has that."

"So four planes? Four kills?"

"There was at least one more. Maybe a sixth as well."

Byrd glanced up. "Well, which is it, Major? Five or six?"

Kipp thought a moment, jingling loose francs in his pocket. "Five."

Byrd licked the lead tip of his pencil. "You were the one who landed and picked him up after his crash?"

"Yes, sir."

"What condition was he in?"

"Bad, Colonel. That's why he's been in the hospital so many weeks. There were bullets in his arms and legs. His cheek had been laid open. Left elbow shot off."

"Any alcohol on his breath?"

"Alcohol? No, sir."

Libby saw the anger rising in her brother, the same anger that often smoldered in her, and she jumped to her feet. "Excuse me, Colonel, it might help us all if we knew why you were asking all these questions? It's rather like an interrogation."

The colonel looked at her and looked at Kipp. "Brother and sister, perhaps?"

"Yes, sir."

"Hmm." Byrd handed the clipboard to his adjutant. "I'm sure I've come across a bit rough. You must admit it appears on the surface to be an act of sheer madness. One man taking on a whole *Jasta* by himself and downing five or six enemy planes. I had to ask about the drinking."

Kipp's face was dark. "Why? The man's barely alive. He saved my life. He saved my squadron. What do all your questions matter? I made my report weeks ago."

The colonel held Kipp's fierce gaze with a sharp one of his own. "They matter because he's been recommended for the Victoria Cross, Major. And only a few get that. Only the very best. Living or dead."

Mrs. Longstaff pushed loose red hairs back from her eyes and ladled stew onto four more plates. "Here's another lot!"

A waiter as thick as a barrel entered the kitchen with a scowl and grabbed the plates from her. "About time. I could've cooked a fresh batch myself by now."

"Good food takes time, Solly."

"This bunch don't know the difference. You're not with the high and mighty anymore. Any slop'll do."

"Not from my kitchen."

275

A tall dark man with a crooked back and a fierce set to his eyes charged into the room and smacked her on the side of her head with his fist. "Not from your kitchen, you say? When did it become your kitchen, hey?"

Mrs. Longstaff covered her face with her hand. "I'm sorry, Mr. Thresher. I just like to cook a decent meal, that's all."

"You take too long. You're six orders behind. Sailors won't pay for what they don't get. I've a mind to throw you back on the street."

"Don't do that, Mr. Thresher. I'm only trying to serve good solid fare."

"You'll not talk back to me! Who do you think you are, hey? Every day I've had to beat you to keep you in line and today's no different, is it?"

Thresher raised his walking stick to strike her another blow. A large hand seized the stick from behind.

"That will do!" snapped a man much taller than Thresher. He was wrapped in a thick scarf that covered half his face and a tattered pea coat was buttoned up to his chin. Thresher fought to get his stick back but the man ripped it from his grasp and flung him to the floor.

"What do you want?" snarled Thresher. "This is my business establishment. How I run it is none of your concern."

"The woman is my employee. I've come to fetch her back. Come, Mrs. Longstaff. Let's be gone."

She was cowering against the wall, ladle in her hand. "I don't know you."

The man yanked his scarf down.

"Sir William!" she gasped. "This is no place for you. They'll skin you alive."

"Aye, we'll do that and more!" Thresher scrambled to his feet. "Solly! Harper! To the kitchen! Lively now! We have a thief!"

Thresher waited until two hefty men appeared in the kitchen doorway before he lunged at Sir William, pinning him to the wall. Sir William struck him on the head and back with the stick. Thresher sank to the floor again, groaning. Solly and Harper rushed Sir William, Harper pulling out a knife half as long as his arm.

"Now we'll cut you!" Harper spat.

There was a gunshot. Then another. The sharp smell of burnt powder filled the kitchen. Harper and Solly sprang behind a table of pots and pans. Todd Turpin and Harrison had stepped into the kitchen. Harrison had a pistol. He pointed it at Solly.

"There are seven shots with one of these," Harrison said. "Eight if I've put one up the spout like I was taught. More than enough for you lot."

"Don't shoot!" hollered Solly.

Sailors and dockworkers fled into the narrow street, where rain was driving against the walls and windows. As chairs and tables were pushed over and men shouted, Harrison gestured at Harper with the pistol. The other man finally got the hint and threw his knife away. It skittered across the floor.

Sir William narrowed his eyes. "I thought we agreed no guns."

Harrison shrugged, not lowering his weapon.

"Where did you come by it?" demanded Sir William.

"Saw it in a pawnshop window. A Yank had traded it in for English pounds. They call it a Colt 1911."

"Never mind what the Yanks call it. Just keep it on these scoundrels."

Sir William already had one arm around Mrs. Longstaff, who had buried her face in his shoulder.

"I'm sorry, sir," she got out. "You shouldn't have come here looking for me."

"It was two days well spent, Mrs. Longstaff, and I'm the one who's sorry. I ought never have turned you out. Never have cut you adrift. I promise to make such amends as I can. I want you back at Ashton Park. We all do."

"Oh, no, sir, I can't. I don't want to offend you —"

"Take my wife to a thousand Baptist meetings and I shan't mind. So long as you agree to come to St. Mark's on Christmas Eve for a good old Church of England candlelight song service."

She laughed a bit, tears on her face. "Why, I do love those, Sir William. I haven't been invited to one for a good number of years."

"That's settled then."

"We'd best leave before the constabulary show up," warned Harrison. He waved the pistol at Solly and Harper and Thresher. "No trouble from you three. Not a word to the police. I'll be nearby."

"We hate the police more than we hate you," growled Solly. "Clear out of here."

The four bustled out of the kitchen, Todd Turpin and Harrison leading the way, Sir William half-dragging Mrs. Longstaff, who was still holding tightly to her ladle.

"Who did you think I was?" asked Sir William as they ran.

"Jack the Ripper," she told him.

He barked a laugh as they hurried past the sailors in the street. "I rather thought I looked like Todd's great-great-grandfather,

Dick Turpin the highwayman. It was not just a question of rescuing you, you understand. It was a matter of rescuing myself."

"Why . . . how's that, sir?"

"The food has been difficult to bear at Ashton Park. It has been a Darwinian survival of the fittest."

She cried and laughed, her face turned toward his arm, as they went up one alley and down another. "I don't know the Darwin chap but I catch your drift. Sally was always a great one for salt if nothing else came to mind for seasoning. It's the seasoning that makes the difference, you see." She looked up at his face. "It's been bad, sir, dreadfully bad. My kin turned me out when I wouldn't thieve for them and Mr. Thresher and his crew beat the heart out of me —"

Sir William wiped at her eyes with fingers that protruded out of frayed gloves. "Never you fear, Mrs. Longstaff. You'll not want for anything again. So long as I am master of Ashton Park you will always be one of us."

13
1919

Summer 1919

Ashton Park was in a stir. A delightful stir, but a stir nonetheless.

Now sufficiently recovered from his injuries, Captain Ben Whitecross was to receive the Victoria Cross from the hands of King George himself.

Harrison stood by the shining black motorcar in his new chauffeur's uniform and cap, hands folded in front of him. Swallows swooped over the manor, and blue sky pushed gray and white clouds to the corners of the estate. Sir William and Lady Elizabeth rushed out the front doors, both of them fussing with his cufflinks as they came down the steps.

"Good morning, Harrison," said Sir William without looking up. "Are Aunt Holly and Sir Arthur in the car?"

"Yes, sir. Lady Grace as well."

"What? Mother traveling again? After so

many years?"

"Apparently, sir."

"Well, well. Will we be able to make Lime Street Station in time for the London train?"

"You will, sir. Though I should like to leave in the next five minutes if we could."

"Of course." Sir William looked from his cufflinks to his wife. "Where is Victoria?"

Lady Elizabeth continued to play with his sleeve. "She keeps changing her dress, William. You know how it is."

"No, I don't."

She sighed. "You have lived among four daughters and a wife long enough. That's how these things are. Especially on such an important day. We are going to Buckingham Palace!"

"I know that —"

Lady Elizabeth put her fingers to his lips. "Hush. What I think you have forgotten is that we have given our consent to the marriage between Victoria and Ben. She has not seen him since 1916. When he left he was our groom and driver. Now he is a captain in the RAF and about to be awarded the Victoria Cross for conspicuous gallantry. Now he is about to be her husband. Do you understand? She will want to outshine the queen if possible. For him."

Sir William paused in his battle with the

cufflink. "All right. I do understand that."

She kissed him on the cheek. "Good. And here is our little princess now. Don't you think it was worth the wait? She is resplendent."

Sir William glanced at the manor. He had expected to see his daughter in green, one of her favorite colors. But she stood on the steps wearing a scarlet gown that lit up the auburn shades in her hair. Everything about her danced as the rays of the sun found their way through the clear sky and the gown burst into flame.

"I say." An astonished Harrison fumbled open a car door. "You look like a bride on her wedding day, Miss Victoria."

Victoria kissed her father and mother and then turned her full smile on Harrison. "Why, thank you. But white for the bride, Mister Harrison."

He doffed his black chauffeur's cap as she approached. "Indeed."

"And you look smashing in that new uniform."

Aunt Holly rolled down the motorcar window and popped her head out. "I've told him that. He's strikingly handsome. Now you've heard it from both Miss Victoria and me."

Harrison smiled. "I'm grateful to you both."

As Victoria stepped into the car she teased, "Though I do miss the fedora and jacket."

"They're hanging on a peg in the Castle. When I'm not driving the motorcar I'll be in my old things and looking after the grass and trees and ponds as usual."

She paused and looked at him. "I'm glad to hear it. Thank you for everything, Harrison. Everything."

He gave a slight nod of his head. "My pleasure, my lady."

Reporters and photographers swarmed around Ben Whitecross outside Buckingham Palace. The medal, with its distinctive burgundy ribbon, was pinned over his heart. Leaning on a cane with his left hand he shook hands with his right.

"Good show, Captain."

"Well done, sir."

"Congratulations, Captain Whitecross. All the best."

Ben smiled and kept shaking hands all around. "Thank you, gentlemen, thank you." He looked up and caught a glimpse of a slim figure standing alone at the edge of the crowd. The sun slipped out from behind a cloud, blazed over the scene, then slid behind another cloud. In those few moments it ignited Victoria's crimson dress, her auburn hair, and her smile. Ben Whitecross felt as if the ground was giving way under his feet.

"Gentlemen. Gentlemen. Excuse me. You must excuse me."

Ben began to lurch through the reporters. He became so frustrated with the cane that he threw it aside and half-ran to Victoria, seizing her hands and gazing into her face before embracing her. He broke away and faced the people who thronged around them, holding Victoria's hand.

"My fiancée. Miss Victoria Danforth."

Scores of hands clapped.

"Well done!" someone called. "When do you expect the wedding to take place?"

Victoria put her arms around Ben and smiled, holding him close. "As soon as I can pry him away from his well-wishers. Once that's done, it's the first church I spot after we leave Buckingham Palace. We've waited long enough."

Standing at the edge of the group, Sir William turned to Libby, who had come from France with Kipp for the big occasion. "All the attention has been on the young war hero and your sister. But you have been absent from our lives far longer than Ben

Whitecross — and you, my daughter, have been sorely missed."

Libby patted her father's back. "Papa, I don't mind. I enjoy seeing her so happy. And you and mother beaming."

"You must know that seeing you and Kipp brings us as much happiness as seeing Victoria and Ben together?"

"Of course I do."

Sir William stood back, holding her hand. "Look at you. You must be a head taller than when you left us. And your complexion reminds me of cream in tea."

She laughed. "Despite the war I have been very well, Papa. French cuisine suits me better than boiled beef and mushy peas."

"It must. You look splendid. I shall go and find your mother and bring the two of you together. Will you be returning to Ashton Park with us?"

"Yes, Father. Though Kipp must return to France for a time."

"Return to France? The war's been over for months."

"He can explain it himself when you both have a quiet moment. It's all about turning aerodromes over to the French and whatnot. He's a major now and there's a fair bit of liaison work."

"All right then. I'll speak with him and

we'll get that sorted out. His mother will want to know. She can't be far. Wait here."

Libby put a hand on her father's arm as he turned to go. "Papa. I wonder if I might ask you a favor."

"A favor? You don't even need to ask."

"I've met someone, Father."

Sir William's eyebrows arched. "What? A Frenchman?"

"Oh, Papa." She laughed and shook her head. "No. Though there wouldn't be any problem if he were, would there?"

"Not at all. They're our allies and all that —"

"As it happens this gentleman is one of our allies too. He's an American."

"American?" Sir William's eyebrows remained in their raised position. "Who is he?"

"He is a Woodhaven. So that should please you, at least."

"Woodhaven? The New York family?"

"Yes, Papa."

Sir William's eyebrows returned to their rightful position above his eyes as his smile opened up. "Well, well. Isn't that something? How is he related? Nephew? First cousin? I'm curious."

"He's their son."

"What? Son? Why, that family is good

friends with the king and queen. And the Prince of Wales." Sir William studied her, putting his hands in his pockets. "They have two sons."

"Mark was killed in the war. This is Michael. The eldest."

"Ah. I'm sorry to hear about Mark. We must extend our condolences. But what of Michael? What can we do for him? What is it you wish to ask of me?"

"Father, I should like to invite him up to Ashton Park for Ben and Victoria's wedding. To meet everyone. If I may."

A smile slowly returned to Sir William's features. "So you are not asking that Jeremiah perform a double wedding ceremony then?"

Libby looked down. "Oh, no, Papa. Nothing like that. But I do very much want him to meet the family."

"And so he shall. We'd never turn away one of our American allies."

He kissed her on the forehead as she put her arms around his neck. "Thank you, Papa."

"You have been gone such a very long time. We have missed you terribly. I know you've prided yourself on being something of a lone wolf. You always lived a bit of your life apart from the rest of the family. But, my girl, you are one of us regardless of where you roam. Your mother and I cherish Libby Danforth."

A plane circled the aerodrome in Amiens, taking its time, a photographer leaning out of his seat as the pilot concentrated on keeping the aircraft steady and level. The sun was bright in the west even though it was beginning its slow fall to earth. Christelle lifted Kipp's hand to her lips.

"When will you take me up?" she asked.

"As soon as he lands. The photographer won't have enough light in a few minutes. By the time we go up the sun will be red and gold. How does that suit you?"

"I like the idea of that."

"Nothing fancy, though. No loops or dives or barrel rolls. I want you in one piece for my sister's wedding."

She lifted her head and he watched the sun fill her eyes. "You have made up your mind? You are taking me to England?'

"You're willing to go, aren't you? Your parents have not objected."

"*Mère et père* — my mother and father would not object to anything you asked."

"Not even your hand?"

"Oh? Are you going to do that?"

He kissed the top of her head. "I will

surprise you."

"And your father and mother?"

"That's why you must come to Ashton Park. Once they meet you they will be charmed."

"I am not French nobility."

"Neither is Ben Whitecross."

She made a face. "Oh, Ben, a war hero, a captain, an aviator, he wears France's Croix de Guerre and Britain's Victoria Cross. What am I?"

"A beauty."

"So a beauty who serves coffee. Nothing more. They will not be impressed."

"A beauty with a heart as big as the sky. They will see it. But there is also one other thing that will come to their attention — I am going to teach you how to fly."

"You won't."

"I will."

She laughed silently at his enthusiasm. The sun put color on her skin and glistened on her lips. He gazed at the effect of the evening light and shook his head.

"It's impossible," he murmured, "not to wish to kiss you no matter where we are or what's going on. I'm helpless."

He put a hand under her head and placed his mouth over hers, taking his time, rushing nothing. She had just had a cup of coffee with sugar and tasted like it. They could both hear the plane landing but did not look up. Finally she pulled away with a mischievous smile like a girl.

"Take me up. Finish the kiss there."

The panorama of a world gleaming with light and green fields overwhelmed Christelle as they flew west. Several times Kipp called from the cockpit behind her but she did not respond. She only whispered, *"Mon Dieu, merci. Merci, mon Dieu."* Crimson melted into emerald and emerald into amber and amber into long stripes of purple cloud. Swarms of blackbirds swept by beneath them.

The harness was tight and would not let her move, so she undid it. Kipp saw what she was doing and yelled at her to stop but she held onto a strap with one hand and leaned out of her seat toward him. He slowed the plane down and shook his head. She smiled and mouthed the words, *"Je t'aime."* Then she waited for him to come to her. Her hair unwound from the collar of her flying jacket and streamed toward him like silver rain.

He released his harness and came out of the cockpit, stretching forward, one hand on the plane's controls, the other drawing her head closer until the kiss was strong, much stronger than the kiss on the ground had been. The aircraft fluttered from side to side and the air rushed over them as the world slipped past under their wings.

"Well, sir?" asked Mrs. Longstaff anxiously. "What did you think?"

Sir William was vigorously shaking hands with people spilling out of the small brick church. "What's that, my dear?"

"How did you find the service and the preachin'?"

"Why, capital, capital." He smiled at an older man. "Good morning, sir." Glancing at Mrs. Longstaff and Lady Elizabeth, he laughed. "You two have been keeping a great secret from me — how wonderful the singing is here, how robust, and how faithful to the Word of God the good parson is. Who would have thought it? A Baptist church?" He began to hum the tune of one of the hymns. "Ah, good morning, sir, a splendid time of worship, I praise God."

"So we may see you here again, Sir William?" asked Mrs. Longstaff.

"Hmm? See me here again? I should think so. That is, if they will have an old dowdy Anglican in their midst."

"What a thing to say." Mrs. Longstaff

beamed. "Why, the people love you. You sang louder than anyone else."

"Did I? Well, there was plenty to sing about, I thank God."

Lady Elizabeth held back a giggle. "Look at you carrying on as if it were election day. I never see you shaking hands like this at St. Mark's."

"Ha. The congregation there would think I was mad." He looked around him. "This is just what I need to shake the dust off my spirit. I would be grateful if we could come again in a fortnight. What do you say to that, Mrs. Longstaff, eh?"

"I would say amen, sir."

"Would you?" He shook another person's hand. "Let us set it in stone then. Two weeks time and we're back. Back and ready to worship the Lord in spirit and in truth." He turned to Mrs. Longstaff and pointed. "Mind you, I don't forget your own promise."

"What's that, sir?"

"Christmas Eve. The midnight service of candles and carols. At St. Mark's."

"Oh, I'll be there, sir, I dearly love a good choir at Christmas."

"Well, that's settled then. We all know where we'll be on December 24th, excellent." He raised his arm. "There's the

293

parson. Hullo! Do come this way, sir, I'd like a word with you, if I may, praise be to God."

Mrs. Longstaff laughed. "What's gotten into you, sir?"

Sir William shook the parson's hand. "God, Mrs. Longstaff, God and the Holy Ghost. Ah, reverend, how pleased I am you chose the text you did for your sermon. I was greatly blessed, greatly blessed, I thank the Lord."

Libby had put on pants and climbed a tree.

Stars showered the leaves. She hugged her knees to her chest as she sat in a fork in the tall ash and had a clear view of the lights of the manor. Ashton Park. It had finally been wired for electricity. Paris had its beauty, even in a time of war, but nothing compared to the sweet green of the Danforth estate, and at night it looked like a magic lantern show. Harrison had mowed that afternoon and the scent of grass sliced open stung her nose. She breathed in deep lungfuls of it.

I want you to love it, Michael. I don't know what you have in America. You probably have a great deal. But here we have oaks a thousand years old. Here we have a castle that withstood Viking raiders. Here we have fields that saw knights clash with sword and shield

294

during the Wars of the Roses.

A couple passed under the tree, holding hands and talking softly. The man walked with a slight limp but still kept up with his companion's pace. She saw it was Victoria and Ben. They made their way to the stables. Libby turned her head to the side and rested it on her knees. Their voices carried in the calm summer air.

"We still have the horses. Papa wouldn't dream of selling them off. We'll use a coach at our wedding." Victoria's voice.

"Would you let me drive the team?" Ben's voice.

"Well, no, darling — you're supposed to be inside the coach with me."

"Couldn't we both sit up front?"

Libby heard Victoria's laugh clearly. "I suppose we could. It's not very regal, though."

"I expect it will be quite a show. Is there anyone who isn't attending from your family?"

"Robbie's signed on for another five years with the army but they've granted him leave to join us. I haven't seen Catherine in ages, but she'll be arriving in a few days. Edward's been at the family's hunting lodge in Scotland since the end of the war — more than six months. He'll be coming down. Only

Catherine's husband won't be here. I gather he's much too busy with the shipyards. I don't expect he'll be greatly missed."

"Not by me, at any rate. My gaze will be fixed elsewhere."

"Oh? You sound like a pilot."

"I am a pilot. And I've made a perfect three-point landing."

Victoria laughed again. Libby could tell she had covered her mouth. "Shh. We're at our old stables. Enough talk."

14

Edward looked out the window at the rain slashing through the ash trees. Gray clouds were racing in off the Irish Sea and covering the estate. He imagined himself standing under one of the trees and Charlotte Squire running out to him again with a cloak to cover his shoulders. He remembered the kiss in the groundskeeper's hut. He saw the beauty of her eyes and hair as she pulled back her hood.

"Edward, my boy. How are you feeling this morning?"

His father clapped a hand to his shoulder from behind.

Edward did not turn. "Right as rain," he said.

"Libby's friend has just arrived from France. Michael Woodhaven IV. Of the Woodhaven family of New York. I'd like you to meet him."

"What's he doing here?"

"Why, your sister invited him to the wedding. She was his nurse when he was shot down over the front. The family has written to express their gratitude for the care she provided. Come and say hello, please. You'll find you like him."

Michael was standing with Libby and Lady Elizabeth in the Great Hall and admiring the large oil paintings of battles during the Wars of the Roses. Sir William introduced Edward and Michael smiled and extended his hand. Edward kept both of his behind his back. Michael dropped his hand but his smile grew wider.

"Nice to meet you, Edward. They tell me you served in the navy during the war."

Edward nodded. "The Royal Navy. Yes."

"And you saw action in the Battle of Jutland? That's great."

"Actually, it wasn't great, Yank. The Germans outgunned us and outmaneuvered us. We lost four times the ships and four times the men."

Michael hesitated. "Still. They didn't knock you out of the war."

"No. We can thank God you boys finally showed up and prevented that. Where would we be today if Uncle Sam hadn't decided to declare war on Germany?"

Michael put his hands in his pockets. "I'm

sorry you feel that way. America never won the war alone. We were allies. We beat Germany and Austria together."

"How splendid of you to say so."

"Edward —" Libby began, a frown growing on her face.

Sir William interrupted. "Edward, might I have a word with you in private?" He put a hand on his son's back and propelled him down the hall to his private study. Once the door was shut, he turned on his son.

"What do you mean by behaving in such a disgraceful fashion? The man is a guest in our house and the scion of a highly esteemed family."

Edward matched his father's glare with one of his own. "When I'm head of the estate, people like Michael Woodhaven will never be guests at Ashton Park again."

"When you're head of the estate? Is that something you expect to happen shortly? The keys of the kingdom aren't handed over to rude and rebellious sons."

"Perhaps you wouldn't have a rude and rebellious son if you hadn't sent the woman he loved into exile while you locked him up in a dungeon on some godforsaken Scottish moor."

Sir William paused and the anger left his face. "I'm very sorry you look at it that way.

299

Your mother and I were only trying to do what was best for you."

"Best for me? You were doing what you thought was best for yourselves and the Danforth name. Heaven forbid I should marry a woman from a poor family no matter what excellent attributes she might possess. Why, her English and her manner of speech are better than mine."

"She was not a suitable wife for you."

Edward sneered. "There's many a woman from a wealthy estate you've introduced me to who didn't begin to approach the breeding and refinement of Charlotte Squire. What do you think your precious Lord Jesus Christ would say? Was he a respecter of persons? Did he teach that the rich were righteous and the poor were evil?"

Sir William labored for words to respond. "It's . . . not a question of . . . of that. You have been placed in a certain position in this world — God has put you there — and we must live within the boundaries He has set."

"He has set? Or we have set?"

"Regardless of how you feel about it, there's no need to take it out on our guest. You do not just humiliate your mother and me by your behavior. You humiliate your sister, someone I know you care for."

Edward folded his arms over his chest. "Is she set on marrying him then?"

"There's been no talk of marriage."

"Why not? It's just the sort of thing you and Mum like. Emma marries Jeremiah and connects the family to the Church of England. Victoria marries Ben and connects the family to a war hero and the British military. Libby marries this Michael Woodhaven and connects the family to the American aristocracy. Isn't that what it's all about? Isn't that how Christianity is lived out in the real world, Father?"

Sir William shook his head, the lines around his eyes deepening. "Why is that you hate your own people?"

Edward's eyes and face grew as dark as his father had ever seen them. "You betrayed me. All for your heartless upper-class principles. I will never forgive you for what you did to Charlotte. I loved her, Father. But that didn't matter, did it? Love isn't as important as keeping up appearances."

Sir William stood at the head of the table in the dining room, a smile warming his face as he looked over his family and the servants who stood just behind them, ready to serve the evening meal.

"It has been a few years," he began, using

301

his House of Commons voice, "since all the Danforths were gathered in one place. And we are not complete yet. We will need Kipp for that. But to have all the rest of you at tonight's meal is something for which I thank God. Emma and Jeremiah are here with the boys. We have Robbie on furlough from Dublin. Catherine — how good to see you, and though it would be lovely to have Albert by your side, we are overjoyed you could join us for the wedding. Edward is down from Scotland. Libby, who has been serving in France for so many years, is at our table again. She has brought to us a good friend whom we heartily welcome into our midst — God bless you, Captain Woodhaven."

Michael smiled and bent his head briefly. "Thank you, Sir William. Thank you, Lady Elizabeth. It's an honor to be here."

Sir William went on. "I cannot overlook the bride and the groom whose love for one another has brought this happy occasion to our estate. Ben Whitecross, VC, and our beautiful daughter Victoria Anne, thank you both for gracing our table."

"And we thank you, Father," Victoria replied. "But I think you should pray. I'm afraid this is turning into one of your speeches in Parliament and we are all rather famished."

Sir William laughed along with his family and servants. "Very well. I wanted to be sure no one was left out. Let us bow before the Almighty."

"Catherine."

She turned and saw it was Robbie. He had emerged from the ash trees and was marching up the path to the sea cliff in his uniform.

"Hullo, Brother," she greeted him. "Have you been following me?"

"Not at all. I suppose we had the same good idea at the same time."

They stood together on the cliff and looked out over the ocean. At different times it flashed, or grew dark, as the sun moved under clouds and through them.

"Can you see Ireland?" he teased.

"On a good day."

"Homesick already?"

"I might ask you the same thing."

Robbie bent down and plucked a long blade of grass, placing it in his mouth. "I do miss Dublin."

"You can't miss the killings that have started up again."

"The Irish Republican Army wants a free country. They'll do to us and we'll do to them, and it's always a nasty twist of the knife from either side."

"Will it be over and done with quickly like last time?"

"It's not like what happened at Easter in 1916. This fight will carry on for a good bit. It's not just a couple of hundred rebels in Dublin anymore. It's bigger than that. It might peter out. But it also might turn into something worse." Robbie took the half-chewed grass from his mouth. "I saw you cross yourself while father was saying grace last night."

Catherine glanced at him. "Is that a crime?"

Robbie continued to stare out at the sea. "Not a crime in England. Not anymore. But odd in a family of Protestants."

Catherine did not respond.

"You should know," Robbie carried on, "that I didn't sign on for another five years with King George out of love for my country. I requested that I be permitted to stay on in Dublin for other reasons. One of them is a young lady."

Catherine half-smiled. "How many Protestant women can there be in Dublin?"

"Shannon comes from a fine Catholic family who've always harbored nationalist sentiments. And I am a soldier of the British Empire. It makes no sense that we should come together."

"Her parents approve?"

"I'm sure they know nothing about it. We've kept it very private. I meet her at one of the churches. The priests are aware and they let us be. When we meet, I'm always in civilian clothes."

"How on earth did this get started?"

"I wasn't out looking. She was nearly trampled by a team of horses. I stepped in. Kept the team back and got the horses under control. Her parents thanked me publicly. Shannon slipped me a note. *Meet me at evening mass at St. Patrick's.* So I went in the dark and out of uniform."

"Sounds risky."

"The IRA could shoot me for a spy and the British could shoot me for a traitor."

"Why do you keep it up? You were never one for the girls."

Robbie decided to sit, drawing his knees up to his chest and resting his arms on them. "At first it was a bit of a lark. She's extremely beautiful and I was certainly flattered that she would pay any attention to me. I was certain it had to do with my saving her life and that she felt obligated to graciously extend a few hours in her company. It became something much more rather quickly. Now I doubt I would break it off even if an IRA gunman put a pistol to my head." He watched a string of white gulls doing loops over a patch of ocean. "I've taken steps to convert."

"What?"

"On the quiet. With a priest at St. Patrick's. Once this latest spot of troubles is over I intend to resign my commission and become a good Catholic boy married to a good Catholic girl. I know it will drive Father and Mother mad but I can't help it. A girl like Shannon is once in a lifetime."

Catherine smiled down at him. "She must be." She settled herself down next to her brother. "And you felt you could trust me with all this news? Thank you."

"You're the quietest of the lot. And you crossed yourself."

Catherine tugged her shawl about her shoulders as a sharp sea breeze cut into them. "All right. Tit for tat. We're both in the confessional today. I moved out on Albert over a year ago. Yes, yes, I know, we've kept up the pretense of a happily married couple. I caught him having an affair and that was that. I have my own money and my own bank account. So I got myself a flat in a Catholic neighborhood in Belfast. Right next to a convent. I've become good friends

306

with a few of the nuns. Father O'Flynn has been taking me through the steps to my baptism."

Robbie stared at her. "Just like me."

"Exactly like you."

"What about Albert?"

Catherine's eyes darkened despite a burst of sunlight that made sea and land blaze. "They don't know about him."

"Cath. You know they'll find out. Someone will put two and two together."

"Why should they? I have birth documents saying I'm a Danforth."

"The Catholic community knows all about him. They detest him."

"So they should. He's become a brute. Always ranting and raving. I'm sure that's why he struck up with another woman. I'm for Home Rule like Papa, and he's a unionist. Albert got sick of coming home to me and my politics."

"You've been out in public with him, haven't you? People will remember that."

"Maybe not. You saw I changed my hair color a bit. You have noticed that, haven't you?"

He smiled. "Of course I have."

"Mum's taken me to task over it but I told her Albert liked it. A redhead. I'm quite a pack of lies these days."

"I hope you get away with it. I hope *I* get away with it. Albert is looking for you. He's bound to be. Eventually he'll need to have you on his arm for some public occasion. What's he telling people? What's he telling your friends? That you're at Ashton Park? That you're bedridden and too ill to show your face? Father will make a trip to Belfast now that the war's over. He'll want a look at the shipyards. How's Albert going to explain your absence then? He has to have you back."

Catherine clenched her fists as she gripped her shawl in another icy gust. "I won't go back. Father and Mother and the Church of England and Ashton Park will just have to get used to it. I've become a different person." She looked at Robbie. "Don't I sound rough?"

"Just Cath acting determined. I'm in the same boat. I'll look like a turncoat. A Papist through and through. Shannon's folks swear the family has been Roman Catholics since Patrick. No different than the Danforths, who swear they've been Church of England since Henry VIII. Well, I don't mind. The Dungarvans are a kind family from what I can see. The time to tell Shannon's parents about the pair of us is when I'm out of the army and a baptized Catholic. I suppose there'll be no good time, so far as telling Mum and Dad goes."

"It may work out with Shannon's parents — unless you kill an Irishman in this new war of theirs."

"You can be sure I'll do my best to avoid that. The Irish rebels treated me well enough when I was their prisoner in 1916. I'll return the favor if I've got one of them at gunpoint this time around."

Catherine shook her head and stared down at the ground. "You can't control war, Robbie."

He scooped up a handful of dirt and pebbles and sifted it until only the pebbles were left. "I can't fret over what may or may not happen. If God doesn't strike me dead for turning Catholic perhaps everything will turn out all right. Even if I'm disowned and disinherited. Like you."

They laughed. Catherine gripped the hand that held the pebbles. "You still haven't told me what she's like."

"The sea runs from gray to green and back again. Her eyes do that. Except when she's in her brightest moods the green is clear as glass, you can see right through it into her heart. You've never seen eyes like hers. She's got small freckles, just here across her nose and cheeks —" He touched his own face. "And her hair is fair. Like light. It's how the sun shines through a rain shower. So sweet to kiss and put my cheek against. It's like dreaming to be around her."

"Listen to you. Do you fancy yourself Lord Byron?"

"All the reading of the classics I did in school is now serving a greater purpose."

She kissed her brother's fist, still curled around the pebbles. "Hail Mary, full of grace."

He responded, "The Lord is with thee. Blessed art thou among women."

The next morning, making Catherine Danforth's bed, Norah Cole found the crucifix and rosary Catherine had forgotten under her pillow. Slipping them into her dress pocket, she plumped the pillows, glanced around the room she had tidied, and left.

Sir William glanced at Kipp over the pieces on the chessboard as they sat in his study. "Lady Caroline has been invited to Victoria's and Ben's wedding ceremony. Did you think of that?"

Kipp kept his eyes on the board. "Perhaps she'll decline."

"Decline? There will be a raft of MPs present. There's even talk of the Prince of

Wales making an appearance. Of course she'll be at the wedding. Her whole family will be at the wedding."

Kipp moved his rook. "I didn't do this in the dark, Father. I told Caroline about it some time ago. I've written her and explained the matter."

"That was a bad move." Sir William captured the black rook with his white bishop.

"I'm sure Caroline and her family will have the good grace to accept it."

"How sure are you? If she's told her family already they will take it as a slap in the face. If she hasn't told them and they see you sitting with this —"

"Christelle Cevennes."

Sir William leaned forward and put a hand gently on Kipp's uniformed arm. "She is striking. I see that. Charming to speak with. Her family have a Huguenot past, she told me. They are Protestants. No one faults her in any way. Your mother and I do not look for French nobility — good heavens, we fought the nobility at Agincourt. But there is the matter of the Scarborough family."

Kipp had moved his knight. Sir William captured it with a pawn.

"We were never formally engaged," Kipp said. "I realize it was expected. But it never

311

took place and it was never announced."

"No matter. Half the nobles in England are aware of your relationship with Lady Caroline. Listen, my boy. You and this Christelle Cevennes make a handsome couple. But I wish you would ask her to return to France before the wedding. You can join her there once the ceremony is over. You have your work with the aerodromes to complete in any case. But I beg the two of you not to make a spectacle of yourselves on Victoria's special day."

Kipp settled back in his leather chair after moving his queen. "I brought her here to meet you and to see Ashton Park. She is properly impressed with the family and the estate just as I expected her to be. You must understand she means more to me than Caroline ever has. Yes, Caroline is handsome, but Christelle is vibrant. Like an essence of life itself. I cannot give her up. England is full of Lady Scarboroughs. But a woman like Christelle is rare."

His father was silent.

Kipp coughed. "Checkmate, by the way."

Christelle was walking with Emma and Libby. The evening light seemed green to her as the sun poured through the leaves they walked under. She was holding James and making him laugh while Peter walked between his mother and Aunt Libby, gripping their hands.

"It's beautiful here," Christelle said. "Will the wedding be outside, Emma?"

"Well, if it doesn't turn into English weather it will be."

Christelle looked at her for an explanation.

"English weather is wet. Perhaps you've brought this lovely sunshine with you from Amiens. If that's the case, it might remain with us for as long as you do."

"Kipp must return and work with the French air squadrons and the RAF. To make sure everything is as it should be. I will leave with him right after the wedding. *J'en suis desolée* — I'm sorry."

Emma seized Christelle's arm playfully. "Tell us the truth. What do you intend to do with our brother?"

"I don't know. So quickly it all happened. We have never talked about — you know — the life together."

"France is so pleasant," said Libby. "I wonder if you could ever consider Ashton Park a home."

"*C'est magnifique* — it's magnificent here, Libby. And you are all very gracious. But I fear your father and mother are not comfort-

313

able with me. Dear Kipp should have written them. They are both surprised to meet me. It would have been better if they had known."

"Mother and Father have had to get used to a great deal since the war began," Libby replied. "They can get used to a great deal more now that it's ended. Just give them some time, Christelle. The changes are coming too fast to suit them. They have no idea what is going to happen next and they're a bit overwhelmed."

Harrison admitted much later to Todd Turpin it was the greatest surprise in his life.

He returned from mowing the lawn for the wedding and wanted only to lie flat on his bed and fall asleep with his clothes on, hat, corduroy jacket, boots, and all. He entered his rooms in the Castle to find they smelled of perfume. Standing in the front room with its couch and chairs and table he tried to identify the source of the scent. But while he might have been good at tracking fox and deer and rabbits, this left him totally perplexed.

Then, to his astonishment, Holly stepped from the small room where Harrison stored the two or three dozen books he possessed as well as back issues of various British outdoor magazines. She wore a simple black summer dress over her slim figure, a silver necklace, and silver earrings. Her smile was bright, her voice taunting.

"The perfume is from France. Kipp's friend, Christelle, brought a bit for each of the ladies at Ashton Park. Don't you think that was kind of her?"

Harrison could say nothing. He took his fedora from his head.

Holly continued. "I know more about what you have done for our family than you think. Actually, I've had my eye on you for years. I'm well aware of what you did for Victoria at Lime Street Station. I know you helped rescue Mrs. Longstaff in London — William shared the particulars and I admit I was looking for that American pistol of yours in that storage room there. I'm also privy to matters William and Elizabeth know nothing about, such as how Machiavellian our Norah Cole can be and how much grief she has caused this family — and how firmly you have stood up to her."

"I do my best for the Danforths, Miss Holly. For all of you."

"Now do you know where the scent is coming from?"

"I expect I do."

"I'm much younger than my brother William, you know. There's fifteen years between us. That's why my hair is still black as night. Perhaps it always will be. You're forty, aren't you, Harrison?"

"Yes. Yes, I am."

"And I'm thirty-seven."

She slowly put her arms around his neck. "I think loyalty and devotion should be rewarded."

"I'm . . . well taken care of . . . Miss Holly."

"Not well enough, I think. You're still a bachelor. And I'm a spinster — terrible word. But it may be we were meant for each other." She laughed softly. "Don't look so terrified, Harrison. I should have said something years ago. But I didn't feel free. The war has changed all that. Or perhaps it's the wedding, with the stable boy marrying the youngest of the Danforth girls. Or it may be the way all the Danforths are pairing off — Kipp with a French girl from Amiens, Libby with an American from New York, Edward still mooning over his chambermaid from the Pendle Hills. Something's in the air. And if the young people can cross boundaries, so can I. Not publicly yet, mind you. But a thousand-year-old castle suits me just fine for now."

She kissed Harrison on the lips. His hat fell to the floor and he didn't know what to do with his hands.

"I hope you love my scent," she purred, "because I certainly love yours. It's so natural. Earth. Grass. Wood. Leaves. Extremely pleasant. I've wasted a lifetime among the lords with their sweet soaps and well-oiled hair and fingers like putty. But it's a new world now, Harrison. If Victoria Danforth can marry a coach driver with a medal on his chest I can marry a groundskeeper who looks like a real man and acts like one too."

Her second kiss was longer than the first. She continued until Harrison responded in kind, much to his own surprise.

"Marvelous." She smiled. "I actually got some life out of you that time. Let's have a third go, shall we?" She pouted a bit. "Or is all this too much too fast for the groundskeeper? Do you want me to leave? I will, you know, if you ask me politely."

Her blue eyes and gleaming black hair were only inches from his face. She waited. Harrison finally cleared his throat and found it was possible to take one of his hands from her back and touch it carefully to her face as gently as if she were a kitten or one of his lambs. She closed her eyes and nuzzled his hand with her cheek.

"Don't go," he managed to say.

15

Reverend Jeremiah Sweet pronounced Ben and Victoria man and wife after a long Anglican service under the shade of the ash trees, Ben lifted the elaborate cream-colored veil and kissed his bride, Sir William spoke a prayer of blessing over the couple, Ben's squadron mates cheered and threw their caps into the air, and a dozen MPs stood in their handsome black morning coats with tails and joined in the applause. Aunt Holly had rushed about making sure as many guests as possible had handfuls of rice to throw, and it began to fly white and thick as Ben, in uniform, and Victoria, in her white and silver gown with a long train held by Libby, made their way back down an aisle between hundreds of chairs set up on the lawn. While they were walking and laughing and ducking showers of rice, three Sopwith Camels roared low over the crowd and dipped their wings, causing everyone to shout and point.

Ben shaded his hand and squinted up at them. "One of them's Kipp. That's his new plane. He didn't even tell me about this stunt. The others look like Hannam and Irving."

Victoria pinched his arm. "I knew. They flew them over from France a few weeks ago."

"Look at Peter and James. Running after the planes with all the might their short little legs can offer them."

Ben looked at her as the Sopwiths swooped down a second time. "I should like our children to be pilots."

She smoothed his curly black hair back from his eyes. "Are we already talking about children?"

"Not this year, of course —"

"Or next. But perhaps we can agree on nineteen-twenty-one or twenty-two."

Ben kissed her softly on lips painted a rich strawberry red. "How utterly fascinating you are."

They kissed and ignored the rice that continued to bounce off their backs until a third pass by the Sopwiths made people stop and glance upward again.

"They're landing in the field there!" someone shouted.

Ben and Victoria broke off their kiss to see their wedding guests crowding around the three aircraft as they rolled to a standstill in a sheep pasture a hundred yards away. They decided to disappear deep into the ash grove. Only Lady Grace, still seated in her white rattan chair, and a few others remained behind to watch them go.

"Bear in mind you are not on your honeymoon yet!" Lady Grace called. They glanced back at her, surprised by the strength of her voice, and she laughed in a cackling kind of way.

"Which one is she?" Lady Caroline Scarborough asked. Her cool gaze made contact with Kipp's sunlit green eyes.

He was standing by his plane, still wearing his leather helmet and white scarf. "Hullo, Caroline. She's with the other two pilots over there by Hannam's plane."

She glanced over, a white parasol above her head against the hot sun. "Their conversation seems quite animated."

"Christelle knows them both fairly well."

"Christelle, is it? So she worked her way through the squadron until she hit upon the squadron leader, did she?"

Kipp's eyes flashed. "Don't, Caroline. You're better than that."

"Am I?" Her eyes glistened. "I love you, Kipp."

"And I loved you. Then the war changed everything, didn't it?"

She turned her face away in disgust as tears struck her cheeks. "You men and your wars. You make them your excuse for everything."

"Caroline. You're a beautiful woman. We both know there's never been a shortage of men."

"Yes. Millions of men. But how many Kipps?"

She held up her hand as he started to speak again and began to walk away as several MPs came around the side of the plane. "I won't be gone from your life. I love you too much. Please enjoy your sister's wedding day."

Kipp watched her drift over the field in her shimmery pale blue dress. She moved with such poise and grace that it was as if a breeze gently lifted her slender figure between earth and sky. His eyes remained on her until a man who said he was Lord Carlisle began to pump his hand.

Edward was sipping from a glass by one of the crystal punchbowls as Lady Caroline walked by and stopped. "Edward Danforth.

It's been ages."

He nodded, his face dark. "Hullo, Caroline. How are you?"

"Not much better than you appear to be. I just hide it better."

Edward looked off across the field at the planes and the crowds of people. "Excuse me. I find the day difficult."

"Why is that?"

"Not on Victoria's account, I assure you."

Caroline shaded her eyes with her parasol to get a better look at him. "You're the eldest son. The world is at your feet."

He gave a harsh laugh. "The world? My youngest sister can marry the groom from our stables and Kipp can prance about with a baker's daughter from France, but I cannot have permission to so much as look at a woman better bred than any of them."

"Your parents are denying you a woman's hand?"

"I shouldn't get into it. I don't mean to spoil your day."

"Edward. I think you know my circumstances. No one could ruin the day for me more than your brother already has done."

He looked at her as he swirled the punch in his glass. "Yes. Of course. Forgive me."

Caroline saw that her parents were engaged in conversation with several of the

MPs just ahead of them. "I have some time on my hands. Would you care to go for a walk? Perhaps we could commiserate with each other."

She smiled gently. Edward stared at her for several moments and watched the light flicker over her dress and hair and pick out the gold in her blue eyes. Finally he smiled back.

"Yes. I'd like that."

The day after the wedding, Holly was standing in front of the Castle keep at six in the morning. She expected to see Harrison emerge from his rooms off to the right but he surprised her by coming around the far side of the Castle, where most of the ruins were. Until he spoke she did not hear a thing, waiting and looking toward his door.

"Miss Holly."

She spun around. "Harrison. You gave me a start."

He took off his brown fedora. "I'm sorry for that. It's how I move. Ball of the foot."

"What are those sticks?"

"Why, one's the staff I've carried for years. I've carved the other for you. From thousand-year oak."

She took the staff from him. It had been shaped and polished so that it glistened as

324

if wet. When she held it upright it rose a foot taller than her head.

"It's lovely." She gave him one of her best smiles. "And quite unexpected. I wish I'd brought you something."

"Well. And you have."

She saw he was gazing approvingly at how she held the staff and how she was dressed — khaki blouse, brown tweed shooting jacket set off by a royal-blue scarf at her throat that picked up on her eyes, a long khaki skirt, tall brown walking boots fastened tight. No jewelry. No perfume.

"Do I pass inspection, Harrison?" she asked.

One side of Harrison's mouth curled up in a smile and his brown eyes smiled too. "You do."

"I'm glad to hear it. Well, let's be off then. I told you I wanted to see the woods through your eyes. We're losing the morning."

Harrison glanced at the oak trees and at the sky where a few thin white clouds were vanishing as the sun continued to rise. He made a soft clicking sound with his tongue.

"It's not six-ten. We've plenty of time. Are you in a rush?"

"Certainly not."

"That's good. You can't rush the forest, Miss Holly."

She had felt in control of the relationship she'd sprung on him until that morning. The moment he had approached her with the two staffs in hand he had become a different man from the one she'd wrapped her arms around the night before the wedding. Then she had overwhelmed him and he had been awkward and hesitant with his words and his movements. Now he was in his element with the earth and the oak trees and ashes, and she was out of hers.

"Come along then, Miss Holly."

They began to walk side by side, at first saying very little. She matched him stride for stride.

"The birds have different songs in the early morning," she said, to see if she could get him talking.

"And different ones at night before they tuck themselves in," he responded.

Then he was silent.

And they kept walking.

For the longest time she felt like a nine-year-old being led about the estate she had thought she knew like the features on her face. He showed her fox dens she had never noticed, rabbit warrens, nests for robins and starlings and blackbirds, old trees full of holes that were homes for bats, tracks in the dirt that showed the comings and goings of field mice and hares.

"Amazing." Her smile was like light in the forest. "Amazing, Harrison."

He kept moving. "I'm very glad to hear you say so, Miss Holly."

Even though her life had been built around the power of being in control, especially when it came to men, and even though she disliked the feeling of not having that advantage, an unpleasant feeling she now had in the forest with Harrison, she also found that what had attracted her to him was not simply quiet eyes joined to a strength in his blood and to ways as natural as rainfall or starlight . . . it was his appreciation for life, all life, his extraordinary kindness, and his ability to utterly calm her spirit and make her feel safe and cherished, as cherished as the plants and animals he loved, sensations no one had ever instilled in her before.

"Look here." He squatted.

Holly stood still and peered down. "What is it?"

"You'll have to get down for a closer look."

"Very well."

She bent by him as he pointed out to her where feathers had fanned the dust and left ripples, where a small spot of dried blood meant a creature had been taken by an owl or a hawk. He seemed oblivious to her as they crouched side by side. But she could not help herself from responding to his warmth and sureness and the manner in which his fingers touched the earth and moved the soil in small circular patterns. She realized she wanted Harrison to remain in control in the best of ways . . . take her up in his arms, marry her on Sunday, lay her down under a canopy of leaves as if she were in a vast canopy bed. He was explaining something about the ash trees, still on his knees, sun daubing his shoulders and hat, while she remained close to him, staring at his hands as he spoke quietly, designs of yellow and green on the backs of her own hands as well as his, and she thought, *Why, I am in a state of grace.*

Harrison straightened, turned around, and looked into her face. His smile left but his eyes filled with enormous amounts of light and spaciousness. She took one of his sun-browned hands and ran a finger over it again and again.

"Care for me," she said. "Be gentle to me."

A hint of his awkwardness around women came back to him momentarily. Then the fact he was in his woodlands with all its creatures, that he was in his kingdom, reasserted itself. She felt a force from him that made her weak. She wanted to cry but did not.

I am never weak. Not with anyone. Not with any man.

His hand was at her face without her noticing he had moved it and his rough thumb was tracing the skin around her eye.

"I'm no duke," he said.

"I'm no duchess."

"Heaven knows what Norah Cole will tell your brother if she's followed us out here this morning."

"I can handle Norah Cole and I can handle my brother. My only problem is, I thought I could handle you."

"Miss Holly —"

"Oh, do stop that. Shall I go around calling you Mr. Harrison for the rest of my life? After the other night? After today?" She put her hand gently on his as he continued to stroke her face with his thumb, following the line of her cheekbone. "What is your Christian name?"

"I don't use it."

"Perhaps I'll use it. Privately."

"I'm Calvert."

"Calvert. I like that. Kiss me, Calvert."

"I want to say something first . . . Holly . . ."

"All right."

He moved his thumb along the smooth line of her jaw, slowly and carefully, as if to be sure he broke nothing, damaged nothing. "I didn't sleep the night you kissed me. When you had gone back to the manor I lay awake and looked into the dark. I wondered about the inside of the Castle. Who'd died in it, who'd given birth, who'd worshipped God Almighty, who'd fallen in love and married. I don't think such thoughts normally. To think of marrying when you're not the marrying sort, to think of the love of a man and his wife when you've no wife to lay down sweet and safe on white linen."

"I've never heard you speak this way. So eloquently. You always play the country rustic who works the great man's estate."

"I keep to myself. In my room I have my Bible and *Paradise Lost* and the poems of Keats. I've written a few thoughts in a notebook." He ran his fingers through her hair as if he were trailing them through the dark water of a forest stream. "I decided that night I would talk to you if you came back. Talk more than I had to anyone." He glanced aside for a moment. "I see I have surprised you, and I don't think you are a person who likes surprises."

He saw that her eyes began turning softer

and softer shades of blue until there was no difference between them and the summer sky emerging through the treetops.

"I have rarely been surprised," she replied. "And it's true I don't like it when it happens. But there are surprises and there are surprises. Yours might be unnerving to a spinster like me, yet they are the sort I would want if I wanted any at all."

"None of what I said is what I wanted to say."

"Try again then."

"Well." He paused. "Well, when I see the pond there in the forest, that deep pond, and it's the autumn that's upon us, November, the leaves all gone and the air sharp — well, the water's blue, not green, for the sky smiles right down into it then, through the bare branches, you see. And Jack Frost comes along and there's a skin of ice on the pond. So I try and take up a piece as large as a good-sized window, without breaking it, a whole sheet in my hands. It's hard to do because as soon as you begin to pry it up from the pond it cracks open. But some mornings I'm lucky. So then I lift up this great sheet of ice that's clear as the air. Yes, clear as the air but it gives you a different picture of things than air and light do on their own. In front of my face I hold it."

331

He brought his hands from her cheek and held them up. "I look at everything. And everything is different. Completely different. Better. It's holy magic, isn't it? Then I lay this window down gently into the pond and it is under the water, and the water is blue, as I said, and against the ice the blue is so light, so thin, like a windowpane made of pale blue glass, but better — if a breeze had color, or if the smallest wind did, or spirit, it would be like that fragment of ice in the pond." He stopped. "So your eyes, Holly, they are like that."

She saw that he was instantly afraid of what he'd said and terrified she would laugh at him and his poetry and his vision. Then she knew it was her turn to take control again, to take control without any grand design on her part, but in such a way that would bring him even more freedom. She placed her hands on either side of his face, a face with uncertain eyes now, her skin smelling of soil and growth and the green leaves she had rolled between her fingers, scented now with air that had moved all over England and had come back again.

"What a perfect man you are," she said and drew his mouth down onto hers.

The waterfall thundered into the stream and

three or four small rainbows shimmered in the white spray. Victoria kicked her feet in the current as she sat upon the bank in a green summer dress. Ben kissed her eyes and her throat and shoulders and lips.

"You know, those rainbows are in your eyes too," he said, sitting back.

She plucked a dandelion and tossed it at him. "They are not."

"They are."

"You treat me as if I were some sort of Greek goddess or some sort of immortal."

"Aren't you?"

"I'm human, Ben. I'll grow old one day and you won't want me anymore."

"Not true."

She gazed at him. "I like seeing you in trousers and a white shirt. You're handsome in a uniform but somehow this is more Ben."

"I wish this were my uniform. I wish the RAF would let me fly in clothes like this."

"What do you think about when you're not thinking of me?"

He grinned. "There's hardly a minute left to think of anything else. What can you do with ten or twelve seconds of free time? Sometimes I think of the repair work they put in for my left elbow and wonder whether

I wouldn't be better off with a cupboard hinge."

She splashed him, kicking with her legs. "Stop lying. Tell me the truth."

"I think about how I was a stable boy and now I'm on top of the world."

"Do you?"

Ben lay back on the grass with his hands under his head. "That cloud looks like a Fokker triplane. Yes, I do wonder — I wonder how I could be a groom one day and then go from one thing to another all the way to where I am now, sitting on a stream bank in the Lake District with you — and you're Victoria Whitecross and my wife. Look. Here comes a Sopwith Snipe underneath that Fokker triplane. Boom. All is kaput. Then I think about how I learned to fly and how I don't want to give it up. But I don't want to stay in the military. I really do want to fly in just a regular shirt and pants and leather jacket and boots."

"So how do we resolve this dilemma? We live in a cave? You return to work for my parents?"

"No. Kipp and I and Michael Woodhaven have been talking. Aeroplanes are the coming thing. Just like motorcars. They'll build more and more roads for cars and put up more and more airfields for planes. So we thought about opening a flying club along with a flying school. Hiring ourselves out to fly mail or important documents or important people."

"You'd work with my brother and Libby's beau?"

"I would."

"And we could all live together in some town or village?"

Ben picked a long blade of grass. "We wouldn't start up here in northern England. Not in Lancashire or Yorkshire. We'd set it up close to London. We'd get more business down there. Kipp's already spoken to your father about it."

Victoria stared at him. "And what did Daddy say?"

"All for it. Reckoned he'd fly back and forth between Ashton Park and London and save hours of travel time. He's got land down by London, you know. Or you all do. All the Danforths."

Victoria lifted her legs out of the water. "I'm quite frozen now. I need a hug." She snuggled down beside him and he put his arm around her shoulders.

"So you're quite serious about this?" she asked. "You three? And Dad helps you get off the ground?"

"Sir William. And Michael Woodhaven III,

Michael's old man."

"No."

"Michael wrote to him about it. Let him know the Danforths were interested in investing. I think his father just wanted Michael to come back to America. Then of course Libby's name came up and that was the golden wand. The Woodhavens believe she was the one that brought Michael back from the brink. So now Old Man Woodhaven is coming over next month to meet Sir William and take a look at the possible site for the airfield himself."

Victoria ran a hand over his chest. "It sounds like the lot of you have thought it all out. Why haven't you told me?"

"Who wants to talk business on a honeymoon?"

"So is that what you want? An airfield? A flying school? A mail service?"

He kissed her forehead. "What I want is to fly and to love you forever."

She traced a pattern on his chin with her finger. "I'm all for that. Well then, since the rest of our life together is settled we can get straight back to the honeymoon."

He began to kiss her again. "Absolutely wizard."

Dear Lady Elizabeth:

I should not trouble you again except that I think you ought to be made aware of certain matters since you are the mistress of the Danforth family. Whilst tidying Mr. Harrison's rooms in the castle just before the wedding I came across the rosary I have placed in this envelope. Only a day or two after, I was fixing Todd Turpin's bed in the servants' quarters and I discovered this crucifix under his pillow. What it all means, I can't say. I leave that up to you and Sir William. However it does seem to me that Mr. Harrison is having an unhealthy influence on old Todd who is quite impressionable. I shall pray for them both. And for you and your husband that you may see clearly to do what is just and right in the eyes of Almighty God and His Son Jesus Christ. This has never been a household that favored the heathenish practices of the Pope's church.

Your devoted servant

Norah

16

The landlady, Mrs. O'Rourke, always left her door ajar so she could see who went in and out. When Catherine arrived with her suitcase and prepared to wrestle it up the staircase to the second floor, Mrs. O'Rourke came out into the hallway.

"How are you, my dear?" she asked, smiling more brightly than she ever did. "How was your visit to England?"

"It was lovely, Mrs. O'Rourke, thank you."

"There is a priest come to see you. He's been here three times while you were gone. Showed up an hour ago. I said I didn't know when you would be back. He told me it was urgent and that he'd sit and wait a bit in case you arrived today."

Catherine put her suitcase on the floor. "A priest? What is his name?"

"Oh — I'm not good with names — Father something or other. I put him in your room — I hope that's all right."

"My room?"

"I couldn't very well leave him in the hallway, could I? Not a man of the cloth."

Catherine left her suitcase behind and hurried up the stairs. She was certain it would be Father O'Flynn, who was leading her through the steps to conversion and her baptism. Tapping on her door, she opened it, and at first saw no one.

"Hullo?" she called out. "Anyone here? Father O'Flynn?"

The priest was in the kitchen putting a kettle on to boil. His back was to her. He was short and in a long black cassock. Instantly she knew it was not Father O'Flynn, who was much taller.

"Father?" she asked.

The priest turned. It was Albert.

"Hello, Catherine." He did not smile. "It's time we set our house in order."

At first she couldn't speak. Finally she was able to respond. "How . . . how did you come to find me here?"

"I finally hired a private detective. He had your photograph. Made inquiries. Straight off he thought that if you were still in Belfast the best place to hide from me would be in one of the Catholic districts. Did you have to change your hair color?"

Catherine folded her arms over her chest.

"I'm not coming home with you."

"You never left me a note. But you must have seen me somewhere with Rose, did you? Well, that's over."

"That's fine. It's over between you and me as well."

Albert shook his head. "Now that the war is done, your father is coming to spend a few days in Belfast. Inspect our shipyards. Meet the employees. Look over new contracts. It won't do for your parents to find out we're separated."

"Let them find out. I'll tell them why."

"You won't. It will jeopardize your future as well as mine."

"My future?" A look of anger moved across her face in lines and twists. "Will you please remove the kettle from the heat?"

Albert took the kettle off the stove and its whistling stopped. "You'll not become a Catholic. I expect you haven't mentioned to your good Father O'Flynn that you're separated from your husband, have you? Your landlady told me how much time you spend next door with the nuns."

"It's no business of yours, Albert."

"It is. You're still my wife. You'll never be a nun, if that's the wild thing you're thinking, and you'll certainly be no convert, if I tell them I'm planning a divorce."

"You won't do that."

"Of course I will. Now let's go home and talk. Patch things up. Invite your father to Belfast so he can see how happy we are. As for your Papist obsession, put that aside. See how good things can be among the Protestants again living in a respectable Protestant home and neighborhood."

Catherine set her face. "I'm not going back with you, Albert."

"Then I'll straightaway head over for a chat with the good Father O'Flynn. I'll scorch his ears, Catherine."

She did not reply.

Albert poured hot water from the kettle into a teapot. "Where's your suitcase?"

Catherine hesitated. "Still down by the front door."

"Good. We're half done. Fetch the rest of your things while I brew you a cup."

Lady Elizabeth stirred the cream into her tea with a spoon. "You don't look well, Holly. Are you all right?"

Aunt Holly hesitated. "I've not been feeling quite myself lately. I don't know what's wrong."

"Shall we summon Dr. Pittmeadow?"

"It's nothing, really. I'll be fine," Holly said, pulling herself together. "You had something you wanted to speak with me about?"

"Yes. I notice you've been spending more time with Harrison and Todd Turpin. Which is nothing to me. I know you're fond of the servants. But I have word that both of them are practicing Catholics. William and I can't tolerate that."

Aunt Holly leaned forward in her chair. The morning sun in the parlor lit up her face so that her blue eyes and black hair flashed. "What nonsense. Harrison keeps the Scriptures — the Authorized Version — in his rooms along with a Book of Common Prayer."

"Well. A maid found a rosary on his desk. And a crucifix under Todd Turpin's pillow at his room in the servants' quarters."

"A maid. Which maid? May I guess? Norah Cole?"

"Norah has been loyal and faithful to this house."

"She is loyal and faithful to Norah Cole, Elizabeth. She is trying to get back at Harrison for standing up to her. You know of course it was she who told William about your church visits with Mrs. Longstaff?"

Lady Elizabeth stared at her husband's sister, taking this in.

"Far from being loyal and faithful," Holly

went on, "she has brought no end of grief to this family. Look at the muddle you're in with Edward now. Are you pleased with how that situation is working itself out? All thanks to Norah giving you private letters Edward had written to Charlotte Squire."

Lady Elizabeth glanced out a window. "William and I are not happy with the situation between us and Edward. He returned to Scotland in the foulest of tempers. He did not say goodbye or wish us well."

"How can you blame him? Everything would have sorted itself out on its own. Edward would have lost interest and moved on to someone else. Or approached you about his affections for her. Now it's a war of wills between yourselves and him." Her fierce eyes sharpened. "Let me see this crucifix and rosary."

"They are right here." Lady Elizabeth slid a small pouch across the table past teacups and saucers. "Now that we've decided to summer at Ashton Park it wouldn't do to have William find these in one of our dresser drawers. I keep them with me at all times."

Holly opened the pouch and the objects tumbled into her hand. Both were made of silver. She ran the rosary through her fingers first. Then held the crucifix up to the light that flooded the windows.

"These are expensive, Elizabeth. And well made."

"I see that."

"Do you really think Harrison or Todd Turpin would purchase costly items like this? Wouldn't Harrison's tastes run more along rustic lines?"

Lady Elizabeth shrugged. "Who knows how men think? They both might spend more on sacred items such as this."

"Well, I know what I think. That these are sacred to someone else. Did you look at the markings on them? Both were made in Dublin."

Lady Elizabeth took them back and examined them more closely. She sighed and closed her eyes. "I confess I don't know what to make of the matter."

"Let me speak with Norah. I believe I can reason with her. I can get to the bottom of this." She stood to leave, then her stance wavered and she sat back down.

"Holly, are you sure —"

"I said I'll be fine." With that she made her way to her room. Norah would have to wait until tonight.

Norah Cole woke from a dream that vanished as soon as she opened her eyes. It left her with an unpleasant feeling. She sat up, staring into the dark. There had been a sound.

"I don't want to turn on the electric light," came a woman's quiet voice. "One moment."

"Who is it?" demanded Norah. "What do you think you're doing in my room?"

"Ah. I have it."

A match rasped and a candle spurted fire. Norah saw Holly, in a black jacket and skirt with a black hat, seated in a chair by her bed.

Holly smiled. "Hello, my dear. I'd heard you were a nighthawk. I'm surprised to find you asleep."

"What do you want?"

"I want you to leave, Norah. Leave and never come back. I want you to get ready and go as if your life depended on it."

"What are you talking about?"

Holly continued to smile but there was no warmth in her eyes. "After Harrison are you now, Norah? Because he's caught on to you and won't let you get away with all your dirty tricks? Where are the crucifix and rosary really from?"

"I swear. Harrison's room and Todd's."

"There are a few things you've missed, Norah. I expect you weren't looking in the right direction. You see, I love Harrison. And when you go after the man I love you cross a line it would be better you had never crossed. So you will do two things tonight. You will get up and leave Ashton Park well before dawn. And you will tell me who the crucifix and rosary truly belong to. Fair?"

Norah glared. "You're as much a bully as Harrison. I'm not afraid of you either. I shall cry out."

Holly moved quickly, yanking a pillow out from under Norah and holding it down over her mouth and face. Then she took Harrison's American pistol from her jacket pocket and pressed the barrel into the side of Norah's head.

"I'm not going to be civilized about this, Norah, my dear. I have a lot of old pagan Lancashire blood in me, and although I may convert to Christianity one day, I haven't yet. You might be younger and taller but you are not stronger than I am. I can take away all your breath with the pillow or I can use it to smother the shot of the gun."

She pulled away the pillow and Norah gasped and pulled more air into her mouth. Holly kept the gun barrel where it was. She coughed and turned away briefly. Then she spoke again. "The hallway is quite empty at three in the morning. I shall drag your body out the back door, put it on a horse I have tethered there, and lead the mare to the sea cliff. Over the side you will go and in the depths you will remain until the sea gives up her dead."

"You witch!" hissed Norah. "You haven't the strength to do that. You're not well."

"Are you willing, then, to wager your life on my capabilities? Now, I'm going to place the pillow over the gun. If you cry out I shall shoot you and all anyone will hear, if they hear anything at all, is a short squeak that sounds like you are having a bad dream. You can leave Ashton Park and live out your miserable life somewhere else, or you can stay here forever at the bottom of the sea. Which would you prefer?"

"God will judge you for this, Miss Holly."

"I rather believe He'll thank me, Norah. For all you know He put me up to it."

Holly had marched Norah out to the main road in the dark. Several miles in the distance they could see lights from the nearest village.

Holly felt her knees buckle, but recovered quickly. Norah caught the movement and said, "You're not well, Miss Holly. God's judgment is falling on you already."

Holly ignored her and said, "You can get a coach or motorcar from there in the morning. Off you go. May God have mercy on your soul."

Norah's eyes were ice. "And on yours."

Norah began to walk toward the village, suitcase in one hand, a bag with a strap over her other shoulder. Holly heard her shoes go *clack-clack* on the stones. She waited a half hour to be sure Norah didn't return. Then she made her way back to Ashton Park, heading through the avenue of oak trees toward the manor.

"Harrison. Wake up."

Harrison shot to a sitting position in his bed. "What's the matter? What time is it?"

It was Todd Turpin holding a lamp. "It's four-thirty. Miss Holly's in a bad way."

Harrison threw on his clothes. "In a bad way? How do you know about that?"

"I was up and about at four and I found her by the front steps of the manor. She was out cold."

"Where is she?"

"In her room. Libby's taking care of her. The doctor's been called for." He pulled Harrison's American pistol from his pocket. "There's this here before ye go."

Harrison stared. "How is it you've got it?"

"Miss Holly had it in her hand."

"What?"

Harrison took the pistol and examined it. Then he put it in the middle drawer of his desk and they left the Castle, making their way quickly to the manor.

"She calls out for ye," Todd told him. "In her fever."

"What is the illness? What does she have?"

"The doctor will have to say. I think it's that Spanish flu that's been giving our folk such a hard go."

"Not that, please, God. You don't know, Todd. You can't be sure."

Todd shrugged as they half-ran up the steps, the lamplight jumping all over them and the oak doors. "I'm sorry, mate."

Harrison sat by Holly's bed and held her hand. The curtains were pulled shut so that even though the day was bright the room was dim.

"I brought you some flowers," he said. "Fresh-cut. They're in a vase here."

Holly lay still. Her face was mottled with red and white patches, her breathing too quiet to hear. Harrison watched the slow rise and fall of her chest.

"I believe she'll live, Mr. Harrison," said Dr. Pittmeadow, standing behind him. "I've seen several of these cases. She'll survive."

"Thank God for that."

"But you must understand that her mind is not altogether there. The last time she was awake she didn't recognize any of the servants. Nor did she recognize you."

"Wouldn't that be a passing thing to do with the illness?"

The doctor put his hands in the pockets of his suit pants and sucked in his lower lip. "The fever broke yesterday. We can only hope it's a temporary lapse of memory on her part and not permanent. But for now we are strangers to her."

Harrison kissed her hand. "She's no stranger to me, sir."

Norah Cole walked into the room carrying a tray of oatmeal and tea. "I have Miss Holly's meal for her when she wakes up. The doctor said oatmeal would be the best thing for her if she could get it down."

Harrison looked up, anger in his eyes. "You! Are you the best they could come up with?"

The doctor looked at Harrison in surprise. "What's that?"

Norah frosted over. "Apparently."

"Where were you? They couldn't find you at all yesterday."

She smiled at the doctor. "Oh, it was my day off and I'd gone in early to the village to do a bit of shopping. I should have told someone. Todd drove Sally in to get some things the doctor ordered for Miss Holly, and she was the one who told me what was going on. So I came back with them. I'm happy to feed Miss Holly if you like."

"Wonderful," replied the doctor.

Harrison shook his head. "Out of the question. I have a half hour. I'll see if I can rouse Miss Holly and get some nourishment into her."

"Suit yourself. I'll be sure to keep an eye on her while you're gone." She smiled at the doctor again. "I'll be back soon, sir, and lend a hand where it's most needed."

The doctor shook his head at Harrison after Norah had left the room. "What's gotten into you, man? Why, she's pure gold. The Danforths are fortunate to have such a devoted servant in their household."

17
1920

May 1920

Robbie straightened his tie and suit jacket quickly before entering the church. He genuflected and took a seat at the back, remaining there when others went up for evening communion. When Mass was ended he left the sanctuary and walked down a long hall, entering a room that was filled with broken furniture and boxes of decorations. There was no window and no electricity. Only the light from the hallway allowed him to see. Everything appeared empty. He frowned and ran a hand through his hair.

Two hands covered his eyes. "Password."

He smiled. "Tipperary."

"Welcome, friend."

He turned around and the same two hands brought his face down. "It's been weeks. Where have you been hiding from me?"

He kissed her lips and put his arms around

her back, the cloth of her coat soft under his fingers. "I'm sorry, Shannon. All the fighting —"

"Shhh. I'm teasing. I thank God you've not been harmed."

He kissed her more deeply and would not stop. Finally she pulled away with a laugh. "I'm drowning."

"I lie in bed," Robbie said, "and every part of my body aches to have you close, take in your perfume, taste your skin and your lips."

She kicked the door shut with her foot. "Does it now?"

"I swear."

"The priests said we could have an hour. Then it's your catechism. Have you been reading the books?"

"I'm ready, don't you worry."

"I don't worry. I pray. Where's that big chair of ours?" She stumbled about in the dark, tripped and giggled, and finally found it, one hand brushing against the stuffing that spilled out of a crack in the leather. "Come. Have a sit. I'll curl up in your lap."

When they had settled themselves in, she ran a finger around each of his eyes and his mouth. "We have so much to say to each other."

"I know that. But right now I'd rather kiss."

Even in the blackness her smile was obvious. "Would you?"

"We can chat later. I'm half-dead from not seeing your face or feeling your hands in mine."

"I've missed you too, Robbie Danforth — you're not the only one who has been feeling out of sorts."

He pressed his lips against her hair as she clasped the back of his head. Then he began to kiss her without stopping. This time she did not pull away for air.

The crash of a machine gun outside broke their spell.

"What's happening, Robbie?" she asked, bewildered.

"It sounds like there's a gunfight going on right outside the church."

The door swung open. It was one of the younger priests.

"Listen to me," he said. "A British patrol has been ambushed on the side street. There's IRA all around the church. Stay here and don't come out. I'll be back for you when it's safe."

"Father —"

The priest saw the restlessness in Robbie's face. "It's bad enough. There's dead on both sides. But the patrol has caught the worst of it."

He closed the door. Shannon found his hands in the dark and gripped them tightly.

"I should be out there," he said.

"But it's not your fight."

"Of course it's my fight."

"It's not your patrol."

"It doesn't matter. I'm British army and those are British soldiers. The Lord knows I haven't any great desire to fight the Irish. But I can't stand by and let my men be butchered."

"Robbie. Listen to me." She released his hands and grasped his face. "Are you listening?"

They saw each other's eyes. He nodded.

"You go out there in your suit and tie with your pistol in your hand and both sides will shoot you. They'll not hear what you shout or care who you say you are. You won't look like a soldier to the British and you won't look IRA to the Irish. They'll both gun you down."

The blast of a bomb going off shook the wall.

"I have to take that chance, Shannon."

"Why? Why do you have to? Your heart's not in this fight. You said so yourself. Running out the front door or back door to save the day won't make any difference. Except to me. They'll kill you and take you from me."

The crackle of gunfire continued.

"I don't know what to do. If I had my men with me —"

"But you don't. Not today. Another day, if you must fight. But not here. Not now, no."

They stood in the dark, clutching each other's hands, while the shooting intensified and then suddenly petered out. The silence seemed worse to them than the sound of the guns. Sirens began to wail far off. They grew louder and louder as the vehicles approached the church.

"So now it's the ambulances," Robbie said in a flat voice.

Special to the *Times* — Londoners will be pleased to learn a new civilian aerodrome has opened just north of the city. SPAD aircraft will provide our citizens with the opportunity for flying lessons or short hops as well as ferrying them between all points in southern England that have access to an airfield or an adequate equivalent. The South England Air Service also has contracts with the Royal Mail, the government, and a number of businesses that wish to move mail, packages, legal documents, and other items as swiftly as possible.

Rates appear reasonable, and the Air Service is run by three men who flew with the air arm during the Great War. Indeed, one of them is a gentleman and an aviator who was awarded the Victoria Cross in the recent conflict. So potential customers can relax knowing their goods or indeed themselves are in the best possible of hands when it comes to flying from one location to another in our country. The SEAS may be contacted by telephone at the number printed at the bottom of this article.

Libby stood by the pole the windsock flew from and watched the two planes coming in from the south. They circled the Park and then dropped lower as they prepared to land. A cool wind made her pull her jacket tightly around her neck.

"It's supposed to be warmer than this in May," she grumbled out loud.

The first plane touched down. It rumbled along the same stretch of pasture that had been used for an airstrip at Ben's and Victoria's wedding. The aircraft was painted in a light gray with blue and red on its tailfin and had two seats, with the pilot in the front one. A man sat behind him in the second seat. She recognized her father as the man in the passenger's seat and Kipp as the pilot. It rolled to a stop, its propeller still whirling, just when the other plane touched down. It had a sky-blue paint scheme and was the same kind of aircraft that Kipp was flying. There was only the pilot in this one — the passenger seat was empty. Libby knew that pilot as well. It was Michael Woodhaven.

She half-ran across the grass once both planes had come to a standstill. Michael lifted her off the ground with a hug and they approached Kipp and Sir William, their arms around each other.

"So these are the planes you and Michael talked our parents into investing their money in," Libby said.

"They are," responded Kipp, tugging his leather helmet off. "And both Mr. Woodhaven and Dad have already received a return on their investment."

Libby kissed her father on the cheek. He was dressed in flying gear just like his son and Michael. "How was your first flight, Papa?"

"Capital. Excellent. It certainly beats long journeys on the train or in a car."

"What sort of aircraft are they?" Libby asked.

"SPAD S.XXs," Michael told her. "Almost like the one I flew in the war."

"But that was a one-seater."

"Right. They had this second seat for a rear gunner. The war ended before the S.XX could be used in combat. So now it's been developed for civilian use. We were lucky to pick up a pair."

"I like its lines."

"Hey. This is the fastest plane in the world. Jean Casale reached 176 miles per hour in one back in February."

"I can't believe that. You didn't fly that fast with Papa on board, did you, Kipp?"

Sir William laughed. "They did not. Or so he assured me."

"We did 150 most of the way. That's fast enough and easier on the gas. Did Harrison fix up that tanker truck like we asked him?"

Libby leaned into Michael's arm. "He did. It's full of airplane fuel now. Why? Are you in a hurry to get back?"

"No. We'll stay the weekend and then get Dad back to Westminster and the House of Commons on Monday. Ben and Vic are holding the fort back at our airfield. We need to work on wedding plans with Mum."

Sir William peeled off his heavy leather flying gloves and slapped them against his leg. "A double wedding in the chapel. Kipp and Christelle Cevennes. Libby and Michael Woodhaven IV. Wonderful."

Michael and Kipp found the heavy wooden chocks at the edge of the field and placed them against the SPADs' tires. Then the four of them began to walk toward the manor.

"Why don't you take your helmet off, Father?" asked Libby. "It's a bit nippy now and then but it's not that bad."

"No. I want your mother to see me in it. I'll pull my goggles down for her too."

"Oh, Father." She smiled and glanced over at Kipp. "And how is Christelle doing in Amiens?"

"She writes that she's fine. Of course she's looking forward to the June wedding. Her parents have said they'll certainly attend."

"Wonderful."

Kipp stopped walking. "Is that Harrison with Mrs. Seabrooke? And Aunt Holly?"

The others paused with him.

"Yes," replied Sir William. The good humor left his face. "Holly is gradually recovering her mental faculties. Ever since she left her sickbed last fall she has spent a great deal of time with Mrs. Seabrooke. The poor woman used to take all her meals alone in her room. Now Holly insists on being served with Mrs. Seabrooke in the front parlor. Mrs. Seabrooke seems to be responding to the extra attention. She has even begun helping the maids with dusting and flower arranging."

"And Harrison spends time with them both?"

"He scarcely left Holly's side during her illness. Oh, he did all his work, of course. But then he was right back at her side. Norah Cole was similarly devoted. So you'll see Harrison walking with the two ladies several times a day."

"Good for him. Bless him."

They began walking again.

"I hope you men are hungry," said Libby. "Mrs. Longstaff has cooked up quite a feast in your honor."

"No worries there. I could eat the bark off a tree," laughed Michael.

"I want the marriage to work, Catherine."

Catherine stood with her arms folded over her chest as Albert prepared to leave for work. He paused with his hand on the doorknob.

"You don't believe me," he said. "After all these months, you still don't believe me."

"I'm a prisoner in my own house. I believe that. I'm a prisoner in my own marriage. I believe that too."

"I've apologized for my affair a thousand times."

"And I'll believe that when I've heard it five thousand times."

Albert's eyes glimmered with anger. "I'll prove it to you. I'll prove that I want a home with you. I'll cook you some fine meals. Sit down with you and a cup of tea and have some fine talks. I'll be here. In this house. With you. And we'll make something of it all again."

"I can't wait."

"Look. If you don't want to give me a second chance you're free to walk out the door as soon as I'm gone. Go on. Head back to your nuns."

"Wouldn't I just love to do that? Everything would be coming up roses until your private detective showed up. Or Father O'Flynn asked me about the divorce proceedings you'd set in motion. No, for now I feel safer here. You'll find me chained to the stove in the kitchen making meat loaf when you're back from work. Unless you'd like to do the cooking tonight."

"Supper will be late if we do it that way."

"I don't mind eating late. I don't have much of an appetite these days. A late supper might help with that."

Albert turned his back on her and opened

the door. People hurried past on the sidewalk while cars and trucks and horses moved up and down the street.

"I'll be home at six-thirty," he said without turning around. "I'll fix the meal. We'll eat at eight."

"Suits me," Catherine responded. "Now I can just lie around all day until you're back and I can get fed."

"It was Max got it, you know."

"What?" Robbie stared at the sergeant major. "He never patrols that district of Dublin."

"He was helping someone else out."

Robbie made a fist and smacked it into his hand. "He had two sons. Just babies."

Surprised at Robbie's burst of anger, the sergeant major waited a moment before finally speaking. "Aye. So the lads have started taking up a collection for his widow. Can we count you in, Captain?"

"Yes. Of course. Put me down for a hundred pounds."

The sergeant major raised his eyebrows. "Very good, sir." He studied Robbie's dark face. "There was a fight out in the country, you know. Close Cork. We gave it to them there, sir. I doubt any of the IRA walked away. If that helps."

"Raising Max from the dead would help, Sergeant Major."

"Yes, sir."

"Who is . . . who is patrolling that district tomorrow?"

"Leftenant Hendricks, sir."

"You can let him know he has another assignment. I'll be taking a squad out there tonight."

The sergeant major nodded. "All right. You'll discuss it with the colonel?"

"Yes, yes." Robbie put a fist to his mouth. "I'll take the same crew back there at dawn."

"Captain —"

"I don't like this war, Sergeant Major." Robbie's eyes were like black stones. "But they want a fight so we'll fight. We'll find out who rules the streets, won't we? We'll find out who rules the dead."

Lady Elizabeth hung up the receiver of the candlestick telephone and smiled at her husband. "Isn't it wonderful young William is doing so well? Three boys now! Emma will never have a moment's peace."

Sir William had been listening to her conversation on the phone with Emma while he read his newspaper. "Born a month early and obviously solid as a rock. Will they be calling him Billy, do you think?"

"Perhaps not a rock, William, but still, it's something to thank God for. Yes, Jeremiah is already calling him Billy. I don't think Emma quite likes it."

He put down his paper after closely reading a few more lines. "I don't think Mum liked it either when I was a lad, but there you have it. When are they coming down?"

"Not till just before the wedding in June. What is it you're reading?"

"Why, there was an incident in Dublin —"

Lady Elizabeth got up from her seat by the phone, waving a hand. "I don't want to hear about any of your war news. Not unless it's about Robbie's regiment being sent back to England to rest and refit."

She walked out of the front parlor just as Kipp was coming in.

"Cheers, Dad," he said, taking a chair by his father. "Michael and Libby went out for a walk so I thought I'd come by and see you. What news?"

"I was just trying to tell your mother. There was an ambush the other day in Dublin. The IRA set upon one of our patrols and killed quite a few soldiers. Well, an unnamed English officer took a squad back to the ambush site that night, lured the IRA into another attack, and trapped them. Killed the lot. Then went back the next

365

morning and drew another group out that was bent on revenge. Wiped them out as well. Took no prisoners."

Kipp's face tightened. "It's getting grim, isn't it?"

"Yes. It's gone past being an uprising. It's a proper war now. As much as it was in France and Belgium. Keep your brother in mind. Your mother's concerned about him, of course. We're praying for his safety constantly."

"Of course you are. We all are. But it's not like Robbie to go in swinging, Dad. You know that. He'll do his bit but he's not a fighter. He'll stay back at HQ and win the war from there."

Sir William nodded. "I expect you're right."

Shannon Dungarvan wrapped the cloak about herself more snugly and adjusted the brim of the hood so it covered more of her face. "It's gotten ugly, hasn't it?"

Robbie squeezed her cold hands. "I'm sorry."

"What do you have to be sorry about? They don't mind killing your men. You fight back and they call you all sorts of names."

"It's not in me to strike out like this."

"Obviously it is. It just needed something

to bring it to the surface."

"They killed a friend — a father with two young children. Something went cold in me — cold and hard — and this anger came —"

"Of course. But my parents don't care about him. It's just the Irish dead that matter to them. They would love nothing better than to see you hanging by your neck from a lamppost. I have to listen to their talk day in and day out. No, they don't pay any mind to the bloodletting the IRA are doing."

"I'm sorry."

"Stop saying that. All you're doing is what the IRA do all the time. You're soldiers. It's all the same thing."

There was no moon. The blackness was on their faces and shoulders and the gravestones that rose up like a forest around them. She suddenly pulled him behind a cluster of tall oaks and began to kiss him with a ferocity that caught him off guard. Then she gripped his face with so much strength he almost winced.

"I don't care. You've become a fighter but that's not all you are. They don't know what I know about you. They don't see it. They don't feel it. I love you. I want us to get out of Ireland and leave all this behind. I don't care about my parents. I don't care about

St. Patrick's. Let's just go somewhere that doesn't know about England or Ireland or the war. You can get us a boat."

"Shannon." He looked at how large and fierce and shining her eyes were despite a night of thick clouds and no stars or moon. "I'd be shot for a deserter. We have to see this through. Ireland can get its independence or get Home Rule. Either way the British soldiers will leave and you must leave with us when we do. I had plans about staying — until those gun battles."

"I know you did. But listen to me. They've targeted you for assassination. Father told me. He knows nothing about you and me, and he's telling me these things, and I have to act pleased. I don't want you shot or wounded. We can't wait. They'll come after you until they put a bullet in your head. There must be some way off this island for us, Robbie."

Robbie leaned forward and kissed her eyes. "If they did come after me —"

"They will come. They are coming."

"— my commanding officer will soon pick up on it. If he decides it puts our men at too much risk they'll reassign me. Send me to India or Palestine or Wales."

"We'd get married and go together."

"I haven't finished my conversion —"

Shannon gripped his arms. "For heaven's sakes, I don't care whether we're married by a priest. It can be a Methodist or a Baptist or a captain on the high seas. If we're not going to live in Ireland under my parents' blessing it doesn't matter about St. Patrick's and the Holy Catholic Church. All that matters is that it's you who swears to be my man." She placed her hands on his face and lowered her voice. "I've seen the nationalists go in and out of my parents' home all my life. Some are good men. Most are good men. But there are a few that would kill and destroy anyone and anything that tried to stop them from having a free Ireland. Those will be the ones they send after you."

"Look." He reached up and held one of her hands and smiled. "We'll get through this. Once our lads find out there's a price on my head, I'm gone. And you with me."

"I pray to God you're right."

Robbie made his way back to headquarters by his own circuitous route. The cemetery was only three blocks from Shannon's home, but she used side streets and alleys before emerging a few hundred yards from her front door. She dropped the hood that covered her head and walked under the streetlamps past handsome houses, a few with columns, some with walls covered in ivy. A man and a woman were talking and laughing and coming toward her. Otherwise the sidewalk and road were empty.

"Good evening," she greeted them.

The bearded man tipped his hat. "God bless."

Then the woman threw her cloak up and over Shannon's head and smothered her cry. They seized her and pushed her into a car that had been parked a few feet away. With the man and woman on either side of her the car drove off. The driver did not speed. When he reached the main street he merged with traffic smoothly and carefully.

Shannon began to fight and the man and woman pinned her arms and legs. The man smacked her head and gripped her tightly where he knew her throat was. Squeezing until he heard her choke he leaned in close.

"You behave and you'll live. You don't and you'll die. Maybe you'd rather be dead by the time we're through with you." He squeezed on her throat harder through the folds of the woman's cloak. "An Irishwoman putting her lips to the mouth of a British soldier! And you a Dungarvan! You're a disgrace to your mother and father! A traitor to your country!"

"Are you ready, Father?"

Kipp walked over from the plane in his jacket and helmet. Sir William had all his flying gear on but was reading the morning paper as he stood at the edge of the field with Libby and Michael. Libby patted his arm.

"Papa? Kipp is talking to you."

"Hmm? Yes, yes, I'm quite ready." He folded the paper up and slapped it against his leg. "Sometimes I am ashamed of our race."

"Why — what in the paper has upset you now?" asked Libby.

"The IRA took an Irishwoman who was the girlfriend of a British soldier. Beat her. Sheared off all her hair. Put a sign around her neck and tied her to a lamppost by the British barracks in Dublin. She was barely alive when the guards found her."

Libby put her hand to her mouth. "Father! That's terrible!"

"I wish that were the worst of it." He looked across the field at the airplanes and slapped the newspaper against his leg again. "Her parents would not come to her because she was in a British military hospital.

371

So they transferred the poor girl to a Catholic one. But they still would not come because she had been consorting with a British officer. They say they will not have her back in the home. Ever."

"That is hard to understand," said Michael, his face dark.

"Wars for freedom are often the most brutal the human race wages," Sir William murmured. "Perhaps it is because people are so desperate. Still that does not excuse such cruelty. So many say their cause is noble, yet they pursue it in the most ignoble of fashions."

Kipp waited a moment as his father continued to stare into the distance. "Any news of Robbie?"

"Robbie?" Sir William turned his head to meet his son's gaze. "We haven't heard from him all week. But I'm sure he's all right. I imagine he's well clear of all this."

18

July 1920

"I'd rather be taking on Baron von Richthofen and his whole crew."

"Stand still." Ben adjusted Kipp's tie. "I saved your life once. But I can't do it this time. All that French girl has to do is smile and you turn into a puddle."

Kipp sighed. "It was easier in Amiens when there was a war on."

"And harder in England now that we have the peace. You'll just have to make the best of it. Jeremiah will be along to fetch us to the chapel in a few minutes, I expect. How are you holding up, Michael?"

Michael Woodhaven IV sat in a chair wringing his hands. "I can't stand the waiting. I want it over and done with."

Ben laughed. "I have two nervous wrecks. And I'm best man to you both. Am I going have to call for reinforcements to keep you lads steady at the altar?"

"Do you think the chapel is crowded?" asked Michael.

"Crowded? It's absolutely heaving. A double wedding — why, I don't think a soul turned down the invitation. They're spilling over into the hallway. The thing is, do you chaps remember your lines?"

"Lines?" Kipp looked at Ben in horror. "Jeremiah will just say, 'Repeat after me,' won't he?"

"Not always. There are things you have to do on your own."

Michael groaned and put his head in his hands. "I'm a dead man."

Holly let a smile Harrison saw all too rarely open her face as Jeremiah Sweet looked from Kipp and Christelle to Michael and Libby and began the long Anglican wedding ceremony. "This is wonderful. I get flashes of another wedding ceremony in Ashton Park's chapel. Whose was that?"

Harrison whispered. "Emma's. The one with the three boys. The minister's wife."

Holly whispered back. "Are you sure it was hers?"

"Yes."

They were seated at the back of the chapel in a corner. The closest people to them were Todd Turpin and Skitt, who ignored their whispering back and forth.

"There was an outdoor one with airplanes —" Holly murmured.

"That was Ben and Victoria. Mr. and Mrs. Whitecross. I pointed them out to you a few minutes ago."

"He was the pilot."

"Ben and Kipp and Michael are all pilots. They all flew in the war. Now they have their own flying business."

"Do they? How are they doing?"

"They're beginning to make money, I've been told."

Holly gestured with her head. "Who is that couple?"

"Libby is marrying an American —"

"I remember *that*. You told me only ten minutes ago."

"Those are his parents from New York. Mr. and Mrs. Woodhaven."

Holly lifted her finger as Jeremiah continued to speak. "And that couple? They are certainly not English."

"The Cevennes. From France. Their daughter is marrying Kipp."

"Ah. That very, very striking young lady. Silver hair."

"Christelle. Yes."

"They do not look very comfortable. I think I need to take them under my wing after the ceremony."

Holly picked up a small stack of photographs that had been sitting on the pew between them. "And these are the family members who are not with us." She selected one. "Edward. Am I right?"

"He is in Scotland."

"And he couldn't make it down?"

"Evidently not."

"This young man in uniform?"

"Robbie. He's a captain in the British army stationed in Dublin."

"All right. You've told me about him. He's caught up in that awful fighting there."

"Let us hope not. Our understanding is he's based in the rear echelon. Far and away from any of the street battles."

Holly tapped Robbie's portrait with her finger. "I like his looks. He has a boyish innocence about him. Does he have a girlfriend?"

"No. He was always quite shy with the ladies."

"They wouldn't give him leave to attend the wedding?"

Harrison shook his head. "The war in Ireland has intensified."

Holly displayed two photographs. "Albert and Catherine. Living in Belfast. Why aren't they here?"

"There have been sporadic shootings in Northern Ireland as well. They didn't feel safe moving about."

She glanced at him. "Is that what they said?"

"Albert has rather strong political opinions when it comes to Ireland. He does not want it independent. He wants it to remain part of Great Britain. The IRA have targeted him."

"What?" Holly almost spoke out loud. Todd flicked an eye toward her then looked back to the front. "Has anything happened? Are the two of them all right?"

"Sir William was just on a business visit there. Overnight. He told us they were safe and sound and still keeping a pleasant home."

"Was it wise for him to go over if there's so much unrest?"

Harrison shrugged. "Your brother is not easily intimidated."

Holly sat back and turned her attention to the ceremony once again. "You're a good friend, Harrison. You have helped me a great deal these past many months. But I feel you are not telling me everything. I'm not an invalid, you know. More comes back to me every day. You needn't withhold information."

"I'm doing my best to tell you what I can of the family, Miss Holly."

"I shall get to it all eventually, you know. It will come back to me, Harrison. With your help or without it."

The nun escorted Robbie to a garden surrounded by high walls at the back of the hospital. He immediately saw Shannon standing alone by a yellow rosebush, fingering the leaves of one of the stalks. He examined the tops of the walls. The nun followed his eyes.

"No one will come in here, Captain. The IRA have guaranteed the safety of the Catholic hospitals. Of all hospitals."

"Thank you, Sister."

"Please try not to stay longer than fifteen or twenty minutes. She is still very weak."

Shannon turned and smiled as he approached her over a flagstone path. One eye was still purplish but the other was a mix of bright green and sunlight. He saw that the fear was gone from it. A white cotton scarf covered her head. She folded herself into his arms.

"I almost didn't recognize you in your uniform."

He pressed his lips against the scarf. "How are you feeling?"

"Much better. The nuns are very pleasant to be around."

He cupped a hand under her chin and gently lifted her head. There were still two large scabs on her lips and another at the corner of her mouth.

"Not very kissable, am I?" she asked.

"That's not true." He touched his lips carefully to hers. "There are no finer lips in all of Ireland."

"What about England?"

"England's not even in the running."

She laughed and winced, putting a hand to her mouth, then laughed again. "It hurts. But I can't help myself. You always make me smile."

"You'll soon be healed up. You're getting all your color back." He bent down and pinched a rose off its stalk and twined blossom and stem into the knot of the scarf. "A few blemishes don't mar your beauty. You rival a summer's day."

"Is that so? You didn't steal that from your Shakespeare? *Shall I compare thee to a summer's day?*"

"I don't know him. Friend of yours, is he?" Robbie peeled back the edge of her scarf. "I see some lovely sun-colored hair."

She put her hand on his as he rubbed the short hairs with his fingers. "It's come along nicely since your last visit," she said.

He smiled. "It's so soft." He touched a scab and his smile was gone.

She squeezed his hand. "You haven't done anything rash. Thank you."

"I'm not sure what you mean by rash. The Black and Tans are still looking for O'Casey. And the Royal Irish Constabulary. And the British army."

"I don't know that it was him. I was blindfolded."

"Our best informants told us it was him. It doesn't matter what you didn't see. Locking him up is only justice, Shannon. There's nothing rash about justice."

"It depends on how it's achieved, doesn't it? He thought he was serving up justice to me. Don't you be like him, Robbie Danforth."

"Making war on women —"

Shannon's hands gripped both sides of his face. They had lost none of their strength. "Don't you be like him. Promise me you'll not act like he acts."

"Look —"

Her one good eye was a hard, sharp green. "Should you come across him. Promise me you'll not be like him."

Robbie hesitated. Finally he kissed her lips again. "I won't be the one to find him. He'll wish I had. The Black and Tans will likely get to Jack O'Casey first and when they do they'll tear him apart."

"No more talk of him." Robbie felt her body trembling as she sank against his chest again. "What did your commanding officer say about getting the two of us out of Ireland?"

"I was about to tell you. It's in the works. No more than a week."

She pulled back quickly and looked at him. "Are you serious? He said that? We're as good as gone?"

"He did say that."

"And you waited all this time to tell me?" She laughed and winced and struck his chest playfully with her fists. "You're a Black and Tan yourself, you are, Robbie Danforth."

Tavy extended a platter to Lady Elizabeth as she sat with her husband in the library. "Your mail, ma'arm."

"Thank you, Tavy. How is everything today?"

"Running like a well-wound grandfather clock."

"Anything from our four honeymooners in France? I wonder if Kipp has taught Christelle how to fly as he promised her he would?"

"I didn't notice any French postage stamps, ma'arm."

She sorted through the envelopes while Sir William read his newspaper. "Well wishes from our wedding guests. Well wishes. Well wishes." She paused. "That's very strange."

"Hmm?"

"There's a note here from Lord and Lady Scarborough."

He did not look up from his paper. "Probably explaining their absence and sending the couples their regrets."

"It's weeks too late for that. No one expected them." She used the letter opener Tavy had put on the tray to slit open the envelope. "I can't imagine what's on their minds."

"Why —" She put a hand on her husband's arm as she read the letter.

"What is it?"

Lady Elizabeth stood up quickly and dropped the letter on the table. "I'm sorry. I can't sit any longer." She crossed the library to stand and look out one of the tall windows.

Sir William folded up his paper and picked up the letter she had dropped. "What's upset you?"

Lord and Lady Scarborough wish to announce the engagement of their daughter Lady Caroline Virginia Scarborough to Edward George Danforth, eldest son of Sir William Danforth, MP, and Lady Elizabeth Danforth of Ashton Park, Lancashire. Information on the date and location of the wedding ceremony will follow over the next few weeks. Please join us in extending our best wishes to the young couple for a wonderful life together. May God bless their marriage and the future that awaits them.

"Now you're operating alone. This isn't an army operation. It's not sanctioned by the British government. You're in plainclothes, so if your luck turns against you the IRA will put a bullet in the back of your head."

"They haven't shot anyone for being a spy yet, Mickey."

"You'll be the first if you muck up."

Robbie was sitting in a civilian motorcar parked on a busy street. He wore rough clothing and a flat tweed cap that made him look like a dock-worker out for a night at a tavern. The man beside him also wore civilian clothes. It was a Friday night in July and a warm drizzle fell over the pavement and cobblestones. Dozens of men walked in and out of a tavern a block away.

Mickey gestured with his chin. "The neighborhood is thick with IRA. We never send patrols here. That pub is an IRA meeting house. You may not see the barrels but you can be sure every bloke is carrying a gun. Are you sure you want to go ahead with this?"

Robbie stared through the raindrops on the windshield. "You were there when the boys cut Shannon down from the lamppost. O'Casey did everything but rape her. What if that were your girl, Mickey? Your daughter? Your sister? The woman you were going to marry? What then?"

Mickey glanced down at his gloved hands a moment. "Do you have his picture on you?"

"I don't need it. I've been staring at it for weeks."

"Don't shoot the wrong man, Robbie."

"I won't."

Mickey nodded. "Right, then." He opened his door and slid out from behind the right side steering wheel.

"Mickey." Robbie extended his hand. "Thanks for your help."

Mickey half-smiled and shook it. "Make sure you have an escape route in your head. I want to come to your wedding and have a grand old time with you and the lads."

"The invitations are already in the mail."

"I'm sure they are. Best of luck."

For the next hour Robbie sat in the car slumped in his seat, pretending he was sleeping. He was far enough away from the pub that no one even looked in his direction. There were cars parked in front of him and in back. For all the men and women who walked by knew, he was IRA. They left him alone.

It was getting dark. An informant had assured him O'Casey would be meeting with other leaders in the pub. O'Casey hadn't left by the front door if he had left at all. As for the back door, Mickey was watching that. He'd toss a few stones at Robbie's car if the man chose the alley.

But O'Casey was in his own territory and he went boldly out the front. Robbie had just looked up from checking his pocket watch. It was twelve minutes after ten, just past 2200 hours. O'Casey emerged from the tavern laughing and in the company of two other men. His beard and bushy hair were unmistakable. He glanced up and down the street and at the people walking near him. The two men with him got into a car. O'Casey waved and turned up his collar to the rain. Bareheaded, hands in the pockets of his coat, he started walking up the street in Robbie's direction. A man Robbie assumed was a bodyguard detached himself from the wall of the pub and shadowed O'Casey from about twenty feet behind.

Surprised, Robbie slid further down in his seat. O'Casey had his eyes straight ahead and kept coming. Robbie tried not to look at him directly. He was sure the man would veer off to the left or right. When he realized the IRA leader was going to pass right by his car he pulled a Webley Mark VI revolver from his jacket pocket. His mind was empty and his hands and body cold. He saw the windshield, the drops of rainwater on its surface, the bodyguard, and the man who had beaten Shannon Dungarvan until she was almost dead.

Robbie threw the door open and it slammed into O'Casey, knocking him to the ground. Then he jumped out and grabbed him by the arm. The bodyguard had drawn a semi-automatic. Using O'Casey as a shield Robbie fired twice and the bodyguard clutched his leg and collapsed in the wet street. Robbie felt O'Casey's hands grasping for his throat and hit him on the side of the head with the Webley. O'Casey sagged and Robbie crammed him into the passenger's seat. Then he ran around to the other side of the car and got in the driver's door.

Men were pouring out of the tavern, trying to figure out where the firing had come from. Robbie started the car and did a sharp U-turn as he spotted fingers pointing. There was the *crack-crack-crack* of gunfire and the banging sound of bullets hitting the trunk. He swerved down a side street to the right and was gone.

There were British army checkpoints at various parts of the city. Robbie avoided them, driving through alleys and across bridges until he parked behind a string of derelict buildings. All the time his gun was on O'Casey, who gradually fought his way back to consciousness. When Robbie came to a stop the Irishman tensed, waiting for the impact of the bullet. There was no shot.

"Get on with it!" snarled O'Casey. "Killing me won't stop Ireland from winning her freedom."

"I don't care if Ireland wins her freedom. My father was always for a season of Home Rule and then full independence."

"So why are you fighting us?"

"You killed my men. You tortured my woman. That's enough reason for any man to fight, isn't it, O'Casey?"

His eyes narrowed and darkened. "The Dungarvan girl. Is that what this is about?"

"I thought of tying you to a lamppost and beating you to death with the butt of this revolver. Or using all the bullets I have left in the gun and then dumping you in the river."

"So what are you going to do?"

Robbie kept the revolver pointed at his head. "Are you a praying man, O'Casey?"

"No. I left God behind with Santa Claus and the leprechauns."

"You can thank God that I am then. And that Shannon Dungarvan is. She didn't want me to harm you. Except for a bump on the head, I haven't. Though I had every intention of executing you for what you have done."

"I'm a patriot."

Robbie thumbed back the hammer on the Webley. "You're a beast, O'Casey! Don't tell me how great your cause is! You don't do what you did to Shannon Dungarvan and have the right to say that anymore! You're just a dirty little killer dressed up as a freedom fighter!" He pressed the barrel between O'Casey's eyes. "It's all the same to your lot. The more important and noble your cause, the more you people feel you have to beat and murder and maim. What

388

are you going to do if you lose the war, O'Casey? Keep on making war on the innocent?"

"I'll fight Britain until the last soldier of King George is off Irish soil."

"That might be a long time if the people of Belfast don't join your country."

"They will."

"What if they don't?" Robbie's eyes flashed and he pushed the barrel into O'Casey's skull. "So help me, I hate your kind. You'll shoot them and bomb them and slaughter them until they do. Am I right?"

"Blood is always shed for liberty."

"So long as it's not your blood."

"Pull the trigger. I don't mind."

"Neither do I."

O'Casey had kept his eyes cold as ice with the barrel cutting into his forehead. But suddenly Robbie's hand began to tremble, and he saw the rage passing in and out of the Englishman's face like clouds scudding over a moon. His eyes opened up in fear. Robbie wrestled with the gun and himself for several moments. Then he placed the hammer down.

"Shannon Dungarvan minds. That's what saves your soul. Someone else somewhere else will kill you. Maybe you'll have made your peace with the God you don't believe in by then."

Robbie kept the revolver on the Irishman. Then he started the car.

"Where are we going?" O'Casey asked, his voice thin.

"Not the graveyard. Your mates are hunting for you on all the approaches to the British and Royal Irish Constabulary bases. But I know this city as well as they do by now. I have a way in they won't be looking for. I'm bringing you back alive, O'Casey. You can rot behind bars. If you win the war the IRA will demand your release and you can come out a hero and the girls will kiss you on the lips. If you're still in a fighting mood by then you can start a new war here or somewhere else. The Russians have a civil war going on. You might want to jump in there with both feet."

"I wouldn't know which side to choose."

"What does it matter to the likes of you?"

O'Casey flared up. "You may not like my methods but I love my country. I'm proud to be standing up for her."

"Is that what you call what you did to Shannon? Standing up for Ireland? She's more of Ireland than you'll ever be, Jack O'Casey. I thank God it's people like her who are the country's future." He pointed the gun at the man's stomach. "Now shut up. We've a bit of a drive ahead of us. And I've been known to change my mind on long drives."

"In the name of our Lord Jesus Christ. Amen."

Sir William raised his head and looked at his wife. She sat beside him in a pew in the manor chapel. Whispering her own amen she opened her eyes but didn't take her clasped hands away from her face. Rain hummed against the panes of stained glass. Sir William stared at the gray color the rain and clouds produced.

"Our second summer at Ashton Park. We really must get away next year."

His wife didn't answer him. She was staring at the large wooden cross over the altar. He leaned back and rested a hand on her back.

"What do you think?" he asked.

She put her clasped hands against her mouth. "All my life I felt it was right that I knew my place. And other people knew theirs. I did not see anything wrong in that. Or anything ungodly. But Victoria has married the man who was our groom and we agreed to the marriage. Kipp has married a French girl and we agreed to that too. It does not seem so very important to me anymore that all our children marry within their class. Perhaps it is enough that Emma and Catherine and Libby have."

"Is that what you felt while you prayed?"

"That. And a number of other things."

"Well. I concur. There seems no good reason to prevent Edward from wedding the woman he loves. If she will still have him."

"Or if he still wants her. Perhaps he really is smitten with Lady Caroline. Heaven knows Kipp was long enough. And there is nothing wrong with her at all or with the Scarborough family. But bringing her into the family now will just wreak havoc with Kipp's marriage to Christelle. I think she still loves him. For all I know she is simply using Edward to get close to Kipp and steal him back. It would be a scandal."

"You don't know that's her intentions, Elizabeth. She may very well love Edward."

"Yes. But both of them wanted to be with someone else. What good can come of a second-best marriage?"

"We need to find out how Edward actually feels about Lady Caroline."

She looked at him. "Haven't we tried? He will not respond to our letters or telegrams and there is no phone line to the hunting lodge yet. Not that he would answer our call if there were one. I'm at my wit's end what to do about the situation."

Sir William cleared his throat and tapped on the back of the pew in front of him with the fingers of one hand. "As we prayed, it came to me I ought to go to her."

"Go to who? Lady Caroline? Edward?"

"Charlotte Squire."

"Charlotte!"

"We have her address, of course. We know the family she serves. It may be she will speak with me."

"And what good would that do?"

He raised his eyebrows. "I don't know. But I was thinking of taking her to Edward."

Lady Elizabeth dropped her hands to her lap. "To Scotland!"

"He hasn't seen her in two years. Who knows? He may find he still loves her. It may change everything for him." He drummed his fingers on the back of the pew again. "I will need to make a few phone calls. Pack a light bag. I can take a ship from Liverpool to the port of Douglas in the morning. What do you say, my dear?"

She gave him a small smile and placed both her hands on his. "If you think it has any chance of healing the rift between us and our eldest son, I say, Godspeed, William."

19

July and August 1920

"Captain Robert Danforth reporting as ordered, sir."

"Very good, Danforth. Stand easy."

The colonel, a tall, lean man with a trim black mustache, got up from behind his desk and extended his hand. "That was a nice bit of work bringing Jack O'Casey in, Danforth. I congratulate you."

Robbie shook the colonel's hand. "Thank you, sir."

"Your promotion to major is effective immediately."

"I'm honored, sir."

"So is your promotion out of this blood-soaked country." The colonel sat back behind his desk. "The IRA will know you're the man to target for O'Casey's abduction in less than seventy-two hours. So you're on a ship tonight headed for Liverpool. That will be your new assignment for the time being. You can expect to see the sights of India or Palestine or Singapore in the new year. Is that satisfactory?"

"Yes, sir, but —"

"But?"

"I'd rather hoped to take Miss Shannon Dungarvan with me. I fear for her safety in Dublin, sir."

"Yes. Miss Dungarvan. More than a fling for you, was it, Danforth?"

"I love her, sir."

"Hm. How much?"

"Very much."

"Enough to marry her?"

"Yes, sir."

"You've thought this through?"

"I have, sir."

"And she'll have you?"

"I hope so, sir."

The colonel drummed his fingers slowly on the desktop. "Does she expect to make a Catholic out of you?"

"That's not important to her, sir. Not after what her countrymen have done to her. And her father and mother."

"I see." The colonel leaned back in his chair. "Is she fit enough to travel?"

"I believe she is, sir."

"Have her here by 1600 hours. Our military chaplain will perform the wedding ceremony. I and Colonel Hotchkiss will stand for you two. The ship sails at 1800. You'll be on it as man and wife. Does that suit you, Danforth?"

Robbie smiled. "Very much, sir."

"Good. We'll see you back here in a few hours then. Dismissed."

Robbie saluted. "I'm grateful, sir."

The colonel got to his feet and returned the salute. "So am I, Danforth. For your service to king and country."

As Robbie half-ran toward the door the colonel called after him. "Oh, and Danforth."

Robbie stopped in his tracks. "Sir?"

"If she wavers at your proposal I shouldn't hesitate to get down on bended knee, if I were you. Politics aside, Ireland has the fairest women I've seen in the Empire, and trust me when I say I've seen a good number of them. Of all those Irish women, Miss Dungarvan is quite easily the most handsome and the most spirited. Don't board that ship tonight as a bachelor, Danforth."

Robbie grinned and saluted again. "No, sir."

"Charlotte?" It was a woman's voice.

"I'm just down here in Lady Thornton's room."

"Come along. There's a gentleman here who wishes to have a word with you."

"A gentleman?"

Charlotte Squire glanced quickly in Lady Thornton's vanity mirror and adjusted her maid's cap, tucking a few loose strands of shining black hair up underneath. Then she left the room and walked briskly down the hall to the staircase. Descending, she could see the front door. A tall man in black coat and top hat with a silver walking stick stood with his back to her, speaking to Lord Thornton. She thought she recognized him by his height and build but could not come up with a name. Lord Thornton spotted her and smiled through his trim red beard and mustache.

"Ah, there she is. The princess of maids."

She smiled as she came up to them. "You are too kind, my lord."

"The truth will out, believe me. Charlotte, I'm sure you remember Sir William Danforth, Member of Parliament for Lancashire? You served in his household briefly."

Sir William turned around. "Miss Squire."

Charlotte's face opened in surprise. "Sir. What . . . what a pleasure to see you again. It's been years."

"Three years. You look well."

"Thank you, sir. I can say the same for

you. I hope the family is in good health."

"Oh, yes. Emma has three young ones now and practically everyone is married off. Ashton Park is quiet — too quiet. Lord Thornton tells me you've enjoyed working here."

"I have. He and Lady Thornton are wonderful and Ramsey is the loveliest town."

"Well, you look splendid, so the manor and the climate must agree with you."

"Thank you, sir."

Sir William coughed into his hand. "Lord Thornton, I wonder if I might have a few words alone with Miss Squire."

Lord Thornton nodded. "Certainly. Barlope here will show you the parlor. After you've finished your business with Charlotte I hope you will join Lady Thornton and me for tea and coffee."

"I'd like nothing better."

Barlope, a craggy man noticeably taller than Sir William, led the way to an oak door he opened on a small room of paintings and mirrors and leather furniture.

"Do you need anything, sir?" he asked.

"Not at all, thank you. We won't be long."

"You may have as much time as you need. After that I will take you to the library."

"Excellent."

The door closed. Sir William placed his

top hat on a chair and leaned his walking stick against the wall. He smiled. "Purely for show, my dear. I get along quite well without it."

Charlotte stood with her hands clasped in front of her. "I'm sure you do, sir."

He bent and pulled back a lace curtain and glanced out a window. "You have a fine view of the harbor here."

"Yes, sir. Lord Thornton has a beautiful yacht. He takes the servants on it every summer. It's quite an outing."

"I'm sure it is. Does he sail the boat himself?"

"He has a crew. But I've seen him haul up and trim the sails right along with the lads. And he insists on manning the wheel."

"Hmm." Sir William straightened and put his hands behind his back. "You wonder why I'm here, I expect. We have had no communication with you all this time."

"I am surprised, sir. I never expected to hear from anyone. I understood your reasons for sending me on to the Thornton estate and I've borne you no ill will. I often told Edward it could not work out but he insisted on maintaining our relationship."

"You have not heard from him?"

"No, sir."

"Not once?"

"No, sir."

"What . . . what are your thoughts concerning him?"

"Excuse me?"

"When you think of Edward — do you think well of him?"

"Of course I do, sir. He always treated me with the utmost respect and kindness. We have gone our separate ways now but I remember him with great fondness and affection."

"What if I told you that the barriers to enjoying a relationship with our son had been removed? That he was free to court you and, if you both wished it, marry you?"

Charlotte's thoughts began to whirl and her mouth chose words independent of her state of mind. "Why, sir, I have heard that Edward is engaged to be married to Lady Caroline Scarborough this summer."

"That's true."

"And I myself have come to an understanding with one of the young men of the yacht crew."

"Has there been a formal engagement?"

"No, sir. Not yet. But he expects to have a ring for me by the fall and declare his intentions to everyone at that time."

"Tell me — forgive me for being so bold — do you love this young man?"

She smiled despite the confusion in her head. "I do. He's very sweet and gentle and treats me like a lady."

"Do you love him more than you loved Edward?"

"I . . . I . . ." Charlotte felt drenched with cold. "Edward and I had an exceptional relationship, Sir William. Something out of a fairy tale. I'll never forget it. Why, he had just survived having two ships go down under him at the Battle of Jutland when we met. It was magical, sir. I don't expect to duplicate that experience with any other man."

Sir William turned back to the window and gazed out at the harbor as he spoke. "Lady Elizabeth and I always thought well of you."

"I know that, sir."

"Over the past few years a number of our children have chosen partners outside of the English nobility. At first, Lady Elizabeth and I resisted. But one after another our sons and daughters won us over. I suppose I could say that God won us over as well. Victoria married Ben Whitecross, who had distinguished himself as a pilot in France. Kipp married a delightful young woman from France. Libby wed an American. In each case Ashton Park and the Danforth name was the richer for it. We saw that God was no respecter of persons and had endowed all sorts of young people with gifts of charm and grace and wit that rivaled and often surpassed that which we had experienced among those of noble birth. I and Lady Elizabeth soon came to the realization you would bless Ashton Park as much as any Kincaid or Fordyce or Rushberry. So that is why I have come. To ask you to return to England and take our son Edward as your husband, 'til death do you part."

"Sir William . . ." Charlotte's tongue and mind stopped working.

He nodded. "Of course it is a great deal to take in. While Lord Thornton does not know the nature of my visit he suspects rightly that I came to ask you to return with me. He thinks for employment. No one can know the truth. Not yet. Not unless you and Edward come to an understanding."

Charlotte did not respond.

"In any case," Sir William went on, "he has invited me to stay over a day, and I told him I would let him know at tea. I do not expect you to give me an answer right now, Miss Squire. But is there any point to my remaining here the night? Might you have an answer for me in the morning?"

"Edward knows nothing of this, does he, sir?"

"He does not. He has been furious with his mother and me since we put an end to your relationship with him and will scarcely speak to us."

"If he loves Lady Scarborough, why would he want me?"

"Because he loved you first. I doubt he has ever forgotten you."

"Would you bring us together then? To see one another? To talk?"

"We would take a ship from the Isle of Man and make our way to Scotland immediately. He has been residing at our hunting lodge in the highlands."

"What if he refuses to see me?"

Sir William shook his head. "Child, if possible, you are more striking than when you lived at Ashton Park. Edward will not refuse to see you."

"Why are you doing this? So many years later? I don't understand."

Lines gathered on Sir William's face. "It is our way of apologizing to you, Miss Squire. Not an easy thing to do. But Lady Elizabeth and I admit we were wrong. We should not have interfered with your relationship with our son. We should have let it take its course. In addition we do not believe Lady

403

Scarborough loves him."

"How can you know that?"

"She was sharply disappointed that Kipp married another woman. We believe Edward, in a state of anger and wishing to hurt us, readily agreed to her proposal that they consider marriage. But she will use it to get close to Kipp once again. We don't believe she cares for Edward . . . and that when he discovers this it will wound him, perhaps fatally."

Charlotte put her fingers to her lips. "You can't mean that."

He shrugged. "You know how volatile Edward is. And unduly sensitive. We thought perhaps if he saw the woman he loves again he might come to his senses."

"I don't even know how I myself would feel if I saw him again, Sir William."

"I understand that. It may be a wild goose chase. It may come to nothing. But Lady Elizabeth and I believed we must try."

Charlotte stared at him a moment longer and shook her head. "You do not need to spend the night, sir. I don't know if I shall regret it in the morning, but I will give you my answer right now."

Lady Elizabeth had her gardening gloves on and was kneeling by a yellow rosebush near the front doors of the manor, when a black cab pulled into the drive. She lifted the brim of her hat to see who it was. Tavy was already walking down the steps to greet the arrival. A man stepped from the car in the uniform of a major in the British army. He was on the far side of the cab helping a woman out of her seat. Lady Elizabeth rose to her feet. The car drove off and Robbie stood smiling at her, his arm around a young woman with a green dress and a green headscarf, whose own smile was quiet and warm.

Lady Elizabeth went quickly to her son, peeling off her gloves, and hugging him. "You didn't call. I had no idea you were coming home."

"I wanted to surprise you. Where's Father?"

"You surprised us so well that he isn't here. He's on a business trip. We hope to see him back in a few days. How long can you stay?"

"Quite a while. I'm posted to Liverpool until January."

She laughed, hugging him again and kissing him on the cheek. "Posted to Liverpool? You mean you're free of that frightful war in Ireland? Oh, I thank God. That's wonderful news."

She pulled back and looked at the woman beside him. "Forgive me. I was so worried. I didn't mean to be rude."

The young woman shook her head. "You weren't rude. You have every reason to celebrate, Lady Elizabeth." She extended her hand. "I am Shannon Dungarvan. Of Dublin. Your son asked that I accompany him to Ashton Park."

Lady Elizabeth took the hand. "I'm very pleased to meet you. Welcome to our home." She looked at her son. "Is there something you should be telling me? I'm sure you didn't meet Miss Dungarvan on the boat."

"No, Mother."

"Is it another surprise? I suppose I can handle any sort of surprise now."

"I hope so. Shannon isn't a Dungarvan this morning. She's a Danforth. Shannon Danforth." Robbie had one arm around Shannon and the other around his mother. "For the past twelve or so hours she's been my wife."

Albert was moving a cast-iron frying pan back and forth over the stove. "I'll have it done in a bit. It's coming up nicely."

Catherine sat at the kitchen table sipping her tea. A thin smile emerged. "That's almost two weeks of breakfasts. Is this still

406

part of your penance? Or are you fattening me up for the kill?"

Albert scowled. "There's no public event coming up where I want you hanging off my arm."

"So it's the penance?"

"I'm no pope. But I think we ought to try and have a marriage again. It's nothing more mysterious than that."

"So bacon and eggs and fried tomatoes should do it?"

"And this morning it's soda bread. I'm trying, Mrs. Moore. I think you're tired of me saying I'm sorry for the affair."

"I am. Sick and tired. The food is better. Though I can't say I trust you yet. Are you sure there isn't some special occasion around the corner?"

"All right. There is. I'm digging a great moat between Belfast and the rest of Ireland. I need your help."

Catherine laughed. "It makes no sense. We almost have a divorce and now you're Sir Galahad."

"I make no peace with you or your father over Home Rule."

"I know that."

Albert came to the table with the pan and scooped a large square of soda bread onto Catherine's plate. "There. That'll go well with butter. My father used to sprinkle sugar on the butter as well."

He placed a square of the bread on his plate next to a fried egg and set the pan down on a folded cloth. Then he took his seat facing Catherine. "That'll do nicely. Shall I pray?"

"It's too much. Really. Don't try so hard. I thought I'd walk out the minute your back was turned. That was long ago. I'm too fat to run out the door now."

"Look. I told you. I've been a fool. Ireland is going up in flames. I'm lucky to have a wife. To have a home. It was like a tomb here all that time you were gone. It was awful. So as sour and short-tempered as I am, I know how to show gratitude. I don't want you becoming a nun and I don't want to be a bachelor. May I pray?"

"Go ahead."

He prayed and they began to eat. Catherine kept her dark eyes on him as he put forkfuls of beans into his mouth. She buttered the soda bread, cut it with her knife and fork, and buttered the edges as well.

"Is it the note?" she asked after a few moments.

"What note?"

"The death note. I saw it, you know. You left it on the chair in your bedroom. Is that what's turned you into Mr. Sweet and Lovely? In case something happens?"

Albert sat back. "I didn't want you to see that. I don't want you to be upset."

"Where was it?"

"In my office. They'd slipped it under the door."

Catherine stopped eating. "You could come out of your building anytime and they might have gunmen waiting in a car."

He shook his head. "No. The Royal Irish Constabulary patrol the docks pretty regularly. In any case, my breakfasts have nothing to do with the note. I only found it on the floor of my office three days ago."

"I know they don't. I'm just having a hard time understanding the change that's come over you."

"Don't think too hard. I'm a complicated man."

"I know that too." Catherine moved her hand, stopped, then moved it all the way across the table and gripped his hand. "I'm still not sure what to make of you, Albert Moore. But I like what you're trying to do. Please be careful. And if you mean everything that you're doing and saying, then promise me something."

"What's that?"

"Promise me. If you mean all this. Don't

even ask what the promise is. Just promise me and I'll tell you."

Albert didn't let go of her hand. "All right. Just to help you on your way. I promise."

"No letters to the editor. Not for the rest of this year."

"Catherine —"

"Not for the rest of the year. It's those that get the IRA worked up. You've made your point a hundred times."

"I'm not afraid of those murderers —"

"You promised."

She thought his anger would burst forth and his face turn into its familiar pattern of white and red patches. But he fought it down and gave her hand a squeeze.

"All right. I won't write another until January. Don't imagine that'll make them forget about me. The nationalists and I have too long a history."

She brought her hand back and used it to sprinkle sugar over the butter on her soda bread. "I like to think the fighting will be over in a few more months."

Albert shook his head and shrugged. "How's the bread? My father's recipe."

"The bread's good." She smiled across at him. "Surprisingly for this house and this marriage, the company is even better."

■ ■ ■ ■

"Where is Harrison today?"

Mrs. Seabrooke looked at Holly as they sat on the veranda at the south side of the manor. Holly bit into a scone and lifted one hand, palm upward.

"You know how punctual he is, Mrs. Seabrooke. If he's not with us for our afternoon tea and stroll then there must be a good reason. I know he was helping young Skitt with the sheep just after lunch."

"I do enjoy his company. I can't say that about very many in this house."

"No? Well, be sure to tell him. It will put some sparkle in his step."

"Isn't it wonderful having Robbie home again? And what a surprise to see him wed! Without a word to his parents or anyone else!"

Holly smiled. "It's delightful. She is such a sweetheart. We really must have tea with her later today."

"I don't know what to make of all her bruises. They say she was roughly handled by the IRA and that's why Robbie married her. To get her out of Ireland."

"She was roughly handled, there's no doubt of that. But Robbie's not the kind to up and marry a woman as a gesture of good will. I'm surprised he's married at all, he's so shy. You may tell the downstairs gossips Miss Holly believes Robbie is deeply in love with Miss Dungarvan and that he has every reason to be deeply in love with her. One day she'll be the toast of England."

Mrs. Seabrooke smiled in a sly way, her eyes smoothing out her face. "I will be sure to tell them exactly that." Suddenly she half-rose from her seat. "Oh, there's Harrison. Running Sir William's dogs."

Holly glanced across the lawn at Gladstone and Wellington, the two blond shepherds. They were chasing sticks Harrison was throwing. Even in the summer heat he still wore his corduroy jacket and fedora.

"I expect he's forgotten about us," said Mrs. Seabrooke, wrinkling her nose.

"I'm sure he'll be along once he's worn out the dogs." Holly sipped at her tea. "I wish I could remember more about him."

"He helped nurse you. It was Libby and Norah and Harrison."

"I know. I've been told that quite a few times."

"There were rumors about you and Mr. Harrison."

"Yes. You've told me."

"I didn't pay any attention to them."

"Wise of you." Holly watched Harrison and the dogs move off into the oak trees by the Castle. "A man and his castle."

"The maids who've cleaned his rooms there say he's neat as a pin. He's quite comfortable in there."

"I wouldn't know."

"One room for books and magazines. Then the bed and chair and desk. A hall that leads into the heart of the Castle itself — it's supposed to be haunted."

"Hm." Holly wiped her hands together briskly to get the crumbs off her fingers. "Perhaps the next time Harrison joins us for coffee and tea we should insist on having it at the Castle keep."

"Heavens, Miss Holly, a gentleman is not going to entertain us in his rooms."

"We could sit just outside if it was a day as pleasant as this one."

Mrs. Seabrooke pointed with her finger. "Oh, now, he's gone and forgotten his stick."

"His stick?"

"You know. The staff he has with him when he goes into the woods. He's left it leaning against that tree."

Holly glanced over at it. "Are you sure that's his?"

"Of course. Who else carries a staff? Todd Turpin doesn't."

Holly squinted. "Doesn't the color seem off to you? And it's rather short."

"Well. There's always been only one staff and only the one person who carries it. Miss Holly. Are you all right?"

Holly was leaning forward in her chair and pressing her fingers to her forehead. "I'm fine . . . don't call anyone . . . just a sudden headache . . . they usually come and go quickly . . . it's all related to the Spanish Flu . . ."

"I can put some water on a cloth —"

"Yes, thank you, just on the back of my neck."

Mrs. Seabrooke poured water from a pitcher onto the cloth in her hand, squeezed it once, and pressed it down gently onto the nape of Holly's neck. Holly continued to lean forward.

"That's very good, Mrs. Seabrooke. That helps."

"I'm glad I could do something."

"These attacks always come . . . when my memory is stirred by something . . . I just don't understand quite yet what it is I'm supposed to be grasping . . . except the front of my head . . ."

"That's a good thing then, isn't it? Perhaps it will come to you, dear, once the headache's gone."

"I . . . I . . ." Holly suddenly sat back up. Mrs. Seabrooke got to her feet to try and keep the wet cloth in place. Holly looked across the grass to where the staff was still leaning against a tree trunk.

"Mrs. Seabrooke," she said. "I have the strongest of impressions that the staff Harrison has left against that tree is mine."

Norah Cole came into the front parlor where Robbie and Shannon were enjoying cups of tea before bed. "There, I've found you two. How are you feeling, Mrs. Danforth?"

Shannon managed a tiny smile. "I'm better. Every now and then since — well, every now and then I get headaches and everything inside acts up. The tea and pleasant company helps." She placed a hand on Robbie's. "Why were you looking for us?"

"I and a few of the others have put the Rose Room to rights as Lady Elizabeth requested. It will be your room for as long as you are at Ashton Park and kept ready for any occasion when you return for a visit."

"Why, thank you, Norah — it is Norah? That's delightful. May we see it now? I should like to lie down and have an early night."

"Tavy has already seen that your luggage was placed there. Please come with me."

They followed her up to the third floor and down a long hall to a room with a massive oak door and cast-iron handle. As Norah prepared to swing open the door she turned to them. "I suppose new is not quite the word to use, is it, Mr. Danforth?"

"It's new to Shannon, at any rate," he replied. "And I haven't played in it since I was eight. We boys broke in and were made to drink castor oil with every meal for three days when they caught us. So we never did it again."

"How old is this room?" asked Shannon as the door swung wide.

"Two hundred years," replied Norah. "Young for England and Ireland. But bits of furniture and whatnot were placed in it from the Castle, including the great bed. Dukes and duchesses have slept in that bed."

"And kings and queens." Robbie smiled. "So we were always told."

The door swung open.

"Oh, my." Shannon's voice was quiet but full. "This is quite a bit more than I expected."

The lamps and candles had been used rather than electric light, and the warm gold color played over high walls painted with red roses twining and intertwining with one another. Oil paintings of red rosebushes were everywhere. As Shannon walked through room after room she saw that someone had placed fresh red roses throughout the suite as well.

"Lady Elizabeth," said Norah, following Shannon's eyes. "She cut and placed them herself. She said to us there had been no time for the two of you to enjoy a honeymoon and we must all pitch in and do our best to make this a bridal suite."

Shannon shook her head. "It's astonishing. I'm overcome. I've never seen anything like this, let alone lived in it. Are we suddenly royalty, Robbie?"

"The gallant answer to that is that you are my queen," he responded. "Which is not so far off the mark."

"Oh, you and your romanticisms."

They came into the bedroom. Candles glowed over the four-poster canopy bed that took up most of the floor space. Each post was carved with roses and leaves, and the canopy and bedding and pillowcases were a rich red. More oils of red roses were on the walls as well as paintings of kings and queens. Shannon put her hands to her mouth.

"We are going to sleep in that?"

Robbie put his arm around her and kissed the scarf that still covered her head. "Sleep, yes."

"Why all these paintings? Isn't that the young Henry VIII? When he was so handsome? And the young Queen Elizabeth?"

"A quick history lesson," said Robbie. "The Danforths were involved in the Wars of the Roses, which went on from about 1455 to 1485. The royal line of Lancaster fought the royal line of York. The Lancaster side had the red rose for their symbol and York had the white. Things seesawed back and forth until finally Henry VII put down the York supporters once and for all. Henry VIII and his daughter Elizabeth I are of the Lancaster line. Legend has it that Henry VII and Henry VIII both tarried at Danforth Castle. And Elizabeth I as well. And other nobles of the Lancaster line. So you sleep among kings and queens tonight when you lie on this bed."

"I can't believe it. I cannot." Shannon turned to Norah. "Has this room never been used then?"

"There are so many rooms at Ashton Park that are never used, Mrs. Danforth. We keep them sealed up for the most part except for special occasions. You and Mr. Danforth are one of those special occasions. This room hasn't been lived in for over a hundred years."

"It smells as sweet as the rose gardens painted over the walls."

"So we've been airing it out and all the windows open. And the fresh roses have been in here all day."

"There are so many hallways off this bedroom."

"To washrooms and wardrobes and sitting rooms, Mrs. Danforth. All sorts of rooms. There's even one where Sir William has arranged some of the most precious relics from the Castle — pikes and swords and suits of armor and carved tables and chairs and tapestries. The tapestries are a wonder. I dusted that room with Harriet and the new girl. We went over every inch. By the time we were done I felt the year was 1485 and if I went out the door I should see the lord of the manor, Henry Danforth, striding down the hallway. And if I stepped onto the lawn there would be knights galloping past on horseback headed for Leicestershire and the Battle of Bosworth Field."

"If it has the same effect on me I doubt I'll ever leave this suite. I could live in these rooms and play the princess for a thousand years."

Robbie pushed back a corner of her scarf and kissed the bright hair growing back underneath. "Why don't we try that?"

20

August 1920

Harrison sat on the edge of his bed in the Castle and tied his boots snugly onto his feet, yanking hard on the laces. He stood and threw on his corduroy jacket and fedora and picked up his staff and headed out the door. The sun was just coloring the sky to the east over the oak trees. Several rooks swooped off the battlements at the top of the keep and rushed past him in the direction of Ashton Park and the ash grove. He followed their flight and thought of the old tree he needed to fell that morning, hoping Skitt had returned the large double-bitted axe to its proper shack in the forest. He wondered what he might carve out of the best of the wood once it was safely down. As he emerged from the oak trees a woman stood in his path, hands on her hips.

"Good day, Harrison."

It was Holly Danforth. She was dressed in

a long brown skirt, khaki blouse, and tweed jacket with a blue scarf tucked into the neck of her blouse. A brown hat identical to Harrison's was on her head with her black hair pinned up underneath it. The only difference was she had small robin feathers tucked into its band, all three of them tinged red. In her hand was a staff.

Harrison took the fedora from his head. "Miss Holly."

She made a face. "Miss Holly, is it?"

"You're up early."

"I've been up early before. Or have you forgotten?"

She approached Harrison, her leather boots treading on the green summer grass. When she reached him she looked up into his face, her blue eyes sharp as the morning light struck them. She gave him her staff to hold.

"I remember everything, Calvert. Everything." She slowly placed her arms around his neck. "Others told me how you cared for me. Now I remember it for myself. Mrs. Seabrooke mentioned the gossip about us before my illness. Now I recall what there was to gossip about. It started with the staff leaning against the tree. The staff you carved for me. Did you leave it against that tree on purpose?"

"I'd forgotten it."

"There seems to be a lot of forgetting still going on. What would you be doing marching about with my staff anyways? You have your own and mine is too short for you."

Harrison did not respond. She gently kissed his ear and whispered, "Did you think it might help? Did you think it might jog my memory?" She brushed her lips lightly over his. "It worked. And now you have another problem to deal with."

Harrison's whole body was catching fire. But he could only stand still and clutch the two staffs for support. He managed to reply. "I don't know what the problem is."

"Of course you do. It's me." She kissed him briefly on the mouth. "And while a lot has come back to me it seems a great deal has left you — what to do with your hands, what to do with your lips, what to say with your words. So we must spend the morning helping you remember. Just as you spent the last few months helping me."

"I . . . there's a tree I must bring down . . . it's dangerous . . ."

"Mm. I like bringing down trees. And a little danger is spice to the soul. Don't you agree?"

"Miss Holly —"

"Hush. It's Holly. And I love you, Calvert.

I intend to marry you even if all the lords and ladies of Britain rise up in arms."

She brought his head down and kissed him with all the strength she could put into her lips and mouth. He dropped the staffs and his arms found their way quickly around her back and pulled her toward him. When the first kiss was finished she smiled and closed her eyes and laid her head on his chest.

"What do you say to that, Calvert?"

One of his hands removed her hat and he pressed his face into her gleaming black hair. "You're the best thing that's happened to me. I thank God you're back. I didn't know if you would ever be all of yourself again . . ."

She didn't say anything. The warmth of his lips and the tears on her hair, she knew, was language enough for both of them. After another minute, it was he who cupped her chin in his large hand and it was he who put his mouth down gently over hers. At that moment everything else that seemed to be missing inside her fell perfectly into place. She let go completely and let him take over, the kisses coming like a sun shower.

Tavy found Lady Elizabeth out with her

rosebushes after a swift rain had made everything sparkle.

"My lady," he said, "Sir William is on the phone for you."

She got to her feet and put a hand on her wide-brimmed hat. "Thank you, Tavy. How did he sound?"

"Cheerful as always, ma'arm."

A maid stood by the phone while the receiver was off the hook and left the parlor as soon as Lady Elizabeth entered. She closed the door behind her.

"William, is that you?"

"It is. I'm calling from Edinburgh. From a private room in a hotel."

"I can hardly hear you. Your voice is so faint."

"Well, I'm picking you up quite well. I won't talk long. You must be wondering what has happened with Charlotte Squire. She is presently in my company and we expect to be at the Lodge tomorrow or the day after."

Lady Elizabeth had been standing as she spoke on the phone. Now she sat down, smiling, and removed her sun hat. "Oh, William, that is such good news."

"Of course there's no telling how Edward will react, but we'll pray and make the best of this opportunity."

"How does Miss Squire feel?"

"Why, she still loves him. She is a bit apprehensive naturally because she doesn't know how he feels about her. But she's willing to talk to him. She's quite a strong young woman, Elizabeth."

"Yes, I know."

"I shared with Lord Thornton very little of what is going on but he's no fool. In any case, he promised that he and his wife would say nothing about their suspicions. He gave me the loan of his personal butler, Barlope, and a maid who is a good friend of Charlotte's, Miss Barrington. They are accompanying us."

She laughed. "You always take such precautions."

"I like to keep my affairs as impeccable as possible. Is all well at your end?"

"Oh, very well. I must tell you quickly that Robbie is home."

"Did you say that Robbie is home?"

"Yes. He has been reposted. He is stationed at Liverpool for the time being. Or he will be once his furlough is over. He is at Ashton Park for a month. And he's Major Robert Danforth now."

"Reposted to Liverpool! A month's leave! Why, the fighting is as bad as it's ever been. How did he manage that?"

"I will have a cable delivered to your address there."

"Tell me now."

"No. Not over the phone. I don't feel comfortable with that. I shall send a telegram as soon as we've hung up. Todd Turpin or Skitt will run it over to the village."

"This is astonishing news. Perhaps it's a good omen for our visit with Edward at the Lodge."

"Wouldn't that be nice? Please give Charlotte the warmest of well wishes from me. God bless you, dear. I will get that cable off to you straightaway."

"Thank you, thank you. I look forward to hearing more about Robbie's situation."

"I'm hanging up now, William. All right? I love you."

WILLIAM
ROBBIE LED A DIFFICULT MISSION. I FIND IT STRANGE TO THINK OF HIM BEING IN SUCH A ROLE. THAT IS WHY HE WAS PROMOTED. IT IS ALSO WHY HE HAS BEEN REPOSTED. HE WOULD NOT GIVE ME ANY DETAILS. I MUST ALSO TELL YOU SOMETHING ELSE. ROBBIE IS MARRIED. SHE IS

A SWEET GIRL AND I ADORE HER.
YOU WILL AS WELL, I AM SURE OF
IT. IT WAS CRITICAL THEY BE
WED BEFORE HE LEFT IRELAND
SO THAT SHE COULD COME
WITH HIM. THAT IS WHY IT WAS
ALL SO SUDDEN. ROBBIE LOVES
HER. AND SHE WORSHIPS HIM.
HAD HE LEFT HER IN DUBLIN IT
WOULD HAVE BEEN HER DEATH.
YOU WILL UNDERSTAND WHEN
WE ALL TALK. I AM PRAYING FOR
YOU AND CHARLOTTE.

ELIZABETH

Norah glanced down from the third-story
window at Robbie and Shannon walking
across the lawn to the ash forest as she
plumped the pillows on their four-poster
bed. She watched as Shannon untied her
scarf. Robbie ran his hand back and forth
over the short blond hairs. They both
laughed and disappeared into the trees.
Norah smiled and bent over to straighten
the bedspread.

"Miss Cole."

The voice made her spin around. She sank
back on the bed and let out a cry. Holly
Danforth stood in the bedroom of red roses
in a white dress and white sun hat. Norah

threw up a hand. Holly came forward quickly and held the hand firmly but gently.

"Don't shout. I'm not here to harm you."

Fear scribbled itself over Norah's face. Holly sat beside her on the bed, and the maid tried to pull her hand free and move away.

"Norah. I know last time I had a gun. I know last time I threatened your life. I remember it all. I'm here to apologize. And I'm here to thank you."

Norah shook her head. "You aren't."

"I am. A great deal has come back to me over the past day or two. It was Harrison's American pistol and I was in your bedroom. I told you I'd kill you if you didn't leave. I walked you out to the road and I sent you on your way." She placed her other hand carefully on Norah's arm. "I also remember you being at my bedside for weeks. Feeding me. Wiping my face with a wet cloth. Helping me sip water." Holly's eyes were the soft blue of a watercolor painting. "I suppose I'm not only here to make amends. I'm here to ask why."

Norah's eyes hunted Holly's face for hints of the coldness and cruelty she knew she was capable of.

"There's no getting around that I said the things I said and did the things I did,"

Norah admitted in a low voice. "I don't understand why I did them and why I wanted to hurt people who had done nothing to harm me — Ben and Mrs. Longstaff and Charlotte. It's the same when it comes to you. I don't understand why I was kind. On the long walk to that village I wanted to murder you. A day later I saw you dying and I wanted to save you."

"You could have put a pillow over my mouth when no one was around."

Norah's face was like rock. "I thought it. I'll not deny it. Had it been the night before I might have done it. I hated you."

"Yet you did nothing to me but feed me and wash my body."

"The first time they left me alone with you I thought I'd whisper in your ear that God had judged you. Then let you cry out for water and do nothing. But I couldn't. I felt like it was God who was watching me. I felt as if He had given me a chance to make up for the wrongs I'd done in this house. That's what went through my mind the first hours I was alone with you. To make things right. Beat the sword into a plowshare like the Good Book says, you know. In my heart was nothing but pity. And a kind of grief that we'd become such enemies that you'd point a gun at me and I'd think of withholding water from you when you were dying. And, of course, I was scared too. I didn't know about your loss of memory. I expected you to recover and to have me turned out of the manor again. And then when you didn't . . . get well, it was all the easier to be kind to you."

Holly was silent. She ran a finger again and again under one of her eyes. Then she leaned over and embraced Norah, kissing her on the cheek and laying her head on her shoulder. Her hat fell to the floor. Moving as if she were made of wood, Norah put an arm slowly and stiffly around Holly's back. With her other hand she began to stroke the black hair pinned up on her head.

"There. It's done now, Miss Holly. We're all done. We can move on. It's a beautiful place is Ashton Park. God has set things right for you and me. A lot of the young people have left but we're still here. We can put some life back in. Holly and Norah. We can do that together. Who'd ever have guessed?"

Edward came around a hedge at the side of the Lodge, past the tall walls of fieldstone and mortar. He had heard a car door slam and the crunch of gravel as the motorcar drove away. There was only a tall figure in a blue cloak and hood standing at the steps that led up to the high wooden door. The person's back was to him but Edward knew immediately who it was. He stood still, trying to grasp what was happening.

She felt someone behind her and turned just as banks of gray mist rolled down off the green hills that surrounded the massive stone building with its numerous chimneys. Edward wore a short black jacket and a kilt with a black and red pattern. Her hood was up because of the damp but it was up for Edward too because she remembered the first time they had kissed at the hut in the rain and the ash trees and she wanted him to remember also. The gray covered them both and hid their faces. Then a breeze broke the mists apart.

"Char," he said.

"You look wonderful, Edward. Every inch the Highlander."

"What are you doing here?"

"I wanted to see you. Your father asked me to come."

"My father?" Lines of anger cut Edward's face. "Why?"

"They think I still love you. And that perhaps you still love me."

"Now? My father brings you here now? I'm to be married in a fortnight."

"And I have an understanding with a young man in Ramsey."

Edward still had not moved. "Then what is the point of us meeting again?"

"Your parents have given us permission to wed. If we wish it."

"After all these years? It's too late."

"It might be. Or it might not."

The anger left his face as if the wind had removed it with the mist. "Do you . . . do you still care for me?"

"I do. Or I wouldn't have come."

"You have feelings? Three years later?"

"I do."

Edward looked around him at the hills as if to clear his head. Then put his gaze back on her. "I can't see your face."

Charlotte paused a moment before pulling her hood back. She saw him react as he took in the blue of her eyes and the line of her face and neck and throat. Her dark hair was loose and about her shoulders, and the breeze moving down from the hilltops began to play with it and swirl it and bring it across her lips and cheeks. She stretched her hands to him.

"Come to me, my love," she whispered.

He crossed the ground between them and took her in his arms and kissed her as if he needed her breath to live.

"I . . . I don't understand," he managed to get out.

"Your parents thought Lady Caroline wanted to marry you — to get back at Kipp — and that you wanted to marry Lady Caroline — to get back at them —"

"I shut you out . . . I smothered my feelings for you — killed them — so it wouldn't hurt anymore . . . but now this . . . I see your face . . ."

He grasped her face in both his hands. Tears flowed from her blue eyes over her skin but she was smiling, almost laughing.

"What is it?" he asked in a worried voice. "Are you all right?"

"I feel so free," she said. "I feel so alive. You're not going to stop, are you? You haven't run out of kisses, have you? Not my Highlander?" She knotted her fingers in his hair and tugged him back into her embrace.

He pressed his face to her hair and cheeks. "It will be a scandal. The Scarboroughs will never forgive us. First Kipp and now me. The father has powerful connections. There will be trouble."

"Your mother and father know that. After we are married they are sending us away. Far from England and the gossips and the Scarboroughs."

"Where?"

"To Canada. To America. Far to the west. Where there are mountains and deserts and animals with the beauty and ferocity of Africa. Just you and I in a vast unleashed wilderness."

"I had forgotten how strong you are. How quick your mind is . . ."

"Shhh. No more compliments. Take me into your castle and dress me in silks and roses and make a lady of me."

Edward suddenly lifted her in his arms. "I shall, Lady Charlotte. How long are you going to make me wait?"

She buried her head against his neck. "Not two minutes. Your parents agreed we could be married here."

"Here? Now?" Edward laughed. "You have everything planned out."

"Your father is parked just down the road. He rang up a Presbyterian minister he knew and asked him to be ready if we needed him. Do we need him?"

Edward swung her about until she shrieked and startled blackbirds swooped off the Lodge's roof in a cloud. "I cannot wait another half hour to make you my wife. I cannot wait ten minutes."

"Try harder," Charlotte laughed. "I think the minister summers in a cottage a hundred miles away."

The minister was only a mile away and came to the Lodge that evening. By a great hearth with a fire crackling red and white, while candles and lamps rested on tables and windowsills, he married Edward Danforth to Charlotte Squire. Barlope stood with Edward and Miss Barrington with Charlotte, and Sir William stood back of the scene, hands by his side, beaming and composing a cable in his mind for his wife. The year-round staff at the Lodge, a dozen servants, were in a semicircle behind him. Large, immaculate stag heads with enormous antlers gazed down on the ceremony with quiet eyes.

"Repeat after me," said the white-haired minister in a voice that rolled about the room and rumbled among crags and burns and woodlands. "I, Edward Danforth, take thee, Charlotte Squire, to be my lawful wedded wife."

Edward, the firelight flickering over his face and over his shining black coat and kilt, repeated the phrase as he took in Charlotte's loveliness. He wanted to add, *You are like a candle, and you push back all my darkness.*

The minister smiled at Charlotte. "Repeat after me, my dear. I, Charlotte Squire, take you, Edward Danforth, to be my lawful wedded husband."

Charlotte faced Edward in a white gown a duchess had worn one evening in the eighteenth century and left behind, a dress stored perfectly by the masters and mistresses of the Lodge so that it shone in the lamplight like a garment newly made. She spoke the words the minister spoke, gazing at Edward, and whispering so that the old minister could not hear, *My lover, my dream, my kiss in the forest and the rain.*

Edward squeezed her right hand and longed to bring it to his lips. "To have and to hold from this day forward, for better or worse, for richer, for poorer, in sickness and in health, to love and to cherish, 'til death do us part, according to God's holy ordinance, and thereto I plight thee my troth."

She repeated the same words to him, adding that she would obey as well as love and cherish him. "And thereto I give thee my troth."

Rings sparkled. Sir William had requested the jewelry of the Lodge be sorted through — *plundered* was the word Edward had jokingly used — until rings that both fit and suited the bride and groom be found.

Edward slipped Charlotte's on her finger as if it had been sized for her at a fine shop in Edinburgh.

"With this ring I thee wed," he told her, "with my body I thee worship, and with all my worldly goods I thee endow. In the name of the Father, and of the Son, and of the Holy Ghost. Amen."

There were no words for the double-ring ceremony Charlotte had insisted on. She pushed the large gold ring fashioned in the 1780s onto Edward's finger and quoted the Book of Ruth from memory: *"Whither thou goest, I will go; and where thou lodgest, I will lodge: thy people shall be my people, and thy God my God."*

"Let us pray," the minister said.

Edward and Charlotte knelt. When the prayer was done the minister brought them to their feet and joined their right hands together again. "Those whom God hath joined together let no man put asunder. Forasmuch as Edward and Charlotte have consented together in holy wedlock, and have witnessed the same before God and this company, and thereto have given and pledged their troth either to other, and have declared the same by giving and receiving of a ring, and by joining hands, I pronounce that they be man and wife together, in the name of the Father, and of the Son, and of the Holy Ghost. Amen."

"A day like this," whispered Charlotte to Edward, *"should never have to end, should it? Can't we make the sun stand still over Gibeon?"*

Edward embraced her. "With your beauty and your spirit, you could."

"Congratulations, my boy."

Sir William and Edward shook hands in front of the fireplace.

"Thank you, Father. I never dreamed when I woke up this morning that I would be returning to my bed with a bride."

Sir William laughed. "Indeed."

"I'll be forever grateful to you and Mum for that."

Sir William put a hand on Edward's shoulder. "I know it's been a harsh season between your mother and me and you, and we take the full blame for that. This may all seem rather plotted and contrived but it had less to do with Lady Caroline than it did with having you marry the woman we believed you still loved. Much has changed for us and our family since the war. Much has changed in the way your mother and I look at England and the circles we move in. We realized it was not right that you be denied the love of a splendid woman like young Charlotte Squire when we had permitted Victoria to wed Ben Whitecross and Kipp to marry Christelle Cevennes. I wish you all the best and the richest possible blessings of God on your marriage. There will be a proper family reception for the two of you once we return to Ashton Park, but for now I hope Mrs. Danforth will find Scotland and the Lodge agreeable."

Charlotte came up and put her arm through Edward's. "I will, Sir William, I will. My head is still spinning from the events of the day, and good Scottish air will set it to rights. I hope we may linger for a day or two."

Sir William smiled and put his hands in his pockets. "Of course. I haven't been up here in years. I should like the opportunity of a stiff hike or two." He glanced at Barlope and Miss Barrington who were standing nearby. "I wonder if Lord Thornton will be able to bear up a few more days without the pair of you."

Barlope inclined his head. "I would dearly love a hunt, Sir William, if that could be arranged."

"A hunt. It can. Naturally it can. I will get off a telegram to Lord Thornton tonight and explain the necessity of your extended absence. Miss Barrington?"

She nodded. "I should like nothing better than to sit out in the heather with a book by Sir Walter Scott, sir. I'm happy to linger, as Lady Danforth suggests."

Charlotte laughed. "Lady Danforth? I carry no title. I'm still good old Charlotte to you, Betty."

Her friend shook her head. "You may still be Charlotte, but things will be different now, my dear. Very different."

Charlotte smiled at Edward. "In a good way, I hope."

Edward held her chin gently with his thumb and finger. "In the best of ways, Charlotte Danforth. I'll make a world for you straight out of Hans Christian Andersen. You'll see."

21
1921

January 1921

January rain lashed the tall library windows. Sir William paused in his comments as he glanced out at a grim dark pierced by the long silver needles. Then he turned back to his family.

"Edward and Charlotte write that they enjoy the snow in the mountains of Alberta more than they enjoy the rain of England." He waved the letter while the others laughed, seated in various places and in various chairs throughout the library. "They admit it is colder but, on the other hand, they can swim outdoors in the thermal springs. And they have recently been taught to ski by a man from Switzerland and to ice skate by a couple who used to live in Quebec. We have set them up in a suite of rooms at a hotel that is built in the Scottish Baronial style. So Edward has not left the Lodge and Scotland far behind, and Charlotte says he is in his element. For which I think we can all thank the Lord, eh?"

Kipp and Robbie and several others clapped.

"But let me turn now to the rest of us. We are all here tonight to say farewell to Robbie and Shannon. I, along with Robbie's mother, and everyone else, am sorry to see them posted out of the country. But we can also take heart that this is not a permanent assignment and that we shall see them back here again at Ashton Park before too long. Do you all have your glasses of hot cider?" Sir William picked his up from a table where Lady Elizabeth was sitting. "To Robbie and Shannon. Cheers and Godspeed!"

Everyone stood and lifted their glasses. "Cheers!" Some called out, "God bless you!"

Robbie and Shannon walked up to Sir William. Robbie shook his father's hand while Shannon gave him a hug and a kiss on the cheek. Shannon wore a silvery white dress that held to her slender figure, a long string of pearls, and a hat with white feathers. Her hair covered her ears and was a lighter blond than it had been before it had been cut. Standing next to her in his uniform Robbie looked at those gathered around him: his mother, Sir Arthur, Lady

Grace, Aunt Holly, Kipp and Christelle, Victoria and Ben, Libby and Michael, Albert and Catherine, Jeremiah and Emma and their three young boys.

"Thank you," he said. "We'll miss you all very much. My rank permits me to bring Shannon along and share lodgings with her and that is an incredible blessing. I must tell you how grateful I am, how grateful we both are, that you accepted her so readily here at Ashton Park. Especially since you had absolutely no idea I'd been married or who I'd gotten married to. She honestly feels like she is one of us now, that she's family, and believe me, that has done her a world of good."

"She's another great Irish asset." Albert bowed toward her. "Shannon and I are the ones God uses to stir the blood of the body Danforth."

Catherine laughed. Everyone but Albert and Shannon were startled at the warmth of the laugh and the sudden gleam of the dark eyes.

"Albert." Catherine grabbed hold of his hand. "Don't carry a good joke too far."

"Who's joking?"

"Well, then it must be the cider."

"Only apples and nutmeg in the cider," said Sir William with a smile. "But an Irish-

444

man doesn't need much to wind himself up. Here or in the House of Commons."

Victoria patted her father's shoulder. "You men want your time in the Nelson Room — Lady Grace insisted we open it up for the first time since at least 1805. It still smells of pipe tobacco even though Norah was after the maids to keep the windows open all last night, regardless of the rain and sleet. The tobacco will not bother any of you, though it would nauseate me now that I'm carrying Ben's son."

Lady Grace crinkled her face in a smile. "You're certain now it's a son, are you?"

"The way it lies, the way it kicks."

Lady Elizabeth sat back in her chair. "You kicked more than the boys."

Victoria shrugged. "Well —"

"August will settle the matter. Now you shouldn't stay up too late, my dear."

"No. And I do want my time in the White Room with the ladies." She clapped her hands. "If you would all sit down I have a song in honor of Robbie's posting. May God be with you and your bride in the Holy City, dear brother."

People took their chairs again and Victoria stood with her back to the storm and her face to her family and the fire roaring at the far end of the library. Ben had lit several

445

lamps while the chatter had gone on, knowing how his wife loved atmosphere, and when she composed herself to sing he turned off the electric lights so that the room settled down into black and gold. Victoria did not look at him, but she smiled and let the music come out of her throat and chest. And up out of her stomach and womb where she rested a hand on her dark dress and on her child.

Last night I lay a-sleeping,
There came a dream so fair,
I stood in old Jerusalem
Beside the temple there.
I heard the children singing,
And ever as they sang,
Methought the voice of angels
From Heav'n in answer rang:
"Jerusalem! Jerusalem!
Lift up your gates and sing,
Hosanna in the highest!
Hosanna to your King!"

And once again the scene was changed,
New earth there seem'd to be
I saw the Holy City
Beside the tideless sea;
The light of God was on its streets,
The gates were open wide,

And all who would might enter,
And no one was denied.

No need of moon or stars by night,
Or sun to shine by day,
It was the new Jerusalem,
That would not pass away.
"Jerusalem! Jerusalem!
Sing, for the night is o'er!
Hosanna in the highest!
Hosanna for evermore!"

Sir William rose to his feet and began to sing the chorus a second time with his daughter. One by one the whole family got to their feet and joined in so that the entire room was filled with the song and the servants heard it thundering through the library door and down the hallway.

"Jerusalem! Jerusalem!
Sing, for the night is o'er!
Hosanna in the highest!
Hosanna for evermore!"

"They did the room over, you see, in about 1799. So that it would resemble an officer's quarters on one of his majesty's ships." Sir William opened the door with a key and flicked a switch for the recently installed lights. The brass and oak jumped into life. Large framed oil paintings of Horatio Nelson in his admiral's uniform and of his famous sea battles hung on the walls. One end of the room had a fireplace and the other a large sheet of wood painted in long black and yellow bands. Large square holes were cut into the yellow wood at regular intervals. Sir William put a hand on Michael's shoulder as the young American gaped. "The paint scheme Nelson favored for his ships. Sir Robert Danforth got that off a real ship of the line that had seen its final battle about 1804. Had it packed up and shipped to Ashton Park. All it's missing are the cannon they used to run through those gun ports, eh?"

Robbie ran his thumb over the brass plaque on the door. "Someone's given this a wipe-down too. It was so tarnished when we were boys no one could read it. Not even Edward the great scholar."

Michael glanced back. "*October 21, 1805.* What's that?"

Kipp shoved him with a grin. "Ignorant Yank. The greatest naval victory of all time. Nelson defeats the combined fleets of the Spanish and French off Cape Trafalgar and stops Napoleon from invading England. Someone always wants to do it, you know."

"Huh. So is this his ship?"

A wooden model with sails and rigging and cannon sat under a dome of well-dusted bright glass on a table in the middle of the room. It had the same paint scheme as the wood at the far end of the room. Sir William bent over the model with Michael and Ben.

"Real sail canvas. Actual iron for the cannons. A figure of Nelson on the quarterdeck. Thomas Danforth did this with one of his sons in the 1850s. Remarkable."

"I've never been in this room," said Ben.

"Neither had we until a few years ago," said Kipp, flopping into a large leather armchair. "I can just imagine what would have happened if we'd managed to jimmy the lock and get our hands on that model of the *Victory*. Penal servitude on some distant island overrun with snakes and spiders and scorpions."

"I think Dad would have had us sent to the Tower of London to rot." Robbie rubbed his hands together. "It's a bit chilly in here. Tavy's had fresh peat placed, so I'll see what I can do." He squatted in front of the fireplace.

"I should like that." Sir Arthur sat down slowly in a chair like Kipp's. "It's the cold and the damp that does you in when you're an elderly Englishman. A sunbaked isle would likely give me another ten years of life."

Kipp laughed. "Oh, you'll get that anyways, Sir Arthur. Keep up your quarreling with Aunt Holly and you'll never die."

"She doesn't fight like she used to. Not since her illness."

"You look very well," Jeremiah chimed in. He was examining an old Bible that lay open on a table in the corner. "This was a naval chaplain's Bible from 1809. Where do people find such things?"

"I bear up well in public," grunted Sir Arthur. "But once I close my bedroom door I sag."

"They said they'd bring along coffee and tea presently." Jeremiah flipped through several pages of the Bible, looking for verses the chaplain had underlined or where he'd put notes in quill-pen handwriting. "And desserts."

"That will help." Albert patted Sir Arthur on the arm. "I need it more than you do."

Sir Arthur slid his eyes over to Albert. "Do you think so?"

"It's a dreek day. A dreek day needs help."

Kipp looked at his father. "So now, what is happening with the other noble families, Father?"

Sir William was bent down next to Robbie. Both were trying to light up the peat.

"What do you mean?" Sir William was pulling the handle that controlled the draft in and out.

"How do the English nobility feel — about the Danforth marriages?"

Robbie was blowing a blue flame to life and Sir William stood up to watch.

"A number of them are fine with the matches. Various lords and ladies congratulate me when I run into them in London." He turned around to look at Kipp and his sons-in-law and Sir Arthur. "There are others, of course. Whenever I cross paths with Lord Scarborough it's only natural there's going to be a confrontation no matter what I do to avoid it. I think they had pretty much forgiven your breaking off the engagement, Kipp, but Edward doing the same thing to Caroline was too much. I'm surprised no blows were landed when he showed up at their estate to inform Lady Caroline and the family in person. But for an act of God they will never relinquish their rage over the double insult of two sons of William Danforth rejecting their only daughter — indeed, their only child. There are those who side with the Scarboroughs against us."

"What are the consequences?" asked Michael. "I mean, what can they do to you realistically?"

Sir William glanced down at the model ship. "They will try to cut us out of noble society altogether. We have not been invited to important balls and receptions. If a family invites us to their home, do you see, they are perceived as siding with us and they risk incurring the wrath and censure of Lord and Lady Scarborough. We are excluded from various weddings and funerals and baptisms." He lifted his head. "We shall weather it, Michael. But that is why it was best to have Edward and Charlotte well clear of England."

"And where is Lady Caroline?" asked Kipp. "Do you know?"

"Spain or Portugal. I'm not positive which. The Scarboroughs have villas in both countries."

Robbie got to his feet and dusted off his uniform, a small fire burning in the grate. "And I've married an Irishwoman from a republican family. That can't help matters."

Sir William looked at his youngest son and put his hands in his pockets. "People will make a noise over anything, Robbie. Shannon is a fine woman. We are not ashamed to bring her in under the Danforth roof."

He glanced at the others. "You've all married fine women. Especially my sons-in-law." They laughed. "It has not been an easy go for my wife and me. We were raised in the old-fashioned way, where parents had as much say or more than their children in who the children married. But God has changed our hearts and inclinations. He is no respecter of persons and shows no favoritism. He would have those who worship Him be as He is. Elizabeth and I have arrived at a place where all our children have married the men and women they loved, and we can only say that it is the Lord's doing and it is marvelous in our eyes. We shall stand by each of you and your children and grandchildren. You need never fear of being without our support."

Ben began to clap. "Hear, hear." The others joined him.

Sir William responded with a slight bow of his head. Then he rubbed his hands together and smiled. "I shall ring Norah for the hot cocoa and coffee that was promised."

The ladies sat in a room of white wallpaper and white furniture, where oil paintings of elegant women in gardens or on horseback were set in white frames. Lady Grace explained to Shannon and Christelle that it had been renovated in the 1870s but rarely used since the beginning of the new century. It was open again at her insistence, just like the Nelson Room.

"All the sealed rooms are opened up twice a year, my dear Victoria," she added as she settled herself into a white chair, chasing away all help with a swish of her cane. "At that time each room is aired and dusted. So you needn't make it sound as if the Nelson Room hasn't seen soap and water since the Battle of Trafalgar."

Victoria smirked. "I apologize, Lady Grace. A slip of the tongue."

"Hm. Up to the same old mischief. Even as a married woman carrying her first child."

Christelle sat next to Victoria on a white sofa with white pillows. "And how is everything with you, *ma soeur,* my sister? Are you still feeling a great deal of the sickness?"

"It comes and it goes, thank you, Chris. I can't abide Ben frying up a pan of bacon, I'll tell you that." She put a hand on her stomach. "The baby reacts. I react."

"But he cooks all the breakfasts for Kipp and Michael."

"Yes. Before they go flying. But no bacon. Not for the past fortnight. I simply can't tolerate the smell of it in the house."

"I'm sorry for the ongoing turmoil in Ireland," Lady Elizabeth said to Shannon. "Sir William had hoped your country might be granted a period of Home Rule decades ago to be followed by full independence. But no one was listening in the Commons or in the Lords."

Norah knocked, wheeled in a cart of coffee, tea, and baked sweets, and left.

Shannon poured herself a coffee and smiled at Lady Elizabeth. "Many would have been satisfied with such an approach. But not all. I don't look forward to news of my homeland while we are in Palestine. This year the fighting will be as bad or worse than the last, and even if the fighting comes to an end I'm certain there will be other conflicts."

"Why do you say that?" demanded Catherine. "Surely enough blood has been shed by now to satisfy even the most violent revolutionaries?"

Shannon drank her coffee. "There are always factions in any country. Even at my parents' home they argued. Sometimes they went too far and my father would have to intervene. The only reason we see so little of it right now is because they are fighting the English. Once that fight is over I'm frightened to think of what might happen next."

"What's this?" Lady Grace looked as if she wanted to bite something. "You think there will be another war after this war is finished?"

"Lady Grace, I'm so sorry." Shannon held her coffee cup in the lap of her white dress, wrapping both hands around it. "I remember the strong opinions. If the present fighting comes to an end in a manner they can all feel good about then I expect there will be peace."

"If." Lady Grace sniffed.

"At least," Lady Elizabeth interrupted, "you will be going to a quiet place for a few years. William and I have talked about visiting the two of you there. We would dearly love to see the Holy City."

"Why, that would be wonderful. Robbie and I would love having you under our roof. What a time we'd have in Jerusalem, the four of us."

The door opened and Emma's face appeared. "Cheers. Am I too late for the party?"

"Jump right in," said Victoria. "How are the three gentlemen?"

Emma helped herself to a small cake, catching the crumbs with one hand while

456

holding the cake with the other. "The three gentlemen of Verona are fast asleep and Aunt Holly is keeping an eye on them. I just peeked in on the men, by the way. What a lovely room with all that brass polished to a gleam and the oak oiled to perfection. They are getting on famously." She glanced at Catherine. "Especially Albert. All his stories. He has the lads roaring. What's gotten into him?"

Catherine sipped her tea. "What d'you mean?"

"Well, honestly, Cath, you two have looked like a couple of rocks on your past visits. If we even got to see the pair of you together. Now you're sitting here with lovely red cheeks and your hair half a foot longer and all black and shining again. Out there in the Nelson Room your husband's the life of the party. What's up? Are you about to be the next couple to have children?"

The red of Catherine's cheeks spread over her face. She ducked her head. "Nothing like that. We've just been enjoying one another more than usual, that's all."

"Even with the fighting in the streets?" cackled Lady Grace.

"The fighting's down south. There's not much in Belfast. A shooting now and then. Not a lot more than that. Bertie has stopped writing letters to the editor and that puts me more at ease."

Libby was seated in a chair next to Catherine. She took her sister's hand and kissed it. "Bertie? And he puts up with it? That's as bad as me calling my man Mikey or Char calling our brother Eddie. I wonder if Christelle calls her man Kipper?"

Everyone laughed and Lady Grace thumped the waxed wooden floor with the end of her cane, causing Lady Elizabeth to scowl.

Libby hugged Catherine as her sister's face colored again. "It doesn't matter. That's wonderful news. Michael says he's been having a great time with Albert's jokes and stories. Seems like you woke something up in that man of yours. Did it take a kiss?"

Catherine smiled. "It took about four dozen cooked breakfasts. And he had to make every one of them. With bacon."

The rain was still slashing down early the next morning when the military car showed up for Robbie and Shannon. Victoria lay in her bed, too ill to get up, and Ben held her hand and sat beside her, but the others stood under their black umbrellas to say goodbye. Since the SPADs could not fly back to London in the bad weather Sir William joined Robbie and Shannon in the car for the ride into Liverpool, where he would catch a train south.

At the dockside, he stood there with a dozen others to see the ship off. It took an hour but finally the troopship began to ease away. Shannon stood beside her husband in the hard rain until finally it drove her inside after a final wave to Sir William. Robbie stayed where he was. Finally, as the ship began to turn, he lifted his hand to his father. Sir William prayed for God's mercy on his son and raised his hand in response. Then it was only the gray stern of the ship and the gray sea and the gray sky.

22

March and April 1921

"It's March first and coming in like a lion." Albert paused with the door to the street half open. The wind tugged at the door, making the doorknob in his hand rattle, and Catherine glimpsed people rushing past with their heads bent and their hands on their heads. "I could open my umbrella and use it as a sail. Fly to work as if I had Ben's or Kipp's SPAD."

Catherine smiled and folded her arms over her chest. "You open that nice umbrella Da bought you in London and it'll end up in Russia in about ten pieces."

"No. No umbrella. Just clutch my hat like everyone else. See you tonight, love."

"You will. God bless you."

"And you."

Albert closed the door behind him and was gone. She lingered a moment, looking at the door, a smile still on her lips, then went to the kitchen to wash up the breakfast dishes. The breakfasts were all cooked by Albert now and were always the fried ones he enjoyed so much. She turned on the tap to fill the sink.

The crash of machine gun fire made her jump. It came again. And again. *Oh, my Lord, it's a killing.* She ran to the door and threw it open. People were crouched behind trashcans and lampposts. A car screamed past. Bodies were sprawled on the sidewalk across the street where the tramcars stopped to pick up passengers. Red was mixing with gray rainwater and pouring over the curb into the gutter. It was where Albert waited for his tram to the docks.

"No!" She ran across the street, ignoring the cars and horses, and fell on her knees next to the first man. She grabbed him by the shoulders and turned him over. The bullets had ripped opened his chest. A torn orange sash drooped over his suit. It was not Albert. The other two were lying face up in the rain with blood pooling crimson under their backs. Neither of them were Albert either. The final man was clutching an umbrella in one hand and his hat in the other. She turned him on his back.

"Cath! Cath! What are you doing here?"

A man's hand was on her shoulder. She

461

looked up and tried to see him through the hair that had plastered itself over her eyes. He dropped down and pulled her roughly into his arms.

"Albert!" she cried, sinking her face into the wet cloth of his suit jacket. "I thought you'd been killed."

"Maybe I should have. Maybe I would have. I slipped into the shop to get a paper to read on the tram."

"They gunned these men down for no reason."

"Sure they had a reason. D'you see they're all four in their Orange Lodge hats and the one had his sash? They killed them because they were Orangemen." He helped her to her feet. "I'll get you back to the house."

"These poor men —"

"They're past our help. Let's go in and get dry and I'll brew you some tea and we'll have a prayer and some talk."

"You have to get to work."

"I'll call in. Tell them what's up and that I'll see them all tomorrow."

"No, you can't —"

"I can. It's better I'm here. The shipyards will not fall apart in one day, will they?"

He got her across the street and through the door just as she began to shudder and great sobs tore through her chest and throat.

Sir William rose to his feet. "Mr. Speaker, the Irish question has been debated in this House for hundreds of years. Yet we have never resolved it. The violence demands we put aside petty agendas and come together across all parties to find a solution. Not in another hundred years. This month. This year. Now, I tell you, now, sir."

Members of Parliament shouted to support him and others shouted to drown him out.

"I have always been a proponent of Home Rule, as this House knows full well. I say this government reaches out with such a proposal this day, this hour, sir. There is not a moment to lose. Every hour more people die — Irish, English, soldiers, civilians. I am certain the IRA are as weary of the bloodletting as we are. Let a reasonable treaty be offered —"

Shouts and cries blotted out his voice. Used to such uproars, Sir William remained standing, his face showing neither frustration nor contempt, and waited calmly for the noise to subside.

"Let a treaty be offered that is good for Britain and good for Ireland. It may be that

463

men like Michael Collins will put their pen to it. It may be it will silence the guns. It is scarcely two years since the cannon of the Western Front ceased their rage and their bellowing. Are we to have another war that lasts until hundreds of thousands are dead and the calendar on the wall tells us it is nineteen-twenty-three or nineteen-twenty-four or nineteen-twenty-five? Is that what the people of England who put you in these seats want? Hm? I think not."

Again the roar. Again the tumult. Sir William remained where he was, his back straight.

"Mr. Speaker. I will close on a personal note. Last week gunmen shot a group of Orangemen waiting for the tram in Belfast. Many of you will remember reading of the incident. Terrible. What the members of the House of Commons do not know is my daughter's husband was waiting at that stop. The only thing that saved him, by the grace of God, was that he went into a store to buy a newspaper. The gunmen opened fire while he was in the shop. When he came out he found my daughter had rushed across the street from their house and was kneeling over the dead bodies, certain he was one of them. Can you imagine, sir, her shock? Can you imagine, those of you who are fathers, my daughter's pain? This has slashed me to the bone like a saber. I could be standing here telling you her husband was murdered. I could be standing here telling you the gunmen came back and shot her."

The House grew silent.

"I have nothing more to add, Mr. Speaker. Mothers and fathers in Britain and Ireland are weeping over their dead today and many more will do so tomorrow. We must have peace."

Sir William:

I was in the Visitors' Gallery at the Commons yesterday. It was a powerful speech. I must see you on a matter of some urgency. May I meet you at your flat tomorrow at five?

Sincerely,
Lord Francis Scarborough

Sir William had a small suite of rooms he used during the week when the House was sitting. He kept it clean and neat, an easy task since the furnishings were spare and he always ate out. Brewing a cup of tea, he checked his pocket watch. It was just after five. He poured the tea into a cup and was lifting it to his mouth when there was a knock at the door. He opened it and Lord Scarborough, a tall, heavy man with a ginger beard and mustache came quickly into the room, his cloak swirling about him, a heavy silver-tipped walking stick in one large hand. He did not take Sir William's hand.

"Sir William." His voice was deep. "I thank you for seeing me on such short notice. This could not wait."

"Of course. Will you join me in a cup of tea?"

"I cannot. You will wonder I did not bring this matter up with you some time ago. Truthfully, I was not altogether confident I could control my temper."

Sir William set down his cup and put his hands in his pockets. "And now you are?"

"No. Not completely. But we must talk."

"Very well."

"Let us get right to the point, Sir William. I sent my daughter to Portugal because she was certain she was with child. After several months there this was confirmed. She went into labor yesterday. During the night she gave birth to a son. Her mother is with her."

"You have a grandchild. Wonderful."

"Yes. I have a grandchild. And so do you."

"I beg your pardon?"

"The boy is Edward's son. Caroline admitted it several months ago, though she

466

would not tell us at first."

Sir William stared. "I cannot believe it."

"You will recall we visited Edward at the Lodge in Scotland last summer. Before he broke off the engagement. It happened at that time. He came to her room in the middle of the night and took advantage of her."

"I have heard nothing of this from him."

"Of course not."

Sir William shook his head. "It is not like Edward to do such a thing. I must write him and hear his side of the story."

Lord Scarborough's face darkened. "Yes. Write the monster. Write the coward. You have him safely away from my hands in Canada."

Sir William's eyes hardened. "I do not care for those words. This is my son you are talking about."

"And it is my daughter who has been so ill used by your family. I cannot seize Edward by the throat. But I will get my satisfaction from his father. Oh, yes, I will get it, Sir William."

"Your satisfaction? What are you proposing?"

"A duel. I will have a duel to satisfy my family's honor."

"A duel! Are you mad? There hasn't been

a duel in Britain for over fifty years. They'd throw us in jail."

"*I* would be thrown in jail. *You* would be thrown in the grave. I don't mind a few months of jail time to avenge this desecration of my daughter's innocence." He smacked the head of his walking stick into his palm. "The coward you raised will not fight. He runs and hides like a cur. So the father must fight for him. Or will you also whimper and whine and flee like a Danforth dog?"

Sir William's hands came out of his pockets. "Control your tongue."

"Or what? I am the injured party here. I will speak as I please."

"Killing me will not help your daughter. And you will be in jail a lot longer than a few months."

"I am sure a good argument can be made for my acting out of character due to the nature of the situation."

"I will not fight you, Scarborough. I am a Christian man."

Lord Scarborough barked a laugh. "A Christian man. Like your Christian son? There isn't a shred of Christianity in your family. You might as well be a pack of jackals or a swarm of hyenas in heat."

Sir William slapped him across the face. A

thin trickle of blood came from Lord Scarborough's nose. He did not lash back with his walking stick. Instead a great smile appeared inside his mustache and beard.

"Now I will have satisfaction. Oh, I will have it. If you will not face me I will stalk your daughters and their husbands. I will send men to harass and frighten them. I know about the silly airplanes just outside of London here. I will have them torched. Oh, I will make life miserable for you, Danforth. Unless you face me. If you do, no harm will befall your house. If you do not, I will do everything in my power to break you. Even if I am broken in the process. I swear it."

"Edward could not have done this to your daughter."

"Are you prepared to meet with my second?"

"He could not have done it, I tell you."

"He has done it. The child is mewling and puking in my daughter's arms as we speak. Are you prepared to meet with my second? Are you prepared to choose a second for yourself? The choice of weapons is yours."

"Scarborough —"

"I will not relent on this, Danforth. I will not. You dogs must be put in your place. I will send my second to this flat tomorrow at seven before the House sits. He will tell you where and when the duel will occur. You must tell him what weapons you favor. Make sure they are fit for a gentleman. When you have your second appointed you may have him arrange a meeting with mine to be sure everything is as it should be." He opened the door and glanced back. "I will crush you, Danforth. Make out your will and ensure that everything is in order for your poor wife. There will be no mercy on my part and no intention of wounding. I will kill you, Danforth. Whether it is swords or pistols. I will tear the heart right out of you."

Sir William was not able to sleep. He read his Bible, prayed on his knees by his bed, paced, and made tea. Finally he collapsed in his leather armchair and fell into a doze about four o'clock. At seven a knock at the door woke him. When he opened it a man in top hat and a dark coat asked to come in.

"I am Henry Bishop. I will be Lord Scarborough's second. Have you given any thought to who your second will be, sir?"

"I have not. Would you care to have a seat, Mr. Bishop? Can I brew you a cup of tea?"

"No, thank you. I am here strictly on business."

"Business? It's madness. I have made up my mind to go to the authorities after I see you gone."

"Ah. That would be a mistake, sir. Lord Scarborough thought you might be inclined in that direction, and I must inform you that actions have been taken against the South England Air Service your son and sons-in-law own and manage."

Sir William's face whitened. "What? Have you harmed them?"

"No one has been harmed, sir. A petrol tank was set on fire and it exploded with no one near. In addition, one of the aircraft was damaged and will require moderate repair."

"You rogues!"

Bishop's face and body were stiff. "It is a matter of honor, Sir William. Something very important to Lord Scarborough and something that ought to be important to you as well. Certainly it is important to our king and country and empire. If you avoid Scotland Yard and carry through on your agreement to meet Lord Scarborough nothing further shall happen to your family, even after your death. But if you renege, the wrath my lord visits upon your sons and

471

daughters will be terrible. May I take it you wish to be a man of your word and face Lord Scarborough on the field of honor?"

Sir William stared at Bishop a moment and rubbed his hands over his face. "Yes, yes."

Bishop brought a folded sheet of paper out of his coat pocket and opened it. "Here is a map with precise directions. You take the main road east out of London here —" he tapped the map "— and at an inn called Old Fellows you turn south. Eventually the road becomes no more than a wagon track and peters out altogether. There is an orchard of wild apple trees a hundred yards ahead. The trees are situated on the banks of a small stream, the Strunk." He looked up. "Dawn on Saturday, April ninth, sir. A little over a week from now."

Sir William took the paper and ran a hand over his uncombed brown hair. "I know Old Fellows."

"Have you given a thought to your choice of weapons, sir?"

"I have not. But it comes to mind I have a brace of pistols in silver and ivory my father left me."

"Are they in any sort of condition to be fired? Are there cartridges?"

"I and my second will make sure the

revolvers are in working condition. And that the cartridges I have in storage are usable."

"I shall test fire both pistols, of course, sir, before the duel commences."

"Naturally."

"How many rounds can each revolver hold?" asked Bishop.

"Six."

"That is well. You appreciate Lord Scarborough sees this as a duel to the death? That he will keep on firing until you are down? That he will go so far as to administer a *coup de grace* if you are wounded and not dead?"

A flash lit Sir William's eyes. "You take a great deal for granted, sir. Suppose it is Lord Scarborough who is lying wounded on the ground? Would it please you if I stood over him and finished him off with a bullet to the head?"

Bishop's smile was thin and laced with ice. "Lord Scarborough was the crack pistol shot of his regiment in the Boer War, sir. The best you can hope for is a swift death and a bullet to the heart. An honorable end. It will appease Lord Scarborough. He has in mind to see your wife receives annual stipends. Anonymous, of course." Bishop tipped his hat. "I should like to meet with your second on Friday, April eighth, at Tollers. Four in the afternoon. I shall be wearing a white rose in my lapel. That is how he will know me."

Sir William stood staring at the closed door after Bishop had left. He began to compose a telegram to Harrison in his head.

"Hello, my boy, how are you?"

"Is that you, Father? The connection isn't much good."

"I'll speak up. How are things at the airfield?"

Sir William could hear Kipp's voice tighten up over the phone. "We've had a run of bad luck. A fuel tank burst the other night, and the next day one of our SPAD S.XXs was vandalized. Someone tore great holes in the wings. It'll be out of service for a week and we'll lose more than a thousand pounds in fees."

"Do the police have any leads as to the identity of the perpetrators?"

"Not at all."

"What steps have you taken?"

"Ben hired on two chums from his army days that he swears by. They're tough Lancashire lads, actually, and so far have proved utterly reliable. One has the twelve-hour day and the other the twelve hour night. They'll switch over every two weeks. I

474

doubt much will get past them."

"I'm glad to hear it. Everyone is all right?"

"We are. No one was injured by the blast. The lot of us were safe and sound in our beds in the village. Though the sound did wake us. We thought it was some sort of army thing."

"How's our Victoria feeling?"

"She still has her moments. Ben was thinking she'd do better at home with mum around. Emma's talked about heading down to Ashton Park with her boys and taking care of Vic."

"I wonder if that might not be best. It's very good that you look after one another. After all, your mother and I won't be around forever."

"What's that? Are you doing all right, Dad?"

"I'm fine. Must get ready for the House now. Give my love to everyone. I'll ring you up again in a few days."

"Splendid. We'll talk to you then. God bless, Dad."

"Yes. God bless, my boy."

Harrison arrived at Sir William's flat on Wednesday, April sixth. He had driven the London car out of its garage and parked it on the street. The revolvers were in his luggage. They nestled side by side in a wooden case with blue velvet under them. The case bore a seal with an eagle on it. Sir William opened it and took one revolver out. Turning it over in his hand he admired the engraving on the cylinder and frame. He sniffed the long barrel.

"How many rounds did you fire?" he asked.

"Six from each, sir."

"How was their accuracy?"

"Spot on. If you aim a tad low."

"Does anyone know you brought the guns down?"

"I don't know about bringing them down. Holly was there when I test fired the pair in the woods."

Sir William's eyes darkened. "How is it that she was there? I told you no one must know about this."

"She pops up everywhere, sir. There's not much I can say, is there? Seeing as she's your sister and I'm the hired man."

Sir William let out a lungful of air. "Quite. I apologize. I gather she is fond of you for helping nurse her back to health."

"Yes, sir."

"How many cartridges did you bring with you?"

"Two boxes of twenty." Harrison finally

removed his hat. "I'd like to know what this is all about, sir. If I may."

Sir William sat down in his armchair with the silver revolver still in his hands. "Have a seat. Tea?"

"I'll brew some up in a minute, sir."

"It comes down to this, Harrison. The Scarboroughs claim Edward lay with their daughter and that now she has borne his son."

"What! Edward?"

"It is what they claim. I do not believe their daughter's story. But there's no point in drawing Edward into the dispute at this point. It will change nothing. So long as Lady Caroline says the boy is his the Scarboroughs will believe her, not Edward."

Harrison stared at Sir William and turned his hat over in his hands. "Is Lord Scarborough insisting on a duel then? Is that what this is about?"

"Yes."

"With pistols at twenty paces?"

"Something like that."

"Why, he's living a hundred years in the past. No one duels anymore."

"I expect he *is* living in eighteen-twenty-one rather than nineteen-twenty-one, Harrison. But if I do not go through with this he will blow up more fuel tanks and tear up more airplanes. And heaven knows what else."

"D'you mean he's responsible for all of that?"

"He swears to do more of it. And worse if I do not meet him on his field of honor as he calls it." Sir William fished the sheet of paper Bishop had given him out of his pocket and handed it to Harrison. "That's the place."

Harrison scanned the map. "Old Fellows. Wild apple trees. The Strunk." He glanced up. "I take it I am your second."

"If you accept."

"Of course I accept, sir. I'd not let you down when we're dealing with the likes of this."

"Thank you, Harrison. If the police lay charges you'll be considered an accessory, you understand."

"I don't care, Sir William. Am I to meet the other second before the date indicated on this map?"

"You'll meet on the eighth. At Tollers'. High tea at four in the afternoon. He'll be wearing a white rose." He leaned back in his armchair. "How are things at home?"

"Fine enough. Victoria came up the other day from the London airfield. Ben flew her. She's less ill in the air than she is on the ground. Emma's down to Ashton Park with James and Peter and young Billy. She's taken Victoria under her wing." He suddenly smiled. "The boys have the run of the estate, with Holly and Norah in hot pursuit."

Sir William thought of his grandsons and smiled too. "What of Lady Elizabeth?"

Harrison clicked his tongue. "She knows something's up. She's no fool. You'd best call her."

Sir William nodded. "I'll do that straightaway."

"Goodbye then, my dear. All the best." Lady Elizabeth placed the receiver back on its hook and gazed at it a few moments.

Tavy poked his head into the parlor. "Can I fetch you a pot of tea, ma'arm?"

Lady Elizabeth looked up. "Tavy. Why, yes. That would be lovely."

"Everything all right with Sir William, ma'arm?"

"Sir William? Yes . . . oh, yes. He and Harrison are getting along fabulously in London."

Tavy disappeared, shutting the parlor door. Lady Elizabeth looked out the window at Holly playing tag with Emma's boys and the two dogs.

Her husband had been pleasant enough. Their conversation had been amiable. But why was Harrison needed down there? To serve as his chauffeur for some pressing engagement? That sounded reasonable enough. Still — something was not quite right in the tone of his voice. Perhaps it was the connection. Perhaps it was her, fretting so much over Victoria's health. And yet Holly had mentioned she'd been with Harrison while he test fired several guns off in the woods.

Rifles? Shotguns? she'd asked.

Revolvers, Holly had told her. *Silver ones with ivory handles.*

His father's pistols? From the American president? Why would Harrison be firing those? To my knowledge they've never been used.

I don't know, Elizabeth. But I fired one of them myself. Lovely things. If they weren't so deadly.

23

April 1921

Harrison woke Sir William in the dark of April ninth with a cup of coffee in his hand. They drank together without turning on any lights, saying nothing. Sir William finally switched on a lamp and read Psalm 23 from the Bible he always kept in his flat. Then the two of them knelt and prayed.

They left in plenty of time. There was no hint of sun in the east. Clouds and stars moved around one another in the early morning sky.

"My will is in order and is with Crofton and Bentley along with all my other legal papers," Sir William said as they drove past buildings and shops lit by the glow of street-lamps.

"Yes, sir."

"I know you will look to Lady Elizabeth's needs if anything should happen to me today."

"I will, sir."

"And you'll take Gladstone and Wellington into the Castle with you and care for them?"

"Yes."

"And my grandsons — ?"

"Sir. Nothing will be left undone. No one forgotten. But, if I may say, sir, I believe you are being a bit premature. Lord Scarborough could back out."

"I hardly think so."

"You were a gold-medal champion three times, sir, and won high silver twice."

"That was a long time ago."

"I showed Bishop the medals. Shook them in his face. Engraved with your name and all. Top shot in the British Empire."

Sir William glanced at Harrison sharply. "You did not."

"I did, sir. That wiped the sneer off his face, I tell you. I couldn't abide his cockiness a moment longer."

"It's good of you to try and avert this confrontation, Harrison. But Lord Scarborough would not step back now if King George himself threatened to take off his head. I must see it through."

"Perhaps you will knock him down first shot, sir. And that will be that."

Sir William glanced at a dog wandering by itself along the street. "My feeling about

Lord Scarborough is that if I wound him he will recover and demand a rematch in July or August. And if I wound him a second time he will challenge me again in October or November. And so on through nineteen-twenty-two and on. Until one of us falls never to rise again. I fear there can be no happy ending to this affair, Harrison."

Victoria tossed and turned and finally sat up. The room that had been hers when she was single was completely dark but she could see Emma asleep in a chair on the other side of the room — she wore a light-colored dress that seemed to glow in the blackness. Victoria reached out for a glass of water on her bedside table, missed, and knocked it to the floor, where the glass broke apart with a sharp crack.

Emma's head jerked up. "What is it, Vic? What's wrong?"

"I just . . . I don't know . . ."

Emma turned on the lamp by her chair and came to her sister's side. The dark rings under her eyes and the sweat on her face made Emma put a hand to her cheek and the side of her neck.

"You're on fire." Emma filled another glass from a pitcher, careful not to step on the sharp pieces under her feet. "Here.

Drink this."

Victoria sipped at it, Emma's hand behind her head. Then Emma let her sink back onto the bed.

"I can't . . ." Victoria gasped. "It makes me sick to my stomach . . ."

"You have to be able to keep down water. You can't live without water."

Victoria shook her head.

"This is not right, Vic. I was never like this with the twins or with Billy."

"I don't know how I can bear another four months, Em."

"I'm going to ring up Dr. Pittmeadow."

"What good will that do? There's nothing he can give me." She grasped her sister's hand. "Lie here. Tell me a story. Pray. Anything. Just don't leave me alone in the dark."

Emma crawled onto the bed and took her sister into her arms. "It will be dawn soon enough. I shall throw open the curtains once the sun is up and flood this room with light." She smoothed her sister's hair, which clung in damp strands to her skin and the pillow. "There was a young woman named Esther, beautiful like you, beautiful as the seven colors of daybreak, but no one knew of her beauty until one day a messenger from the king spotted her drawing water from a well."

Bishop fired the second revolver at an apple tree fifty feet away. The bullet entered the trunk just below a large bole. He grunted and handed the gun to Lord Scarborough.

"It shoots slightly low, my lord, as Sir William advised. But it is dead-entered. There are five more shots. Both revolvers have five cartridges."

Lord Scarborough felt the weight of the revolver, turning it over and tossing it in his hand. "A pleasant balance. Even with the long barrel — what is it, seven, eight inches? What did you say this was called, Danforth?"

Sir William stood nearby in the semidarkness, the other revolver in his left hand, the barrel resting along his pant leg. "It is a Samuel Colt invention, Lord Scarborough. 1873. The Single-Action Army. It is a forty-five caliber cartridge."

"How did your father come by this matched set again — Roosevelt, you said?"

"He was asked to be part of a group from Her Majesty's government that traveled to the United States. He got along well with the president, Theodore Roosevelt, and was asked to join a hunting expedition. This was a gift from the president."

"I wish I'd had this at Mafeking during the Boer War." He tossed it in his hand once more and glanced at Sir William. "I'm sorry we must use them on each other."

"We need not."

"Blood for blood, Danforth. I cannot forgive what your son has done. Look to yourself."

A morning wind moved the young leaves on the wild apple trees back and forth. The east glowed silver. Bishop opened the lid on his watch.

"Ten minutes," he announced. "Conditions will improve rapidly. Please prepare yourselves. Once again, I will count out twenty paces. When I am finished you are free to turn and fire. Lord Scarborough has indicated he will not cease firing until his opponent is dead. What are your intentions, Sir William?"

"I shall match Lord Scarborough shot for shot."

Sir William listened to the birds waking up and calling to each other and to the sky. The Strunk was not a swift stream, yet he heard its slow passage between the banks clearly — the gurgling, the splashes . . . he even heard the rise of fish.

"Gentlemen." Bishop's face gleamed amber and gold. "I'll ask you to stand by me here. Sir William, if you would face south, Lord Scarborough, if you would look to the north, please."

Sir William clapped Harrison on the shoulder. "There it is. Thank you for your help in all this. If things should go ill for me, care for my family and Ashton Park in the same noble fashion you always have."

"I will, sir."

Sir William walked up to Bishop. Lord Scarborough gave him a slight bow and Sir William returned the bow. Then they stood back to back. Sun broke over apple orchard and stream and the fields of bright-green grass.

"We have dawn," said Bishop crisply. "I begin the count. Do not turn and fire until I reach twenty, if you please. One. Two. Three. Four. Five."

The two men began to stride away from each other, each holding their revolver up at their chest, one finger on the trigger guard.

"Eleven. Twelve. Thirteen."

The sun shone on the left side of Sir William's face. The warmth felt unusually strong to him and the light unusually bright. There was nothing in his mind but the steps he was taking, the scent of damp grass, the roll of the stream, and the gun at his chest.

"Eighteen. Nineteen. Twenty."

Lord Scarborough wheeled and fired, his right arm extended, holding the gun. Sir William turned and felt air move past his head. Lord Scarborough fired a second shot. Bark flew into Sir William's face from a tree trunk on his left. Then he lifted his hand as if he were a machine, seeing only Lord Scarborough's figure, and fired three quick shots, thumbing back the hammer automatically each time. One shot clipped the shoulder of Lord Scarborough's gun arm and made him flinch. The second made him clap a hand to his ear, his right hand still holding the revolver as he slapped it to his head. The third shot threw him back five or six feet, hurling him to the ground. Sir William kept his gun on Lord Scarborough and waited for him to rise. But he did not move.

Bishop knelt by Lord Scarborough's body. "God help us. You've killed him."

Sir William's eyes changed and he seemed to come out of a trance. Dropping his revolver he ran to his opponent's side along with Harrison.

"No. He's breathing yet." Sir William tore off the coat and shirtsleeve to look at the wound high on Lord Scarborough's right shoulder. "The bullet went clear through. But there is dirt and fabric in the hole. And we must stop the blood." He whipped the tie from his neck and tied it as tightly as he could on the shoulder above the wound. "We must get him to the nearest hospital immediately."

The three men half-carried and half-dragged Lord Scarborough's heavy body to the car he and Bishop had been using. They laid him in the backseat but had to bend his legs to make him fit.

"We will follow you." Sir William took off his jacket and put it over Lord Scarborough's chest and stomach. "Drive as swiftly as you can."

"No." Lord Scarborough raised his head, breathing heavily. "It was a shooting accident . . . my shooting accident. You were not involved, Danforth. Or your man there. That is my story . . . and true enough as it goes."

"We must help you —" Sir William protested.

"You have done enough." Lord Scarborough gritted his teeth in pain. "If I want you at the hospital I shall have Bishop ring you . . . now leave us."

"I cannot."

"Leave us." Lord Scarborough was still gripping the revolver and he pointed it at Sir William's stomach. "I will have my honor, Danforth."

"Tavy! Tavy!" Emma flew down the hallway. "Mama! Holly! Norah! Victoria's bleeding — her bedsheets are covered in blood!"

Norah and Tavy were already up and in their uniforms. Tavy phoned the physician and Norah ran to the room with an armload of towels. Holly arrived a moment later in her dressing gown and started placing the towels between Victoria's legs to staunch the flow of blood. Norah was out and back again with clean blankets, which she placed over Victoria after removing the ones streaked red. Lady Elizabeth rushed in, hair askew and dressing gown barely tied.

"What is it?" She looked at Victoria's chalk-white face. "What's wrong?"

"She's having a miscarriage." Blood spattered Holly's face. "We must get the baby out for both their sakes."

"That is something for the doctor to do."

"We don't have time to wait for the doctor! Help me or we will lose them both!" Holly looked around her. "Norah. Get down here and keep her legs apart. I must get my hands up there. Elizabeth. Come here."

"Is she breathing — ?"

"Yes. She is unconscious but she is breathing. Get down here beside me and Norah.

If we work together we can save them. Now, Elizabeth."

Sir William and Harrison drove to the hospital as soon as Bishop phoned them. He met them in the hall outside Lord Scarborough's room.

"How is he?" asked Sir William.

"They are going to remove his right arm at the shoulder."

"What?"

"There is too much damage. He wanted to speak with you. Harrison and I will wait out here."

Sir William stepped into the room. The curtains were drawn. Lord Scarborough turned his head as he lay on the bed.

"Danforth?" The voice was weak.

"Lord Scarborough."

"Take my hand, sir."

Sir William gripped Lord Scarborough's good hand.

"I have my honor, Danforth. We . . . fought well . . . jousted with our lances. I lose my arm . . . for my daughter . . . I do not mind that. If I should die after the amputation . . . honor is all I have left to meet my God with."

"Christ's sacrifice is sufficient for your soul. Take that with you instead."

Lord Scarborough grimaced through his beard. "Are you preaching . . . Danforth?"

"Sound advice. From one Englishman to another."

"Danforth." His voice became a rough whisper. "We need not have fought. A telegram reached me from Portugal . . . last night. Caroline said she was . . . acting out of spite. It was not Edward . . . it was the head groundskeeper at the Lodge."

Sir William went rigid. "What? Buchanan?"

"Steady, Danforth. The issue at hand is . . . I should have called off the duel as soon as I received . . . this news. Should have rung you at your flat. I did not. I cannot tell you why . . . I don't know why. So I am judged for my treachery. Can your Jesus cover that?"

"His love fills the universe and the entire world of men."

"Well. I would rather stay . . . and find out if that is true. I may not . . . have that choice. Will you pray for me, Sir William?"

"I will. I will, Lord Scarborough. God have mercy on you. On us both."

"She will live." Dr. Pittmeadow looked down at Victoria as she slept. Color had slowly begun to return to her cheeks and face. He glanced at Lady Elizabeth, who was slumped in a chair by the bed, holding her daughter's hand. "She will be able to give birth to another child."

She did not raise her eyes to his. "Are you sure?"

"I am. I have, unfortunately, seen a great deal of this over the years. She has not been damaged physically, Lady Elizabeth. It will be her emotional scars that need healing. Have you contacted her husband?"

"Ben is coming up by aircraft. He's in the air now. We will see him in less than an hour."

"I am glad to hear it. That will help enormously." He checked his watch. "See that you give her coffee with plenty of sugar. Tea with honey. Sweet biscuits. Oatmeal with dark cane sugar and cream. As much as she will take. I will come by again this evening to check on her."

Holly had been standing in a corner of the room. She followed him into the hall. "Thank you, Doctor."

"You did the saving, Miss Holly. If you'd waited for me it would have been a far worse day than it has already been." He began to walk toward the staircase. "Where will you . . . ah . . . bury the boy?"

Holly kept pace beside him. "The grave

will be just by the chapel. Generations of Danforths have been buried under the ash trees there. The Church consecrated the ground in the eleventh century."

"Yes, of course. I expect the little one will be under the earth by the time I return tonight?"

"Yes, Doctor. We're just waiting on the father, Ben Whitecross."

Sir William hung up the phone in his flat. His face was bleak. "My daughter has lost her baby."

Harrison stood up from his chair. "I'm so sorry, sir. So sorry."

"It was a boy."

"I don't know what to say, sir."

Sir William sank into his seat, staring at the door. "She's pulled through. The doctor said she can still bear children."

"I'm glad to hear it."

Sir William lifted his left hand and looked at it. "Do you believe in God's judgment, Harrison?"

"Why . . . I do, sir . . . though I don't like to dwell on it —"

"How do I know He did not slay my fourth grandson because I shot Lord Scarborough?"

"Ah, no, sir. Scarborough himself accepted the outcome. Why, he tried to kill you, sir. You fired to wound. He knows that. God Almighty must know it."

"Still. It was a sin, wasn't it? I should not have agreed to the duel."

"Sir, we've been through all that. Scarborough would have gone after your family, as he threatened. You agreed to the duel to protect them. As any good father would."

"There's no denying I fired the shot that forced them to remove his arm. Bishop's last call did not put Lord Scarborough out of harm's way yet."

Sir William stood up and went to the closet. Finding one of his top hats he reached inside for a pair of black silk gloves. He pulled one onto his left hand and did not put on the other.

"I shot him with the left hand, Harrison. I shall wear this black glove to remind me of that. Eating. Sleeping. In the House. At Ashton Park. I shall remove it the day I deem Lord Scarborough has fully recovered."

"Sir —"

Sir William looked at Harrison but stared right through him. "If he does not recover I shall wear it for the rest of my days. To remind myself how I took another's life and, by so doing, took my grandson's life at the same time."

Emma tucked Billy into bed after the other two boys. Then she switched off the lamp and told them a story in the dark. The deep quiet told her the three of them had fallen asleep. She stayed in her chair a few more minutes. Finally she got up and drew aside a curtain to look out over the lawn and the ash trees. There was no moon. She leaned her head against the windowpane.

Lord. I prayed my heart out for Victoria and her son. Look, here are the three young men You blessed me with — why couldn't You have blessed her as well? What has she done wrong? What have I done wrong that You would not hear my prayers? Now I must go back to being a minister's wife and help my husband put faith in the lives of others. How can I do that when my heart is so barren? It feels like it has been burned over and that now it is nothing more than a scorched and blackened field where nothing can grow.

Yes, You spared her life — just. Why could You not spare her son's? Why could You not spare me? For now I have no desire to return to Ribchester and the church there. No desire to play the role of the clergyman's wife. No will to put up a brave front. You have visited Ashton Park with sudden death. And now once begun, I fear You will not leave off until the grass by the chapel is filled with graves that I and others could not prevent from being filled. I wish You would stay Your hand. But You are God and I am not, and You no longer listen to me.

24

December 1921

Dear Sir William:

I write to tell you that the doctors feel I have almost reached the stage of full recovery. It has been difficult learning to write with my left hand but you see I have mastered it pretty well. I thank you for your prayers and your many kindnesses, which have been much appreciated by Lady Scarborough and myself. We hope to visit Ashton Park in the new year and will let you know our plans once the doctors agree it is safe for me to travel.

I trust you and your wife and children are in good health. We are doing splendidly here and Caroline and the boy are getting along very well at our villa south of Lisbon. Now that I am much improved Lady Scarborough will be embarking later this week for Portugal. She intends to stay with Caroline and young Charles until Easter.

Most sincerely, I remain,
Lord Francis Scarborough

Lady Elizabeth sat in her chair in the library and read the note a second time. "It's wonderful news. You'd never know you two had quarreled, let alone shot at each other." She looked up at her husband, who stood with his hands clasped behind his back, staring out of the tall library windows at the brown leaves that rushed past with the November wind. "Will you not feel free to remove the black glove now? There is much gossip about it among the servants, Tavy and Norah tell me."

Sir William did not reply to her question about the glove. "You know I must return to Westminster this afternoon. Kipp has deliveries to make in Manchester and will come west to collect me after lunch."

"I am aware of that."

"The bloodshed in Ireland maddens me. We have had meeting after meeting with the delegates from the *Dail Eireann,* the Irish Parliament. This evening I need to attend one of the special committees."

"You were hopeful last week a treaty might

499

be signed before Christmas."

"I still am. But it can't come soon enough. Thirty people were killed in Belfast this week. I fear for Albert and Catherine. And that is only Belfast. Three years of violence have solved nothing." He brought his left hand out from behind his back and stared at the glove covering it. "Violence begets violence."

"William. Stop torturing yourself over that. Lord Scarborough was in such a temper that nothing less than a duel would do. You know what his plans were had you not responded to his challenge. He is hale and hearty and acts as if the incident never occurred. Why can you not do the same?"

"I have —"

"Why can you not remove that glove? I only see your left hand when you wash up. It is pale as a gull feather compared to the right one now."

"I am committed to seeing the treaty signed. I can tell you what you must not tell anyone else — I believe they will consent to dominion status such as Canada enjoys."

"They don't insist on full independence?"

"They see it as something to be achieved later on. This is the approach I have always argued for. A small step now, a larger step later. They become a self-governing state within the British Empire and the king is their head."

"Why, that's marvelous."

Sir William turned from the window. "It would be marvelous if all the Irish would agree to it. I don't know if that will be the case. Still we must try. Perhaps Michael Collins has enough authority to sway all Ireland to his side. He is for the dominion status. The six northeastern counties will not be party to this, however. Albert will have what he has always wanted — a Northern Ireland that remains fully connected to Britain with Belfast as its capital."

Lady Elizabeth stood up and took his right hand, the hand without the glove. "You look so troubled. Why not thank God, William? He has put you in a position where you have done as much as any to bring about this peace. The guns in France fell silent in nineteen-eighteen. Now the guns of Ireland will fall silent soon. You are helping to save hundreds of lives."

"I wish to. I pray to. But there are bound to be those who will oppose the treaty, the nationalists who will not go along with Collins. You remember what Robbie and Shannon wrote in their last letter from Palestine. They're convinced there will be fresh fighting among the Irish themselves if I cannot help draft the best treaty possible."

"You put too much on your shoulders. People like Jack O'Casey will never be satisfied unless they become the rulers of Ireland. You can never appease such men." She looked into his eyes. "What becomes of prisoners like him?"

"He will be released if he agrees to the terms of the treaty."

"Just like that?"

"I'm afraid so."

She grasped his gloved hand. "And does this come off if a treaty is signed?"

"No. The glove has nothing to do with the Irish treaty."

"Then when will you remove it if Lord Scarborough's health is not a good enough reason?"

"That is up to God."

"God? It's up to God now? What has to happen that is up to God?"

Victoria folded her arms over her chest and hunched up her shoulders under one of her husband's old fleece-lined flying jackets. The leather handled the scattered snowflakes and the fleece handled the cold. A leather cap that was lined in the same way covered her head and flaps covered her ears. She thought she looked ridiculous but didn't care. Staying warm was the thing.

Ben's plane was coming down on the brown grass field that was home to the South England Air Service. He was finishing up a courier run between London and Coventry only a few days before Christmas. The SPAD touched, bounced twice, then rolled to a stop. He jumped out and came toward her, taking her in his arms.

"Look at you!" He kissed her. "Rosy cheeks. Bright red lips. Flashing eyes. And not a dab of makeup. Does the cold weather bring out the best in you?"

"No. You bring out the best in me. The cold weather just makes me play dress-up with your old clothes."

"Are you warm enough then?"

"Not really."

"So why aren't you back at the house waiting? I'd only be another half hour."

"I couldn't wait that long."

"A half hour? You're acting like we're on a second honeymoon."

She placed gloved hands on both sides of his face. "It is a second honeymoon. I saw Dr. Honeycutt today. Ben . . . we have another child, another boy, alive inside me."

"What?" Ben's face opened with surprise and delight, a sudden smile tugging at his lips and eyes. "Is he sure?"

"Yes, he's sure. Merry Christmas, love."

Ben hugged her with a burst of strength, laughed, kissed her, and laughed again. "Is that why all the color in your face?"

"That's part of it. Are you happy?"

"Of course I'm happy. I never thought . . . I didn't know . . . after we lost —"

"It's all right. We were both scared of trying again. Now I'm even more scared. But I'm happier than I am scared."

The snowflakes thickened and Ben wrapped his arms more closely around her. "I'll get the lads to put the plane in the hangar. The mother here I'm getting home. Did you bring the motorcar?"

"I walked."

"You did not."

"I did, actually."

"You can't walk. You need to sit in the hut and wait for me to bring it round."

"I won't. The baby has a better chance if I'm healthy. I'm not made of bone china, love. Hold me tight so the wind doesn't carry me off to France and I'll be fine."

They dropped by the hut with its fire and Ben asked two of his helpers to put the plane away for the day. Kipp and Christelle had flown to Liverpool earlier and were settled at Ashton Park now for Christmas. With one arm strong around her he began to walk her along the road into the village.

He laughed. "Won't your mum and dad be caught off guard!"

"They really will. They've been so busy thinking about Christelle's baby coming next March and Char's coming next June in Canada they haven't thought about me at all. And father's been so excited about the treaty signing and its passing in Parliament —"

"The news of you bearing another child will throw them for a loop. When is the baby due?"

"May."

"How do you know it's a boy?"

"It is. Believe me, it is."

"I won't argue with the mother. Look, we'll head for Ashton Park right after my flight tomorrow. I have some special deliveries we've been paid handsomely to take care of before Christmas Day, and once that's done we're off."

"If it socks in?"

"It won't."

She pinched his arm. "If it does."

"I suppose we'll make a cozy home until it clears. If it won't clear then we're off to Liverpool by train."

"Even if you lose the fees?"

"We'll make up the fees. It's more important we get you to the estate. And I have news too. Not as big as your news but —"

Snowflakes flew into her face like feathers as she lifted her face away from his chest to look at him. "What news?"

"We've decided to expand. We're bringing some other fliers in to handle the south while Kipp and Michael and I start up another airstrip in the north. Right by Ashton Park."

"What? You're not!" She stopped walking. "You're not, Ben!"

"The Lancashire-York Air Service. With service to Cumbria, Durham, and Northumberland."

"You're not joking!"

"No, my love. We'll handle Wales and up to Glasgow and Edinburgh. And Cheshire. The Midlands and South and the occasional hop to France will be the other lads' job. Your father's already given us the land. A field that's lain fallow for thirty years. This was all meant to be a Christmas Eve announcement, so you really will have to keep it to yourself or I'll get thrown in the Tower."

"So how far — how far is the field from the manor?"

"About three miles."

"Is that all?" She seized him in her arms and kissed him with the sort of ferocity he

remembered from their midnight ron
in the stables. "Oh, I love you! How wonc
ful that will be! Where will we live?"

"In the village by Ashton Park. Or your
father says we can build on a corner of the
estate. It's really up to you and Libby and
Christelle."

"Oh, a corner of the estate. Near the sea.
With our own ash trees. Please, please!" She
kissed him again, almost knocking him
down.

Ben laughed. "Who can argue with you?
I'm sure your father will give you any corner
of the estate your heart desires."

"I want some figgy pudding too! And a
cup of good cheer!"

"That I can take care of. Let's get you out
of the storm, my apple-cheeked beauty."

25
1922

March 1922

"So good to see you, Sir William. Now we both shake with the left hand."

"We do, my lord. Not a bad thing. Welcome to Ashton Park."

"Thank you. We have not been here since Victoria's wedding to Captain Whitecross, I believe."

Lady Elizabeth had her brightest smile for Lady Scarborough as they stood together on the steps of the manor, Tavy holding the doors open for them. "I'd love to have you join me for a fresh pot of tea in the parlor, my lady. We can leave the men to their conversation and meet up with them again at dinner."

"I'd like that." Lady Scarborough, tall and blond like her daughter Caroline, turned to her husband. "Now don't exhaust yourself, my dear. I'm sure Sir William can offer you a room for a nap if you feel faint."

508

"Of course —" Sir William began.

Lord Scarborough had lost weight but none of his height or commanding presence. "I feel like an absolute rocket. There's too much to talk about to sleep through our visit. I shall see you at dinner, Madeleine."

Sir William took his guest to the private study with its chessboard and books and newspapers. Lord Scarborough settled himself in a chair, leaning his walking stick against its leather side, and took a pipe from his pocket.

"Do you mind if I smoke, Sir William?"

"Not at all, my lord."

"I must congratulate you on your work with Ireland. The treaty was passed by their Parliament in January and now they have their Irish Free State. An end to the bloodshed."

"I hope so. The vote was close, only sixty-four in favor, fifty-seven opposed. There have been armed clashes between pro-treaty and anti-treaty forces."

"I expect that will peter out with the June elections once the pro-treaty Irish win a majority."

"That is what I pray for, my lord."

"Please — let's dispense with the formalities in private." Lord Scarborough stuffed tobacco into his pipe's bowl, the stem in his teeth. "After all, we almost killed one another. That should afford us some sort of intimacy in our relationship." He struck a match and lit the pipe, puffing rapidly to get the tobacco burning. "Though I would have preferred it happen through marriage."

Sir William sat down opposite him. "How is Caroline — how is she feeling, Francis?"

Lord Scarborough blew smoke into the room. "Very well, thank you. Charles is a year old now and growing by leaps and bounds. The photographs are impressive. Of course Madeleine is just back and has wonderful stories to tell me about the boy. I thank God he looks more like his mother than he does that blackguard Buchanan. What did you do about him, by the way? Did you sack him?"

"Yes."

"Any idea where he is now?"

"None at all."

Lord Scarborough puffed. "A great deal seems to be going on here at Ashton Park, William. Lorries passed us going in and out of your estate when we drove up — the ones going out had loads of dirt and the ones coming in were filled with bricks and lumber."

"The boys are setting up a new air service a few miles from Ashton Park."

"Is that the aerodrome I spotted from the main road?"

"It is. They've left the other in the hands of three of the lads Kipp flew with during the war. This one will serve Yorkshire and Lancashire and on into Scotland and Wales. They've made the decision to take my offer and put up homes on the estate rather than buy in the village. Elizabeth and I are overjoyed naturally. The houses should be up by next year."

Lord Scarborough took the pipe from his mouth. "So this flying business has been going well for them, I take it?"

"I and a few others have received handsome returns on our investments."

"Royal Mail contracts?"

"They get some of those. A great deal of it is packages from various business firms or legal documents. And passengers. Men will pay a good fee for traveling rapidly from London to Birmingham or Liverpool to York. So they have a number of two-seaters at the London field now and are starting with two up here. SPAD S.XXs. Not all brand-new but they run well. The boys operate flying schools as well."

"You continue to invest, I presume?"

"I do. And others. Such as Michael Woodhaven III in New York, the father of

Libby's American husband."

Lord Scarborough set his pipe, still curling smoke, on a table and ran his hand through his beard. "This may be something I should like to get into, William. Yes, I believe I might. Tell me, how is Kipp?"

"He's well, thank you, Francis. His wife and he had their first child in March. He's a month old now and doing very well. A boy."

"Wonderful, wonderful. I hold nothing against him, William. Or against Edward. That is water under the bridge. Neither of them had anything to do with Caroline's disgrace. Will we see them at dinner?"

"Kipp, yes. All of them are living here in the manor until their houses are built. But Robbie is in Palestine, as you know. And Edward is still in Canada."

Lord Scarborough shook his head. "No, no, William. Water under the bridge, I say again. Bring Edward home. He has nothing to fear from me. I am sorry he broke off the engagement but he did nothing to harm Caroline. Bring him back to Ashton Park." He looked at Sir William's gloved hand. "I had heard of this. No one knows what it's about. They think your hand is scarred from some accident. I know the truth. You wear it because of the duel, don't you?"

"Partly."

"Then off with it, William. We ought never have fought once I knew Buchanan was to blame, but fight we did and it was honorable. You carry no guilt. Please remove it for my sake, sir."

Sir William half-smiled. "Thank you. I cannot."

"Why is that?"

"It is not just about you and me."

Lord Scarborough studied Sir William's face. "But still this matter has to do with the duel."

Sir William nodded. "It does, Francis. I will say that much."

"When I was not yet sure if I would die or live, you told me your God would forgive much."

"I believe that, yes."

"Is it not true in your case? Or does the forgiveness you spoke of have well-established boundaries with high walls?"

Sir William did not respond, only returning Lord Scarborough's gaze.

The pipe was lifted again, tapped against the table so that ash fell out, refilled, lit, and was soon pouring a fragrant smoke into the room that reminded Sir William of cherrywood burning.

"Never mind, sir. We all have our secrets."

Lord Scarborough drew on his pipe quietly for a few minutes, staring up at the white ribbons that made their way to the ornate ceiling. "So. No word at all on Buchanan's whereabouts?"

"I knew nothing about the duel until it was over, Elizabeth."

"Neither did I."

Lady Scarborough brought her cup to her lips and then withdrew it. "I really thought it *was* a target-shooting accident. Once he had recovered from the bout with pneumonia following the amputation he told me the truth. You must understand, my dear, he blames himself for the whole thing. He knew your son had not done our daughter any wrong, yet he thought it would be dishonorable to back out of the engagement at the Strunk. Oh." She set down the cup in its saucer, almost spilling it, and threw her head back. "He has the most complicated views on this idea of honor. Francis would have been most at home at the court of King Arthur. However, with his willingness to fight at the drop of a gauntlet, I doubt he would have lived long enough to enjoy the Middle Ages."

"But you say he is well past it all then, Madeleine?"

Lady Scarborough looked out the window and watched Harrison walk past with Todd Turpin. "With your family, yes — he feels honor was satisfied that morning. I see no ill will residing in him. But with Buchanan — well, that is something else again."

"You don't —" Lady Elizabeth started and stopped. "Buchanan was let go immediately, you know."

"If Francis were to query you concerning his whereabouts, would you be able to reply?"

"Not at all. We have no idea where he is. We refused to give him references to another house after what he had done to your daughter."

Lady Scarborough's eyes glistened as she smiled, lifting her teacup again. "Thank you. Though I must say the boy is lovely. Lovely."

Lady Elizabeth smiled in return. "How often God grants us beauty out of our tragedies."

"If He did not, how could any of us remain standing from one day to the next?" She drank her tea. "I fear my husband will go after Buchanan, Elizabeth."

"No. He is not thinking that, is he?"

"Oh, he doesn't say it in so many words. But he's acting exactly the way he was

515

before he went off on this duel idea with Sir William. I didn't know it at the time, of course, but now I see the same pattern asserting itself — the gestures, the expressions on his face, the phrases he employs over and over again, the pacing. The word *honor* coming up in his conversation countless times. The darkness in his eyes when he sits alone in his chair by the fire. What should I do?"

Lady Elizabeth leaned forward, the fingers of both hands laced together. "Will he not talk to you about it if you ask him directly?"

"I tried. Once." A tear moved along the line of her cheek. "I'm sure he's making inquiries everywhere. Unless this Buchanan has taken a boat to the Orient, Francis will certainly find him. Then we will go through this all over again. I don't know how to stop him. I pray but he is not a man of faith and my prayers bounce off the armor of his heart. Is it possible . . . do you think . . . I wonder if your husband could get through somehow . . . before there was another —"

"My dear Madeleine. Your daughter and our son could have married and made us family. I will ask William. Of course I will ask. He will want to help." She reached over and took Lady Scarborough's hand. "For all we know, William may have picked up on your husband's mood on his own and is considering what is the best step of action to take. You remain committed to an overnight stay, I hope? I may have something to tell you in the morning."

"Ah." Lady Scarborough clasped both her hands around Lady Elizabeth's. "That gives me a touch of hope."

Kipp ran his hands through Christelle's thick hair and kissed her with so much strength and ardor she began to laugh and pushed him back.

"What has gotten into you, husband?" she teased. "You're a father yet you act as you did when you first romanced me in France."

"You're even more beautiful now. Look at the color in your face and eyes. You're irresistible."

"Yes? Am I? Most women need months to look themselves again after a birth."

"You don't look yourself. You look twice yourself, three times."

"Oh, you crazy man, come kiss me again then." She opened her arms. "Our angel is still napping."

"You smell like heaven," he murmured, burying his face in her hair.

"Yes? And you smell like gasoline."

"I washed my hands."

"But not your hair or your body. You haven't had your bath yet, have you?" She rolled over to face him, smiling and pinching his cheek. "*Je m'en fiche.* I don't care, *mon cher,* you know I don't. You could smell like a farm and it wouldn't matter. I love you."

Kipp began to kiss her shoulder. "Our son needs a sister."

"Oh-ho, is that true? I have not even recovered from giving you Matthew and now what? We need Marianne?"

"It's an idea."

Christelle kissed his lips. "Wait. Give me a year of peace. Then we'll see. Let us get into our house first. Oh." She pulled away and picked up a telegram from the table on her side of the bed. "I almost forgot this. It came while you were doing your flight to Birmingham and back."

"Who is it from?"

"I did not open it. I am a better wife than that." She watched as he hesitated with it in his hand. "Go ahead. Read it. Please. I need a rest."

Kipp opened it. She saw his face tighten.

"What is the matter?" she asked, immediately reaching out to touch his arm.

Kipp handed the telegram to her. "It would be better if you read it for yourself."

Christelle sat up, throwing her long hair back over one shoulder. She squinted in the half-light of the room, glancing over once at Matthew, who was sleeping by their bed in a small wooden crib. When she finished she looked at Kipp.

"What can I say to you? Lady Caroline is being stalked by this Buchanan. She is afraid to tell her family because she is certain Lord Scarborough will kill him. She asks for your help as a friend." She shrugged. "You must go to her."

"How can I go to her? She is in Paris."

"And you have planes that fly over the Channel to Paris every week."

"There's nothing I can do. I'm not the police. And you have just had the baby."

She took both his hands. "I had Matthew over a month ago. I am fine. There is a house full of people here to take care of me. Darling, you cannot ignore this. You cannot. If something happens to her and we did nothing? And she has her little boy with her?" She shook her head. "*Non.* You and I are not that sort. Go and talk with Michael and Ben. You will need to be in Paris at the address she gave you as soon as possible. If not today then tomorrow."

"Christelle —"

"Shhh." She laid her head on his chest.

"Your feelings are for me, aren't they? Not for her?"

"Of course my feelings are for you. How can you ask that?"

"I don't ask it for me. I ask it for you. I see that it is you who are worried. If you love me, it will be all right." She reached her hand up to his face. "But we cannot have her father and mother dining with us here and smile and do nothing for their only child. *C'est impossible.* Get Caroline away from this Buchanan and bring her back here. Bring her and her boy to Ashton Park." She kissed him softly. "My Kipp. I'm sorry. But you must. It is *la guerre* — another kind of war for you."

Michael put the phone down. "All right. You're flying to our London airfield at dawn. They'll refuel you there and you can take some packages to Paris for us. Use the civilian field at the west end of the city."

Kipp sat beside Ben in the parlor while Michael stood facing them. "I think the SPAD can handle her and the boy when I bring them back."

"I'm sure it can too." Michael coughed. "Look. I don't know this Buchanan —"

"He's a big tall Scot," Kipp replied. "Haven't seen him in years."

"Don't kill the guy. Or let him kill you. Just get her out of that hotel and back to England. It would be better if he never knew you were there until after you were gone."

"I still don't understand why she didn't stay at the villa in Lisbon." Ben looked at both of them. "Wouldn't that have made more sense? The servants are there to protect her."

Kipp glanced down at the floor. "She said they couldn't stop Buchanan if he wanted to break into the house and abduct her or the boy. So she left at night and took trains all the way up to Paris."

He paused a moment and put a hand on Ben's shoulder. "When's Vic due? May twelfth?"

"Any time now."

"So you have enough to worry about. I'll handle this. You handle the birth."

Ben laughed. "I won't do the delivery, if that's what you mean. But I'll be pacing outside the door until Pittmeadow puts him in my arms."

"It could be the first girl of the bunch."

"Whatever we get, I'll be happy."

Michael remained standing, hands in his pockets, his eyes dark. "I'll be happy when the baby's born, Ben. And when you touch down with Caroline and her kid, Kipp. Not before."

Sir William stood in his dressing gown in the doorway winding his pocket watch as Lady Elizabeth sat up in bed reading. "I wanted to say goodnight, my dear. I believe the dinner and conversation went well, considering all that's happened between our two families."

Lady Elizabeth set her book down on the bedspread. "I think so too. Madeleine and I had a good talk when we were in the parlor. Did you find Francis quite open?"

"Yes. He was all right. Well, goodnight. We'll see you at breakfast."

"William. Did he mention his daughter?"

"Oh, yes. He's quite happy about his grandson, Charles."

"Did he ever bring up the boy's father? Buchanan?"

"Hmm? Yes. He wondered where the man had got to."

"What did you tell him?"

Sir William raised one shoulder in a shrug and made a face. "There was nothing to say. I haven't any idea where he is."

"Why do you suppose he wants to find him?"

"No idea."

"Madeleine is worried he means to duel again."

"What?" Sir William put the watch in the pocket of his gown with his gloved hand. "Is that what you think?"

"I don't know what to think. It's what she thinks. She says he's acting exactly the way he did before he challenged you. She's convinced he's transferred his animosity toward our family and our boys to Buchanan. I wonder if you might have a word with him about this."

"We're not that close, Elizabeth. I expect he'd just raise his drawbridge and lock everything up tight if I asked. Surely there's nothing to this."

Lady Elizabeth played with the cover of the book. "It might be a wife's anxieties, nothing more. But he has been shooting again, William."

His eyes narrowed. "She's certain about this?"

"He told her he needs to be as accurate with his left hand as he was with his right. As accurate as you, he said. That was just before they drove up here from Oxfordshire." She watched her husband take this all in. "I wish you would find some way to talk some sense into him."

Sir William glanced at the blind pulled

tightly over her window. "I don't know that I can."

"Right, I've got Wynken, Blynken, and Nod trussed up safely in the motorcar. Are you ready?" Jeremiah put a hand on each side of the doorframe and leaned into the vicarage, turning his head to the right. "Hullo. Where are you?"

A voice came from far inside the house. "I said I'd be there."

"Do you need help with anything?"

"I don't."

Jeremiah stepped back outside and squinted up at the May sun. Fast steps behind him were followed by a rush of air as Emma swept past clutching several pieces of luggage. She glanced back over her shoulder. "I thought you were in an all-fired hurry."

Hands in his pockets, Jeremiah walked to the car, opened the driver's door, and slid behind the wheel. Emma stared rigidly ahead from the passenger's seat. He looked at her as the boys began to squabble.

"So how long does this go on?" he asked.

"Does what go on?"

"You punishing me for being an Anglican minister."

"Oh, don't be ridiculous." Emma whipped

her head around. "That's quite enough you three. No more of it. I am out of patience today." She faced front again. "Hadn't we better get going?"

"Not until you talk a bit more civilly."

"For heaven's sake." She exaggerated a smile and turned it on him. "Reverend Jeremiah Sweet, will you please put the motorcar in gear and take us to Ashton Park before God kills another one of my sister Victoria's children? Thank you and may the good Lord bless you."

"Emma!" he hissed. "Must you act this way in front of the boys?"

"I'm not acting. Please put the car in gear."

"Emma —"

"I've heard all your sermons, Jeremiah. Over and over I've sat in that hard pew and let them fall on my ears. Let me work this through in my own way."

"Work it through? You've been going on like this for the past two months."

"Not quite."

Jeremiah turned the key and the car engine rumbled. "If Vic has a healthy baby, will that be the end of your performance of Job?"

"Do you think I'm performing?"

"I'm just wondering what it would take to

see you friends with God once more."

She leaned her head back and closed her eyes. "A lot more than you have to offer. I'd sooner be married to a bricklayer who spent his Sundays smoking cigarettes and drinking beer."

"Emma —"

"Stop this *Emma* rubbish, will you? And be grateful I haven't packed up the children and moved to the Lodge in Scotland, far away from your pulpit and parish. Don't talk to me anymore. You boys settle down. I am going to have a nap while we drive. You may wake me up when there's a proper adult to speak with."

26

April 1922

It was late in the afternoon when Kipp finally made his way from the airfield to the address Caroline had sent him. The street was busy with cars and trucks and horse-drawn wagons, and people swarmed over the sidewalks. He stood across from the hotel and ate a croissant sprinkled with almond slices while watching the faces going past for ten minutes, but he saw no sign of Tanner Buchanan in the crowd.

Eventually Kipp wiped his hands on his pants and made his way through the traffic. The hotel lobby was empty and a clerk promised to ring Michele St. Laurent, the name Caroline was traveling under. He stood by a window and glanced out while he waited.

"Kipp."

She stood at the bottom of the staircase dressed in rough clothes — a long brown skirt full of creases, a tweed jacket, a rumpled white blouse, a limp blue scarf, scuffed leather boots. Her hair was in disarray over her shoulders and there was no makeup on her mouth or over her cheeks or around her eyes. But to Kipp's surprise he found the same beauty in her that he had found in Christelle since she had given birth to a child, a look that was softer and more luminous and much richer.

She saw the look that came into his eyes and smiled almost shyly. "Please come upstairs and meet Charles."

He followed Caroline up the staircase. Her hands hitched up the hem of her skirt and her hair tumbled down her back. It had not been brushed. Nor could he smell any perfume. Instead he caught only the scent of cigarette and pipe smoke on her clothing, and a trace of soap from her skin when her hand was near his face. She glanced back at him once as they climbed.

"We are on the seventh floor. I'm sorry. You must be tired from your flight."

"I'm fine."

At the door she knocked and opened it a crack. "It's mummy." She stepped inside, smiling at Kipp. "I knew you would come. I knew. I've told Charles all about you."

"What have you told him?"

"I've told him you were a pilot in the war and a great hero. Not that he understands much of what I say. He's only thirteen months old."

"It was Ben Whitecross who won the medals, not me."

Her shy smile returned, a smile new to her. "Medals don't matter, Kipp. Heart matters. And spirit." She looked at him. "What's wrong?"

"I've never heard you speak like this before. Or look like this."

"Well, we've been on and off trains for days and I've scarcely slept."

"You . . . seem so natural . . . and down to earth. I'm not used to it."

"I suppose the years have changed me. I suppose I have nothing to put on airs about anymore." She looked away and her smile widened. "Here's my little man."

A boy with hair as bright as hers and Kipp's toddled slowly over and she scooped him into her arms, hugging and kissing him. "Charles. This is the nice man I told you about, the brave man who flies airplanes in the sky."

Charles examined Kipp with deep blue eyes — *eyes,* Kipp thought, *that are as blue as the sea at sunrise.* Then a soft smile came, exactly like the new smile he had seen on Caroline's face. He smiled back.

"Hello, Charles," he said. "Your mummy is an old friend."

Charles thought about this and smiled again.

"Would you like to go up in the air like a bird, Charles?" Kipp asked. "With mummy holding you in her arms?"

"Oh, I was hoping we would fly. That explains why you have arrived so quickly." She kissed Charles on the cheek. "We will get our bags and then we can go. There are not many. Caroline and Charles are quite the vagabonds. It's a two-seater, isn't it?"

"Yes."

A sudden roar filled the hotel room and the windows rattled. Kipp rushed over and drew back the lace curtains. Rain slashed across the glass and dark clouds filled a sky that had been clear a half hour before. He leaned on the windowsill with his hands and stared.

"I would have crossed over from England sooner except for a downpour that lasted two or three hours. This looks like another of the same. If it lasts it will soon be too dark to fly."

"We have been here almost three days. All the rainstorms have lasted a long time."

"We have to remain in Paris until I get

decent flying weather." Kipp sat on the windowsill and faced Caroline and Charles. "Have you been taking all your meals in the room?"

"Yes. We haven't left the hotel."

"How did you get a telegram off to me?"

"I paid one of the hotel staff to deliver it to a telegraph office."

"Do you think he has followed you from Portugal?"

"I don't know. He would not have stayed there once he knew Charles and I had fled." Charles buried his face into her shoulder. "He's tired. Let me put him down for his nap."

She held the boy close, whispering and smiling to him, and took him into the bedroom. As she laid him in the middle of the large four-poster bed her hair fell down over his face, and he giggled and clutched at it with his small hands. Caroline tickled him and then sat down on the bed and began to tell him a story while she smoothed back his blond curls. The boy continued to play with the long strands of her hair until his arms fell back on his chest and he was asleep. She kissed him on the forehead and walked out to Kipp, closing the door behind her.

She stood awkwardly in front of him.

"Thank you again, Kipp. I'm sorry about the weather. I feel better with you here."

Kipp had meant to look back out the window at the storm and try to spot a break in the cloud cover, but he had ended up watching her with her son. As she stood before him he felt he was looking at a much different woman than the one he had courted during the war. Her walk was different, her eyes, how she talked, what she talked about, the hair that wasn't combed and pinned, the clothing that wasn't immaculate, a face that was bare and open to the wind and light, a mouth that was its own fresh pink color without a stroke of lipstick added.

If she noticed he was staring she did not say anything about it. She sank down on a sofa and kicked off her shoes and threw her head back.

"I didn't sleep a wink last night." She put a hand over her eyes. "I was too anxious. I suppose Charles picked up on it because he was restless until about three. Here you've come all the way from Lancashire to rescue me and I'm possibly the worst host ever."

"Caroline. Get some rest if you need to. A clear dawn and we're out of Paris at four or five."

"Perhaps just a nap then . . ."

In a moment she was breathing deeply and her head sagged to the side. He got off the windowsill and gently placed his hands underneath her neck and laid her head down on a cushion. Then he straightened out her legs. He took a blanket off a table and spread it over her, carefully tucking it around her chin. That close to her face her breath moved softly over the backs of his hands. That close he could take in the lilac scent of soap on her skin. He could not resist brushing her cheek with his fingers. A shock went up his hand at the touch. Her sunlight hair was strewn over the cushion and sofa and came in waves over her shoulders.

There is so much simplicity to you now. So much of air and morning. You are not the woman I left behind.

He checked that the door was locked and bolted and sat down on the floor with his back to it. That way he was between Buchanan and the woman and the child. That way he could not see the perfection of the woman's face as she dreamed. There was only the rain on the glass and the thoughts of Christelle and his son, Matthew.

It was so dark that Kipp could not see a thing when he opened his eyes. He could smell Caroline's hair. Her head was against his shoulder, the blanket pulled over the two of them. His leather flight jacket was damp where she was breathing onto his arm. As his eyes adjusted to the darkness he saw that Charles was asleep in her lap with her arm over him. But he knew that none of this had woken him. He waited.

Footsteps. Slow. Going up the hall outside the room. Stopping. Then coming back. The person was trying to move softly but was too heavy. It was someone walking the way a man walked.

The hair on the back of his neck spiked. He could feel it sticking into the collar of his shirt and jacket. It was exactly the sensation he'd had when he sensed the presence of enemy aircraft in the sky over France. His whole body tightened.

Pressure came against the door. It stopped. Then came again. The knob was turned slowly and the lock tested with a piece of metal. Not a key but something else. If he succeeded in opening the lock there was only the bolt on the door. A good kick could bring it down.

I have to get the two of you into the bedroom.

At first Kipp was going to put his hand over Caroline's mouth and whisper in her ear. But he felt it would cause her to panic and lash out with her arms and legs, especially since she'd believe she was fighting for Charles as well. There was no time to think everything through. The wood of the door was pushing into his back again. Quickly he lifted her chin and put his mouth to hers. Her lips were soft and warm and in a moment he knew she was waking up. A hand clutched his arm. Another came to his face. The kiss deepened as she responded.

"Kipp," she whispered.

His hand was still holding her chin as he put his mouth to her ear. "Caroline. There is a man outside the door. Take Charles into the bedroom immediately. Put furniture up against the door."

He could see the whiteness of her eyes in the dark. "Is it — ?"

He nodded. "Who else? Take Charles into the bedroom."

She hesitated, still looking at him. Then she gathered her boy up and moved silently and swiftly. The bedroom door was closed softly and firmly. He heard a chair being dragged up against it. Carefully he got to his feet. He put his hands in his pockets and curled them around two large flat stones. One had been given to him by Ben and the other by Ian Hannam.

"He's a big bloke," Ben had said. "Saw him the once at Ashton Park a few years before the war. Don't play around. If it's him or you and the woman and child are in danger do what you have to do, mate. We'll tidy things up afterwards."

Kipp stepped back and faced the door as the knob turned again. He was in his cockpit and the Hun were roaring through wisps of white cloud at his squadron, guns flashing, crosses black and fierce. His mind emptied. He waited for the door to crash back on its hinges under Tanner Buchanan's shoulder.

Suddenly there was a stream of rapid-fire French in the hallway. Kipp could distinguish enough of the words to make out that someone was challenging Buchanan's presence. There was the thud of running feet. A shout in French and more running. Quiet.

Kipp counted to sixty before cautiously unlocking the door, drawing back the bolt, and peering out. The hall was empty. He closed and locked the door again. Then he crossed to the window. Light silvered the east in a line like a paint stroke. Just the sight brought a smell of petrol to his nostrils and the brassy scent of belts of machine gun bullets being loaded into his Sopwith Camel. He put his hand to the white silk scarf he still wore whenever he flew.

I never feel this way flying mail. But Tanner Buchanan does not stand between me and my aircraft when I am carrying letters and parcels.

He tapped on the bedroom door. "Caroline. It's all right. He's gone for now. Someone surprised him in the hallway and he ran."

She opened the door a few inches. "Are you sure, Kipp?"

"Yes. But now it's our turn to run. The rain's over and the sun's coming. We need to get down and into a cab. I'm sure he'll be expecting us to take a train to Calais and a boat from there."

Her blue eye in the door opening was dark. "He knows you're a pilot, Kipp. He knows everything about the Danforth family. He wants to get back at the lot of you for sending him packing. Almost as much as he wants me and the boy."

"He can't fly a plane, Caroline. We're going to be airborne in an hour and he won't be a passenger. Or diving at me out of the clouds."

"Tanner will just follow us to England."

"We'll deal with that in England. At least you'll be safer at Ashton Park than in Paris or Lisbon."

"Is that where you plan to take us?"

"Yes. Your parents are there."

"And your wife and child."

"It's time you met. Chris is French, not English. She can handle old lovers better than a British wife could."

A smile came to Caroline's eye. "Meaning me if I had wound up the British wife?"

He shook his head and smiled back. "The old Caroline might have had trouble perhaps. Not the new one."

"Is that how you see me now? As the new one?"

"You're not any Caroline I ever spent time with. I don't know how else to look at you except as someone I've just met and decided to help out of a jam."

"I'm not sure what to think about that."

"You can think in the cab. Now give me your bags, pick up Charles, and let's get to the airstrip and away to London. If he's watching the aerodrome on the west end we'll have to move quickly." He turned away and then turned back. "He's not the type to carry a gun, is he?"

"I don't know what he'd do. I don't know him anymore. He's become so . . . so predatory."

"Well. There's a comforting thought."

Her hand came through the door and grasped his arm. "You won't hurt him, will you? He's still my son's father."

"Hurt him? I just want to fly away. I worry more about him hurting me." He half-smiled in the dark of the hotel room and then the smile left. "I worry about him hurting you and Charles. I won't let him do that, Caroline."

Kipp kept them in the lobby until the cab pulled up at the hotel. Then he rushed Caroline and Charles into the vehicle, threw in their luggage, and jumped in beside the driver. The streetlights were still shining when they started out over the wet and glistening streets but by the time they reached the airfield the sky glowed and the lights were out. Kipp kept glancing behind the cab but no one was following them.

The feeling of having escaped a dogfight with Richthofen's Flying Circus vanished when he looked across the aerodrome to where his SPAD S.XX was parked. A tall man stood beside it. He glanced at Caroline, who was hugging a sleeping Charles to her chest. Her lips tightened.

"Yes. It's Tanner."

Kipp glared at the French official next to him. *"Pourquoi avez-vous permis que l'homme près de mon avion?"*

The official grew flustered. "He said he

was one of your business partners, Captain Danforth. From England."

"He is as much a business partner as the German ace Hermann Goering, *monsieur.*"

The Frenchman's face reddened. *"J'en suis desolé."*

"Never again. Please call the *gendarmes.*"

Kipp waited a moment while the sun rose clear of the spring fields and stared at Buchanan, who remained perfectly still by the plane. Then he made up his mind and began to stride across the damp grass. Again his thoughts took him to 1917 and 1918 and the walk to his fighter plane under an early morning sky. The memory made every muscle in his body tense.

"Kipp!" Caroline ran after him. "Wait for the police to handle Tanner!"

"I don't need the police."

"Please."

"I policed the skies and aerodromes of France four years ago, Caroline. I can do it today."

Caroline realized she was dealing with a different man than the one she had known in England, all smiles and gentle words and gallantry. This was the man she had never seen, the one who had climbed into cockpits every day of the war knowing he might never land again, might never see her again, a man who might take bullets to his chest or be burned alive when his plane caught fire but who still flew east to the sun and challenged the Germans to a duel with wings and guns. She stopped running.

"Who are you?" she whispered. "We are both strangers to each other this morning."

"Tanner Buchanan." Kipp stopped in front of the tall Scot with burning blue eyes and hair like black water in a stream. "Have you cut the fuel line?"

The Scot's face was rough-cut but handsome. He shook it quickly once. "There is no honor in that."

"I'm putting Caroline in the plane with Charles."

"You're not taking my son. Or my woman."

"I'm taking both."

"I'll kill you, Danforth. I'll snap you like a dry branch."

"Stop it!" Caroline came up, still holding a sleeping Charles. "Tanner, I'm going back to England. Back to my father and mother. If you want you may visit us there at the Scarborough estate. Though you must understand my father may take exception. He is wild enough to challenge you to a duel."

"A duel." The words rolled in a thick

brogue off the Scotsman's tongue. "I'd like that."

"I wouldn't. Charles would lose his father or his grandfather. Or both. If you still love me you won't let it come to that."

"Love you? I'd die for you."

"I don't want you to die for me. I want you to live. We will never be husband and wife. But you will always be Charles's father."

Tanner sneered. "So are you going to marry this Englishman?"

"No. He's already married to another."

"Perhaps he fancies you for a weekend lover."

Kipp lashed out swiftly and struck him on the chin with his fist. Tanner's head snapped back. Before he could recover Kipp hit him three more times in rapid succession. The Scotsman's eyes glassed over and he fell to the ground under the wings of the SPAD.

"No more!" cried Caroline, seizing Kipp's arm.

"He's down. There is no more."

"You shouldn't have hit him."

"Someone had to hit someone if we were going to get on board that plane."

"He'll never forgive you. He's as medieval about honor as my father."

"It might be that I am as well." Kipp

turned eyes of fire on her. "No one can talk to you like that."

Startled by the strength with which he spoke his words, Caroline did not reply for a moment. Then she said quietly, "You love someone else now."

"I have a great deal of love in me."

Confused, Caroline took the sentence in. "What are you saying? Is it possible you think you can love us both? No man can do that."

"Here are the *gendarmes*."

Six policemen arrived and picked Tanner off the ground.

"Are there any charges, Captain Danforth?" asked the officer in command

"Just keep him away from my airplane until we've taken off."

"Of course. Did he have a fall?"

"Yes. A fall from grace."

As they dragged the big man away, Kipp dug out a flight jacket, helmet, and goggles from the rear seat and handed them to Caroline. "Put this on, please. *Tout de suite.*"

"Whose are they?"

"Christelle wears them whenever we go up."

"Kipp, I can't put those on."

"Chris knows you're going to use the helmet and jacket. She was the one who offered them. 'For heaven's sake, *mon cher,* you cannot put the poor woman in clothing four times her size. She has been through enough. *Laissezlui quelque chose d'usure dans laquelle elle ressemble et se sent merveilleux.*' "

"I'm afraid my French isn't quite as good as my Portuguese."

Kipp took Charles gently from her arms. *"Let her wear something in which she looks and feels wonderful."*

"Your woman has a good deal of space in her heart." Caroline picked the flight jacket off the grass and pulled it on. "More than I should ever have if you were my husband."

Kipp was wrapping a sheepskin blanket around Charles. "The old Caroline maybe. I'm not so sure about the new one."

"Why do you keep saying that? I'm the same person. Yes, a few changes, life does that, but I'm still Caroline Scarborough."

"No." He kissed the top of the boy's head. "Four years ago you would have said you were *Lady* Caroline Scarborough."

She stood still as she took this in. Dawn found her and lit up her bright hair and blue eyes. Kipp smiled.

"What is it?" she asked, the flight jacket fastened up to her throat. "I look foolish, don't I? I have no doubt your French wife

544

is absolutely smashing in this."

If Caroline was confused about her feelings and the man she had once known as Kipp Danforth, then Kipp was just as confused about the woman who used to be Lady Caroline Scarborough. He let his eyes linger as the light showered her body and face. The brown leather gleamed and held her shoulders and hips snugly. She filled the jacket perfectly, her hair falling loose over its front and back.

"Vous êtes magnifique." With one hand he held the boy to him and with the other he took Caroline's arm. "Let me help you into the rear cockpit."

"I know that much French. You shouldn't be saying it if it's not true. And you, my old friend, should not be saying it at all."

She lowered herself into the cockpit, his hand on her back.

Kipp gave Charles to her once she had strapped herself in. *"Christelle dirais la même chose — et vos yeux sont d'azur, pas simplement bleu, mademoiselle."*

"What?" Caroline half-laughed. "You sound like a man selling apples and oranges on the Champs Elysees."

"I merely said that Chris would agree. And that the proper word for your eyes is *azur,* not *bleu."* The *gendarmes* had brought up the luggage and he placed it in the back with her and her son. "Please put on the helmet and goggles. I will be flying low so that Charles is not distressed for lack of oxygen but you'll see more and be more comfortable with them on."

His head passed near hers as he stowed the bags. They looked at each other.

"Kipp. When you kissed me in the hotel room —"

"I had to. I didn't want you to cry out. And I felt that placing my hand over your mouth would make you panic."

"So it meant nothing?"

"I didn't say it meant nothing. The last twenty-four hours have made my life difficult."

"Why?"

"I don't have to tell you."

"I want to hear it from you."

"Are you afraid?" he asked.

"A little," she replied.

"Are you afraid of flying?"

"A little."

"You will be all right." Kipp jumped into his cockpit and began to check all the gauges. "And Chris will have to come up with the answer because it's beyond me. I can't understand anything that happened in the hotel from the moment I saw you at the foot of the staircase. But she will."

"No woman can understand your feelings for another woman."

"Chris can."

"She will not want to."

"Yes, she will."

"No woman is so free or so gracious."

"Get your helmet and goggles on. We're leaving. First to London. Then from our airfield there to Ashton Park."

"All of this is quite mad." Caroline began fighting to get her hair under the leather helmet. "I think we are both suffering from lack of sleep."

The French ground crew came up and pulled the chocks away from the SPAD's wheels. Kipp leaned down to one of them. *"Mélange complet — radiateurs fermés — un accélérateur troisième place au chaud."*

"What was that you said?" she asked.

"Petrol mixture full. Radiators closed. I'm going to start the engine and then open the throttle a bit to about one-third. Two minutes or so of warm-up and we're off." He turned around to face her. "You're sitting where the tail gunner is supposed to be. Let me know if you see Tanner coming after us in a Fokker D.VII, all right?"

"That's not funny, Kipp." She stared at his goggles. "They make you look like

547

someone else." She pulled hers over her eyes.

"So do yours. *Démarrer le moteur!*" On the propeller's second spin the engine caught and roared. After a couple of minutes Kipp gave the thumbs-up. *"Radiateurs à mi-chemin. J'ouvre le papillon des gaz mainte-nant — merci — au revoir."*

"What?" asked Caroline again.

"You don't have to know everything."

"This is my first time, Kipp."

"Radiators are at half. I'm opening up the throttle." The plane began to roll forward. "We'll get the RPMs up. Head into the wind. Once we're going fast enough we'll lift off. The principles of aeronautics."

"Motorcar engines are always failing."

"I've never had a plane engine quit on me yet, Lady Caroline."

"Please don't call me that!" She had to shout above the engine.

"It's your title. Your parents will insist on it once we land at Ashton Park."

"I prefer being ordinary."

"Your father will think I'm insulting you. It will be matter of family honor. There will be a duel."

"Stop it."

"There will."

"Oh, use my title when we land in Lancashire, if you must. Until then, I'm Caroline."

If he replied, she did not hear it above the rush of wind and the howl of the engine. Green grass and plane hangars were flashing past. They bounced two or three times and began to leave the ground. Charles opened his eyes, looked around him, looked at his mother, looked at the clouds and blue sky, and began to laugh.

His mother was terrified. "How can you laugh? We're hanging in the air with nothing underneath us."

The SPAD flew low, heading north and east. They could see the tiny farms and roads and cattle and people. Soon they were over Amiens and the skies Kipp had patrolled. Again the feeling of war came over him. Then it was Calais and the Channel, a rugged blue with whitecaps and gulls that turned over and over. Caroline's mouth opened as they soared over the water and the cliffs of Dover drew closer and closer, flaming a pure white in the early morning air.

It's like the beginning of the world, Kipp.

"What's all the commotion?" Victoria stood at the head of the staircase and looked down at Christelle as Lord and Lady Scarborough rushed out the door with her father and mother. "Is it the king?" She laughed, holding one hand over her large stomach.

"Oh, much better than the king, *ma soeur.* Your brother is back and he has the Scarboroughs' daughter with him. And their grandson."

"Is that where Kipp flew off to the other day? To get them from Portugal?"

"Not so far. They were in France."

Victoria pouted. "No one would talk to me about it."

"They didn't want you to worry."

"Kipp flies like a wizard. Why should I be worried when he is in the air? There will never be German planes diving on him again."

Christelle came up the stairs and took her free hand. "The man who caused the scandal. The groundskeeper at your hunting lodge in Scotland."

"Buchanan."

"He was making life, ah, *très difficile* for Caroline and the boy. So Kipp brought them here so that they would be safe."

Victoria looked at her. "I'm sorry, Christelle. This must be . . . *très difficile* . . . for you. She was his fiancée once."

"I know that. And I have always wanted to meet her."

"Why on earth would you want to meet her? I should think you'd want to avoid Lady Caroline as much as possible."

"*Oh, non, non.* We both love the same man. It has always been my wish to spend a day with her and talk about nothing but Kipp." She laughed at the expression on Victoria's face. "Well, who else can I do that with?"

"I am astonished. But what makes you think she still loves him? Caroline was going to marry Edward."

"That was only to . . . to, how will you English put it, *modifier le nez Kipp* — tweak your brother's nose. A game of wits between lovers."

"What?"

"He still loves her." She smiled. "Maybe he knows it now that he sees her again. But I always knew. And she is *impuissants pour lui* — helpless for him. It will remain that way so long as the sun rises and sets."

Victoria was too surprised to speak at the calm way in which Christelle talked about Kipp loving another woman. Christelle laughed softly and took Victoria in her arms and kissed her on the cheek.

"*Vous êtes si anglais* — you are so English. I am not troubled. Kipp loves me like the wind. He will never prove unfaithful and he will never dishonor me. Oh, he will gaze at her beauty — for Caroline is the sort of woman who will look *moins mignon,* less cute, but far more beautiful as she grows older — like a day that grows warmer and brighter. And now and then there will be a kiss, I don't care. *Il ne me dérange pas.* No, Victoria, truly it does not upset me. We have a saying among our women — *une partie de son cœur est avec elle, mais de tout son cœr est avec moi* — a part of his heart is with her but all of his heart is with me. I believe Caroline and I will become good friends once we have had the talk we need to have. Now God has given us the opportunity."

"God?"

"Yes, of course, why not? If anything should ever happen to me I find it comforting to know she would love him and care for him and that he would not be left alone. Despair and grief and loneliness would not rob him of his life for she would take him into her arms with my blessing. Perhaps such a day will never come. But if it does I want my man to be loved by someone I love — and someone I trust. I thank God she is here." She kissed the confused and troubled Victoria a second time. "I must go and peek in on Matthew and Norah. I hope my words do not upset you too much."

Bewildered by the conversation, Victoria shook her head and a small smile came. "Not too much, Chris. I expect I'd have to be French to fully appreciate your point of view."

"There must be some Norman blood in the Danforth family line. You could draw on that."

"Norman blood? Don't tell my father that." Victoria made an *"oh"* with her lips. "Now I've had a contraction. Could that be the Norman blood responding or the Danforth blood taking exception?"

"*Non.* Truly?"

Victoria looked at her with widening eyes. "The last one was only ten minutes ago."

Christelle put an arm around her. "Come. To your room. To your bed." She called down the staircase. "Tavy! *Monsieur Tavy!*"

Tavy showed up immediately. "Ma'arm."

"Please to call Dr. Pittmeadow. Victoria is going into labor."

"I will ring him up straightaway."

"And the others. They are all out on the front lawn hugging and kissing Lady Caroline. Tell them as well. I will take her to her room. We do not have long. Dr. Pittmeadow will have to fly to be with us before the baby comes."

"I was having them an hour apart," Victoria added.

"And you told no one?"

"They were so mild — but these —"

"Come along."

"I'm — I'm a bit frightened, Chris," Victoria said as they moved quickly to the room she shared with her husband. "Last time —"

"No, my dear, *this* is this time. *This* is a new time. You will be fine. You are birthing a healthy boy to be friends with my Matthew."

Victoria laughed and winced, holding her stomach. "You and Kipp and your boy. I should have said something yesterday — I suppose it was my water that had broken — but I thought it was something else —"

"Shhh. Now it is one of the most exciting times of your life. Everything will come off beautifully."

"Last time —"

"*Non.* There is only this time. This is your beginning, *c'est tois début,* and you are ready. You are strong, so beautiful, so loved by your man and your family and your God. This will be a wonder."

"The pain —"

"Squeeze my hand until it falls off. I give you my hand for your pain. That is my birth gift to you."

"Thank you," gasped Victoria. "I believe I will make good use of it."

Emma and Libby were on either side of Victoria when the baby was born. He was cupped in Dr. Pittmeadow's large hands, and everyone laughed as the doctor slapped the child and he began to cry.

"Listen to him." Victoria was crying and smiling. "He is so full of life. It's wonderful."

Emma watched as the doctor tied off and severed the umbilical cord. Then he placed the boy in his mother's arms.

"Oh, dear God, thank You," Victoria cried, "thank You." She kissed the baby's head again and again.

Lady Elizabeth rushed from the room. "I must tell the men."

Sir William and Ben were seated on chairs far down the hall. The crying of the baby had made them both look at each other and smile and Sir William had wrung Ben's hand — "Thanks be to God, my boy."

"Come along, you two." Lady Elizabeth was gesturing to them. "Come, Ben — quickly, you're a father."

Tears sprang to Ben's eyes as he saw Victoria in the bed holding the child that Libby was wiping clean. "Vic, I can't believe it."

Her wet face glistened in the light. "It's a miracle, love. Would you like to hold him?"

"Can I?"

"Of course you can."

Ben took the boy as if he were made of glass and the women laughed. He gazed into the tiny face the way Victoria had seen him gazing at constellations at night or the swift flight of wild geese at dawn. He pressed his lips to the baby's forehead. Then he turned to Sir William.

"Sir," he said, "would you like to hold the child?"

"Very much. Thank you." Sir William glanced at his left hand. "One moment." He peeled off the black glove and dropped it to the floor. Then he took the infant from Ben. "Heaven bless the child."

"Has your hand healed then, Papa?" asked Victoria.

"Yes, it is quite healed now, thank you, my dear."

27

Summer and Fall 1922

"So Kipp and his wife have Matthew." Catherine stood in the kitchen holding a letter while Albert sat at the table sipping tea and reading the newspaper. "Vic and Ben have Ramsay. And now Char and Edward have young Owen. We are being overrun with boys."

"The election results from Dublin are very encouraging. The Free State has a majority. The anti-treaty forces will not have their way. The treaty will stand. The Irish Free State will come into being in half a year on December sixth."

Catherine ran a hand through his hair. "Did you hear me?"

"It's good news for Ireland. North and South. But better news for the six counties of Ulster because we're free of all that and still united to Great Britain. Fine days, Cath."

"Yes, I'm glad. But I can't see the anti-treaty Irish just going home and drinking Guinness and letting go of their dream of independence. No more than you let go of your dreams, love."

Albert put down the paper and picked up his mug of tea. "I suppose not. But the British army won't be out until the Free State is established in December. All that time they'll be making sure the legitimate government gets the guns and planes and armored cars. The anti-treaty lads will have nothing to fight with but a few old rifles."

"They made a fight with those old rifles during the war against the British."

"Hm. Well, maybe they've had their bellyful and will choose a pint of Guinness over another year of pitched battles on Irish soil."

She sat down at the table with him. "When have the IRA ever had their bellyful unless they get their own way? Promise me you'll shy away from mounting a letter-writing campaign to keep Ulster with Britain once the Free State becomes law on December sixth."

"Why —"

"You don't need to be involved. Northern Ireland will vote to remain united to Britain without your help. Ulster will never choose to join the Free State. Please stay out of the

558

debate."

"I'm not afraid of the republicans."

"Well, I am. There's more killing to come, Albert Moore. You can be happy about your election results but the IRA won't lay down their guns. You know better than I how many clashes there's been down south between pro-treaty and anti-treaty lads. It will be Irishman against Irishman and it breaks my heart. I don't want to stand by your grave because the IRA got fed up with your letters to the editor."

"I stopped that when you asked me to."

"But you're thinking of doing it again, aren't you?"

He drank his tea and avoided her eyes.

"Look. I want life, Albert Moore. Not coffins and clay. And I don't want to wait to hear that Libby and Michael have the next child. Or Robbie and Shannon. I want you and me to be next. And I want us to have the first girl of the lot. That's not much to ask, is it?"

He laughed. "D'you know you argue more like an Irishwoman every day? Do you think it's up to me to decide whether we'll have a girl or a boy? Do you imagine your husband's the Almighty?"

"Let's just try, that's all. Others can write the letters. The IRA have forgotten about you. So stay forgotten and make a family with me. Starting with a little girl."

"All right, all right." Albert poured himself more tea. "We'll populate Ulster with a crop of Moores. I won't take up the pen. I'll take up fatherhood. Does that suit you?"

She grinned and grabbed his hand. "It does suit me."

"Good. Now maybe I can have a moment's peace. Do you mind if I read up on the rugby and football scores?"

"If you will say you agree with me."

"About what?

"Taking up fatherhood. And motherhood."

"I said yes, already." He stared at her. "We're in a race of some kind now, are we?"

"We are. A race against Libby. And a race against Robbie. I'll not be at the bottom of the barrel on this one. I lost enough contests against those two when I was a girl at Ashton Park."

"What?" Albert's mouth was open. "D'you suppose this is some kind of childhood game, Cath?"

"It is. Are you with me, Albert Moore? Or against me?"

Her hand tightened on his.

"The Lord save me." He stared at her. "You're more Irish than the Irish."

Sir William was supervising the unloading of the final pieces of baggage from the summer at Dover Sky. Lady Elizabeth came down the steps from the house quickly, a letter in her hand and a smile opening her face. Seeing her expression, he laughed and put his hands in his pockets.

"What news?" he asked. "Banff? Jerusalem? Belfast?"

"It's from Catherine."

"Ah. It's a child on the way, isn't it?"

"Don't spoil my surprise."

"Very well." Sir William smiled. "Is Albert's football team making a grand start to the season?"

Lady Elizabeth waved the letter in the air. "Don't spout nonsense. We have our seventh grandchild. Catherine's almost two months along."

"Two months? Ha-ha." Sir William swung his wife off her feet. "How we've been blessed. How we've been blessed by the Lord. We really must have a time of worship in the chapel tonight."

"The child is due in March next year. Late in March or in early April."

"Excellent. Splendid. That's the Easter

season. How wonderful that would be."

He put his wife down but kept his arms around her. "The new airfield a going concern. Babies underfoot. Robbie and Shannon back on a three-month furlough in October. Edward and Charlotte and young Owen home for Christmas. The new houses almost up. Such a year. We never saw such a year."

"Perhaps Mrs. Longstaff will bring out the ice cream for us at dinner tonight."

"In celebration. Of course she will. There must be lorry loads of it. The household has been away since June."

"Well, our airmen didn't come down to Dover with us, my dear. That's three families. Heaven knows what's left."

Sir William headed up the steps into the manor. "I will ask her directly." Tavy opened the doors. "Good to be home, eh, Tavy?"

"It is. You have news, Sir William?"

"Do you know your Bible, Tavy?"

"The Bible, sir? I should think so, sir."

"I have my quiver full. Do you take my meaning? My quiver full."

Tavy watched him stride into the manor and thought a moment. Then he turned to Lady Elizabeth. "Another grandchild, my lady?"

"Indeed, Tavy, indeed. Catherine and Albert."

"My goodness, ma'arm." Tavy barked a laugh. "That's the best news we've had out of Ireland all summer."

"It is, isn't it? Civil war and the Irish at each other's throat. It's desperate. And here we have our Anglo-Irish child. A new life, Tavy. It's so much better than the killing and the dying."

"So it is. So it always is. Only sometimes our race does forget, my lady. We forget, to our shame."

She smiled. "And God reminds us with a baby. Thank you, Tavy. You're quite the theologian today."

He smiled back, smoothing his black dress jacket over his frame. "Just the Danforth butler, Lady Elizabeth."

Emma was standing by the Ribble as it surged past the vicarage in a wide sweep. Sheep were grazing on both sides of the flow, their white vivid against the September green. She was thinking about the Romans who had maintained a garrison in Ribchester for three hundred years. How the soldiers must have missed the climate of home and the women they loved and their families. When they prayed to Jupiter, what did they ask for? The same things Christians and Anglicans asked for? How successful were their prayers?

A year ago when Vic lost her baby I would have said my prayers were quite unsuccessful. Now she has a boy and my brother Edward in Canada has a baby and Kipp and Christelle have their Matthew. And Cath, of all people, Cath is expecting. Here I have been railing against God for months — and against my Anglican minister husband — and God has opened womb after womb. If this were a parable it would be about grace. If it were a sermon I would be Job or Jonah or Mary Magdalene. I deserve nothing really. Yet all these blessings have been poured on my family. Why?

"It's a lovely evening."

Emma turned when she heard her husband's voice. "Thank you for joining me. The Hinchcliffes are still at the vicarage with the children, I take it?"

"Everyone's getting along fine. They told us to take our time." He handed her a thick blue shawl. "I thought you might need this."

"I do." She tugged it over her shoulders. "Can we walk?"

They went along the bank of the river, both her hands knotted in the shawl as the sun dropped into the fields, Jeremiah walking beside her in a dark suit with the white Church of England collar at his throat. For several minutes she did not speak again until a rolling cloud of starlings made her look up and stop walking.

"Not a care in the world." She drew the shawl more tightly around her. "I do not know what to make of Victoria's baby boy. And everyone else's. If God was looking to punish me —"

"Perhaps He is not."

"No sermons."

Jeremiah looked out over the river. "I am not preaching."

"It wasn't just the loss of Vic's first child that put me over the edge. There was the war. There was Ireland. Blood and death and mayhem. How many mothers' prayers were not answered in Dublin or Belfast today? The constables will show up at the door and say, *Sorry, we're sorry, but.*"

Jeremiah did not reply.

"I thought about taking the children and leaving. I thought I should suffocate if I had to attend one more church service and smile and smile."

"I know."

"How do you know?" she demanded.

"The expressions on your face and your silences made it plain. And you mentioned

565

separating yourself from me and the Church more than once."

"I ought to have done it. Now I feel even more lost without all my anger."

"I don't understand what has been so pent up in you. You always acted as if you had a beautiful life at Ashton Park."

"I did. But I also slipped the things that didn't make sense under the carpet — the hurts, the deaths, the prayers that went unanswered. Something about the child's death set me off. The things I'd stashed away erupted."

Jeremiah went to put a hand on her shoulder and then pulled it back. She saw the movement but didn't say anything.

"Now we have the kindness of God again with all the babies." Emma sighed. "The brightness that comes with them and all the colors of childhood. I don't know how to bring the two together, the dark and the light." She bent and picked up a handful of pebbles. "Libby is none too well off because of the babies."

Jeremiah frowned. "What do you mean?"

"Don't worry. She's not about to burst apart. But she can't bear children. The doctors don't know what's wrong. She and Michael have told no one. Not Mum and Dad and not his parents."

"I'm sorry, Emma. I am. I may be a minister but I don't pretend to understand it all. I only know there will always be both — dark and light, wheat and tares. Victoria lost a baby, now she has a second baby, but that doesn't mean it can't grow ill or that one of our own boys can't contract a lethal disease, God forbid. Will you fly apart again when the next bad thing happens?"

"How should I know?"

"Good and evil, Emma. Year in, year out. But underneath it all there is still the love of God. It undergirds our world or there would be no world. There would be nothing left. So take heart at the blessings of infants born to Ashton Park. Thank God if you think of it. But tomorrow one of the people we love could be dead. One of the children could be dead. Yet still the love of God would be underneath it all."

"That's what you believe." The river was shining in the twilight. "Why does there have to be wrong and brokenness at all if God is as much a God of love in this world as you say He is?"

"Why do we have a choice?" Jeremiah looked up at a sky that was darkening rapidly. "And why do some choose hate over kindness? Murder over forgiveness? While others choose love over revenge and mercy over destruction? We've landed in a world of decisions, Emma, and we want so badly to make all the right ones. But we don't always do that, do we? Yet sometimes, it seems, it happens. I believe the grace of God covers all our choices, good or ill."

"The Holy Bible speaks of judgment."

"Our courts judge. God judges. I leave it at that."

Emma folded her arms over her chest, clutching her shawl. "I wish I could live the way you speak. I wish I could live by the grace of God. I wish I could believe all things, even the worst, are covered by this love and that nothing good is lost, nothing fine forgotten, no sacrifice diminished."

She looked at the sky as he was doing. Small stars began pierce to the dark and it looked to him as if she were counting them.

"I can't pretend to have thought it out like you, Jeremiah. I don't see the straight lines. I don't see them converging in the distance. But I grant you the world isn't all darkness even if it's not all light. And God is not always hidden even if He's often a great riddle to me."

"As He is to me."

Jeremiah felt her arm slip through his for the first time in over a year.

"Take me home," she said. "I want to see

our boys. I want to watch them play rough and tumble. I want to kneel beside them at bedtime and ask them to say their prayers. Take me to that."

"Are you going to let me open my eyes yet?"
"I am not."

Albert had Catherine firmly by the hand, carefully leading her out the door of their house onto a street wet with rain. People who noticed what was going on stopped to watch.

"Now?" she asked.

"All right."

"You mean you weren't going to tell me unless I asked?"

She opened her eyes. In front of her was a car of deep blue with flashes of gold trim. She put one hand to her mouth and the other on her stomach where she was just beginning to show.

"Albert Moore!"

"The young mother needs to ride in comfort. No more trams or cabs."

"I don't know how to drive."

"I'll teach you. Until then I'm your chauffeur." He put on a black cap with a visor.

She laughed. "We can't afford this."

"Of course we can. Business is booming. Your father agreed it was high time we got one, especially with me being the head man over here."

"The head man, are you?" She ran a hand over the front of the car. "I think it's the loveliest motorcar I've seen on the streets. Everyone will notice you."

"Don't fret." He put an arm around her and walked her into the street. He opened the passenger door. "The Irish Free State will soon gain the upper hand. All this nonsense will be over. Slide in beside the driver. I'll take you for a spin. That's what the Americans say."

"Oh, no, I've got potatoes and carrots ready to go in the pot."

"Come along, Cath. A half hour of your time. We'll get out into the country. Take in the good air."

Albert climbed in behind the wheel and started the engine. After ten minutes in traffic he began to steer them past villages and stone fences and long green fields. Dairy cattle grazed in pastures glittering with light as the sun broke free of the cloudbanks. The roadways shone like mirrors. Catherine rolled down her window so she could take in the scent of hay and of the sharp November trees and of air rinsed of dust.

He glanced at her. "So what do you think then?"

She smiled, leaned her head back, and closed her eyes, one hand instinctively resting on her stomach and her baby. "I'm not thinking, Albert Moore. I'm just dreaming now."

Libby placed her head against Michael's chest.

"Are you going to be all right?" he asked.

Libby brushed at her eyes with her fingers. "I need a few minutes."

"We shouldn't go on keeping this to ourselves. We ought to tell your parents."

"No. They'll only worry."

"They'll pray too. And you'll have your mother to talk to about it."

She shook her head. "It will upset them. And I have Em to talk to. That's enough. Too much talk only makes it worse. There's nothing anyone can do. I can't bear children and that's that."

"I love you so much." He cupped her face with its tears and its pain in his hands. "Think of the crazy way we met."

She laughed while she continued to wipe her fingers across her eyes. "We should never have fallen in love. I don't know how you did that to me."

"Listen. British doctors are great. But we have some pretty incredible physicians in

New York and Boston and there's a medical center in Rochester, Minnesota, I've read about. I want to take you there."

"We can't."

"Of course we can."

"Ben and Kipp count on you."

"They can bring Irving or Wales or Hannam up from London. Or train Edward if they need another pilot."

"Please. I can't keep laughing and crying at the same time. Edward flying? In any case, he's told Father he wants to go into politics."

"The airfields will make out okay. Let's do it, Lib. New York is amazing. You'd love it. And the docs might find something the fellows here missed."

"I don't think we can."

"You keep saying that. What we can't do is delay the welcome-home dinner for Edward and Charlotte and Owen. Your dad will be champing at the bit to give his speeches and his prayers."

Libby sat up. "So he will. We can discuss America and her doctors later."

He helped her to her feet. "So long as you come up with a better argument than simply saying, *We can't, Michael, we can't.*"

"I'll work on it while I'm acting perfectly happy downstairs. Owen makes it easier. He is such a lovely baby boy."

Michael grinned. "Just wait until you see yours."

"Do you know something the best doctors in London don't?" She patted him on the cheek. "Thanks for cheering me up. But I'll need a moment to clean up my face."

"You look great."

"You always say that. I look like I've been dropped on my head."

"And I look like I've been flying upside down. We work well together. We'll steal the show from Eddie and Char."

Libby sat down at her vanity and began to dab at her eyes with a soft cloth. "Eddie, is it? He'll absolutely love that. Do try and get on better with him than you did the last time you two met, shall we? It's Edward. Edward. Nothing else will do."

Sir William tinkled his glass with a spoon. "So a toast." He stood, glass in hand. "To Edward and Charlotte, who have returned from their sojourn in Canada with a greater gift than any of us could have imagined — young Owen."

"Cheers."

"God bless you."

"Well done."

"And they have returned to an England

where my good old Conservative Party is finally in power again. All the best to the new prime minister, Mr. Bonar Law, who is, in fact, Canadian-born like Owen."

People clapped and someone shouted, "Hear, hear!"

Edward looked at Charlotte, who smiled and nodded, one of her hands resting on Owen's arm as he sat happily in his high chair. Edward rose to his feet.

"Father." Edward lifted his glass. "I look around the table and here is my brother Kipp with his lovely wife, Christelle, and their beautiful boy, Matthew, hardly a few months older than Owen. Across from me, my sister Victoria with her husband, Ben, and their bright lad, Ramsay. Down at the end are Emma and Jeremiah and their strapping young boys Peter and James and Billy. Here beside me are Michael and Libby — I know they are just waiting for the right moment to pounce and surprise us with triplets."

Everyone roared. Libby offered a small smile.

Edward carried on. "Once Catherine and Albert join us this weekend we'll have their child with us as well, although she's still in hiding. I say *she* because we're still looking for the first granddaughter in the Danforth family and it may be that Belfast wins the prize. Though Robbie and Shannon might have something to say about that. A granddaughter born in Jerusalem — what do you say to that, Father?"

Sir William smiled. "Amen."

"It will be a full table once Robbie's and Shannon's ship docks at Liverpool. It will be an early Christmas indeed." Edward raised his glass higher. "Father and mother, Sir Arthur, Lady Grace, Aunt Holly, my brothers, my sisters, my brother Kipp's wife, my sisters' husbands, and all my wonderful nephews — it's good to be home."

As those seated at the table cheered Sir William gestured to Tavy and whispered something. James was seated to one side of his grandfather and Sir William put an arm around the young boy's shoulders.

"Ice cream!" he announced. "We never have enough of it. Always the best ending to any feast. Especially if you are five, eh, Peter and James?"

"Yes, sir!" they both shouted at the same time.

Emma laughed. "Hush. You'll soon be as noisy as the adults in this family."

"No, it is a night for noise, a night for celebration. Elizabeth, I'm not exaggerating, am I?"

Seated at Sir William's other side his wife patted his hand. "Not at all. Everyone agrees this is a time to lift our voices. Edward and Charlotte are back here among us with their son, all three looking splendid — the mountain air truly agreed with them."

Maids and footmen began serving dishes of vanilla and chocolate ice cream that Mrs. Seabrooke wheeled in on a cart. Conversation and laughter continued as spoons clicked. Tavy stepped up to Sir William's chair as he matched his grandson James spoonful for spoonful.

Sir William did not lift his head. "What's that, Tavy? I'm in a race here."

"The telephone, Sir William."

"What's that? Can't it wait a moment?"

"Scotland Yard is on the line, sir."

Sir William put down his spoon. "Are you sure, Tavy?"

"Yes, sir."

Sir William rose. "Excuse me. I must get to the telephone." He glanced at his grandson. "You can finish that bowl and we'll start on another once I'm back."

"What is it, Father?" asked Victoria.

"I don't know, really."

He left the dining hall with Tavy. The talk at the table had been so loud no one but Lady Elizabeth had heard what Tavy had said to her husband. She poked at her white ice cream with her spoon, turning over in her mind why the police from London might be calling. Was it something to do with Parliament? The new prime minister? She hoped nothing had happened to Lord and Lady Scarborough or their daughter Caroline — had Tanner Buchanan popped up again and committed some crime?

When Sir William returned he stood very tall and still at the head of the table, looking at the far end of the room, until one by one people noticed and quieted down, realizing he had something to say. Lady Elizabeth laid down her spoon, then picked it up again.

"What is it, my dear?" she asked. "What was the call about?"

"Why, it was . . ." He stopped. Then started again. "It was Scotland Yard." James stared at his grandfather's face and reached up with his small hand. Sir William took it. "Albert was ambushed this afternoon when he left his office at the shipyards. He was getting into his car. They were parked nearby." He gazed around the table, bewildered, his eyes drifting from one face to another, finally coming to rest on his wife. "Catherine was at home. The Royal Ulster Constabulary came to the house. He's dead.

Our daughter's Irishman is dead, Elizabeth."

28

December 1922

St. Mark's-among-the-Starlings was packed on the day of the funeral, Wednesday, December twenty-seventh. Despite the driving rain and sleet people spilled over onto the steps and grounds of the church and huddled under enormous black umbrellas. Inside sat King George V and his son Albert as well as the prime minister, Bonar Law. Jeremiah led the service in his black robes with white Geneva bands tied at his throat. Catherine's sisters and family crowded around her in the front pew, Emma holding her hand.

Although there had been talk of burying Albert at a cemetery in Belfast it was Catherine's decision that his body be placed in the consecrated ground by the chapel at Ashton Park. "I will not be staying at the house in Belfast," she said, "but I will always return to Ashton Park wherever else I may

be. I want him to be there waiting for me."
The hearse led the procession of motorcars
over the roads to the estate, all the head-
lights gleaming in the rain.

Harrison and Todd Turpin had dug the
grave the day before and covered it with a
canvas tarpaulin. The burial ceremony was
private, so many of the people who had followed in their cars parked at the side of the
road and either remained in their vehicles
or stepped outside to stand under their
umbrellas. The grave could be seen if a
person stood farther up the road past the
oak trees, and that is where scores of cars
ended up and hundreds of men and women
and children. Many wanted to see the king
and the prime minister. Others were
touched by the tragedy of the young Danforth woman, carrying her murdered husband's child, standing in the rain with her
head bowed, dark red roses in her arms.

The king and his son stood by the grave
along with the prime minister and other
members of the government to which Sir
William also belonged. The pallbearers
brought the black coffin from the hearse to
the cemetery under the leafless branches of
the ash trees — Kipp, Ben, Edward, Robbie, Michael and, in a rare act by a member
of the clergy, Jeremiah, disdaining the

weight of the coffin and the rain that pounded on his bare head and robe. They set Albert down by headstones that had been placed in the earth a thousand years before, names and epitaphs washed away by hundreds of storms.

Water covered Jeremiah's round glasses so he removed them. He did not bring the Book of Common Prayer out from under his robe but recited from memory. *"I am the Resurrection and the Life,"* he began. *"He that believeth in me, yea, though he were dead, yet shall he live. And whosoever liveth and believeth in me, shall not die forever.*

"Man that is born of a woman hath but a short time to live, and is full of misery. He cometh up and is cut down like a flower; he flieth as it were a shadow, and never continueth in one stay. In the midst of life we be in death: of whom may we seek for succor but of thee, O Lord, which for our sins justly art displeased. Yet, O Lord God most holy, O Lord most mighty, O holy and most merciful savior, deliver us not into the bitter pains of eternal death. Thou knowest, Lord, the secrets of our hearts: shut not up thy merciful eyes to our prayers: but spare us, Lord most holy, O God most mighty, O holy and merciful savior, thou most worthy judge eternal, suffer us not at our last hour for any pains of death to fall

from thee."

Harrison and Todd Turpin pulled the canvas tarpaulin aside. The pallbearers lifted the coffin and set it down on two ropes that Harrison and Todd and two footmen held taut. Slowly Albert was lowered into the grave.

"You do not have to be the one to cast earth on his coffin," whispered Emma. "Let your brothers do it."

Catherine's eyes behind the black veil were as dark as her clothing and the umbrellas and the storm. "Do you think he would have done less for me, Em?"

One hand on her stomach she bent and took up a handful of mud and clay. She dropped it onto his coffin, now at the bottom of the grave, and spoke words only Emma could hear: *"The Lord giveth and the Lord taketh away. Even as it hath pleased the Lord, so cometh things to pass. Blessed be the name of the Lord."*

Kipp and Edward and Robbie also scooped up handfuls of wet earth and let them fall onto the coffin. At Edward's encouragement, Ben and Michael did the same, and finally Sir William. Jeremiah, still reciting from memory, stood at the head of the grave and, looking at Catherine, said, *"Forasmuch as it hath pleased Almighty God of his great mercy to take unto himself the soul of our dear brother here departed: we therefore commit his body to the ground, earth to earth, ashes to ashes, dust to dust, in sure and certain hope of resurrection to eternal life, through our Lord Jesus Christ, who shall change our vile body that it may be like to his glorious body, according to the mighty working, whereby he is able to subdue all things to himself."*

To everyone's surprise, the king, shrouded by a large umbrella wielded by an army officer in full dress uniform, spoke the next set of words of the burial service: *"I heard a voice from heaven saying unto me, Write, From henceforth blessed are the dead which die in the Lord. Even so saith the Spirit, that they rest from their labors."*

"Amen," responded Sir William.

The king looked toward Catherine. When she saw his gaze she mouthed the words *thank you* and bowed her head to him. He nodded and lifted his hand in a gesture of blessing and sympathy.

"Shall I sing now, Cath?" Victoria was beside her. "Or would you prefer I didn't?"

"Prefer you didn't?" Catherine smiled through the rain and the veil. "It was one of his favorite songs. He loved whenever you sang it, though he always complained you didn't sing it often enough. Now's the time, Vic. Please."

Ben held the umbrella over her while Victoria stood at the grave and sang to the king and the prime minister and Catherine and all the mourners who listened in the gray light and December showers.

The ash grove how graceful, how plainly
  'tis speaking
The harp through its playing has
  language for me.
Whenever the light through its branches
  is breaking,
A host of kind faces is gazing on me.
The friends from my childhood again are
  before me
Each step wakes a memory as freely I
  roam.
With soft whispers laden the leaves rustle
  o'er me
The ash grove, the ash grove alone is my
  home.

The Great Hall with its vast oil paintings and fireplace capable of burning eight-foot logs had been prepared to receive the guests after the service. The heat from the fire soon dried and warmed all those present, while the enormousness of the space seemed to

584

make people speak in low voices. The king and his entourage lingered for half an hour before leaving by car for Lime Street Station and the royal train. During that time Kipp spoke with Albert, the king's son, who had just had his twenty-seventh birthday on the fourteenth. Albert had been in the RAF during the war and the two of them had met once at an aerodrome near Amiens. The king spent a few minutes with Ben, on whose chest he had pinned the Victoria Cross, and Edward, whose survival of two sinkings at Jutland in 1916 was still fresh in the king's memory. Just before his departure the king was introduced to Robbie, who was in the uniform of an army major, and Shannon.

"The sun has been on both your faces," the king said. "It cannot have been in Ireland, even though they tell me you served in Dublin for a number of years."

"I did serve in Dublin, Your Majesty. I was there during the uprising of Easter 1916 and I also served in the years before the treaty was signed. The sun is from Palestine." He introduced Shannon. "My wife was born and raised in Dublin."

She curtsied. "Thank you for lending our sister your sympathy in a time of sorrow, Your Majesty. It is an honor to have you at

585

Ashton Park."

"It is the least I could do for Sir William and his daughter. The Irish conflict goes on and on. But those in favor of the treaty seem to be gaining the upper hand. If they triumph will that end it, Mrs. Danforth? My advisors give me many opinions."

Shannon was in black from head to foot but her emerald eyes gleamed out from behind the dark fabric. "There is always hope."

"But?"

"My parents are republicans and nationalists. They have disowned me for loving an Englishman. Many of the leaders fighting each other once sat and debated in our home. I can tell you this, Your Majesty — even if the IRA should lose this fight they will never give up. Not in Dublin. Not in Belfast. They will lay down their arms once they have achieved a united Irish republic and not before."

The king put his hands behind his back. "Another Hundred Years' War?"

She thought about this, the green eyes sharp in a face bronzed by desert sun. Then she replied, "Yes, Your Majesty."

"I pray to God you are wrong."

"I pray too, Your Majesty."

Lord Scarborough was standing with Sir William at the doors to the manor as the king and prime minister drove off in their motorcade in a sudden downpour of sleet.

"It was good of him to come," said Sir William. "It was good of both of them."

"You have served England well, William. You shouldn't be surprised to have the king stand with you in a time of tragedy. You worked hard to bring about the peace in Ireland."

"The peace did not last long, I fear."

"You gave them the opportunity. Our troops have left for good. Now it is up to the Irish to sort it out."

"Albert had long ago stopped writing letters in support of an Ulster separate from the rest of Ireland."

Lord Scarborough put his hand on Sir William's shoulder. "A longing for independence can often breed the worst hatreds and atrocities the human race is capable of. The IRA keeps lists. And holds on to its grievances. Ulster became a separate nation on December seventh, divorced from Ireland and united to England instead. Albert supported that. They did not forgive him."

"The child is due in the spring. He ought to have had a father. He ought to have had his own father."

"I know that, old boy. This whole household will have to be the child's father." He patted Sir William's back. "Come back inside out of the damp. I have something I must tell you."

They stood in the hallway. It was empty.

"Listen. Tanner Buchanan has surfaced again. I'd rather not bring this up on a day of mourning. But it's better you hear it from me."

"What? Where is he?"

"Not skulking about my estate looking to get his hands on Caroline or the boy. Not hiding in your bushes either. You know I have been brought into the House of Lords? Well, I received this note from the prime minister ten minutes ago. I shall destroy it after you have read it."

I have appointed a number of people to act in an advisory capacity and report directly to me. They hold no government post but I shall rely upon them heavily. They will be my assistants. When it comes to Scotland and the Highlands I look to a number of gentlemen. One of them is a Mr. Tanner Buchanan. I understand you have a history with this man. I ask you to lay that aside in the interests of the nation. I would appreciate it if you approach Sir William on this matter as well, for I believe there has been an incident between one of his sons and Mr. Buchanan. Pray let this all be put to rest. At a time when there is turmoil in Ireland and India and Palestine, the king counts on your placing Crown and Country above all lesser concerns.

"It isn't just a matter of Arab versus Jew." Robbie stood by the Fireplace with his brothers and brothers-in-law: Ben, Michael, Edward, Kipp, and Jeremiah. "I don't mean to belittle that. The Nabi Musa riots in the Old City of Jerusalem a couple of years ago were bad enough. And there are clashes all the time really. With Hajj Mohammad Amin al-Husayni as Grand Mufti the riots between Muslim and Jew are only bound to get worse. He hates the Jews and their desire to make Jerusalem the capital of a Jewish state. No sharing of the ancient land so far as he's concerned. Muslims only. No Jews. No Zionists. No British for that matter. No one but true followers of Allah."

"That sounds grim." Kipp sipped at a mug of tea. "What else is there that makes things worse?"

"Jew against Jew. It's exactly like we're seeing in Ireland. There are Jews who favor a state that is a mixture of both Muslims and Jews. Those Jews who want a pure Jewish nation hate them. They will kill them if they can, just as the IRA kill those who don't want an Irish Republic."

Jeremiah removed his glasses and polished them on his robe. "What about the Arabs then? What about the ones who are Christians? What about the ones who don't want an Islamic state?"

"The Muslims who want an Islamic Republic governed by Islamic law — not British law — will do the same to the Arabs who oppose them as the Jews do to those of their kind who resist a Jewish state." Robbie made a gun with his finger and thumb and pulled the trigger.

"What do you think ought to happen?" asked Edward. "What's your political solution?"

"Mine?" Robbie stared into the red and orange of the fire. "There were Jewish kings reigning in Jerusalem thousands of years before Islam came into existence. The Jews came by conquest. There have been Islamic rulers in Palestine for fifteen hundred years. The Muslims came by conquest too. So eliminate the extremists on both sides and let Jewish and Muslim moderates form a nation together."

"The trouble is," Michael spoke up, "it's the extremists who eliminate the moderates, not the other way around."

Robbie shrugged. "If they can't make one country of Jews, Muslims — and Christians — then let them have two states side by side. Except I think they'd be at each other's throats even if they did that. I believe that would have happened if the South had won the war in your America, Michael. Two nations, North and South, constantly having border conflicts and outright clashes." He looked up from the blaze. "One nation of Muslims and Jews hammering matters out in political debate and compromise. That's what I'd want. If that doesn't come to pass there will be civil war within each group. And full-blooded hostilities between Jewish and Muslim armies."

"Aren't you a wealth of good cheer?" Ben inched away from the fire. "You must miss the heat. How does Shannon like Jerusalem?"

"She loves the climate, surprisingly. I thought she'd wilt. Loves the people too. But not the intrigue. Not the two battles for nationhood going on. That's too much like home."

"Can't go on in Ireland forever." Edward smiled and put his hands in the pockets of his dress pants. "Won't go on in Palestine forever either."

"How is Kipp?" asked Lady Caroline.

Caroline and Christelle were in black with their veils lifted.

"Ah, Caroline. Our Kipp is well. Distraught over what's happened to Catherine of course. But he's a good father, doting on Matthew, and doing all his flying safely, no war stunts, just delivering mail and packages. How is your boy?"

"Oh, Charles is coming along tremendously, Chris. He's with his grandmother upstairs in that child's playroom you've set up. Mum and Dad are both wonderful with him."

"Any sign of our dark foe, Buchanan?"

"Papa has hired extra servants who follow me about like detectives from Scotland Yard. I don't know whether Tanner has lost interest because Kipp bopped him on the nose or whether the extra protection has made him keep his distance. Perhaps he's just waiting for an opportunity."

"I hope not. I pray he has moved to Calcutta or Bombay. Far away. Listen, my dear." Christelle put her hand under Caroline's arm and drew her close. "A number of us are going over to Belfast to help Cath move back to Ashton Park. Emma, Libby, Aunt Holly, Victoria, Char, myself — Shannon, if she's still here. I would like you to join us."

"Why . . . I would love to help the poor thing, of course . . . but I'm not family —"

"Of course you are. Your father and Sir William are good friends now, *n'est-ce pas*? Look at them standing over there and talking together. Our children are playing with one another upstairs. If this were a different culture — Africa, yes? — then you and I would both be Kipp's wives. Sisters really. So in my mind you are family. Will you not help us? There is so much to do. It would be wonderful to have another pair of hands."

"But Charles —"

"Bring him here to Ashton Park where he can be with the other children. Your mother can come and keep an eye on him and spend a few days with Lady Elizabeth. Why not?" She took Caroline's hand. "I would love to have you with us in Ireland. In truth, I'm a bit of an outsider, *la femme française* — lovely as the sisters are to me. I only feel the kinship with Charlotte, the one who was a maid before marrying Edward. And Shannon — the Dubliner and Catholic."

"Yes, of course, I know Charlotte and Shannon."

"With you I will feel more at home, yes, more myself."

"With me? Your rival for Kipp's affections?" Caroline smiled and shook her head. "You are so different. This is all so strange. And Kipp just over there by the fireplace."

"So you will come? We need you. Most of all, I need you, my dear."

"You're not like any woman I've ever known. Yes, I'll come. Of course, I'll come. Who can say no to a person who puts things the way you put them?"

Robbie was standing by himself, still near the fire, when Harrison and Todd Turpin and Tavy brought in a six-foot deadfall trimmed of its branches and rolled it into the flames. Sparks flew and all the men danced back except Robbie.

"You'll not want to get a burn, sir," warned Tavy.

"I don't run much anymore, Tavy," responded Robbie. "Been through too much. Seen too many things."

He watched the ash log erupt into yellow heat. A hand touched his back. He turned to see a young officer wearing the same uniform he was. The officer grinned and saluted.

"How are you, sir? Major Mickey Gilfillan reporting for duty."

"Major Mickey —" Solemn as he felt and solemn as the day was, Robbie smiled and pumped the man's hand vigorously. "How in heaven's name did you get to be a major, Mickey Gilfillan?"

"Why, I just bowed and scraped to the same generals you always did, Robbie, and here I am."

"God bless you, what brings you here, Mickey?"

The smile dropped from Mickey's face. "I'm here to pay my respects, sir. I'm very sorry. Some of the old boys wanted to be remembered to you as well. I have a card for your sister signed by all of them. Albert was a brave man, sir. A grand Irishman and a fine Ulsterman."

"Thank you, Mickey. It will be a hard go for Catherine in the days to come. A card from those who thought well of Albert will help out, I'm certain of it. Shall I give her the card?"

"Oh, no, I'll do that myself, sir, in a moment. I did want to say hello. It's been years."

"Yes. Ever since Jack O'Casey and my on-the-spot marriage to Shannon and our midnight passage from Dublin to Liverpool."

"Aye. I'm glad to see you've kept yourself fit, sir. I hear you've been assigned to Jerusalem."

"I have. It has the makings of another Ireland, I'm afraid, unless the people can learn to work together. Well, it may be that things will sort themselves out just as I pray they will in Ireland."

"We just shipped out of Ireland on the sixth, sir. Left all our guns and artillery with the Free State forces."

"Hmm."

"God save Ireland, sir. I pray she has a brave future."

"I do as well, Mickey. There's no more I can do for her now but pray."

Mickey did not respond. Robbie noticed he was practically standing at attention. He put the mug of coffee he'd been holding on the mantle of the fireplace and faced Mickey squarely.

"Right. What is it, Gilfillan? What's on your mind today?"

Mickey glanced about to be sure they were alone. "We know who murdered Albert Moore, sir."

596

Robbie felt the coldness in his head and chest. "Go on."

"It wasn't the IRA. It was an assassination squad called the Crew. Led by Jack O'Casey. We know O'Casey was in on the ambush. We know he pulled the trigger."

"I see. Let the Ulstermen deal with him then. Let the Royal Ulster Constabulary track him down and hang him."

"Oh, they're hunting him, sir. Perhaps they'll get him. But there's something else you should know."

"What's that?"

"When the Crew claimed responsibility there was a personal message."

"From who?"

"From O'Casey to you. He wrote, *How does it feel to be one brother less? And I'm just starting, Englishman.*"

The coldness reached down into Robbie's stomach and out into the tips of his fingers. "Did you read this for yourself?"

"I did, sir. I have the note here."

He handed it to Robbie. Robbie glanced over it and put it in his pocket. "What do you want from me, Mickey?"

"O'Casey's a loose cannon as far as the IRA are concerned, sir. No one would be surprised if he started his own military unit and opposed both the republicans and the

Free State men. He has a bone to pick with those who support the treaty and those who are against it."

"So?"

"Even by the cruel standards of the civil war he's brutal, sir. Worse than he was during the War of Independence. They say he's tortured and murdered two IRA lads and a couple of men from the pro-treaty army. Both sides are hunting him. Whatever course the new Ireland takes, it's better off without the likes of him."

Robbie turned away. "Let the Irish deal with the Irish."

Mickey was silent a moment. "The RUC, the Royal Ulster Constabulary, well, they apprehended a member of the Crew yesterday, sir. He says O'Casey's out to get your kin, for sure. No mistake."

"He said what they wanted to hear. The RUC were probably beating him."

"This was in his shoe."

Robbie turned back and reluctantly took the slip of paper. On it were written the names of his brothers and brothers-in-law as well as their wives and his sisters. And their children. Underneath the names was written Ashton Park Estate, Lancashire. The writing was the same as the writing used in the note that claimed responsibility for the killing of Albert Moore.

A sudden moan, quiet as it was, went through the room like a black wind. Robbie and Mickey looked to the far end of the Great Hall to see that Catherine had collapsed into the arms of Sir William. He struggled to keep her off the floor. Kipp and Ben and Edward came running.

"We must get her up to her room," they heard Sir William say. "The day has broken her heart. I fear for her and the baby."

Robbie looked back at Mickey, his eyes turning to stone. "Who will help me?"

"It's unauthorized, of course. You and I, sir. No one else. Completely off the books. Just like the last time we went after O'Casey. Others are aware of what's going on but you'll get no help from the IRA or Free State. They'll not come after you if you get him. But they'll not lift a finger to point you in the right direction either."

"It's not my war, Mickey."

"Right enough it's not, sir. Ireland will sort it out. But you're not fighting Ireland, sir. You're fighting a murderer."

Robbie watched them carry his sister up the staircase. It struck him that four of the men bearing Catherine to her room had been pallbearers that day for her husband — Edward, Ben, Kipp, and Michael. A coal leaped onto the floor, glowing a bright red. He nudged it back toward the fire with the toe of his boot.

"When?" he asked.

"Just say the word," replied Mickey, "and it's a go."

"We'll take a ship from Liverpool to the Isle of Man first." He was still prodding the hot coal. "Then get a boat for Belfast."

"Yes, sir."

"You don't have to do this with me, Mickey."

"Oh, I do, sir. Yes, I do. Albert and I are both Ulstermen." He saluted. "God bless you, sir, on this hard day."

Robbie straightened and returned the salute. "Thank you, Mickey."

"How is she?"

Emma was just closing the door to Catherine's bedroom when Jeremiah came down the hall. "She's resting. Mum's with her and I decided to let the two of them be. Where are the boys?"

"Your father slipped out the back with them. The four are taking Gladstone and Wellington for a walk."

"That's good."

"And how are you, Em?"

"Considering the sort of day it is, I'm well

600

enough." She gazed up at his dark eyes. His robe was gone and he only wore his black suit with its white clerical collar. "I'm not about to jump off a cliff and curse God, if that's what you're worried about. I've made my choice. Just like you said I should."

"And what's that?"

"I'm going to open the windows and let in more air. I'm going to draw the curtains and let in more light. That's what God has put in me to do. That's what I want to believe anyways."

He smiled. "That's beautiful to hear on a day that has so little beauty to it."

She grasped his hand and her grip was hard. "Only . . . I wish . . . in one part of me — that there would be justice — for what has been done to Albert . . . even vengeance . . ."

"That is not for us, Em. *Vengeance is mine, I will repay, saith the Lord.* It's in God's hands."

"Murder is a crime. A sin."

"So it is."

"You said there would be judges. That God would appoint judges."

"It's up to God to appoint them. Not you or me."

"And how does he do that, Jeremiah? He put it in me to open the windows of my soul as far as possible. What does he put in the heart of those who must pass judgment?"

Jeremiah looked down at the floor and shook his head. "I don't know."

29
1923

January 1923

Shannon lifted her head from the pillow. There was a tapping of sleet and ice on the window of the Rose Room. It had not been that — something else had woken her. She reached over to touch Robbie in the dark. He was not there.

"It's all right." Robbie's voice. "I was just about to wake you."

"What's going on? What time is it?"

"It's three. You need to go back to sleep after I'm gone. I hope you can." She felt the weight of his body as he sat beside her on the bed. "I'm going to switch on the lamp. All right?"

"I've got my eyes closed."

She sensed the brightness through her eyelids, waited a moment, and opened her eyes, blinking. Robbie put an arm around her. He was dressed in the rough and simple gear of a groundskeeper. The clothes reminded her of Harrison but the flat tweed cap made her think of Todd Turpin.

"What's happening?" she asked again.

"I'm going over to Ireland. There's something I have to do."

"Ireland? But the British army have left."

"I'm not going as British army."

She shot up to a sitting position. "What are you doing, Robert Danforth? They'll shoot you in Ireland."

"Here's a list. It's a kill list. A gunman was carrying it. Look it over."

Shannon read the names of her sisters-in-law and brothers-in-law and their children. "Oh Robbie! Who wrote this?"

"Jack O'Casey."

Her face whitened and the skin tightened over her cheekbones. "No."

"He was the one that killed Albert. His group claimed responsibility."

"What group?"

"The Crew. He's gone wild, Shannon. He's even killed IRA men. They're hunting him."

"Then let the IRA deal with it."

"So far he's eluded them."

"Give them time."

"We don't have time." He handed the other note to her. "I've told Harrison to go about with that American pistol of his in his pocket. Todd's old but he's sharp as a tack and you'll see him toting a shotgun about — he'll say it's to deal with foxes that are after the sheep."

"O'Casey wants revenge." She looked up from the note. "Have you only told Harrison and Todd?"

"All the men know. My brothers. My sisters' husbands. Dad. Tavy. Let's leave it at that."

"I . . . I don't know what to say. I realize someone has to do something. I just don't want it to be you."

"O'Casey killed Albert because Albert wanted Ulster to stay out of an Irish republic. But he also killed him because he was my brother-in-law and he was the easiest one to reach."

"But — you'd have to kill his entire gang. They probably all have the list. How many are there?"

"I don't know."

"Robbie —"

"I can't sit here, Shannon. And we can't return to Jerusalem until this is settled." He took her hand and interlaced his fingers through hers. "I had mercy on him once. I can't this time. You know that."

"He won't have mercy on you if he catches you over there."

"And he won't have mercy on my family if he catches any of you here." He kissed her on the cheek. "I love you. I have to defend my family."

"Many an Irishwoman's heard those words before, believe me."

"Shall I stay then?"

She shook her head slowly. "You can't." Suddenly she seized him in her arms. "Oh, God go with you, love. You must come back to me, Robbie Danforth. I shall never forgive you if you choose an Irish grave over my kisses and my bed. I want to bear your sons and daughters. I want us to live to a hundred. Promise me."

"Shannon —"

"I don't care how impossible it is. Promise me. Say it."

He hugged her back and kissed her on the lips. "I promise." Then he stood up, gently removing her arms. "Mickey Gilfillan is waiting for me at the Castle. He helped me with O'Casey the first time. We make a good team. I'll be back soon." He turned off the lamp and moved across the room in the dark. The door opened and closed.

Shannon drew her knees to her chest. She prayed and tried not to think.

Robbie had been gone a week when Harrison woke up one morning and decided it was past time to go and see Sir William. It was still dark but he knew Sir William was an early riser just as he was. He dressed in his usual clothing, including his corduroy jacket and fedora, sat on the edge of his bed and laced his boots tight, placed his American pistol in his pocket, picked up his staff, and headed to the manor, where several lights were already burning. Tavy met him at the door.

"G'day, Tavy," Harrison greeted the butler. "Is he up?"

"He is. Listening to his new radio in the parlor."

"Ah."

"I'll let him know you'd like a word."

"Thank you, Tavy."

Sir William had headphones on and was listening to a broadcast when Harrison came to the door. He saw his groundskeeper and smiled and lifted a finger to indicate he would only be another moment. He finished listening and took the headphones off.

"Marvelous invention, Harrison. I prefer it to the telephone. Just listened to the news from London." He rubbed his hands together. "I should like some tea. Can I interest you in a cup?"

"No, sir. Thank you. I'll state my business

and then be on about my work."

"Hmm. This sounds serious. All is well? No intruders? No one lurking, I hope?"

Harrison noted the ivory handle of one of the revolvers that had been used in the duel sticking out from a pocket inside Sir William's morning jacket. "All's well on the home front so far, sir."

"I'm glad to hear it. I confess I'm a bit restless. I need to get back to Westminster but I swore I wouldn't move an inch until I'd heard that O'Casey and his rogues had been dealt with."

"Well, sir, the IRA are after him too, so are the Free State folk, and neither side have been able to run him to ground. So far as your son goes I'd say we are looking at weeks rather than days before he catches any scent."

"I pray for him all day, Harrison. All day, every day. I don't mind saying I'm worried for his safety."

"Of course you are, sir. But you can thank the Lord he has a good mate with him in Mickey Gilfillan."

"I am, thank you, I am."

Harrison cleared his throat. "Sir. There's something I've been meaning to talk to you about for some time."

"I see." Sir William got up and closed the

door and stood facing Harrison with his hands in his pockets. "What's happened?"

"Ah . . . well . . . there's this . . ." Harrison paused and blew out a mouthful of air. "I'm not good at beating around the bush, sir."

"Then out with it, man. It can't be that bad."

Harrison fixed his gaze on Sir William. Sir William returned the gaze. Neither man looked away or blinked.

"It's this, sir." Harrison breathed in. "Holly. Your sister."

"What? She's all right, isn't she? No one's mentioned anything to me."

"She's fine." Harrison gripped his staff more tightly and took the plunge. "So fine that it's important I marry her."

Sir William had been jingling change in one of his pants pockets. He stopped. "I beg your pardon?"

"Marriage. I need marriage."

"You need marriage?"

Harrison nodded. "To her. Only to her."

"Why —"

Anticipating a protest, Harrison cut Sir William off. "It's all this trouble that set me to thinking. Life is short, Sir William. We don't know how many years the good Lord will allow each of us, do we? It's best not to squander the days we're given."

"Naturally not."

"Holly and me — well, we love each other, sir, your sister and I. We'd like to spend the rest of our years together. I know she's of the manor born and I'm but a grounds-keeper but —"

"No small thing to look after Ashton Park's lands and forests, Harrison."

"No, sir. It's grand. But it would be grander if I could do it with her by my side."

"Harrison —"

"I love her, sir. I never thought I'd love a woman. But I adore her. She likes the woods and all the animals and the stars and at sunrise she's as wide awake as I am and she can walk all the miles I can and more and she, why, she herself is something, when you think of the ash trees at the height of summer, it brings to mind the way she is, stately, full of grace, tall, beautiful —"

Sir William had begun to smile, and his smile grew wider and wider as Harrison spoke as though he didn't notice, rushing headlong with his words, hoping to over-whelm Sir William and convince him that if he permitted Holly to marry him she would be marrying a man that would treasure her and honor her despite his lowly birth. Finally Sir William laughed out loud, so loud that Norah on her way past the parlor almost dropped a pitcher of cream. Then he slapped a hand to Harrison's shoulder.

"You needn't go on. Elizabeth and I may be getting on in years but we've seen that you two have been spending considerable time together. We have discussed the matter. This is not 1899, Harrison. Our children have married who they wished despite our objections. In all cases our objections were erroneous. What I'm saying is this: Holly is a mature woman and certainly doesn't need my permission to marry whoever she likes, but if she wishes to marry you then I say thanks be to God — I can think of no better man for my headstrong younger sister than you."

Harrison looked as if he had been hit by a tree. "What?"

"I say, Christ be with you. Elizabeth and I would be thrilled to see you marry my sister. And if you'd like, I'd stand with you. It would be an honor, sir, an honor."

Harrison looked as if he might topple over at any moment. "You have no objections?"

"None, sir." Sir William seized Harrison's free hand — Harrison's other hand was gripping the staff with so much strength the knuckles and fingers were white — and shook it. "God bless you, Harrison."

"Why . . . thank you, sir . . . thank you . . ."

"We'll be brothers-in-law, Harrison. I look forward to that. I look forward to it very much."

"Thank you — thank you — d'you think . . . is Miss Holly up, do you know, sir?"

"She is. She was lingering at breakfast with Elizabeth and Lady Grace and Victoria only ten minutes ago."

Harrison almost walked into the door. "I should try and say something —"

"By all means."

Harrison finally got a grip on the doorknob. "I'll be out on the grounds presently, sir."

"Take your time. I'm sure Todd Turpin has matters well in hand."

"Aye — he would . . . thank you, sir . . . thank you . . ."

Harrison stood in the hallway with his staff in his hand. Suddenly everything sank in. He broke into a run and almost knocked over two maids carrying bed linen. The dining-room door was open and he burst upon the four ladies still at breakfast like a gust of wind and rain. Spotting Holly he fell to his knee beside her and grasped her hand. She looked at him in shock and delight, her lips curving into a full smile and her eyebrows rising.

"Why, Harrison, what's this, what — ?" she asked but he broke in on her.

"Marry me. I love you."

Her eyes flew wide as did everyone else's at the table. "Harrison —"

"Your brother is all for it. He said the Lady Elizabeth was too. Not that they needed to be for us to get married, he told me, but it's nice all the same, don't you think?"

"Why, I am —"

"I love you, Holly." He suddenly dug into a pocket. "I have this."

He pulled out a diamond ring.

Holly rose to her feet. "Harrison!"

"It was my mother's. I've kept it for years. It's as old as the hills. It's not much but I tried to polish it up."

"Not much? You tell me your mother's ring is not much?"

"I mean —"

Holly bent down and took his face in her hands. "It means the world to me."

"Will you — will you take it — will you wear it — will you — ?"

His words stopped as she kissed him. When she pulled back he took her hand and pushed the ring up over her finger. It was too large. They both laughed.

"She was a big woman," he said.

"We'll make it work." She smiled through tears that made their way down her face. "We've made it work so far."

Lady Grace began to cackle.

Lady Elizabeth was still holding onto the teacup she'd been raising to her lips when Harrison had run in. "I am greatly astonished."

Victoria's eyes gleamed. "I don't think there's been a better breakfast at Ashton Park. Not one I've been in on at any rate." She lifted her juice glass as sunlight glinted off the glass of the windows. "To your marriage and your future. God bless you both. And may your love for each other sweeten us all."

Lady Grace lifted her cane. "I say."

Lady Elizabeth paused and then got to her feet holding her glass. "Happiness and abundant love. Do we need to start a house for you two as well?"

Holly's eyes remained on Harrison, who was still on his knee. "A castle suits me just fine."

"What?" Lady Elizabeth stopped the glass at her mouth. "That damp, musty place? It's full of ghosts."

"My man will slay any and all ghosts for me." Holly cupped Harrison's face in her hands again, the diamond throwing off light every time she moved her fingers. "Won't you, my love?"

He grinned and finally remembered to take his hat off his head. "A short morning's work, m'lady."

"Ah. Edward. Come in and sit down, my boy." Sir William tapped a finger on the radio. "I can't seem to tear myself away from this contraption. I was listening to a march with pipes and drums. Astonishing."

Edward shook his father's hand and sat down. "We had a radio in Canada. One day they'll be in every home."

"Do you think so?" He smiled. "Thank you for coming by. Have you heard the news?"

"Aunt Holly and Harrison? I'm frankly amazed. Char is totally delighted. It's much in keeping with all the barriers Ashton Park has had to breach over the past five years."

"It is indeed." He placed a large hand on his son's arm. "Have you given any more thought to entering the political arena?"

Edward's face lit up. "Why, yes. I've thought about little else besides Char and Owen and running for office."

"Good. Good. Things began well for me with the new prime minister, Mr. Bonar

Law. Since New Year's that has changed. I expected to be in the Cabinet but that has not happened. I anticipated appointment to various committees and sub-committees — I have, after all, been a very loyal party man. And Mr. Law hinted last fall such anticipation on my part would not be out of place. But nothing has come to pass."

Edward narrowed his eyes. "Why do you think that is?"

"I have an enemy who is close to the prime minister. I suppose he is the family's enemy. Do you recall hearing how your brother brought Lady Caroline home from France? When she was being threatened by a man who used to be our groundskeeper at the Lodge in Scotland?"

"Of course. Buchanan."

"That same man is now an assistant to the prime minister."

"Buchanan?"

"Yes. An assistant on Scottish affairs. Heaven knows who recommended him or how he was selected. But he's at the prime minister's side on a daily basis." Sir William leaned forward. "I don't know how long he will exert an influence on the prime minister's office. But I'm sure he has his ear when it comes to myself and to the Danforth name. It is his way of getting back at us, you see. He'll damage and thwart us any way he can." Sir William smiled. "But I am not unduly troubled. God provided us with a prime minister from Canada. He has provided me with a special assistant from Canada. It all balances out, you see."

"What, sir?"

"You, sir." Sir William smiled. "If you will take it. I am bringing you on board as my special assistant. We shall work side by side on a daily basis."

"But how — ?"

"I was placed on a committee by Prime Minister Lloyd George before we Tories pulled out of the coalition government and Bonar Law was put up for PM instead. I remain on that committee. Policies related to agricultural issues in the north of England — Lancashire, Yorkshire, Cumbria, Durham, and Northumberland. And the borderlands — so Scotland and Wales. You have spent some time at our hunting lodge in Scotland and are not unfamiliar with the Highlands and their practices and needs especially with regards to sheepherding. It is my desire we produce recommendations of such breadth and wisdom that Buchanan's attacks against us would eventually be dismissed by the prime minister as being no more than a personal vendetta against our family. Why, perhaps he will dismiss Buchanan altogether. We shall meet the devil's fire with the Lord's grace and at the same time groom you for a political career — what do you say?"

Edward smiled. "When can we begin?"

"You will return with me to Westminster. Does that suit you, my boy? Are you ready to touch your heels to the horse's flanks?"

Edward laughed and spread his arms over the back of the chair he was sitting in. "I am, sir. I am." He threw back his head. "Tally ho! Hounds away!"

30

Winter and Spring 1923

"I want to know what's up, Ben."

Victoria was holding a bawling Ramsay, her hair askew and her face flushed in exasperation at her child's ill temper. Ben took all this in as he opened the door to their bedroom at Ashton Park, but despite the blaze in her green eyes and the red splotches on her skin he could only smile at how incredibly beautiful she was. The smile was not what she wanted to see however.

"What are you grinning about?" she demanded.

"Nothing."

"Had an easy day of it, did you?"

"Why, I had to fly to Manchester and York and back. I wasn't exactly snoozing in the back of the hangar."

"So that's what you do on slow days, is it?"

"There are no slow days, love."

She rocked Ramsay in her arms but his crying only grew louder. "And none here at the manor either. Especially when there's villainy about."

Ben flopped in his favorite chair and held out his arms for his son. "Villainy?"

She promptly deposited the screaming child in Ben's arms. "What else would you call it when you men skulk around and keep secrets from your wives?"

"What secrets?" asked Ben.

The baby looked at him, put his hand to his father's face, and immediately stopped crying. This seemed to upset Victoria more than the crying and the villainy of the husbands of Ashton Park put together.

"Look at that!" she exploded. "Everything's against me today!"

Ramsay laughed as Ben made faces. "What's happened?"

Victoria glared at him. "What hasn't happened? Ramsay's off and Mrs. Longstaff's food's been off and then we're told we can't pop over to Belfast to fetch Cath's things and put the house up for sale. We've been making plans for weeks and — just like that!" She snapped her fingers. "Belfast is too dangerous, he says."

"Who says?"

"Papa. Who else. Him and the High King

of Ireland, Lord Edward himself."

"Eddie was never in Ireland."

Her green eyes threw sparks. "No. That was Robbie, wasn't it? And where is Robbie?"

"Army business."

"Army business. Where?"

"I don't know."

"You *do* know. All you men know. Do you take your women for fools? We eat together and walk together while you're up there flying in the clouds. We talk to each other and we know that every one of you men know where Robbie is and you know why we're not going to Belfast."

Ben kissed Ramsay who giggled. "Well, you said it yourself, didn't you? It's too dangerous."

"I didn't say it. Papa did. People shop in Belfast. Go to church. Take walks in the park. It's not dangerous for them."

"Ireland's caught up in a civil war, Vic, and it's a nasty one. Best you wait out this jaunt to Belfast a bit."

She pointed her finger at her husband with a sudden sharp movement. "You see? You're all in on it. The only woman who isn't frustrated is Shannon and that tells me she knows something the rest of us ladies don't. Why is Belfast dangerous for the likes of us? We aren't Irish. We don't live there. We're not on one side or the other. The IRA don't drive down streets spraying bullets randomly. They choose targets. And we're not targets."

The words came out, surprising Ben himself and his wife, as he bounced Ramsay in his lap. "Yes. You are."

Victoria stopped her rant and stared at him, strands of auburn hair dangling over her face. The blaze died in her eyes. "What?"

Ben puffed his cheeks and blew out his breath. He looked at his laughing son. "There's nothing for it now, Ram," he said to him. "The lads'll have me for dinner, spit and roasted, but there you are. They're not married to Victoria Danforth." He looked at her. "Here it is then — it was Jack O'Casey killed Albert. Admitted to it. Swore he'd come after the whole Danforth family, all the wives and husbands and children —"

Victoria's mouth opened. "Why . . . what . . . he wouldn't dare —"

"And children, Vic. And *children.*" He kept his eyes steady as she stopped arguing and fear found its way into her face and body. "O'Casey has his own gang of gunmen. They've run afoul of both the IRA and the IRA's enemies. But he wants us. Because Robbie captured him a few years back and almost killed him for his beating of Shannon. Oh, yes. It was her O'Casey stripped of hair and dignity and left tied and bleeding to a lamppost in Dublin. Robbie could have shot him but gave him over to rot in prison instead. Until the treaty set him free. Now he's running amok in Ireland. Murdering Albert was the opening shot in his war against us."

Victoria fell into a chair, still staring at him. "Robbie's gone after him."

"Yes."

"And you're afraid gunmen will cross over to Liverpool and come to Ashton Park."

"One already tried. The police caught him in Belfast and found a list he'd hidden in his shoe. All our names. All our children's names."

"Oh, dear Lord."

"We shall have to tell all of the ladies now. The idea was to spare you, Vic. To keep the fear from you. From mum."

"I . . . I'm sorry."

Ben kissed Ramsay and got up and carried him to his mother where he happily snuggled against her chest. He went to the window that was already dark with night. He looked at nothing for a moment. Then leaned against the window frame.

"But I'll tell you what I think, love. I think

that everything O'Casey's done has nothing at all to do with his lot coming after us."

"What, then?"

He turned and their eyes met.

"It has everything to do with getting Robbie to come after him. To get Robbie back to Ireland. It's your brother he wants. And now he's got him where he wants him, doesn't he?"

"They're in there. They're all in there." Mickey squatted down behind the bushes next to Robbie, revolver in his hand.

It was still dark, at least an hour before sunrise. Morning damp beaded Robbie's beard and mustache. "How do you know?"

"Our informer's always been good as gold. And so he should be, for that's the coin we pay him in. I got a glimpse myself through one of the windows of the farmhouse — I counted five or six. There's supposed to be no more than seven of the Crew altogether."

"Right." Robbie peered through the branches. "I see they've lit the lamps. Let's get on with it."

"Are you going in the back?"

"No. You can, if you like. I'm going in the front door."

"That's risky."

"Anything we do from now on is risky."

"Wait." Mickey gripped Robbie's arm. "There's the devil himself."

Robbie looked. Two men were standing at the front door and smoking cigarettes. One of them was O'Casey — leaner, a longer beard and longer hair, a limp when he moved, but Robbie knew it was him. The flare when he drew in on the cigarette showed his eyes. The same eyes.

"I'm going," Robbie whispered.

"I'm right behind you."

They crept out from behind the bushes and kept out of the two men's line of sight, crouching and moving swiftly in the blackness, guns ready. When O'Casey's eyes swung to him Robbie was already running up and pointing the revolver at his head.

"Good morning, Jack," he said.

O'Casey's man tried to lift his rifle but Mickey spoke up. "Through what's left of your heart, mate, if you bring it up another inch."

O'Casey kept smoking. "Major Robbie Danforth. What are your intentions?"

"You won't be going to prison this time."

"No, I don't think I will either."

Men emerged all around them with rifles pointed at Robbie and Mickey.

O'Casey smiled. "We spotted you an hour ago lurking in the bush. Just a chance glance, but there you are. I thought it best to let you come out in the open rather than waste men going after you. I know how mad you can be." He blew out a mouthful of smoke. "I told the lads you'd come right to us."

Robbie didn't flinch, his Webley still on O'Casey. "I can kill you before one of them shoots."

"Aye. You could. If you were me. But you're too much like our late lamented Michael Collins. Too, too British. Too sporting. Fair play. Marquess of Queensberry rules — no hitting below the belt. You'll not shoot me because I have no gun. You wouldn't shoot me in the car and you'll not shoot me here." O'Casey barked a laugh. "That's how you'll lose your Empire, Danforth. And your life." He drew on his cigarette and his face glowed white. "Kill them both."

The crash of gunfire. Robbie winced. Glanced at Mickey. Saw the shocked look on his friend's face.

They both looked at O'Casey's men falling to the ground dead.

O'Casey stared at Robbie. The cigarette fell from his fingers, a spark in the blackness. He pitched forward on his face.

A group of men with Thompson submachine guns walked slowly up. They prodded the bodies with the toes of their boots. One man with a neatly trimmed beard and mustache came out of the dark and approached Robbie.

"We were fairly certain if we hitched our wagon to your horse you'd eventually take us to O'Casey." He turned his head to the others. "Check the house and the trees." Then he looked back at Robbie. "I should kill you too. We're old enemies we are, the English and the Irish. But you led us to the beast. And he was the greater enemy. You're a foe. But he betrayed his people. He put a knife to Ireland's back when we thought he was one of us. He shamed Ireland. Cigarette?"

Robbie shook his head. The man lifted an eyebrow to Mickey.

"Oh, I will — thank you, I will," said Mickey quickly.

He put the cigarette between his lips and the man lit it with a lighter from his pocket.

"I'm Brynn O'Shea," the man said. "Major in the Irish Republican Army. Thank you for your help in setting Ireland free. Now be off. Take ship back to England. None will lift a hand against you. Go now. If we meet again I pray the guns'll be done with."

"What about our revolvers?" asked Robbie.

"It's wild country between here and Dublin harbor. Keep them on you and stay sharp."

Robbie and Mickey began to move away as the east brightened.

"Danforth."

Robbie stopped and looked back.

"I was at the post office when they brought you in during the Easter rising in 1916. I know your father's always been for Irish independence. And I once courted Shannon myself." A small smile came to O'Shea's face. "Oh, yes. A fine woman. I swore I'd kill O'Casey for what he did if I ever got my hands on him. Now I have. Go. And tell her to think gently of Brynn O'Shea if I ever come to mind."

Robbie nodded. "I will."

He and Mickey walked off through a patch of tall grass, waded a stream, crossed another field, and climbed a stone fence before reaching their motorcar. They looked at each other once they were in their seats. Mickey shook his head. Robbie started the engine and they drove in the direction of Dublin. Within five minutes the sun was up and in their eyes.

Catherine was told Robbie was back in England and had been picked up by Harrison in Liverpool. She wrapped herself in a warm cloak and went down to her husband's grave and stood there for the longest time. Finally she knelt. She heard the car when it pulled up in front of the manor. She imagined Shannon rushing to him and the two of them holding each other and kissing. She saw him hugging their mother and shaking father's hand. Ben would be there. And Edward and Michael and Kipp. He would greet them all.

Then came the footsteps. She heard them on the stone path and on the wet winter grass. They stopped.

She didn't look up. "Is he dead?"

"Yes."

"By your hand?"

"I found him. But the IRA followed me. It's they who killed him."

"The IRA killed him —"

"A man named Brynn O'Shea and his squad."

"And they let you walk away?"

"He admired Father's politics. And he knew Shannon." He put a hand on his sister's shoulder. "He wanted O'Casey more than he wanted a British soldier."

She put her hand on his. "God save Ireland. I feel my baby's safe now. Thank you, Robbie Danforth."

He squatted and took her in his arms. She began to weep, her shoulders and back shaking with her sobs. He kissed her and held her closer.

"It's all right. Go on as much as you like. Go on as much as you like, Catherine Moore. But it's peace to you and your child now, Cath. Peace."

The women finally had their trip to Belfast. There they gathered Catherine's and Albert's things and put the house up for sale. Robbie and Shannon said goodbye and took ship from Liverpool to Palestine. Catherine refused to be kept back from the dockside parting despite a heavy rain shower, and her and her brother's eyes remained on one another until the boat was gone.

The baby was born on Good Friday, and Sir William declared an early celebration of Christ's resurrection by having the black crepe taken down and replaced with daffodils and the windows opened to the light. Mrs. Longstaff quickly put aside the simple fare Sir William demanded and cooked up a goose and ham, to everyone's delight including his.

On Sunday morning when everyone thought she was in bed Catherine slipped out of the house and headed down to the family cemetery, her baby bundled in thick blankets. Sun was beginning to burn off the haze from the damp grasses. Todd Turpin and Harrison were standing by the front steps to the manor and tipped their hats to her.

"Now, do you see, love?" She held the child toward Albert's headstone. "Not the girl for the Danforths and Moores. Not yet. But a man. A good strong man for you. See how perfect he is? He's got you and me in him. You can see that, can't you?" She brought the child back to her chest. "Sean Moore. Sean Albert Moore. What do you think of that? Isn't that fine? Irish and English. A beautiful name. He'll have your fight. You'll see. Your courage. You'll never have cause to be ashamed."

The sun made its way through the treetops and robins took flight from branch to branch.

"I do love you," she said.

31

May 1923

Charlotte Danforth had never been to London in her life. The cab dropped her off in front of the Houses of Parliament and she stared up at the Gothic towers and Big Ben as if she were a tourist from another country. Placing Owen in the stroller she had brought with her, she walked around the buildings until she found the public entrance at the west end that Edward had told her about. She entered the central lobby and was overwhelmed by the ornate ceiling and chandeliers and statues.

"Look at all this, Owen," she said, gazing about her. "Isn't it something, darling?"

At first the lobby was empty but then she saw her husband approaching along a corridor. Owen reached out his arms to him and began to laugh. Edward kissed his wife and scooped up the boy.

"So you both made it here safely." Edward

hugged his son and kissed him on the cheek. "How was the flight?"

"Marvelous. Owen didn't fuss. The sky was as blue as —"

"Your eyes?" Edward glanced quickly about him. Seeing the lobby was still empty he drew Charlotte to him with one arm and kissed her with so much strength he pulled her up on the toes of her shoes. Her cheeks were flushed when he let her go.

"I . . . I'm surprised you dared in this place."

"I haven't seen you in weeks."

"I know but —"

"I shall do it again."

She stepped back and thrust out her hands. "No, Edward, don't do anything mad. We're not at the hotel in Canada anymore."

"It's almost as fancy."

"Oh, far more fancy. But some person will come in off the streets or from one of the Houses any moment."

Edward's eyes glittered. "They won't, my beauty. There's a great fuss in both Houses today. I just came from the Strangers' Gallery in the Commons. The prime minister resigned on Sunday. It appears Stanley Baldwin will take his place today."

"What? Mr. Law resigned? Whatever for?"

"Why, to keep everyone in their seats and out of the lobby here." One arm still held Owen while with the other he swept her off her feet and kissed her deeply again. She tried to push away but finally wrapped her arms around him and responded to his kiss with just as much energy and strength.

"I've missed you," he said, catching his breath before kissing her again.

She laughed and pretended to beat him with her fists. "Stop it. You're confusing Owen."

Owen tangled his fingers in his mother's glossy black hair while his father kissed it.

"Law was feeling poorly all through April and May," said Edward. "So he's stepped aside. Once Baldwin takes over, Buchanan is gone. He was Law's personal assistant."

"Is that why you're so perky?"

"Not at all. The papers Father put forward in committee and the speeches he made in the House showed he was far better informed about Scottish agricultural affairs than the prime minister was. Buchanan was already losing favor. I've been perky for some time. The sight of you made my kettle boil over, that's all."

She patted him on the back. "Right. There's a crowd coming along the corridor."

Edward broke away and gave Owen to Charlotte after a quick kiss on his head. "I see. I expect they're breaking for lunch." He put his hands behind his back. "That's Buchanan in front."

"Oh. He is tall, isn't he? But not ugly."

"Not ugly on the outside, you mean."

"I did mean that."

"Hmm. There's his lady friend to greet him. I see her in the lobby every day."

Charlotte squinted. "Who is it, do you know?"

"Buchanan is not in the habit of introducing any of his friends to me, my dear."

But after Buchanan had kissed the lady's hand and tucked her arm under his the pair of them approached Edward and Charlotte. Tanner Buchanan had his long dark hair pulled back in 1700s style and fastened with a silver clasp that was a Celtic knot — Charlotte noticed this when he turned his head to speak to his lady companion. As he stood in front of them his shoulders were broad and his eyes gray under thick eyebrows. He nodded to Edward.

"Mister Danforth."

Edward inclined his head slightly. "Mister Buchanan. May I introduce my wife, Mrs. Charlotte Danforth? This is my son, Owen."

Buchanan bowed his head and smiled.

"An honor, Mrs. Danforth. A handsome boy."

"Thank you," she replied.

"My companion," said Buchanan, "is Lady Hall."

The woman, who seemed to be about half Buchanan's height, smiled brightly and extended her hand. "My name's Kate. I'm very pleased to meet you both. Tanner calls you his worthy opponent, Mr. Danforth."

"Among other things I'm sure, Lady Hall." He took her hand.

"Hello," said Charlotte. "You're American, Lady Hall?"

"Kate. Yes, I'm from Natchez in Mississippi originally. But Mum married an Englishman, Lord Hall, and now here I am."

"Well, I'm Char from Lancashire. How do you do?"

"Baldwin's in, Danforth."

Edward raised his eyebrows. "Is he?"

"And I'm out."

"Sorry to hear it."

"Will you two ladies excuse us a moment?" Buchanan walked several feet away as men filled the lobby, some from the visitors' galleries, some from the House of Commons, some from the House of Lords. "You're not rid of me so easily, Danforth."

"I didn't think we were."

"I'll run for office. There's bound to be an election in a year or less. Baldwin will want a majority. Not a coalition or a minority government. I mean to get my seat."

"So do I."

"I'll tear you apart in debate."

"I take it you won't be running for the Tory Party then?"

A thin smile came to Buchanan's lips. "Not any party the Danforths are members of, you can be sure. I'll run for Labor."

"All the best then."

Buchanan gripped Edward's arm. "I mean to have my son. I mean to have him by my side just as you have yours."

"Surely that is a matter between you and the Scarboroughs. Though I do not think you will have much luck there."

Buchanan's eyes flamed. "I know that Caroline and Charles spend a great deal of time at Ashton Park."

"They are family friends."

"I'll have him back. And if your brother Kipp stands in my way again I shall lay him low, be sure of it."

"Will you? Last time you two met I understand he was the one left standing."

"That won't happen again."

"We'll see. Good day, Buchanan. I expect we won't have you here at Westminster again for quite some time then?"

"Oh, I'll be here, Danforth. Cementing my alliances. Rallying my support. One day you may see me the first man in the kingdom. Then what will you do?"

Edward walked back to his wife and Lady Hall. He gave the American lady a short bow. "May I wish you well until our paths cross again, Lady Hall?"

She extended her hand once more. "Oh, I'm positive they will. Tanner assures me we shall see a lot more of you two in the future."

Charlotte smiled. "I will look forward to that then, Kate."

Buchanan took Lady Hall's arm under his. "Good day to you both."

Edward had his hands behind his back. "Until we cross swords, Buchanan."

Charlotte slapped him lightly on the arm after the couple had left. "They couldn't have been friendlier. Why did you have to say that?"

"No damage done. She sees it merely as a quip."

"And is it?"

"For my part? No."

"Edward —"

"And not for Buchanan's part either."

Sir William came striding across the lobby through the throng of bodies. "Ah, Charlotte, my dear, how splendid! How was your flight down?" He took Owen from her arms. "How are you, young man?" The boy looked carefully at Sir William and then smiled and put a handful of fingers on his nose.

"It's so good to see you, sir," said Charlotte with a smile as he kissed her cheek.

"I hear Baldwin's in, father," spoke up Edward.

"Indeed he is." He lifted Owen high in his arms. "But I bear greater tidings."

"What's that?" asked Edward.

"You will recall the anti-treaty forces called for a ceasefire in the civil war at the end of April?"

"Of course."

"Well, I have a reliable report, confidential naturally, that the anti-treaty forces are laying down their arms tomorrow. Tomorrow, praise God, the twenty-fourth of May, Queen Victoria's birthday. The slaughter's done. See here." He held Owen with one hand and dug into his coat pocket with the other, eventually producing a sheet of paper that he unfolded. "Frank Aiken, the IRA

Chief of Staff, is going to call upon his men to dump arms — not surrender them, mind, but at least to stop the fight after dumping them. And that's tomorrow. Éamon de Valera is going to support Aiken's order. I have his statement. Not a word of this to anyone. I will speak on behalf of this in the Commons once it is public knowledge."

Edward took the paper his father offered him.

Soldiers of the Republic. Legion of the Rearguard: The Republic can no longer be defended successfully by your arms. Further sacrifice of life would now be in vain and the continuance of the struggle in arms unwise in the national interest and prejudicial to the future of our cause. Military victory must be allowed to rest for the moment with those who have destroyed the Republic.

Éamon de Valera

The house was white with a green roof and trim, nestled in among the ash trees as if it had grown up among them. Libby was delighted to see a starling hopping along the eavestrough. Michael walked ahead of her as if to open the door and then looked back.

640

"Coming?" he asked.

She shook her head. "No. I think not."

"But you helped plan this."

"I know."

"Ben and Vic have already moved into theirs. And Kipp and Christelle are doing the same this evening."

"They're staying, Michael. We're not."

He looked at her. "Why — we'll be back, Lib. I swear it."

"Do you? Then that'll be soon enough."

"Hey. I thought we had agreed on this. To try and get help from physicians in America, to visit with my family —"

"Yes, yes," Libby turned away. "I'm sorry, Michael. I was in France for so many years my family thought I'd never return. Sometimes I didn't think I would either. But then I did. With you. And I saw all this and I remembered how much I loved it and I wanted you to love it too."

"I do." He stood behind her. "Do you think I want to just take you away to America and never bring you back again?"

She looked up at the sun making its way through thousands of leaves. "Will you climb a tree with me, Michael?"

"What?"

"I loved to do it as a girl."

"You're in a dress."

"If it tears you'll buy me another, won't you?"

She kicked off her shoes and reached up for the lower limbs of an old ash tree. Gnarled and twisted and rough, the tree offered many handholds and footholds. She moved rapidly and was fifty feet off the ground before Michael had even thought about beginning the climb.

"Aren't you coming, Yank?" she called down.

"I never saw you do anything that fast before. Except outrun everyone to my airplane the day before the war ended."

"I was excited. And I'm excited now. Race you to the top."

"To the top? The top's hundreds of feet off the ground."

"You fly airplanes higher than that."

Michael grinned and stripped off his leather flight jacket and began to work his way up. They were both high in the crown of the tree among leaves and thick branches before he was close enough to stretch out his hand and tap her on the foot. She laughed and held open her arms.

"No one's ever kissed me in a tree," she teased.

"That will be kind of tricky even for an American."

"The branch I'm on is sturdy enough. Don't hang back. You tackled the Flying Circus over France."

"I actually never ran into the Flying Circus."

"So then show me your courage now if that's the case."

He eased his way onto the limb. She kept backing up as she faced him until she had nowhere else to go. Laughing, she kicked at him playfully until he managed to pin her legs and pull her down toward him. Then he took her in his arms and kissed her while the bough waved back and forth in a breeze.

"There," he said.

"How brave you are."

"I don't think I've ever been this high in a tree before. Once you can see past the leaves it's almost like the cockpit of a plane flying very low. Treetop level, we call it."

She nestled against him. "Now we can pretend we're robins or starlings."

"We could put a house up here, you know."

"We couldn't —"

"I mean like a tree house or playhouse. I'd build it. My brother and I built two or three in the woods back home. Then you could leave the house whenever you wanted to get away and climb up here. All alone."

"Oh, I like the sound of that. If you could actually do it. Vic has her house close to the cliff because she loves to gaze at the sea. Kipp has his close to the Castle because Chris loves the old tower and battlements."

"And yours is in the heart of the forest."

"Yes." She put her hand on his chin and brought his eyes to hers and away from the view of trees and meadows. "Will you bring me back? Or will you make an American out of me?"

"I'll bring you back. I'm part owner of two British airfields after all. And I love England, Libby."

"We might return with a child. We might, Michael."

She imagined a girl with ginger hair standing at the base of the tree and staring up at them, smiling from ear to ear, freckles spotting the bridge of her nose and her cheeks. Libby called to her and the girl began to climb and climb and climb.

32

June 1923

Harrison was awake at three.

Everything was still asleep. The birds, the deer, the rabbits. And the hunters appeared to have called it a night as well. The owl that often flew from its nook at the top of the keep had already returned and Harrison, peering up at it in the summer dark, was certain its eyes were closed.

"Ye are not running off, are ye?"

Harrison smiled as Todd Turpin approached. "If I was marrying you, I might."

"Is the Castle ready?"

"Well, the women have been in and out of it for two weeks, and for some reason Lord Scarborough is practically living in the keep, so I can't see as it wouldn't be. I'm not allowed a peek. Neither is Holly. Neither are you for that matter."

"What's the harm?"

Harrison shook his head. "Gave my word.

And I'm a poor liar. They'd ask me and I'd stammer. No matter, Todd. Only a few hours to go."

"So let's be about that hike through the woods you wanted. Your last walk as a free man."

Harrison patted Todd Turpin's shoulder. "Old Todd Turpin. If you only knew how she unpinned my wings."

Todd Turpin snorted. "Mine have never been pinned. So they don't need fixing, do they?"

"I have no idea what sort of woman would be needed to help you out of your deep, dark hole."

"I'm just fine."

"A matter of opinion."

"Let's be off. I've used up enough words for one day."

They went into the oak trees and when they had passed by the oldest ones, Harrison touching them with the tip of his staff, they headed toward the ash grove and the sea. Todd Turpin began to hum.

"I know that tune," said Harrison.

"I'll sing the verses and ye can join me on what they call the chorus then."

"You said you were done with talking for the day."

"Singing's not talking, is it?"

646

They disappeared in the blackness of the woods but their voices carried back to Ashton Park, where Holly Danforth slept with her window up. She opened her eyes and listened until the song became too faint. Then she smiled and closed them again. The rough voices and plaintive music worked its way into her sleep.

Here's forty shillings on the drum
For those who'll volunteer to come
To 'list and fight the foe today.
Over the hills and far away.

O'er the hills and o'er the main.
Through Flanders, Portugal and Spain.
King George commands and we obey.
Over the hills and far away.

Then fall in, lads, behind the drum,
With colours blazing like the sun.
Along the road to come-what-may.
Over the hills and far away.

O'er the hills and o'er the main.
Through Flanders, Portugal and Spain.
King George commands and we obey.
Over the hills and far away.

33

Sir William bent over the cables in the front parlor while his valet brushed at his jacket.

"Here. This is from New York City. Libby and Michael are doing extraordinarily well. They invite Harrison and Holly to join them on their honeymoon. And now we have the one from Jerusalem as well. Beautiful weather. Palm trees. Robbie asks us to pray for the peace of Jerusalem. Of course we will. Confound it." He snapped his head around to glare at the valet. "Have you quite finished brushing me off, Liscombe?"

"Sorry, sir. A lot of long blond hairs, sir. Stiff. Hard to get off. It's like they're glued on."

Sir William sweetened. "Ah. My dogs. Forgive my ill temper, please. I seem to be more worked up over marrying off my sister than I did seeing all seven children to the altar."

"That's all right, sir. I'd sooner go back to

648

the Somme than to the altar."

"Ha." He tucked the telegrams in the pocket of his morning coat. "What time is it?"

"Just on eleven, sir."

"Eleven! The ceremony starts at noon. I must get over to the Castle, Liscombe." He smiled and patted his valet's back. "I'm grateful for the brushing but it's time to go over the top."

Liscombe, a thin man with silver hair, returned the smile. "Give me leave and I'll blow the whistle, sir."

Tapestries had been brought out of the Rose Room and returned to a well-washed and dusted Castle keep. So had suits of armor and swords and pikes polished to a brilliance. At the moment Holly Danforth approached the altar, Lord Scarborough signaled to a half dozen footmen to peel sheets off windows high in the tower that had been open to rain and wind for centuries. Stained glass had been set in place under his direction and paid for out of his pocket as a gift to the bride and groom and the Danforth estate. Rainbows of green, blue, purple, scarlet, and gold streamed down over Holly's head, a head displaying hair that was, for one of the few times in her life, piled high and interlaced with ribbons that were encrusted with diamonds. Harrison watched her come as if she were floating on a river of crystal.

"Your mouth is open," she whispered as she came up to him in a cascade of light.

"There's no help for it. You're more beautiful than the forest and all its trees."

"You're given to hyperbole, Harrison."

He smiled. "Never."

She slipped her white-gowned arm under his. "This is the first time I've seen you in a morning coat. You look dashing."

"The way they've decorated this place I feel as if I ought to have jumped into one of those suits of armor."

"I should have liked that. Will you do that for me when we're all alone here, love?"

"I will."

Jeremiah smiled at them. "Are you two ready then?"

She nodded. "Yes."

Harrison winked. "Can't get there fast enough."

Lady Elizabeth and Norah stood for Holly, while Sir William and Todd Turpin stood for Harrison. Sir William glanced out over the faces of family and servants seated on benches that had been hauled out of a dry dungeon, where they'd sat like great stones from the time of Oliver Cromwell. His children with their children. Servants that had been with them for ten years, twenty years. Ben the stable boy, now his youngest daughter's husband. Charlotte the chambermaid his oldest boy's beautiful wife. Kipp married into a French family and the French family married into the Danforths. His sister marrying the groundskeeper — as fine a man as Sir William had met in or out of Westminster or Buckingham Palace.

"Are you ready to take your vows, Mr. Harrison?"

"I am, Reverend."

"Miss Holly Danforth?"

"I am, Reverend."

Sir William's eyes went beyond the Castle erected by Danforths a thousand years before in a time of war and hazard and found the graveyard by the chapel. There lay Victoria's first child. There lay Albert, Catherine's Irish husband. Fathers and mothers were there. Dozens of his ancestors had been placed under the ash trees — where were they now? How many had gone home to God? He was no judge of that. But he and his wife had carried their family forward on prayer and faith and they would continue to do so no matter what hardship befell Ashton Park or what bitter grief they yet had to bear. The moment came for him to pronounce a benediction on his sister and her husband, and he spoke out clearly.

"I wish you the beauty and grace of God, my sister, in this new life He has given you," he said, looking at her.

She smiled. "Thank you, William."

He looked at Harrison. "And I wish you all the wisdom and strength the Lord wishes to bestow. Receive it."

Harrison nodded. "I will, sir."

"From the book of Isaiah, chapter 30, verse 21: *And thine ears shall hear a word behind thee, saying, This is the way, walk ye in it, when ye turn to the right hand, and when ye turn to the left. Amen.*"

Mrs. Seabrooke could not recall much of what had happened before the air raid that killed her husband in 1917, but she had found her way back to the one thing she loved to do — organize. Tavy no longer had to manage the household and play butler. With the wedding Mrs. Seabrooke had been reinstated as manager of the manor's staff and put in charge of arranging the reception. When the people spilled out of the Castle keep there were tables and chairs set up under the oak trees, with the table of honor for Mr. and Mrs. Harrison set under the thousand-year oak with the Viking spearhead embedded in its trunk.

Mrs. Seabrooke clapped her hands at the servants. "Come along then, see the people seated and served. A storm could brew up. This is England. Table of honor first, then see to the rest. Lively, lively."

Red tablecloths fluttered in a warm June breeze like banners on a field where medieval knights might gallop armored horses. Emma and Jeremiah and their boys sat with Catherine and her baby, Sean, the infant taking everything in with startled eyes. Mrs. Longstaff had been cooking for three days and Holly thought her husband would jump out of his chair with joy at finding toad in the hole, cock-a-leekie soup, and rabbit stew on the menu.

"Why, it's amazing," he said as he dug into the meal. "Did you have anything to do with this, Holly?"

"Not a bit. But I think Mrs. Longstaff knows you pretty well after all these years."

"We scarcely ever get things like this at table downstairs."

"Maybe we can change that. What would you say to a Saturday-night meal once a week in the Castle? Of the sort of simple fare common when the keep was built a thousand years ago?"

"I'd love it. But will your brother agree to such a scheme? Every week? I can't see it."

"Let me handle my brother."

"All right. What shall I do then?"

She smiled. "Handle me."

Sir William had just stood up from his seat at the table of honor with a glass in his hand, when the roar of a motorcycle made him pause. Kipp and Ben had talked about getting a pair of motorcycles for the nearby airfield, and both stood up to look as the bike found its way along the road between the oak trees.

"It's a Douglas," said Ben.

"It is," responded Kipp.

"Lovely."

The rider stopped in front of the keep. He was clothed in a long leather coat, leather helmet, and boots. Peeling off gloves that were more like gauntlets he yanked the goggles up off his eyes and looked at the scores of guests seated at tables on the vast stretches of grass around the Castle. Finally he approached Sir William.

"I'm terribly sorry to interrupt, sir," he said, every eye on him. "But I do have an important message I was asked to deliver today."

"Very well." Sir William set down his glass. "Have you come from the village?"

"Liverpool, sir." He reached into a leather satchel that was slung over one shoulder. He handed Sir William a flat package tied with string. "Here you are. My lord."

Sir William tried to open the package, struggling with the string. "Just sir, my boy. I'm not entitled to any sort of lordship."

The courier did not reply. Sir William continued to wrestle with the string. Finally, his face red, he handed it back.

"They might as well wrap these things in barbed wire. If you will do me the honor."

"I know what's in it, my lord."

"Young man. Please stop that. I am Sir William."

"And it please you, my lord, you are not. Not anymore." The courier straightened. "The documents come from Buckingham Palace. King George V wishes it to be known in what great esteem he holds you and your family. In particular for your help spread over many years in bringing the Irish crisis to a peaceful resolution. As a measure of that esteem he appoints you First Marquess of Preston. The investiture ceremony will be held in August."

"I . . . ah . . . Preston . . . why, I'm often in Preston. Our textile business is there. A charming spot." Sir William remained rooted behind the table with its red tablecloth, the unopened package by his plate. "I don't know what else to say."

The courier touched his hand to his helmet. "May I wish you every happiness, The Most Honorable The Marquess of Preston." He walked back to his Douglas motorcycle and straddled it, adjusting his goggles over his eyes and starting the engine. The bike growled and rumbled and he sped down the dirt track, past the oak trees that bent over his head.

Edward stood up at his table. "You were going to toast the bride and groom, Father. And you should. But first I think we must toast you and Mother — Lord and Lady Preston of Ashton Park."

Lord Scarborough was on his feet, glass raised. "Hear, hear."

Everyone rose.

Edward drank from his glass. "God bless you!" He began to clap. In moments the applause was thunderous and prolonged.

Sir William remained standing, but he reached down to take his wife's hand. He smiled at his family and friends and his servants as they clapped and called out. The breeze picked up and parted the branches of the oak trees and he caught glimpses of

Ashton Park and the ash grove that surrounded it. Looking up to the top of the Castle he saw a Union Jack flying for the first time from the battlements and beneath it the ancient flag that bore the coat of arms of the Danforth family of Lancashire. A thought sprang into his mind . . . he saw the floor of the central lobby at Westminster, a floor he had crossed ten thousand times over the years. It had been laid down in a complex pattern with Minton tiles. Among the tiles lay Latin words he had grown accustomed to — they came to him with unusual force, so that he almost gasped.

"Nisi Dominus aedificat domum in vanum laboraverunt qui aedificant eam," he said out loud in astonishment, but no one heard him.

It had never occurred to Sir William that the words might apply to his family and his house, that they might apply to Ashton Park and a castle that had been built almost a thousand years before. But now the feeling pressed in on him that they did — and that the day was not only about Holly and Harrison or about what had been bestowed on him and his wife, but about the honor due the One who had been with his family through war and peace in all generations. And he began to clap along with the others because he saw and understood what a great work had been done.

Nisi Dominus aedificat domum in vanum laboraverunt qui aedificant eam.

Except the Lord build the house, they labor in vain that build It.

ACKNOWLEDGMENTS

My thanks to my great editor at Harvest House, Nick Harrison, and the crew he works with who helped bring *Ashton Park* to light — special people like Shane White, Paul Gossard, Georgia Varozza, Katie Lane, and Laura Knudson. Thanks also to my agent Les Stobbe for his ongoing and tireless support and my publicist Jeane Wynn of Wynn-Wynn Media for her bright spirit and hard work on my behalf. I'm always grateful for my wife Linda's love and encouragement and the enthusiasm of my son Micah and my daughter Micaela for their father's writing. And to Brendan and Jacqueline Cook and their sons who always make a home for me whenever I'm in England — cheers and thanks for making the green hills of Lancashire come to life every time I visit you there.

A final word. If the accomplishments of Ben Whitecross in his Sopwith Camel seem incredible, my readers should know they are based on the exploits of World War I ace William George Barker of my home province of Manitoba. On October 27, 1918, Barker tangled with scores of enemy aircraft and single-handedly shot down four of them in a short span of time before being shot down himself. He survived and was awarded the Victoria Cross by King George V at Buckingham Palace in 1919.

ABOUT THE AUTHOR

Murray Pura earned his Master of Divinity degree from Acadia University in Wolfville, Nova Scotia, and his ThM degree in theology and interdisciplinary studies from Regent College in Vancouver, British Columbia. For more than 25 years, in addition to his writing, he has pastored churches in Nova Scotia, British Columbia, and Alberta. Murray's writings have been shortlisted for the Dartmouth Book Award, the John Spencer Hill Literary Award, the Paraclete Fiction Award, and Toronto's Kobzar Literary Award. Murray pastors and writes in southern Alberta near the Rocky Mountains. He and his wife, Linda, have a son and a daughter.

Visit Murray's website at www.murray pura.com/